SEK

BOOK TWO OF THE UNWELCOME TRILOGY

R.D. BRADY

Scottish Seoul Publishing, LLC

BOOKS BY R.D. BRADY

The Belial Series (in order)
The Belial Stone
The Belial Library
The Belial Ring
Recruit: A Belial Series Novella
The Belial Children
The Belial Origins
The Belial Search
The Belial Guard
The Belial Warrior
The Belial Plan
The Belial Witches
The Belial War
The Belial Fall
The Belial Sacrifice

Stand-Alone Books
Runs Deep
Hominid

The A.L.I.V.E. Series
    B.E.G.I.N.
    A.L.I.V.E.
    D.E.A.D.

The Unwelcome Series
    Protect
    Seek
    Proxy

Be sure to sign up for R.D.'s mailing list to be the first to hear when she has a new release!

"Knowing yourself is the beginning of all wisdom."
- Aristotle

"Not until we are lost do we begin to understand ourselves."
- Henry David Thoreau

1

Lyla Richards stood in the remains of Attlewood. Three piles of dust were being slowly taken away by the wind. One was Angel, one of her Phoenixes. She wasn't sure who the others were, but they had six people missing altogether. Six dust piles had been spotted, so they were all accounted for, though who was who would never be known.

There was no time for a proper burial. But Jamal Nguyen, another Phoenix and one of Lyla's best friends, was collecting their ashes into a wooden box. When they reached their new camp, they would have a ceremony.

Right now, though, time was of the essence. They had defeated the Unwelcome contingent that had attacked the camp. It was only a matter of time before someone came looking for them. Lyla had sent Frank and Miles ahead with the wounded and those who would be moving slower, those with children and the elderly. She'd sent most of her Phoenixes with them as well. All that remained was a skeleton crew that was now combing through Attlewood for any supplies they might be able to use. It killed her that they had to leave most of what they had built behind. She and Frank had led Attlewood for years, finally achieving some safety, until the Unwelcome had ripped it all apart.

"Lyla?" Her nephew, Riley, stepped from between two cabins that had belonged to the Carolinas and the Hallidons.

Once again, she was struck by how grown he was. She still thought of him as her little nephew, the love of her sister Muriel's life.

She pictured him as he had been before the Unwelcome had arrived: tousled brown hair, blue eyes bright with mischief. Dirt smudged across his face and knees. He'd been adorable. Completely aware of her own bias, she still thought he was the most beautiful little boy she had ever seen.

But that little boy wasn't who walked toward her now. At seventeen, he had the strong muscular build of a man, although the smoothness of his face gave away his youth. And those blue eyes, once filled with such mischief, looked at her with determination. She shook off her remembrances, clearing her throat. "Yeah?"

"We've done the last sweep. We found a few more supplies, blankets, a bag of oats in the back of the barn. I tied them to Jamal's horse."

"Good. Well, I guess that's it." She took one last look around and headed for the entrance. A tall muscular woman with skin the color of rich chocolate turned at her approach, wearing a green-and-brown Phoenix cloak. Addie Hudson, one of the Phoenixes and Lyla's other best friend, stood holding the reins of two horses. Next to her, Jamal secured the box of ashes to one of them. Addie's eyes were bright, no doubt from holding back tears. Losing their people and leaving Attlewood wasn't easy for any of them.

But Addie's voice was steady as she spoke. "You sure about this?"

"Yeah. You guys catch up with the group. They'll need all the help they can get. We'll be along as fast as we can."

"You sure you don't want the horses? It would probably speed up the trip." Addie looked over Lyla's shoulder to where the group who would be accompanying Lyla stood: Riley, Petra, Adros, Rory, and two Unwelcome, bound from hand to foot. Arthur would also be joining them; he was scouting ahead, making sure there were no more Unwelcome nearby.

Lyla turned back to Addie. "No. You need to get to the rest of the camp quickly. That's more important."

Lyla wasn't sure how long it would take for the Unwelcome to respond to the missing ship and liaison, but they had to be aware by now. And they would send someone to check soon. Everyone from Attlewood needed to be long gone before that happened.

Jamal nudged his chin toward the two prisoners. "What if they don't cooperate?"

Lyla flicked a glance over both of them. The male had blond hair. The female had short red hair, just like her brother. She was glad Arthur wasn't nearby right now to hear her words. They were bringing the Unwelcome with them for questioning. They needed to learn all they could about what the Naku knew and what they planned. Killing them before, when they offered no threat, felt like murder. Even now, the thought of it felt cold blooded. But if they in any way endangered the people with her?

She looked Jamal right in the eye. "Then they die."

2

The lights that lined the dark-gray metallic floor emitted a soft hum. Xantar's gray body was covered in a white tunic, and he wore slipper shoes on his feet, the material of both almost weightless. The fragile Naku bodies could not handle the friction of any heavier material against their skin.

The hum followed Xantar as he made his way slowly down the hall. His legs ached today and had begun to shake even before he reached the end of the hall. He paused, one thin gray arm resting against the wall. In the muted white light, it looked even a few shades paler than the normal gray. His long fingers rested there, his large bony knuckles stark in the light.

He tapped his wrist unit, and a door slid open down the hall. A whirring noise approached him. He turned as his glider lowered to the ground next to him. Grasping the railing along the top, he slid his body through the opening and sat down with a sigh. The foam on the seat cushioned his aching bones. More foam slid from the wall of the glider, encasing his legs and massaging his aching muscles.

Ah, much better. He directed the glider to the control room. He had been notified that there was a problem with one of their veerfinah. The doors to the control room slid open at his approach. All Naku inside turned to him, placing one finger to their forehead before returning their focus to their work.

Windows lined the far wall, providing a view of New City below and the land for miles around. Xantar did not even glance at it. Views were not important factors. Why the makers of the ship had thought to create a glass wall was beyond Xantar's understanding.

Fejel stepped away from his console. He was a younger Naku, with far fewer wrinkles on his face and an ability to stand for much longer periods of time. But his mind was not as finely attuned as Xantar's. At one thousand three hundred years old, Xantar had accrued the most knowledge of any Naku on the ship, making him their leader. When he passed, the next oldest would take the mantle of authority. There was no ambition, no jealousy. Efficiency was the key to the Naku society—efficiency and unemotional reason.

But in Xantar's opinion, that lack of emotion was their one flaw. It made them reliant on others when dealing with more emotional species, like the humans.

There were always risks with such species. They could not be trusted. They often said one thing and meant another. Their liaisons were kept on a tight leash, with constant mental probing to make sure their actions were being conducted in the best interest of the Naku. The probing, however, damaged their brains beyond repair within a few months, rendering them nonfunctional. But there were always more humans that could be utilized.

Xantar focused his energy on Fejel, pulling his mental signature from the others in the room.

One of their liaisons had disappeared with a contingent of avad, the Naku's slaves who the humans had dubbed the Unwelcome. *Has the liaison been found?*

Yes, Esteemed Leader. He is dead.

By whose hand?

Unclear. His contingent is dead as well.

All of them?

Two are missing, and based on the other avads at the scene, we deduce they are dead as well.

Xantar paused at the unexpectedness of Fejel's words. They had created the chelvah to be powerful. Their uniforms were designed to further protect them, as were their weapons. And they had been bred to follow the Naku's orders unquestioningly. They could be killed. In fact, the Naku regularly did so when they reached a certain age. But them dying without the Naku's orders was extremely unusual.

How were they killed?

Fejel frowned as he looked at his screen. *Three were killed with a romag.*

The weapon of the chelvah. Shaped like a spear, it emitted a bolt of energy that reduced humans to ash. The uniforms of the chelvah insulated them from most of a romag strike unless in very close contact.

Fejel continued. *The other seven were killed by severe trauma, resulting in internal bleeding and broken necks.*

Xantar narrowed his eyes, Fejel's words setting off a flurry of analysis within Xantar's mind. That was not possible. There were no creatures on this planet capable of breaking a chelvah's neck.

The human liaison was killed as well. He was stabbed.

His death was of no consequence, but the method of death suggested a human was responsible.

Where were they found?

A human camp called Attlewood. It is affiliated with Lyla Richards.

The woman they were searching for. There was something special about her, something she had in common with the Cursed. Which meant she and the Cursed were the reason he had lost a contingent of avad.

Have them detain all members of the camp.

The camp was deserted when the chelvah arrived.

Have them search the area. Find the members of that camp. He paused, calculating the options. *And send for the hunter.*

3

The forest was still as Vellum walked through the undergrowth. His footsteps made little noise. Normally such a stillness would make Vel pause, knowing that the forest was warning him of danger ahead. But this danger he was expecting. Still, he paused behind a large Spanish moss before he reached the clearing, taking stock of what lay ahead.

Four Unwelcome stood halfway between Vel and the middle of the clearing. They were spread out—two facing him and two with their backs to him. And in the middle of them sat the veerfinah, the Unwelcome ship, its ramp down. He eyed each of the Unwelcome. As always, they were completely covered from head to toe in their dark-blue skintight suits. The suits did nothing to hide the strength of the occupants they covered, although the dark helmets concealed their faces. Each Unwelcome was at least eight feet tall.

Vel, who stood at six foot six, had never been in the company of any beings taller than him before the Unwelcome arrived. He was used to being the largest man in the room. He supposed he still was, because whatever the Unwelcome were, they certainly weren't men. No man grew to those heights or widths. Vel was strong, extremely so, but even his muscles paled in comparison to the Unwelcome before him. And these weren't even the largest Vel had ever seen. He'd seen one monster who easily stood ten feet. Although that Unwelcome had been unnaturally slow, and from the way the others treated him, most likely stupid. Apparently whatever genetic formula they'd used to create that one had not worked according to plan.

Vel scanned the clearing once more, looking for any additional Unwelcome or a stray human, but there was no one. He stepped out from the trees and strode toward the Unwelcome. The two facing him whipped their heads toward him as he approached but made no move and no sound. The two from the other side of the ship moved to the base of the ramp. As Vel passed by the first two, they fell in step behind him. The other two headed up the ramp. Vel followed them. Once inside, the two Unwelcome disappeared into the cockpit. The other two closed the ramp behind him.

Vel caught sight of his reflection in the metal that lined the ship's wall. A ragged scar ran from his ear to jawline on the right-hand side of his face. On the other, a burn went from the edge of his eye down his neck. He glared at the image as he passed, curling his fist. *Bastards.*

He walked to a seat and strapped himself in as the ship began to vibrate. Two Unwelcome sat across from him, strapping themselves in as the ship took flight. The only sound was the slight hum of the engine.

No explanations of what Vel needed to do were offered. But no words were needed. After all, this was not Vel's first trip on a veerfinah.

∾

THE FLIGHT to New City only took twenty minutes. On foot, it would have taken two days. Vel felt the change in height as they began to ascend. For just a moment, the faint stirrings of fear fluttered in his gut. He didn't like going to the mothership. Normally he only had to deal with that rat of a human Chad Keyes.

But apparently whatever the Naku wanted, it required a special audience. He slowly reached down and stroked the hilt of the serrated knife at his waist. The feel of the cool ivory under his fingertips calmed him. They needed him. He did not need them. He would be fine. And if he wasn't, well, he had learned through trial and error that the Unwelcome had a weakness in their armor: the spot where their helmets met their suits. It was unprotected. And he would not hesitate to exploit that weakness if needed.

The ship slowed, and two minutes later he felt a small jolt as they landed. The Unwelcome across from him unbuckled. Vel did the same. He cracked his knuckles as they lowered the ramp. Without a glance toward him, the two Unwelcome headed down the ramp. Vel followed as the other two emerged from the cockpit. Both followed him down the ramp, and one started to check the outside of the ship while the other stayed behind Vel.

Another veerfinah flew over them, heading for the exit, the downwash rustling his hair. It only emitted the slightest of hums. There were about a dozen other veerfinah lined up silently along the bay. This was only one of twenty landing bays on the mothership. He didn't know what the other ones looked like, as they always brought him to the same bay, obviously not wanting to give away too much.

The only reason he knew how many landing bays there were was he had spent two weeks camped out below, just watching the mothership, taking note of the number of ships flying to and fro. Watching the lights to see if there was any pattern. He'd learned a few things but nothing too critical. But information was always helpful. The Unwelcome veered to the left at the end of the row of ships, heading for a single metal door.

The Unwelcome on the left waved his arm over the door, and the bracelet at the cuff of his uniform lit up for a second before the door slid open with a puff of air.

The Unwelcome slowed as they started down the hall, needing to duck a little to compensate for the ceilings, which stood at eight feet. Dark tiles lined the floor, contrasting with the bright white of the walls and ceiling. The Unwelcome continued down the hall, their shoulders hunched the entire walk. This ship hadn't been created for the Unwelcome. Which begged the question: Who exactly *had* it been built for? It was possible it had been built for the Naku, who were smaller in stature, but Vel wasn't entirely convinced of that.

The hunching meant a slower pace, which meant he was able to keep up easily with his guard. Doors lined the hall, but Vel only knew that from past experience. Walking by them, the outlines of the doors were completely hidden.

At the end of the hall, the Unwelcome turned right. Here the ceiling sprang up to fifteen feet, allowing the Unwelcome to straighten to their full height. They passed open archways that led to comfortable seating areas with glass windows. More proof in Vel's mind that this ship hadn't been created for the Unwelcome. He had never seen one sitting down. He certainly had never seen one socialize or relax. No, this ship had had a different purpose in the past. The hallway was long and lined with the archways on both sides. While the left held the seating areas with the long windows, the right held small tables and chairs. It looked like an eating area. Vel had never seen the Unwelcome do that either.

Ahead, a set of ornate doors stood closed. They looked like they were made with wrought iron over ivory. The wrought iron wove in and around it, creating intricate patterns that resembled vines and flowers unlike any seen on Earth. The ivorylike substance behind it almost seemed to glow.

The Unwelcome strode toward it. Once again the Unwelcome on the left waved his arm over a panel outside the door. The door did not spring open immediately. Vel came to a halt behind them just as the doors opened inward.

One of the Unwelcome glanced back at him before stepping inside. The ceiling in here was even higher, reaching to at least thirty feet. The room was circular, with seven additional doorways, equally ornate, on this side. A platform had been raised on the far side of the room, hovering five feet off the ground. Six additional Unwelcome stood guard at the edge of the platform. The Unwelcome that had accompanied Vel moved to the side of the doorway and stood at attention. Vel strode toward the platform. His footfalls, though slight, seemed to echo off the material of the floor. It looked like shiny concrete in blues and greens. Every once in a while it would change color, adding a pink, orange, or yellow.

He continued walking until he reached a black spot on the floor in front of the platform. He stopped there, waiting.

He waited for ten minutes before a door at the back of the room opened. The lights went out, but Vel stayed where he was, used to the theatrics of the Naku's entrance. A minute later the lights flared back to life, causing him to blink hard. A large throne now sat at the edge of the platform. Xantar, the Naku leader, sat in it. He did not cut an imposing figure, standing somewhere around four feet. He was extremely gaunt, his pale gray skin hanging from his bones, and wrinkles piled upon wrinkles on every piece of observable skin. He was slumped to the side, as if the effort of sitting straight was simply too much.

At a glance, most would probably write him off as no threat. But it wasn't his body that told of Xantar's strength. It was his eyes. They pierced through the ruin of his face, dissecting everything about the human in front of him.

"I have a job for you."

Although the words came from Xantar, the voice did not. A man, tall and wraithlike, slid from around the back of Xantar's chair. He was so thin his cheekbones dominated his face. His eyes were sunken back into his skull, his fingers long and spindly as he clutched his velvet robe to his chest. His voice was raspy as if his mouth was too dry to form the words. "There is someone we need you to find."

"What can you tell me about them?" Vel kept his gaze on Xantar as he spoke.

"It is a woman. She is the leader of a camp called Attlewood."

"I've heard of it. Their leader's name is Lyla. Is that who you're looking for?"

The man paused, tilting his head to the side, like a dog listening to his master's commands. And that was exactly what he was—a lapdog of the Naku. When they communicated with you, their thoughts burrowed through your mind, leaving holes. Over time, that damage removed things. Emotions first, then intelligence, then your very life. The man in front of him would not survive much longer. He had obviously already stopped feeding himself.

Vel felt no pity for the man, only contempt. He was weak. Better he should die than bring more of his weakness into the world. People thought the Naku were the evil ones. But humans ... they were no better. They had been preying on one another long before the Naku arrived. And they would continue preying on one another long after the Naku left.

Vel held no ill will toward the Naku. They had never taken away anyone he cared about. Not that he had actually ever really cared about anyone. But humans, they had hurt him. He had seen their true colors when he was a boy. When he was weak. But that hadn't given them pause, so he had no qualms about tracking down humans for the Naku. They deserved whatever was coming to them.

"Yes. We are looking for Lyla." His voice slithered over the words, as if the man were morphing into a snake before his very eyes.

"Do you need her alive?"

The man tilted his head again, getting his orders. Xantar's gaze met Vel's as the man's words slid from his mouth. "We would prefer if she were alive. We have plans for her."

4

Three Weeks Later

The sign Lyla passed from the Before proclaimed that visitors should inquire at the ticket box or gift shop for a membership to the zoo. She didn't stop, but her eyes were drawn to the image of the smiling children, some holding stuffed animals, others ice cream. It was such a different world those children had lived in compared to the children of today. They seemed to have a carefree existence. Today, children would be lucky if they had food, never mind toys or an outing to go visit incarcerated animals. Lyla wasn't even sure some of them would know what an ice cream cone was.

Not for the first time, Lyla wondered who she would have been in the old world if that company Bytertech hadn't put profit above safety and pulled the asteroid into the Earth, setting off worldwide catastrophes of tsunamis, volcanic eruptions, and earthquakes. Half the world's population disappeared in the first month. The subsequent outbreaks of disease and crime helped whittle down those already diminished numbers in the following months. Some thought it would be the end of the human race.

But we survived, Lyla thought as she rounded the path past the old front entrance to the zoo. She nodded at the two Phoenixes on guard there. *Although it was to see to a much-changed world.*

Electricity, plumbing, all the comforts of the old world were gone. Humanity was thrown back to the dark ages. And then the Naku and their slave race of soldiers, the Unwelcome, had arrived, making everything a whole lot worse.

Lyla spied the primate exhibit, or at least what was left of it. She and the people of Attlewood had taken up residence in an old zoo. Half the fences had survived, along with a few of the exhibits. It was one of the fallback locations she and Frank, the former leader of the Attlewood Camp, had set up years ago. She'd originally thought if they had to use them, it would be because of a natural disaster. But there was nothing natural about the Unwelcome's attack on their camp.

She glanced over at the large chimpanzee enclosure. The male Unwelcome, whom they called Thor, was still out. They had gotten his name out of him but that was all. His full name was actually Geothorxed, but they had shortened it to Thor. With his build and blond hair, it suited him. She was surprised he'd told them. But her surprise was nothing compared to his when he'd said his name. Arthur told them that after the shedar, they never used their names again, only a number.

Thor glared at Lyla defiantly as she passed. She was pretty sure he'd made sure he was out when she came by, to solidify his hatred for her. He was close to eight feet tall and was about half as wide. Lyla wasn't sure even a blast from an Unwelcome spear would slow him down. She made sure each of the Phoenixes who guarded him knew they were expected to take every precaution and use whatever force was necessary to protect themselves and the camp.

She broke off the contact with the large Unwelcome to nod at Montell and Eddie, who stood with Unwelcome weapons in their arms. The Unwelcome had guards at all times, and the guards were switched out every two hours. Lyla didn't want to chance fatigue or inattention to lead to an escape attempt. The Unwelcome were stronger, taller, and could easily overpower anyone guarding them. Which meant the humans needed to be on their toes at all times.

One of the good things about the old zoo was that it had plenty of places to hold prisoners. They had two: one male and one female Unwelcome. Lyla made a habit of seeing them first thing in the morning and asking them questions.

Not that they answered them. She sighed, knowing their presence was becoming a problem amongst the rest of the camp. Food wasn't exactly abundant right now, and feeding two very large prisoners wasn't going over well.

Otto Swingler, who at six foot five had once been the tallest member of their camp, stood at the entrance to the chimp house. He nudged his head toward the entrance as Lyla approached. "He's in there."

"Figured. Any change?"

Otto shook his head. "No."

Lyla's shoulders slumped. She'd wanted him to get a little reaction, something that would help justify the Unwelcome's presence and the chance they'd taken sparing them.

"Please, I just want to help." Arthur's voice cut through the air. Silence was the only response. Lyla slipped into the shadows to watch. Arthur and Anixquold were the same height at seven feet, making them smaller than most Unwelcome. Both had the same light hue of blue skin, red hair, and blue eyes. Arthur was more muscular than his sister, but not by much.

But that was where the similarities ended. Arthur was considerate, friendly, giving. His sister was the opposite. She hadn't spoken, barely ate, and wouldn't even turn in the direction of the person speaking to her. Even Thor was more responsive than she was.

But Arthur visited her twice a day, trying to get her to say something, anything. This morning, he spoke of their limited childhood. She never said a word or even looked at him. Finally Arthur turned and walked out.

Lyla let him go without revealing her presence. He looked so dejected. She stepped toward the cage when she knew Arthur was gone. Inside, Arthur's sister had her back to the door, and Lyla had no doubt that she hadn't even looked at him.

Sparing the Unwelcome had been an act of mercy. But Lyla had hoped that perhaps, like Arthur, they would be willing to help them. But without the benefits of Arthur's education, all they knew was what the Naku had drilled into them for years. Dedication and duty to the point of death were their prime motivators. And if they couldn't find a way around that, then the difficulty in holding the Unwelcome would soon far outweigh any potential benefits.

And Lyla didn't like her options if it reached that point. Protecting the humans under her care was *her* primary motivation. Having three of her Phoenixes guarding the Unwelcome left her with three less to protect the camp. Without anything to show for it, she couldn't justify that, especially not now when they needed every hand to help set up the camp and shore up their food supply. The grumbles from unhappy camp members were getting louder every day.

"He just wants to help you," Lyla said. The tightening of Anne's shoulders was her only response. "He's your family. He cares about you."

Anne took one step closer to the far wall.

Lyla sighed, knowing today's questioning would go no better than any other day's and also knowing that she didn't have the time or patience for it.

With one last look at Arthur's sister's back, she stepped outside, looking around. "Where'd he go?"

Otto pointed in the direction of the tents. "I don't know why he tries so hard."

"She's his family, what else can he do?" She headed in the direction Otto had indicated.

It didn't take long to spot Arthur. He must have been walking incredibly slow. He headed for a water barrel, his long-legged stride eating up the distance. He reached for the long ladle and took a drink. Judith Carolina, who had been holding a bucket and walking toward the barrel, stopped suddenly as she caught sight of Arthur.

Arthur either didn't notice the fright that crossed her face or chose to ignore it. He smiled. "Let me help you."

"Um." Judith clutched the bucket to her, but her son Tagger grabbed it from her hands and ran over to Arthur.

Arthur smiled down at the youngest Carolina. "Why, thank you, Tagger."

Tagger grinned up at him while Arthur filled the bucket with water. Arthur looked at Judith after filling it. "I could carry it for you."

"No, no, that's okay." Judith took the bucket, some of the water sloshing over the side as she all but snatched it from him. She backed away, starting to turn before seeming to recover herself. "Thank you, Arthur."

"You're welcome."

Tagger hurried to catch up with his mom, but he turned and waved back at Arthur, who returned the gesture.

As Tagger turned around, the smile slipped from Arthur's face, and a look of wistfulness crossed it.

Lyla watched the whole interaction with mixed emotions. She knew it would take the camp time to adjust to Arthur's presence. She understood that. But when it came to his need to feel a sense of belonging, Arthur was almost like a child. He wore his emotions on his sleeve, and he wanted nothing more than to be accepted. Human looking though he was, his height and blue skin made it hard to forget his otherness.

"Morning," Lyla called out.

Arthur turned, the smile returning. "Good morning. You were up early this morning."

She nodded. "I needed to check over the crops, and there was a small issue with Thor last night."

"Oh no. What happened?"

"Nothing big. He just refused to return his food tray."

"You should have called me. I would have helped."

"I know. But you've been putting in long days. I thought you could use the sleep," she said lightly.

"Is that the real reason?" he asked quietly.

She shrugged, not meeting his gaze. They both knew that Arthur could help subdue their prisoners. But his presence was just as likely to rile them up more.

"Was anyone hurt?"

"No. The tray was returned. It was fine." She paused. "Any ideas though about how to get through to them that we're not the enemy?"

"I don't know. I had hoped with a little time they might begin to see that this life, even locked up as they are, is much better than what they had received under the Naku. Can you give them more time?"

"A little. But people are not happy. Having those two here, it scares them."

He looked down at her. "You mean having us three here."

She wanted to lie but found herself nodding her head. "Yes."

"Are they all scared of me?"

"Most, but some don't want to be. Emma and Edna have come around. Those that you interact with, they aren't as afraid, but just your size scares people."

"I can understand that."

"The children love you, though. None of them are afraid of you."

Arthur smiled. "They are a constant source of joy."

"That they are. I was thinking maybe you could help out at the gift shop today. Riley was going to start clearing it out."

He nodded. "I can do that. Are you still heading out?"

"As soon as I round up Miles and Petra."

"Be careful, Lyla. The Naku will be looking for you."

A shiver ran through her. "I know."

5

A whistle sounded through the trees. Vel changed direction, heading toward it. They'd made it to the Attlewood, but the place had been deserted. Some sort of battle had taken place. Scorch marks lined the fence and some of the buildings.

But while no one remained, there were also no goods, no supplies. Whatever had happened, the camp had had time to pack up before it disappeared.

Which didn't make any sense, unless they had known in advance the Unwelcome were coming. But then why the scorch marks? Why would anyone stay behind?

Unless they won the battle. Vel shook his head almost as soon as the thought crossed his mind. He'd taken on an Unwelcome or two in the early days and lived. But a battalion? While protecting innocents? There was no chance humans could win that interaction.

He made his way through the brush surrounding the camp, spying Grit waiting for him. He stepped out. "What is it?"

She nodded away from the camp. "An Unwelcome ship landed back there. The grass was really matted down, so it sat for a while."

Vel frowned. That was unusual too. What had happened here?

"I found a body."

Vel's head whipped toward her. "Show me."

Without a word, she led him thirty feet away. But as they approached he could make out the purple of the body's robe. The man's extremities and face had been gnawed on by the wildlife. "One of the liaisons?"

Grit nodded to the body's hands. "I think it's Chad Keyes."

Vel noted the rings, picturing the liaison for New City. He also noticed the rip down the center of the tunic, lined in blood. "Well now, Chad, who did you piss off?"

"It wasn't an Unwelcome."

"No, it wasn't." Unwelcomes didn't use swords or knives. They used their spears or their hands. They had no need for any other weapon. Vel stood, looking around.

"We need to find out what happened here. Contact the boys. I want everyone to split up. Visit all the encampments nearby. See what people know."

"Okay." Grit hesitated. "You don't think the camp actually won this battle, do you?"

Vel narrowed his eyes at her. "Lyla and her camp have over two hundred people in their charge. Most of them aren't fighters. With that baggage, there's no chance they won. No, something else happened here. We need to find out what. And we need to find that woman."

6

Riley wound down the path leading to the kitchens. The zoo had been almost completely destroyed in the years since the Incident. Seven enclosures remained, but only three of them were fully standing. The frames of other enclosures were still there and some of the pathways leading from exhibit to exhibit stood.

Riley meandered along one of those pathways now, trying to imagine what the zoo must have been like in its heyday. Animals had been caged and watched by humans for pleasure. Riley couldn't really understand that. Although, seeing as how most of the animals had come from other lands, he supposed he could appreciate the curiosity. They'd had elephants at this zoo. Riley would have loved to see one of them.

With that thought, he supposed he could understand the attraction of viewing different species. But what he couldn't really grasp was people spending a day or even an afternoon just wandering around, talking, laughing, and eating. No goal in mind. No job to achieve. Just relaxing.

And he realized with a jolt that maybe he had been indoctrinated as strongly as the Unwelcome. His life, like everyone's in the camp, was about survival. Oh, they might take some time off to swim or play baseball, but survival was always there. Always their focus.

But it was those little bursts of freedom, of relaxation from the everyday grind, that helped make the grind more bearable. The Unwelcome had none of that. There was never a day off or even an hour off. Riley knew Miles, Maisy, and Lyla were a huge part of why he worked so hard. He wanted them safe. He wanted them protected. He wanted them happy. They wanted the same for him. But for the Unwelcome, connection to others was not part of their life. What must it be like to never experience happiness?

Even knowing that, he couldn't let himself feel empathy for the Unwelcome. They felt none for the humans they killed. And at this point, after suppressing their emotions for so many years, maybe they couldn't feel any emotions at all.

He curled his fists, rolling his fingers and remembering the feeling of warmth flowing over him the first time his abilities had manifested. He'd been trying ever since then to figure out how he'd survived the fall from the bridge. How he'd survived being under the water. He'd had *gills*, for God's sake. That wasn't normal. And Miles. Miles had his arm back. How was any of that possible?

He'd been trying to reactivate those abilities ever since the attack at the old camp, but the only time he'd managed was on the walk to the new camp when Thor had tried to attack Arthur. But as soon as the danger had passed, just like all the other times, the strength had flowed right out of his body.

He had been wracking his brain trying to figure out what exactly triggered it. He'd thought maybe it was the presence of the Unwelcome, but when he'd been underwater, there'd been no Unwelcome. They'd been up on the bridge, but still. Besides, when he was around Anne and Thor, his abilities didn't material-ize. They'd tried fighting with Arthur, thinking maybe the threat of violence might bring them out. It didn't work. Of course,

Arthur as a threat wasn't very convincing. He winced every time he threw a punch. Half the time he called out what he was going to do before he did it. He simply didn't want to hurt anyone.

Riley had been batting around the idea of going a few rounds with Thor. Of course, if his abilities didn't kick in, he'd be in for a world of hurt. And possibly a world of dead, so Lyla had warned him against that avenue of investigation in the strongest terms possible.

Of course, Lyla was the other problem. She shouldn't have abilities. And yet she did. And from her time in New City, they now suspected his mother had as well. He ignored the bloom of grief and anger that appeared at the thought of his mother dying, sacrificing herself again to save her family. He shoved those feelings aside and focused on the bigger question: How did his mother and aunt, who weren't Cursed, have the abilities of the Cursed?

They needed to get those answers. He knew it was only a matter of time before the Unwelcome tracked them down. They'd been too interested in Lyla to simply let her go. And no doubt the reports of humans being able to fight off the Unwelcome had made it up the chain of command to the Naku.

They would be coming for them. And they needed to be able to fight them. They needed answers. The problem was, he had no idea where to find them.

And they were running out of time. The grumbles in the camp were getting louder. Frank and Lyla had managed to keep a lid on most of the angst, but it was an undercurrent adding to people's fears.

Riley turned a corner, and Adros called out to him. Riley stopped, waiting for Adros to jog over to him. His face looked mutinous. Riley frowned. He and Adros had come a long way in the last few weeks. The anger that had surrounded Adros before seemed to have almost disappeared overnight. But right now, he looked like he wanted to kill someone.

"You know where Lyla is?" Adros demanded.

"She went to find Maisy. What's wrong?"

"Some kids upset Alyssa and Rachel."

Alyssa and Rachel were Adros's sisters. Their father, Brendan, had abused them, and when it was discovered, he'd been banished from the camp, which led to him turning Lyla in to the Unwelcome. The girls had lived with Lyla, but when they switched camps, Adros had wanted them to live with him. So far, the arrangement seemed to be working out.

"What happened?"

"They're saying I'm a freak and that they're sisters of a freak."

"A freak?"

Adros nodded. "Because of our abilities. So I went to talk to the kid's dad."

"Who was that?"

"Sheldon Barker."

"Oh crap." Sheldon had stirred up trouble back in Attlewood before. He was one of those people who always thought everyone was against him.

"What's his issue now?"

"Our abilities."

Riley frowned. "But we saved everybody because of them."

"Yeah, but apparently Sheldon's saying that because we have them, the Unwelcome are definitely going to come for us."

"They were always gunning for us. We're Cursed. That hasn't changed."

"Well, Sheldon is telling people that we should all be kicked out so that the camp can be safe."

Riley's mouth fell open. "Kicked out? That's crazy."

"Yeah, well, his son was talking about it at school, and he got both Rachel and Alyssa upset that I might be kicked out like, well, you know."

Like their dad. Riley sighed. *Great.* "Look, let's keep Lyla out of this for now. She's heading to Meg's this morning. I'll find

Frank and tell him what's going on. You tell Rachel and Alyssa you're not going anywhere, okay?"

Adros's shoulders slumped in relief. "Thanks, man. I appreciate that."

"No problem. See you at training later?"

"You got it." Adros gave him a tight smile and headed back down the path.

Riley watched him go, not sure what to think. Sheldon was a pain, always stirring up trouble. But with people already upset with the presence of the Unwelcome, he could cause a lot more problems. The camp felt like its bonds were already tenuous. Sheldon stirring up trouble could rip right through them.

7

The sky was blood red with long, thin gray clouds streaking through it. Geothorxed grabbed Xechulia's hand. It felt so tiny in his, so fragile. He could feel all of her bones. "Hurry," he said.

She stumbled, but he caught her before she fell. Tears streaked down her face. Her blue skin looked gray under the layer of sand and dirt. He wiped her tears away. "Come, Xe. We can make it."

"I can't."

"You can, and you will." He yanked her to her feet and pulled her forward, then glanced over his shoulder. The sand stung his eyes as the storm grew closer. Lightning slashed across the sky, and thunder roared. Every now and then, the ground trembled as the lightning made contact.

Fear tore through him. Where was it? He scanned the landscape. It was a barren wasteland. Hills rose in the distance, reaching for the angry sky. Smaller hills and rocky outcroppings dotted the land between here and there. They did not need to reach the far range. He'd found a closer hiding spot just two days ago.

Focusing on the distance, he missed a new obstacle in front of him. Xe yanked him back before he hit it. His gaze barely registered it as a child. Bits of meat still clung to parts of its bones, a few pieces of clothing and hair all that the scavengers had left. It hadn't been there two days ago.

He didn't waste time trying to see if he knew who it was. There was no time for that and no purpose. No one mourned here. He pulled his sister to the side and caught sight of the small opening. "There!"

He yanked her forward, small rocks peppering his back and legs. "Hurry!"

He held her tightly. She was so thin he was afraid she would blow away with the wind. Already she struggled to stay with him, and the full storm wasn't even on them yet. He pushed on, each step harder than the last. A branch flew at them, and he ducked, barely managing to avoid it. With one last push, he stumbled into the small opening and pulled Xe in behind him. Her small body barely weighed anything. "Climb past me. It gets bigger farther in."

She did as he asked, and he rolled the rock by the opening across it, further protecting them. Sand began to pile up outside, and for a moment he worried they might be buried inside. But better to be buried inside than to be caught out in that storm.

"Baya?" His little sister's voice trembled from farther in the dark.

"I'm here, Xe." He reached his hands straight out and after two steps touched the top of her head. Her hands quickly captured his, and he pulled her trembling body into his. "Shh, shh. It's okay."

She sniffed. "I need to be tougher."

"Only with them. Never with me."

He felt her shoulders sag in relief. And he was content to hold her for a few minutes. Xe was three years younger than him. He should have been taken by the Naku two seasons ago, but he could not leave her behind. So he'd hid with her, and together they'd managed to avoid them. But he knew he would not be able to keep it up. He needed to teach Xe everything he could before he was taken.

He was not sure even that would be enough. There was a softness to Xe that the Naku would not want. He swallowed down the knowl-

edge of what would happen to her at the culling. Her only hope would be to be chosen as a breeder. She would never make it as a soldier.

He pulled away from her. Reaching into his pocket, he handed her two small, thin rocks and some dried wood. "Show me what you've learned."

With a large sigh, she took the objects from him. Stepping back, she crouched down low. Thor reached behind him and after a few steps felt the wall of the cave. He leaned against it, listening as rock struck rock. At first there was nothing but the sound. But soon, small sparks appeared. Finally, a small spark leapt onto the dry wood.

Xe let out an excited squeal.

"Gently," Thor cautioned as she leaned forward and began to blow on the flame. The small flame started to take hold. Xe scrounged around, gathering some additional wood and quickly building a small pile above the flame, careful to leave space for air to reach the flames.

She watched it, her eyes large, biting her bottom lip. She looked up at Thor. "Baya?"

He smiled. "It's good, Xe. Very good."

She wrapped her arms around her legs, smiling as she rocked back and forth, watching the flames.

Thor sat across from her. Neither spoke, both entranced by the fire. Sitting in the cave, the storm blowing outside, he felt safe. He knew it was an illusion. He knew there was no such thing as safe. But for just a few moments, he wanted to believe it. He wanted even more for his sister to believe it.

A flash of something in his sister's hand caught his eye. It was the object they'd found yesterday. It was round with some sort of picture on the face of it. "Baya?"

"Yes?"

"Will we ever see each other again after you are taken?"

She didn't say if he was taken. There was no doubt in her voice that he would be taken. There was no doubt in his mind, either. He wanted to lie. Avoid the question. He wanted to go back to just a short time ago when he'd almost felt safe. But the Naku controlled every aspect of their lives. Even here. "I don't know."

She nodded as if she expected the answer. And he didn't doubt that she did. She picked up a long, thin stick from the ground and slipped the object onto it. Then she held it over the fire.

"What are you doing?"

But she didn't answer, focusing on the object as it began to glow. Then she pulled it from the fire. Using the edge of her shirt, she grabbed it and plunged the face of it into the underside of her wrist.

"Xe!" Thor leaped around the fire as she cried out. He yanked the object away, dropping it to the ground as he inspected her arm. It was red and had taken on the vague outline of the face. "Why did you do that?"

Tears rolled down her cheeks as she looked up at him. "So you'll have a way to recognize me, even if I'm grown when you see me again."

Tears pressed against the back of his eyes as he looked into the face of the only being he had ever loved. They had been dropped here four years ago. Xe had barely started walking when they had been removed from the ship. He had cared for her all this time, keeping her alive. And she had repaid him by showing him what it meant to be loved. He'd seen the other children who'd been dropped, the ones alone. They were barely more than animals by the time of the culling. Thor had already had to kill a few of them himself.

Now, as he looked into his sister's face, he knew their time was coming to an end. Soon he would be taken, and she would be left alone.

He turned and reached for the ring. He placed it on the stick and put it into the fire. When it glowed, he pulled it out of the fire. Taking a breath, he plunged it into the same spot on his own arm, then looked at her. "So you will know me as well."

THOR'S HEAD jerked up from the pillow. The sky was still a pale pink, not the angry red of his dream. This sky looked pretty, peaceful. His home planet's sky had always been red with a dark haze covering the land, the smell of smoke always in the air. He sniffed. Here he could smell flowers.

He rolled to his side, and his sleeve fell back, revealing the scar. It had turned white long ago. He had not looked at it in years. Not since he had put on his uniform. He had not thought of Xe in years, either.

He sat up, taking a breath, the dream sliding through his mind. He could not remember the last time he'd dreamed. In the battalion, they were given a pill each night before they went to sleep. It ensured that they did not wake up, that they did not dream. During the day, all their thoughts, all their actions were directed by the Naku. It was ingrained in him to follow orders, to focus on his duty and nothing else.

And he had done his duty. But here there were no pills, no orders, no duties to follow. Here, there was nothing but time.

He pictured Xe's little face. They did not keep track of years the way the humans did on Earth, but he figured by Earth time, he had been eight and she had been five. They had taken him in the next culling. Xe had screamed and cried, even though he had warned her that she could not, that they would take it as weakness.

He had never seen her again. By the time he put on the uniform, he knew family and emotional attachments were weaknesses. And he did not think about her again. But here, she slipped into his brain. He knew she was grown up now, but in his mind she would always be that little girl in the cave. Maybe it would be better if she had become a skeleton on that planet than what the Naku put the females through.

He stood and walked along the edge of his enclosure, stopping in front of the hill where the little girl always sat. Every day she sat on the hill and read or ate her lunch or sang. Her name was Maisy, the daughter of the camp's leader. She was bigger than Xe had been, but she was no doubt the reason he'd been thinking of her. She had that same softness, that same weakness.

He turned his back on the hill, striding across the enclosure. He would not think of her, nor would he think of Xe, who was no doubt long dead. Weaknesses, both of them. He had no time for weaknesses. He began to do push-ups. He needed to keep up his strength. The Naku would find them.

And Thor needed to be ready to help destroy these humans.

8

The staff swung over Miles's head. He barely managed to duck to avoid it. He felt the breeze as it passed too close to his hair for comfort. He rolled, coming to his feet, bringing his half arm up as well.

Petra, her dark-brown curls pulled back in a messy bun, her pale green eyes watching him, a slight sweat on her tanned skin, stopped with her staff raised. "Nothing?"

Miles shook his head, lowering his arms, his legs feeling like jelly. "Nothing."

Miles and Petra had been sparring for a good five minutes. Petra had not once relented in her attacks. Miles had tried to return the favor, but between him and Petra, there was no competition. She was the better fighter. But this sparring match wasn't for training or to improve their skills. It was to see if they could somehow activate the abilities that had appeared during their battle with the Unwelcome.

Miles blew out a breath, staring at his half arm. He could still picture his arm full as he'd battled the Unwelcome that had been trying to reach the people of the camp. A surge of strength had spread through his limbs, and then, as if by magic, his arm had been whole again. And he'd had the strength to fight the Unwelcome. But as soon as the fight was finished, so too were both of those abilities.

The smallest Unwelcome Miles had ever seen was seven feet tall, but he'd heard reports that some grew as large as ten feet. Humanoid, they were extremely muscular and powerful. No humans could fight them.

Or so they thought. Now they knew the Cursed, who the Unwelcome were tracking down, *could* fight them. Strength, speed, the manifestation of an arm, and in his adopted brother Riley's case, the ability to breathe under water, had all aided them in fighting the Unwelcome and protecting humans from them. They just couldn't figure out how they'd triggered those abilities.

"I don't understand. Why isn't it working?" Petra asked, barely breathing hard.

Miles took a few deep breaths, shaking his head. "I don't know."

The fact that he couldn't figure it out was driving him nuts. He'd been thinking about it for the last few weeks since the battle had ended. On the long walk to the new camp, he'd turned every single moment of the fight, and the minutes just before the fight, over in his mind. He knew that somehow the adrenaline he'd felt must have released the abilities. But attempts to replicate it had failed every single time. "Maybe it's because I don't really fear you."

Petra raised an eyebrow. "I can take care of that."

Miles raised his hand, taking a quick step back. "I'm not saying you're not a good fighter. But I don't believe you would kill me ... because you wouldn't, right?"

She shrugged. "Probably not." A smile hid around the edges of her mouth.

"But during that fight with them, I didn't think that. The fear was real. I knew if I lost that fight, I'd be dead. The people of the camp would be dead. There is something about that fear that I think helped bring out those abilities."

"So what? We need to be in fear for our lives?"

He frowned. "Maybe. Or maybe we need to be fighting an Unwelcome and be fearing for our lives."

Petra glanced over her shoulder to where Arthur was carrying two bales of hay on his shoulders. His blue skin shone in the sunlight, as did his red hair. Maisy, Miles's eight-year-old adopted sister, was skipping along next to him, talking nonstop, her red hair just a shade lighter than Arthur's. With a shock, Miles realized that if not for Arthur's size and blue skin, he might actually be mistaken for Maisy's father.

Arthur smiled down at Maisy, looking completely enamored in whatever she was saying. And he probably was. He'd led a life completely absent of social contact, even though he'd been surrounded by other Unwelcome. Now he hated to be alone. Despite that difficult, stark life, he was easily one of the kindest people Miles had ever come across. Miles had found him with tears in his eyes the other day when he'd found a baby bird that had fallen from its nest.

"Yeah, I don't think fighting Arthur will put the fear of anything into us." Petra stepped next to him, a small smile on her lips as she watched the unusual pair head down the path.

Miles nodded. Arthur had started them all down this road of understanding. He had actually saved Riley and Miles's lives when an Unwelcome patrol had come across them. And that had been the beginning of their friendship and their better understanding of the Unwelcome. He was a good fighter, but he had no interest in hurting anyone at the camp. At the training sessions, it was clear he was holding back.

Petra's gaze strayed in the direction of the old chimpanzee holding. "Of course, the prisoners might not be as reserved."

Miles snorted. He had no doubt that was true.

Lyla appeared from the barn, leading two horses. She waved Petra and Miles over.

"Looks like it's time to go," Petra said.

Miles swallowed. "Just how mad do you think Meg is going to be about us skipping out on her?"

"Oh, she'll be mad. But hopefully Lyla can smooth it over."

"I hope so."

"Besides. Lewis helped us out. He deserves to know what we found out about the Cursed."

"Well, let's get this show on the road. Lyla said if we set a fast pace, we can hopefully be back tomorrow."

9

The trip to Meg's land took a few hours. Miles wanted to say he enjoyed the trip. It was gorgeous land that they were traveling through. Rolling hills of green dotted with tall trees full of leaves with rocky hilltops in the distance. Deer scampered here and there. They'd even spotted a few wild horses. And yet he couldn't relax. And he wasn't experiencing the normal be-on-your-guard-at-all-times kind of focus.

He kept waiting for an Unwelcome ship to appear in the sky. Or to hear and feel the heavy footfalls coming up behind them. At night, his dreams had been taken over by images of the Unwelcome swarming the camp. He knew Riley was having practically the same dreams, even though they never spoke about it.

"Miles, you still with us?" Lyla called.

Miles's head jerked up, causing him to pull hard on the reins of his horse. The horse danced around for a few moments at the action. Miles struggled for a few seconds to get her back under control. "Uh, yeah, yeah. I'm here."

Lyla raised an eyebrow. "We're almost there. Maybe a little less daydreaming. And remember, when we get to Meg's, you follow my lead. Do not speak unless I indicate it's all right."

"But we've been there before," Miles said.

"Yes, and we ran out on her before," Petra reminded him. "She's not going to be happy."

"But that was to save Lyla. She'll understand, right?" He didn't give either of them a chance to answer before he rushed on. "Are we sure we even have to do this? We'll probably never even run into Meg again."

Lyla shook her head. "Look, Meg can be a good ally or a ferocious foe. And Lewis, he's a good man. If he has a daughter who is Cursed, then we need to warn him about the abilities she might develop."

"But we're still not telling Meg, right?" Petra asked.

Lyla was silent for a moment. "For now, no. She'll want to know what you found, and she's no doubt heard about the attack at the camp. We will tell her about everything except your abilities."

"You mean our abilities," Petra said.

"Right," Lyla said.

Miles's nervousness only ratcheted up at Lyla's words. "Seriously, can't we just leave?"

Lyla shook her head. "That's no longer an option."

Miles frowned at her serious tone. "Why?"

"They already know we're here," she said softly.

"What?" Miles's head turned from side to side, but he didn't see anything.

"On the ridge," Petra said just as quietly, as she curled her lip.

Lyla nodded. "How long?"

Petra kept her gaze straight ahead, her shoulders relaxed, although there was a little strain in her voice. "They've been following us for about the last half mile."

"Very good," Lyla said softly. "It's Meg's people. But let's let them make the first move."

Miles nodded, bobbing his head and trying not to glance at the ridge.

The valley they cut through had tall cliffs on either side and a river running through the center.

It was the same spot where he and Petra had run into Cal's men. He glanced over at Petra. Her lips were tight, but he wasn't sure if it was because of the men on the ridge or if she was remembering what had happened here the last time they rode through.

"Heads up," Lyla said, bringing her horse to a halt. Petra and Miles did the same.

At the end of the valley, just where they'd appeared last time, a cadre of horsemen appeared. Miles scanned the group but didn't see Meg amongst them. Or Lewis, for that matter. But he did spy one familiar face.

"Oh, crap," Petra muttered.

"What is it?" Lyla asked.

"One of those guys, his name is Ham. He was one of the guys who we escaped from."

Lyla said nothing, just nodded.

The horses barreled toward them. Goosebumps rose on Miles's skin. They were actually going to stop, right? They weren't just going to run over them, were they?

At what felt like the last possible second, the three riders yanked their horses to a stop. Dust flew in the air, as did the horses' hooves. The riders pranced angrily in front of them before the horses settled. Ham leaned forward. "Well, well, well. Look who's come back."

Lyla ignored his tone. "I'm Lyla, leader of the—"

"I don't care who you are," Ham shot back. "You're trespassing. Drop your weapons and put your hands up."

The men on either side of Ham put a hand on the hilt of their swords but neither looked comfortable with Ham's words.

Miles glanced at Lyla and recognized the look on her face. It was the look she had before she explained in a very physical way why she was the head of their camp. *Ah, Ham, you poor, poor, stupid schmuck.*

Lyla looked over at Ham. "No."

Surprise flashed across Ham's face. "What did you say?"

"You may escort us to speak with Meg. But we will *not* be disarming."

Ham glared. Miles could swear he could see the wheels turning in Ham's mind, albeit incredibly slowly, as he processed Lyla's words.

Ham reached for his sword. "You damn well—"

Lyla's horse bolted forward. Her sword was at his throat before he could do much more than widen his eyes in fear. "Don't." She glanced at his companions from the side of her eyes, keeping her attention on Ham. Petra moved to Lyla's right to keep an eye on the other horsemen. Miles kept his attention on the guy on the left.

"We need to speak with Meg," Lyla said slowly. "We do not mean any harm, but we will not allow any of you to harm us, either." Lyla removed her sword from Ham's throat, backing her horse away a step.

Ham fumbled for his sword.

"No." The rider next to him lashed out. "You've made enough of a mess of this. Cool it." The rider turned to Lyla, bowing his head for a moment. "We'll escort you to Meg. But you will have to disarm before meeting with her."

Lyla inclined her head. "At your camp's gates, as is your policy, we will disarm."

The young man nodded back. "Thank you. Ham, lead the way."

Ham glared at Lyla before fixing his glare on Miles with a promise of payback in his eyes. But then he turned his horse without a word and started forward.

Miles let out a shaky breath, glancing over at Petra, who gave him a small smile in return.

"What's your name?" Lyla asked the rider who had ordered Ham forward.

"Pierce."

Lyla nodded. "Lewis's son."

"Yes." Pierce flicked a gaze at Petra and then Miles, another look full of meaning. "My father was hoping to see you again."

Miles returned the look. "We're looking forward to speaking with him again as well."

10

It took them another hour to reach Meg's camp. At the gate, they left their weapons, though Miles knew both Lyla and Petra had knives hidden in their boots. Meg's camp looked the same as it had the last time they'd been here. The color purple was everywhere. Most people wore tunics and lived in fabric tents. It looked like a medieval camp.

Most of it looked the same, which surprised Miles. It felt like a lifetime since they'd last been here, but it had only been two months.

To his right, in the distance, he could see fence repairs underway. The crop fields looked like they had been destroyed. Debris from tents still littered the area. Lyla nodded toward it. "Tornadoes?"

Pierce nodded. "Yes. We lost seven people."

"I'm sorry," Lyla said.

Pierce looked like he wanted to say more, but he closed his mouth.

Miles walked next to Petra, following the same route they'd walked to see Meg the last time. The water wheel still gave him a little thrill. It had so many possible benefits.

The doors to Meg's castle were held open as they approached. Lyla didn't slow. She strode toward it, stepping over the threshold without hesitation. Miles and Petra followed a little more cautiously. The foyer was the same: long with skylights lining it, making it feel bigger.

Lyla paused at the end of the hall beside the double doors that led to Meg's throne room. She held up a hand as the guards began to open the doors, then turned to look at Miles and Petra. Petra tugged on Miles's sleeve, pulling him forward. Lyla nodded at the guards, who opened the doors wide.

Meg sat on her throne, her face expressionless as they approached. Her white hair was once again pulled into a long braid, which was draped over her shoulder. Lewis stood at the right of her throne, just behind her. His face was equally expressionless.

Lyla stopped a few feet in front of the base of the throne. She inclined her head. "Meg, it is good to see you."

"Well, Lyla, you have more lives than a cat. You escaped the Unwelcome?"

She nodded. "With a little help."

Meg snorted. "Modest as always, I see."

"They had this with them." Pierce knelt, offering her the Unwelcome weapon. Miles's nerves rattled as Meg's hand closed around it.

"Consider it a gift," Lyla said. "A token of my thanks for helping Miles and Petra reach the university."

Meg hefted the weapon with a grunt. "A bit lighter than I thought it would be."

"The trigger is on the underside, but I would advise against using it in here. You wouldn't want to destroy such a beautiful room."

Meg nodded, her gaze not leaving the spear as she ran her hands over it. Her gaze shifted to Miles and then Petra. "Ah, looks like my two new friends have finally returned. I believe you were supposed to return with my men, were you not?"

Miles opened his mouth but found himself unable to speak.

"We were," Petra said, her gaze meeting Meg's.

Meg nodded with a small smile. "I see you haven't lost any spirit, despite your recent encounters."

"They were supposed to return to you, but when they realized that my life would be forfeit, they raced to my side," Lyla said.

Miles kept his face blank but couldn't help but glance at Lewis. They had discussed what they were going to say before they arrived. Lyla didn't want to mention the difference in the blood, even though they had told Lewis.

"A strong bond you have with your family and your followers," Meg murmured. "I heard your camp was attacked as well."

"That is true. The Unwelcome followed me back."

"And from what I hear, you were victorious."

"That is also true."

"I would like to hear the details of that fight." Meg stood and nodded at two of her guards along one wall. They pulled open a set of doors Miles hadn't noticed before. Beyond them was a long table, food already placed upon it. "Let us eat, and you can tell us this story. And then we can decide what punishment these two will experience."

Miles's mouth fell open. "Punishment?" he said, his voice coming out as a squeak.

Lyla squeezed his arm gently. "We would love to join you in a meal."

11

"You need to eat."

The Unwelcome in the enclosure said nothing, moved nothing. She just stood, her back ramrod straight as she stared at the wall.

Riley watched her, not sure what to do. Lyla had left this morning for Meg's camp. They didn't expect her back until tomorrow at the earliest, so Riley had taken over her duty of checking on the prisoners. Arthur's sister had barely eaten in the time she was here. Riley knew how much Arthur ate, so he knew she had to be feeling it. But still she refused.

The other Unwelcome ate everything on his plate.

Anne was being held in an old orangutan enclosure. There was a glass wall on one side and concrete walls on the other three with a single door. One Phoenix was stationed outside the glass wall and another at the door. Even with the glass walls, Anne couldn't see the other Unwelcome.

Riley sighed, looking at Anne's back. They had offered her new clothes, but she had refused. Thor, on the other hand, had agreed. Petra had shot the male Unwelcome at one point with one of the Unwelcome spears when he lunged at Arthur during the walk from the old camp. The action had spurred both the Unwelcome into being more cooperative, and they had walked the rest of the way without too much resistance. He hadn't been badly hurt, just some close burns, but his uniform had been shredded.

Riley wasn't sure if Thor eating and accepting clothes was a sign he was softening a little or if he'd decided it was just the most practical approach. No point starving yourself or walking around in rags if you didn't have to.

But Anne, she was a different story. She had refused to eat these last two days.

Riley had hoped that maybe with time away from the Unwelcome, and with seeing Arthur again, that maybe Anne would soften a little. But it hadn't happened.

So far she had only said one word to Arthur in all her time here: "Traitor."

"You're safe here. It's okay to eat."

"She won't."

Riley looked over his shoulder, not surprised to see Arthur. Riley nudged his chin away from the enclosure. With a look at his sister's back, he followed Riley.

Riley walked until they were out of earshot of Anne. He wasn't sure how to begin this conversation. "Your sister, were you guys raised together?"

Arthur hesitated. "I'm not sure 'raised' is the correct word. Our home wasn't like this. This is a paradise compared to where we lived. On my world, no care was given to children. Most didn't survive, so why waste the resources? Children were on their own. Only the strong survived."

Riley shuddered at the images he conjured in his mind. It was a miracle Arthur was as decent as he was.

"But ..."

"But?" Riley asked.

"Anne and I, we worked together to survive. For the first five years, we had each other's backs. Even when we first entered training, for the next five years, we looked out for one another the best we could."

"Then what happened?"

"We went to separate training areas. It was another three years before I saw her again. I almost didn't recognize her. And the same for her with me."

"Really?"

"When we were younger, food was scarce. All of us, we were little more than shadows. At age ten, once they've determined our potential, we begin a new physical regimen—specialized food, medical intervention, chemical regimens. It's called rovac. I grew three feet between the ages of ten and thirteen and gained nearly two hundred pounds. It was a very painful process. Our bodies are not meant to grow that quickly."

"You all go through that?"

"Yes."

"Why aren't they happy to get away from the Naku, then?"

Arthur sighed. "You have to understand, I was lucky. I was an interpreter. I was exposed to humanity's range of emotions. Your joys, heartaches, love. It was an education that helped encourage the small light of hope burning in the corner of my mind that our lives could be better. My sister ..."

Arthur took a deep breath, looking away. "She never had that. She was trained to be a soldier. Their lives are nothing but pain, isolation, and training. The views of the Naku are taught to them and repeated over and over and over again until my people cannot think any other way but the Naku's. They have never been shown kindness. They have never owned anything. They have never been allowed to make any choices for themselves."

"They're slaves."

Arthur nodded. "Yes."

Now it was Riley's turn to look away. He didn't like being reminded of how horrible the lives of the Unwelcome were. That they were the slaves of the Naku. It was easier to hate them. And he did. But it didn't change the fact that Arthur's words had affected him.

"How much time do I have?" Arthur asked softly.

"What do you mean?"

"I have seen the turmoil our presence causes. People do not like us being here, and they like using Phoenixes to guard us even less."

"I don't have a time frame. But if you can figure out a way to get through to them, you need to do it. They're a risk. And if they aren't providing us with intel or at least aren't a threat ..."

Arthur's head hung a little lower. "I understand."

"I'm sorry, Arthur."

"It's not your fault. And you have given them a chance. Not everyone would do that, so thank you." Arthur gave him a tight smile and walked back toward his sister's enclosure.

Riley watched him go with a heavy heart. He knew Arthur would spend the next hour talking to his sister, reminding her of their times together. And he also knew his sister wouldn't say a word. If Arthur was right, and she hadn't been allowed to think for herself for years, he didn't think there was any way he was going to be able to get through to her.

He glanced toward the monkey enclosure holding Thor. And there was absolutely no chance anyone would get through to Thor.

We should have killed them back at Attlewood. It would have saved us a lot of difficulty. He turned, heading for the kitchens.

And it would seem a lot less like murder.

12

The meal was simple but delicious. During dinner, Lyla told a carefully edited version of her rescue and the attack at the camp. Lyla made the spears out to be the factor that enabled them to win against the Unwelcome. Meg seemed satisfied with her story, though Miles had to dig his nails into his palm to keep himself from revealing anything.

Finally, Meg sat back. "That still leaves the issue of restitution. Miles and Petra did go back on a promise."

"What did you have in mind?" Lyla asked.

"Well, Miles here is as close to a doctor as we've had. I think he should stay with us for a month, teach my people what he knows, and then he can return."

Miles's mouth fell open. A month?

Lyla smiled. "You already have a doctor. Or is Sylvia no longer with you?"

Meg smiled. "Oh, she's with us. But it's always good to have two on hand. For emergencies."

"Well, as Miles is our only doctor, I don't think that will work for us."

"Perhaps Petra could be one of my guardsmen, just for a few months."

Petra's gaze met his, and he knew she was about to agree. "The water wheel," he blurted out.

All heads turned toward him. "What's that?" Meg asked.

"Uh, the water wheel. When I was here last time, we talked a little about what else it could do. I, uh, I think there's a way I could rig it so it could produce a small amount of electricity."

No one spoke for a moment. "You really think you could do that?" said Meg.

"I ... I think so. I'd be happy to try."

Meg banged her hands on the table. "Excellent. First thing tomorrow, you create electricity for us, and we'll consider your debt paid. And if not"—Meg smiled—"then I guess we'll get to enjoy both your and Petra's company for a little bit longer."

13

Riley grabbed the large wooden plank and threw it onto the back of the cart. His shoulders ached, and he wondered, not for the first time, where the heck those powers of his had disappeared to. They sure would make this whole task a lot easier.

Rory Hallidon, a Phoenix only slightly older than Riley, wiped the sweat from his brow and leaned on his pitchfork. He ran a hand through his dark hair. "There is nothing fun about this."

"Nope, there isn't." He and Rory had been tasked with emptying out one of the structures toward the front of the zoo. The roof had partially collapsed in one section, and the wind had blown debris in, which practically covered it to the ceiling.

Frank said the structure had once been a gift shop, which was apparently a place that people spent money on things they didn't need to remember a place they would probably visit again. Riley really didn't understand why the people of the Before did some of the things they did. He grabbed the end of a large tree branch. "Give me a hand with this."

Rory helped him pull it from the pile. They pulled slowly, the debris shifting as they moved it. When they reached the end, Rory grabbed it and helped push it on top of the cart.

"Getting a little full," Rory said.

Riley nodded behind him. "Well, here comes the new cart."

Arthur walked toward them, his shirt off, showing off his muscular physique. He pulled the large cart behind him with very little effort. Otto walked next to him, all six foot five of him looking tiny in comparison, making Riley not even want to think of how puny he must look in comparison to Arthur.

Arthur pulled the cart to the side of the other one and then walked around to join Riley and Rory. Rory handed him a water sack without a word. Arthur took a long drink, wiping his mouth with his arm when he was done and handing it back. "Thanks."

"No problem. You guys need a break before you take the next one?" Riley asked.

"Nah, we're good." Otto attached the leather straps to the front of the cart, and then he and Arthur stepped in between the straps and started to pull.

Riley and Rory stood side by side watching them. "They're like an extra set of horses," Rory said.

Riley laughed. "Yeah, Clydesdales."

Rory stretched out his back. "Well, enough break time. Back to work."

Riley grabbed his gloves and followed Rory. "Rory, where did you and your sister start out from again?"

"Out west. We were in the mountains. We spent a good year walking."

"Must have been a tough trip."

"It wasn't easy," Rory said. His tone held the smallest hint of warning for Riley not to ask any more about it. Riley heeded the warning.

"When I was a kid there was a guy who came through the

camp. He said something about some places having electricity out west."

Rory nodded as he grabbed hold of what looked like an old door and put it to the side. They could probably use that at some point. It was actually in pretty good condition. "Yeah. I saw a few places. It was never much. Maybe lights at night, but that was about it. Why are you asking?"

Riley hesitated, not sure how to respond. Rory was one of the Cursed, and so was his sister. He knew about their abilities, although his hadn't manifested at Attlewood. He didn't know about Miles's idea that it was something in the blood. He studied Rory from the corner of his eye. Rory was a good guy. He'd protected his sister for years, and he pitched in whenever help was needed.

"Miles, he has this idea that the answer to our abilities is in our blood. I guess I'm hoping we can find a way to answer some of the questions he's come up with."

Rory stopped what he was doing. "Do you think it will help fight the Unwelcome?"

Riley nodded. "I have to think that the more we know, the better off we'll be. We still haven't been able to use them again."

"You don't think ..."

"What?"

"You don't think it was just a one-time thing, do you? Like you used them and they're just gone now."

Riley's mouth fell open. He'd never considered that. Was it possible the abilities weren't a part of their DNA but just a fluke? Something with an expiration date? "I don't know. Miles definitely saw something in our blood sample, but he needs better equipment to figure it out."

Rory frowned. "You know, when we were passing through this one camp, someone mentioned something about a lab."

"A lab?"

"Actually they said *the* lab. They said the docs who were there were crazy smart."

"Do you remember where it was?"

"No. I'm not sure I'm even remembering that correctly."

"Would Tabitha know?"

"I can ask her. If you think it's important."

"Actually, I think it might be extremely important."

14

Meg walked at the front of the procession toward the water wheel. She and Miles were discussing what was possible and some of the materials he would need. Petra was right behind them.

Lyla stayed to the back of the group, walking near Lewis. When she was sure Meg was far enough away, she said, "Lewis, I was hoping I could speak with your blacksmith. Perhaps we could work out a trade for some of his work."

"I'll take you to him." Lewis nodded to the guards near him, which included his son. "Stay with Meg."

Lyla said nothing as she fell in step with Lewis. They walked along the path. A group of children ran past them, the dog that accompanied them barking and jumping with their laughter. Lyla watched it with a smile. She wanted that for the children of her camp again.

She saw the blacksmith ahead, but Lewis veered off in between two tents, leading Lyla to the edge of the camp's boundaries. He stopped and turned to Lyla, waiting.

Lyla glanced around to make sure they weren't being overheard, but Lewis had chosen a good spot. "There are some things you should know," she said. "Things we haven't told Meg."

He frowned slightly. "I don't keep secrets from Meg."

"I understand. And I'm not asking you to. I am just providing you with the information, and you can tell Meg if you wish. But it involves your daughter."

Lewis's whole body stiffened. "They found something else?"

Lyla shook her head. "No. The answer is probably in the blood, but the effect can only be seen in battle, battle with the Unwelcome."

The crease between his eyes deepened. "I don't understand."

"The fight that I recounted to Meg was mostly true, with one large exclusion: The weapon that turned the tide wasn't the Unwelcome's spears. It was the Cursed. *They* are the reason we were able to defeat the Unwelcome."

Lyla told Lewis about the battle and the abilities that manifested in the Cursed. His face remained largely expressionless while she spoke, the barest twitch of an eyebrow the only indication he was surprised by what he was hearing.

When Lyla finished speaking, Lewis remained quiet. She didn't rush to fill the silence. She had known Lewis for years. They had even fought side by side on a few occasions. He was a man of few words. And she knew right now he was picking and prodding at the information she had just provided him.

And she had a feeling he would come to the same conclusion she had.

"Meg cannot be told this," he said softly.

She nodded. "I agree."

Meg was a good leader. She took care of her people. But there was a ruthlessness to her that had only grown these last few years. If she knew the Cursed could be used as weapons, she would require each of them to fight. And then she would go looking for more. Meg's ambitions were held in check by the Unwelcome and by leaders like Lyla, who wouldn't stand by and allow her to run over other camps. But she was always pushing those boundaries.

Lewis eyed Lyla. "There's something you should know as well. The Naku are increasing the rewards for the Cursed."

Lyla frowned. "What are you talking about?"

"After the tornado swarm, we received a visit from the Naku liaison."

Lyla grimaced. She had killed the last Naku liaison.

"They offered us a full year's supply of food in exchange for four Cursed."

Lyla's mouth fell open. That kind of offer would be the difference between life and death.

"Meg hasn't said yes yet, but she's getting pressure to say yes. Four lives for three hundred is not a difficult argument for people to make."

Lyla felt a little light-headed at the thought. If the Naku liaison was making this offer to other camps, then things were going to get a lot more difficult for the Cursed.

"The Naku must know what the Cursed and you can do. It must be why they are looking so hard for them."

"I'm not sure that's entirely true," Lyla said. "They know our blood is different, but I don't think they know what our abilities are. I think that's why I was taken—to figure it out. And all the Unwelcome that attacked us were killed, as was their human liaison. There is no one to report back."

She didn't hesitate telling the lie. Lewis had a daughter who would be affected by the information on the Cursed. And he had, in his way, helped save her. So she owed him. But she wouldn't reveal anything about their two captives or Arthur.

"But they're still looking for you."

"Yes. It's why we moved camps."

Lewis was quiet for a long moment as he studied Lyla. "That might not be enough. If what you say is true, if the Cursed can fight and defeat the Unwelcome, the Naku will stop at nothing to destroy them, to destroy you once they learn the truth. You may not be able to run far enough."

Lyla met his gaze unflinchingly. "I know."

Lewis's gaze shifted in the direction where Miles and Petra were. "They'll think they're safe for now, but if Meg learns what they can do ... you guys need to get out of here. And don't come back for a while."

Lyla studied Lewis. "How many Cursed do you have?"

"Four."

"You can come to us if you need help, if you need to hide them."

"I hope it doesn't come to that."

"I hope so too," Lyla said softly.

And yet they both knew that one day it would come to exactly that.

15

She's late.

Thor sat in the shack at the back of his cell. There was a cot with sheets, a blanket, even a pillow. The covering was made of wood and had three sides. The fourth side was open to the former monkey enclosure. Surrounding him in a circle were bars twenty feet high, with more covering the top. Concrete, grass, and dirt covered the area. There was one tree in the middle with a rope and an old tire attached to it.

They had put him in a cell that at one point had contained animals. He expected no less of the humans. They were a brutish race. His guards stood twenty feet apart on the other side of the bars. Both held romags, the weapons of his people. The humans couldn't hurt them on their own, but they could do damage with a romag, maybe even kill them.

He had to admit, though, that he was surprised that he was still alive. He didn't know why they'd decided to spare him back at their other camp and then drag him with them to this new camp. But he knew eventually they would kill him.

But still, they were treating him better than he had expected. His cell was clean. They provided him food three times a day.

And the food ... He had never tasted food so good. On the ship, they had sustenance. It was vitamin infused and fulfilled all of their nutritional requirements. But this food was actually enjoyable to eat.

A burst of laughter reached his ears. He turned his head as a group of children raced by, a man with them smiling and laughing at their antics. Thor frowned. He did not understand this aspect of humanity. Their smiles came readily to their faces as if searching for the opportunity to do so.

And laughter. He'd heard it occasionally since they had arrived on this planet. But it still surprised him. He himself had never laughed. He did not know any of his people who did.

All except one.

He frowned as an image of the traitor crossed through his mind. They called him Arthur, their tongues too primitive to say his true name, just as they were too primitive to say his own name and called him Thor instead.

The traitor visited his sister every day. And every day he walked away looking dejected. He visited Thor as well, but Thor would not even give him the dignity of eye contact. By his estimation, the traitor was below even the level of humans.

He glanced at the sun. It was high in the sky. *She's late.* She had never been this late before. Perhaps she was not coming. A feeling of disappointment wafted through him. He jerked to his feet as if he could banish the emotion.

I will not be made weak by these humans. I am stronger than—

The song started soft, like a whisper on the breeze. Then it grew in volume and strength. Thor stepped to the edge of his enclosure. He could just make out the girl's pale red curls as she sat down on the hill behind his enclosure. He did not know the song. Before this girl, he did not even know humans could make such noises. He had never known there was such a thing as singing. He'd only learned the word by overhearing humans speak of how gifted the girl was.

He did not think it was weak to admit he had never heard a sound so beautiful. He closed his eyes, listening as the girl sang of love and loss. Her emotions filled the song as it made its way through the bars to him. He pictured Xe, her little hand in his as they struggled together to survive. At this moment, he felt closer to her than he had in years.

The last of the notes died away. He shoved aside the feeling of loss that accompanied them. He did not know why the girl chose to sing there every day. It could not be for his benefit.

Besides, he only liked it because it broke up the monotony of his day. He did not truly enjoy the sound. Nor the feelings in his chest they evoked. But when she sang, for those few moments, he was no longer in his stupid cage. He was somewhere else. He was somewhere free.

He started at the thought. What was wrong with him? Ever since these humans had taken him, he'd had these thoughts filling his mind. Thoughts about how he felt, what he wanted. He'd never wanted things before. He needed to get back to his people. He needed to get back to his duty. Duty was life. Here he had nothing but time on his hands, and it was clearly clouding his mind.

The tree in the middle of his enclosure shook as wind cut through the bars. Thor frowned as he stared at the sky. Dark clouds were rolling in incredibly fast, shifting and turning until they seemed to reach for the ground.

A tornado swarm. He followed the track of the clouds, realizing they were pointing right at the hill where the girl had been singing. Before he could do more than recognize the danger, they touched down. Branches and debris flew in the air. He hurried to the edge of his cage to see if the tornado would hit his enclosure and free him. Wind howled through the air, drowning out any other noises. Tree branches slammed into his cage and bounced off, some breaking though with the force of the gusts propelling them.

He held on to the bars, wind tugging at his clothes and hair. His gaze darted to where he'd seen the girl last. Funnels swirled across the area, heading away from the camp.

As quickly as they appeared, the funnels dissipated. The air slowly went silent as the white noise of the swarm died away. For a few minutes, all there was was silence. Then people began to emerge from their hiding spots realizing the danger had passed.

Thor gripped the bars, staring at the hill where the girl had been. There was no sign of her. Movement from a bench at the base of the hill caught his eye. The girl emerged, her hair wild around her face, twigs and dirt caught in her curls.

She met his gaze and offered him a small smile as she stepped toward the enclosure. Unbidden, the corners of his own mouth started to rise.

A cry from behind him caused him to whirl around. A group of people were gathered together, pushing the debris off a woman who had been buried. It took only a few moments to reach her. A man pulled her up and clasped her to his chest. Thor curled his lip. *Weakness.*

He turned back in the direction of the girl, but she was gone. But a new object had appeared. A small white bundle sat between the bars of his enclosure. His guards were watching the rest of the crowd and not paying any attention to him. Thor walked casually toward the bundle, waited until both guards were not looking, and then grabbed the bundle, easily hiding it in his fist.

He continued his slow walk of the boundary of the enclosure before returning to his cot. When he was sure no one was paying him any attention, he laid the bundle on the cot. It was small, filling less than a quarter of his hand. And it was light. It was covered in a thin piece of white fabric. Carefully, he pulled back the fabric. Two small round objects lay there.

He frowned, staring at them. They looked soft. Definitely not weapons. He picked one up, inspecting it. There was a red-colored line in between two sides of a pale yellow. On one side was a thin covering of white. Was it food? He'd never seen anything like it, although it did resemble something they called biscuits.

He brought it close to his nose and sniffed. He smelled raspberries and something sweet. His mouth watered in response.

He placed it back down quickly, looking around again. The guard glanced at him. Thor glared at the man until he turned away again. He watched the two objects from the corner of his eyes. He did not think they were dangerous. In fact, he was pretty sure it was the girl who had left them for him. Was she trying to trick him? Had they sent her, thinking he would be fooled? Were they trying to poison him?

No, that was not the game these humans played. Their leader had a directness to her. When she wanted him dead, she would do so herself. She would not hide behind a child. Weighing his actions for a moment longer, he picked up one of the objects, and after sniffing it again, he took a tentative bite. He gasped as sweetness burst across his mouth.

Holy Naku, that was delicious. He gobbled down the rest of the object, savoring the explosion of fruit, tartness, and sweetness that spread throughout his mouth.

He reached for the second one and halted his hand mid-grab. He would wait. Make sure they were not trying to poison him. And then he would eat it later if he suffered no ill effects. He wrapped the other object back in its fabric and placed it under his pillow. Then he lay down, disturbed to find a smile had somehow wormed its way onto his face.

16

The smell of lamb stew filled the air. Four members of the kitchen crew were finishing up the last of the setup for lunch—carrying out the tables and lugging the bins of silverware, cups, and bowls over to where Emma, Edna, and Saul would serve in another ten minutes.

Arthur scooped up the last of the stew in his bowl and swallowed it down. "Thank you. That was delicious. You sure it is not a problem for me to eat before everybody else?"

Emma waved away his concerns. "Edna, Saul, and I always eat before the onslaught. We get too busy otherwise."

"Besides, it's nice to have some new company. I've heard every story these two have," Saul said.

"Speaking of stories." Edna reached into the bag under her table. "I brought you a new book. It's called *The Power of One*."

Arthur took the book from her with a smile. "Oh, thank you. And I finished that book you suggested as well, Saul. I gave it to Miles. I know you said I should let Maisy read it, but it didn't seem appropriate for someone her age."

"Why? What was it about?" Edna frowned.

Arthur's brow furrowed. "It's a tale about a very disturbed

young child. He destroys his parents' home and has delusions of grandeur and frequent hallucinations. He shows no inklings of guilt or conscience at the destruction he brings. His only thoughts are about himself. I think he may be a child psychopath."

Emma frowned, turning to Saul. "What on earth did you give him?"

Saul looked like he was trying really hard not to laugh. "*The Complete Works of Calvin and Hobbes.*"

Emma's mouth fell open. "The comic strip?"

Saul nodded.

A small chuckle burst out of Edna.

Arthur looked between them. Were they laughing at him? "It was a truly disturbing accounting."

"Oh, oh, Arthur. That's ... It's funny," Edna said.

"Funny? He thinks his stuffed animal is real. He has no respect for his parents. He—"

"No, no, he's a child. Children's brains work differently. They are self-involved but not out of malice. It's a developmental stage. They're also full of joy, wonder, laughter. It's our job as the adults to teach them right from wrong."

"Well, Calvin's parents were certainly failing."

Emma smiled. "He was a difficult child. But his imagination, that was wonderful, not scary. You must have children where you're from. You were a child once."

"I ... I don't remember much from that. I began my training when I was very young. And we were not allowed to be children like Calvin or like any of the children I've seen here."

Edna reached over and squeezed Arthur's hand. "I'm sorry, Arthur. We didn't mean to bring up difficult memories."

He shook his head, gently placing his other hand over Edna's. "No, it's good to see how you treat your young. You protect them, love them. We had no adults to look out for us. It was only us children. It was not an easy time."

"But you had your sister, right?" Emma asked.

Arthur smiled. "She was so tough. From the very beginning, she was tougher than me."

"Has she spoken to you?" Edna asked.

"No. Not yet."

"Well, she will. You keep trying. That's what you do for family." Emma stood. "Now, I'm afraid we need to get dinner out before the savages grow restless."

"Oh, of course." Arthur stood quickly. "I'll carry the stew pots out for you." Before anyone could say a word, he strode toward the kitchen. He didn't like thinking about the time on his home planet or those early years of training. Honestly, he didn't like thinking of any of the time before he met Miles and Riley.

But there were moments with his sister that were branded in his mind. Moments of connection. As he'd told Riley, she'd had his back, and he'd had hers. For years, they'd had only each other to rely on. They had been sent to the same training battalion. But then he'd been sent to a school to learn the languages of Earth, and he had never known what had happened to her. Not until he saw her at Attlewood.

Arthur grabbed the giant stew pot. Normally it took two people to lift it, but Arthur could manage it on his own. He walked toward the table and placed it carefully on top.

"Thank you, Arthur," Emma said.

"I'll get the other one." He turned, heading back for the kitchen.

"They shouldn't let that thing near the food."

The words reached Arthur's ears when he was only a few steps away. He kept walking, but it was like a wave of cold water had been splashed over him, reminding him that as enjoyable as his meal with Emma, Edna, and Saul had been, he was not one of them.

He grabbed the other stew pot and put it on the table next to the first. A line had already formed. Emma gave him another distracted thank-you before starting to serve.

Arthur backed away, but Saul grabbed his arm, handing him a small bag. "Dessert," he whispered. "And don't you listen to them. You're good people, Arthur. We know that."

"Thanks, Saul." Arthur took the bag and skirted around the line. A group of men were at the back of the line. He felt their eyes on him as he passed. He kept his head down, not wanting to meet their gazes.

He'd never experienced this feeling before. With the others on the ship, he was accepted. He had never been hugged or welcomed in any real way, but he always knew his place. Here, he had friends and people who honestly cared about him for the first time in a long time, and yet he didn't know where he belonged.

Maybe it would be better for everyone if he did find some other place, far away from the camp. But even the idea of being on his own again opened up a hollow pit in his chest. He felt like he'd finally had a drink after dying of thirst for his whole life. And he couldn't imagine voluntarily giving up water.

He walked past Thor's enclosure. Thor glared at him from the other side, but Arthur just continued on to his sister's enclosure.

"Hi, Anixquold," he said.

Her back stiffened, but that was her only response. He sighed, his shoulders feeling so heavy. He just wanted her to look at him. He wanted to look into her eyes and explain why he had left his unit. He wanted her to understand that they were meant for more than just following the orders of the Naku. But she didn't turn.

"I'm sorry. I wish you would listen. I wish you could understand. The humans, they are not what we thought. They can be violent, but they have a great capacity for kindness, for joy as well. I think we do, too."

To his astonishment, she turned toward him, anger and hate in her eyes. "You betrayed everything we stand for."

But even as he read those emotions, he was happy she was at least *showing* emotion. It was a start. "No. It's not what we stand for. It's what the Naku stand for. We mean nothing to them. We have nothing. No relationships, no joy, no life beyond serving them. We are slaves."

She raised her chin. "I don't know what 'slaves' are, but if that's what we are, then I am proud of it. I serve the Naku, as I was created to do."

Arthur's heart sank. And this was the problem. His brothers and sisters were not educated beyond what they needed to do their duty. Getting them to understand that there could be more to life than just what the Naku wanted ... He didn't know how he was going to do that.

He unwrapped the package Saul had handed him. Inside were six cookies. They called them snickerdoodles. He took out three and placed them in between the bars of her cell. "There is more to life than what the Naku have told us. If you can at least accept that, then it's a start."

She turned her back on him again.

Arthur sighed. He put the remaining cookies in his pocket, not in the mood to eat them right now, before turning and walking away from his sister. If he couldn't convince her, who could he convince? Would he be the only one of his people amongst a group of humans?

He wanted more for her than a life of death and duty. There were no older Unwelcome. Growing old was not an option. He did not know what happened to the Unwelcome as they aged, but he knew they were never seen again. His moment of joy that she was interacting with him gave way to despair at the hate and anger in her eyes.

"Well, well, look who's conversing with the enemy."

Arthur's head snapped up. Three men stood in front of him. They were three of the ones from the back of the line. "I'm sorry?" Arthur said, not sure what the man was suggesting.

"You will be," one of the other men said.

Arthur frowned. "What—"

Pain lanced across the back of his skull. He pitched forward onto his knees, turning his head in time to see the large metal bar come flying at his face.

17

The grunts and muffled shouts drew Thor to the edge of his enclosure. He squinted, trying to make out anything, but whatever was happening was out of his view, closer to the enclosure where the other Unwelcome was being held.

A human flew into view, stumbling backward before getting to his feet. Thor moved to the edge of the bars as the man charged, and the object of his attack became clear: the traitor. Blood was splattered across his face and arm. His clothes were ripped and stained. Three men surrounded him. Two flew off as he backhanded them and lunged forward. A third charged with a metal pipe, slamming it into the back of his legs.

The traitor stumbled to his knees. He managed to get a forearm up, blocking the pipe with his hand as it swung at his head. He grabbed onto it and yanked it away. The humans didn't try to retrieve the pipe. They started kicking and hitting the traitor. And even though the traitor held the pipe, he did not swing it at them.

Thor grunted, not surprised at the violence. These were the humans he expected. The Naku had told them how primitive and brutish they were. That they looked for any opportunity to inflict damage upon one another. That their violent tendencies over-whelmed any other considerations.

The Naku were right. These primitive beasts did not deserve this planet.

"No!" The cry came from farther down the path. A small figure darted toward the men.

Thor sucked in a breath as Maisy threw herself on Arthur, using her body to shield him from their blows. In their anger, or perhaps just not caring, one of the men slammed his fist into the side of her face.

A roar erupted. With no small amount of shock, Thor realized it had come from himself. Feet pounded down the pathway. Maisy's brother grabbed the man closest to him, flinging him away before slamming him to the ground. Other Phoenixes grabbed the men, yanking them away from the traitor.

The man who'd hit the girl was flung against the bars of Thor's enclosure. He started to straighten, but Thor reached through the bars and slammed his head into them, dropping him to the ground. No one even noticed, except the little girl, now enclosed in her brother's arms as she watched Thor over his shoulder.

18

Riley clasped Maisy to his chest, his heart pounding. When he had seen her crumpled over Arthur, his heart had stopped.

Jamal slammed one of the men onto his knees. "You stay on the ground, and if you move so much as a muscle, I swear I will end you."

Addie kicked one of the men forward. "On your stomachs, all of you."

Adros knelt down next to Arthur. "He's in bad shape, Riley."

"Get him to Simon."

Adros nodded, grabbing one of Arthur's arms while Otto grabbed the other. Riley blanched as he took in his face. *Damn it.* He wished Miles was here. Simon wasn't nearly as gifted but he was all they had at the moment.

He looked down at a still shaking Maisy. Almost half her face was swollen. "Did one of them hit you?"

She ducked her head into his chest before nodding.

Riley tensed, trying to calm the anger rolling through him. They'd gone after Arthur and hit a child.

Addie reached for Maisy. "Give her to me."

"I've got her."

"Riley, I'm going to take her to Simon and have him check her cheek. Also, if I touch one of these men knowing they hit her, I'll probably kill them."

Riley took a long look at Addie and recognized the anger bubbling under her surface. And the fact that she was as angry as he was helped calm his own temper. He handed Maisy over. "Jamal and I will to lock these guys up, and then I'll find Frank."

"Lock us up? For what? That thing killed our people," one of the men sneered.

"*He* didn't," Jamal said.

"You know that for sure?" Justin Barker, Sheldon's brother, taunted. His pale blue eyes were scrunched tight, his lips a hard line.

Riley ignored him and glanced over at the unconscious man next to Thor's enclosure with a frown. "What happened to him?"

"Maybe he knocked himself out?" Jamal asked.

Riley looked at Thor, who stood on the other side of the enclosure. "Maybe. Come on, let's lock these guys up and find Frank."

THEY LOCKED the three men up in the only other fully standing enclosures. It had been used for penguins and had tall smooth walls. The men had complained about being treated like animals, but neither Riley nor Jamal cared.

Addie found them after they had locked them in. Arthur had sprained his hand and had a ton of cuts and contusions, but he would be fine. Maisy was all right as well, but she was going to have a really bad black eye. Emma and Edna were sitting with her and Arthur in the med tent. Maisy refused to leave Arthur's side.

Addie tugged Jamal's arm. "We're on duty. You good?" she asked Riley.

"Yeah. I'll find Frank and then go check on Maisy and Arthur."

"Okay. See you later." Jamal and Addie headed off. Jamal linked his hand through Addie's as they headed for the front of the camp.

Riley had just started for Frank's place when Frank appeared on the path ahead of him.

"You heard?" Riley asked when Frank reached him.

"I heard. What the hell happened?"

"It looks like Justin and some of his buddies jumped Arthur."

"They still alive?"

"Yeah, Arthur took the brunt of the damage."

Frank frowned. "Even with a group, Arthur would have been able to overpower them. They're not trained fighters."

"He was in no shape to talk when I saw him, but I'm guessing he didn't want to hurt them."

Frank shook his head.

"Maisy threw herself over Arthur to try and keep him safe."

Frank sucked in a breath. "She okay?"

"She took a hit to the face."

Anger flashed across his face. "God damn it. Where were the guards?"

"We switched the patrols, remember? Adros was on duty. He got there the same time I did."

"Oh, right." They had decided it was a waste of manpower to have guards just standing outside the Unwelcomes' enclosure. So now they had someone just patrolling nearby and checking in on them every few minutes.

Riley glanced back at the enclosure. "So, are we going to give them a chance to gather their stuff before we banish them?"

Frank looked at Riley and then looked away. "I'm not sure that's the plan."

"What? But that's the rule: No violence against any members of the camp. These guys meant to hurt Arthur. If we hadn't shown up, they could have killed him."

"I know, I know. But Arthur's not really a member of the camp."

"So what, he doesn't count? It doesn't matter if anyone tries to kill him? Are you kidding me right now?"

"It's not that simple, Riley. People are not happy the Unwelcome are here. We haven't gotten any good intel from them. And Arthur ... his presence is making a lot of people uneasy."

"But he hasn't hurt anyone."

"But his people have. Everyone here has lost people to the Unwelcome. When they look at Arthur, they see the enemy. They see the beings that robbed people of their family."

Riley supposed he could see that. But all it took was spending a few minutes with Arthur to know he wasn't like that. "What about you? Do you see him that way?"

"Arthur? No. But when I look at the other two, I can't help but think about David. He should still be here."

Riley pictured his best friend from that time before they knew of the Unwelcome's existence. He had been killed in the first camp attack, the one that had introduced all of them to the Unwelcome. He'd been only eleven years old and had been Frank's grandson. "But Arthur's not responsible for that. His people are slaves."

"True, but he's also the only one who seems to be unhappy about that. The rest are still following orders. And I have no doubt those two we're keeping in cages would kill us if given half a chance."

"None of that makes what they did to Arthur right."

Frank sighed. "You're right, it doesn't. But people are scared. They don't understand how you guys were able to defeat the Unwelcome back at Attlewood. They're still unsettled from that fight and from the move. They're all waiting for the Unwelcome to find us again. And then we throw three Unwelcome into the middle of all that. If we banish these guys, I'm worried it's going to break the camp. That they'll think we're siding with the enemy over the humans. So we need to be very careful about what we do next."

Riley knew Frank was right, as much as he hated the idea that Arthur was some sort of second-class citizen. God, Arthur had had a crap life. He'd risked his life to save both him and Riley. And now in repayment for that, he was being beaten by a group of Neanderthals. "So what are you going to do?"

Frank blew out a breath, running a hand through his hair. "I don't know. Let's table everything for tonight. Maybe tomorrow morning we can come up with an answer."

Riley looked past Frank to the figure moving rapidly up the path toward them. "Not sure that's going to fly."

"Why?"

He nudged his chin at the figure. "Lyla's back."

19

The trip from Meg's camp took three days. They'd managed to get some hunting in. Lyla was hoping some full bellies might help tamp down some of the uneasiness in camp. She also managed to trade some game for a bag of flour, oats, and even sugar at the trading post. Edna and Emma were going to be very happy.

So as Lyla rode through the front gate, she was optimistic that maybe they could turn things around. She just needed to provide the camp with a sense of security, if not hopefulness.

Then she saw Addie and Jamal's faces as she dismounted, and all that optimism fled. She had stopped in quickly to check on Maisy and Arthur and then headed right out to find Frank.

Anger boiled low and deep in Lyla. Someone had hit her child. Someone had hit Arthur. And from his wounds, she knew he hadn't fought back much. With his strength, he could have hurt or even killed any of the attackers with little effort. But he'd let himself be hurt to avoid hurting them.

Lyla took some deep breaths, knowing her anger was only going to get in the way, but it wasn't easy. The image of Arthur's bruised and battered face stayed in her mind. And even Maisy was going to have a nice shiner. But even as she looked at her little girl's face, a part of her was so darn proud of her. She had stood up to those men. She'd tried to protect her friend. She'd done the right thing. And that sense of pride helped cool her temper ... a little.

She rounded the path and spied Frank and Riley ahead outside the old penguin exhibit. The paintings of playing penguins were faded but could still be made out on the walls. She picked up her pace, coming to a halt before them. "What happened?"

Riley quickly recounted what he knew, including where Justin and his friends were now.

"It was Justin?" Justin was Sheldon's brother, but honestly, he was usually the less annoying of the two of them. "Justin's a complainer, but it's unlike him to take matters into his own hands. What changed?"

Frank shook his head. "Not sure. He lost his daughter to the Unwelcome and his wife. Seeing Arthur and the other two, it must have snapped something inside him."

Lyla hadn't known that. All she knew about Justin was he was a royal pain but a good worker. She looked at Riley. "How badly did you hurt them?"

He shrugged. "They're fine. Won't even need a doctor."

"Even with your powers?"

Surprised flashed across Riley's face. "Actually, they didn't appear."

"Huh." She'd thought for sure they'd appear when the danger was real. But if Riley's hadn't manifested when he was trying to protect both Maisy and Arthur, then maybe they were gone for good. A shudder ran through her at the thought.

That means the next time we see the Unwelcome, we're on our own.

But that was a worry for another day. "Riley, can you go see Maisy?"

"I'm sure Miles and Petra are with her now. She's fine."

Lyla stared at him. "Fine. Then just go away so I can speak with Frank in private."

Riley rolled his eyes. "I'm not a kid."

"No, but you're also not in charge. Go," Lyla said.

With an annoyed grunt, Riley headed in the direction of the med building. Lyla shook her head as she watched him go.

"He did well, Lyla. He wasn't lying about those boys. They're not hurt too badly. And we both know that he and Adros could have really done some damage."

"Guess they went and grew up on me."

"Kids tend to do that when we're not looking."

Lyla sighed, turning back to Frank. "So what are we going to do?"

"I don't know. But in the time you've been gone, more and more people have been reporting how uncomfortable they are with the Unwelcome being here."

"I get those two." She waved toward the area where their Unwelcome prisoners were. "But Arthur? He's a good guy."

"It's human nature to fear what you don't understand. And with the Unwelcome, there's more than enough to justify that fear."

"But Arthur's not one of them. He saved the boys, me, Max's grandson, and all those kids. He didn't have to do any of that. He could have just stayed with the Unwelcome or run away and stayed away from all us humans. But he didn't. He put his life on the line to save the boys before he even knew them."

Frank put up his hands. "You don't have to convince me. I know who Arthur is."

"Do you trust him?"

"I don't think he'd hurt us, no."

"But?"

Frank sighed. "But he's not one of us, Lyla. He's still one of them."

Lyla stared at him, her mouth dropping open. "How can you say that? You know he's not like them."

"But he's not exactly like us, either. And if *I'm* struggling to trust him fully, imagine how much more difficult it is for everyone else."

"But why?"

He paused. "I keep forgetting you don't remember anything of the old world. Discrimination, us versus them, it was a huge part of our world in the Before."

Lyla knew all about those times. Discrimination based on race, religion, gender. She'd read about the civil rights movement, the MeToo movement, the discrimination throughout time, depending on which religion was currently dominant. But judging someone by their skin color or gender or religion was more foreign to her than the Unwelcome.

"But that's not part of our world anymore," she said. "We've moved past those ideas."

"Since the Incident, people have been focused on surviving. There's an old saying: There's no atheist in a foxhole. But I think that applies just as well to us today: There are no sexists, racists, or bigots when it comes to survival. We band together to get through. Those other factors are way down the list of concerns. But now, we *are* surviving. Oh, we're struggling. But it's not like those first few years or even those first decades."

"So we're comfortable enough to be bigots again?"

He shrugged lightly. "So it seems."

Lyla shook her head. "I guess that's a warped sort of progress."

"And there's another problem."

"What?"

"People aren't just scared of the Unwelcome." He paused. "They're scared of you and the Cursed as well. Your abilities, they frighten people."

Lyla was at a loss for words for a moment. "But we used those abilities to *save* everyone."

Frank put up his hands. "Again, you're preaching to the choir here. But people don't understand why you can do what you can do. And it makes them nervous."

Lyla kicked a stray rock and watched as it rolled down the path before it hit a crack in the path and got stuck. And that's how Lyla felt: stuck in world not of her own making. She shook her head. "I mean, I get that to a certain extent. But they *know* us. And no one wants answers to how we have these abilities and why more than us. But no one's exactly stepping forward with any answers."

"Actually, Riley had an idea about a place out west. It's called the Lab. Rory and his sister heard about it on their trip here. Allegedly there are still scientists there. Maybe they could offer some answers."

"Maybe. But 'somewhere west' isn't much to go on."

"No, it isn't," Frank agreed.

Lyla scanned the zoo, watching people walking in small groups. Unlike in the old Attlewood, people walked quickly, their eyes darting around. "How scared are people?"

"Very, and it's spreading. This incident isn't going to help settle things down."

"No, it's not." Her gaze strayed in the direction where the two Unwelcome were being held. She still believed sparing them had been the right thing to do, but their presence had brought nothing but trouble. No intel, no information. Arthur hadn't even been able to break through to his sister yet, and Thor, well, he was Thor. They were not going to get anything from him. Good intentions had gotten her only trouble.

Frank sighed. "So now we have a rather small problem that's beginning to morph into a larger problem. And we need to decide what to do with Justin and his group. And what do we do with the Unwelcome?"

Lyla didn't answer him right away. She focused on one of the penguins behind his shoulder. It was hard to make out, but it seemed to be dancing with some other smaller penguins. The zoo could be a good spot for them. But it wasn't home, not like Attlewood was. Crops hadn't been planted. Roots of any kind hadn't really been established yet. There hadn't been time to set up anything permanent.

But it had the makings of a good spot. It was large, had a strong fence that covered half the facility. The cages actually could be converted into homes, as difficult as that might be for some people to accept. Montell and Lyla had found it a few years back. She had pictured in her mind what it could become.

But she knew now that would never happen.

"We need to split the camp."

20

As soon as the words left Lyla's mouth, she knew that was the answer. That was exactly what they needed to do: split the camp. Not just because of the Unwelcome in their charge, but because of the Unwelcome in general. After the attack, the focus had been on getting everyone out and safe. There'd been no time to think beyond that. But now that the initial panic had passed and the move was complete, it was easier to take a step back from everything and evaluate where they were at.

The Unwelcome would come for them, but not all of them. They wanted the Cursed. They wanted Lyla. They wanted their people. And anyone nearby would simply be collateral damage.

Frank nodded. "We should. We'll send Arthur and the Unwelcome to a different site. It will calm things down and allow us—"

"No. That's not what I mean. You need to take the camp somewhere else. Myself, the Cursed, and the Unwelcome will head in a different direction."

"No, no. That's not the answer."

"Frank, you know the Unwelcome are trying to find us. None of you needs to be at risk. *We* have no choice. So you need to take everybody else and keep them safe. I'll take the Cursed and see if we can track down this lab."

"Lyla, I'm not letting you go out there on your own. There's safety in numbers."

"Against humans, yes. But against the Unwelcome, the safety comes in smaller groups that are tougher to track. If we're gone, the Unwelcome will have no reason to target you. You guys can head to the other location we scouted."

"I don't like this."

"I don't either. But it won't be forever. And hopefully when we come back, people will have calmed down and will be able to view things a little more clearly. Besides, it will be safer for all of you."

He looked down at her. "But it won't be safer for you."

She broke off from his knowing gaze. She had been fooling herself ever since the Unwelcome had targeted her. She kept thinking they just needed to get away from Attlewood, away from the Unwelcome, and they would be safe.

But now she couldn't hide from the truth. She looked back at Frank. "There is no safe for us."

21

Vel and Grit had searched every inch of the Attlewood Camp one last time. They'd found some clothes, a few broken dishes but nothing that explained what had happened. He'd instructed his men to wait outside the gates while they searched.

He had twelve men, and he'd seen each one in battle over the last ten years. Most would trade their sister for a few bucks, and for that he trusted none of them. But they all feared him, which kept them in line. Once the search was concluded, he gave them each a direction and sent them in packs of two to find out what they could about where the Attlewood Camp had gone.

He and Grit headed for Meg's kingdom. Meg knew a great deal about what happened in her section of the world. Her people were loyal and reported everything to her. If Lyla and her people had passed through Meg's lands, she would know.

It took about six hours to reach the edge of Meg's land. He and Grit camped on the border, waiting for nightfall. When the darkness was complete, they packed up their small camp and headed in, using the moonlight to guide them. It only took an hour before they came across the first patrol. Two men stood warming themselves by a fire.

Vel and Grit moved to a series of trees nearby so they could listen.

"I'm not going to put up with him much longer. I don't care who his daddy is."

"Yeah, he thinks he knows so much."

"Meg only likes him cause he's giving it to her on the side."

The other man was silent for a moment.

"What?" the first demanded.

"Man, you can't talk like that. If Meg ever heard you—"

The first man spread his hands out wide. "Who the hell's going to hear us? There's no one out here." He took a swallow from the flask he kept gripped in his hand. "You know, one day, Meg won't be in charge."

The other man laughed. "You think you're going to be in charge?"

"Shut up, Aaron." The first man shoved the other one, who fell on his back.

He scrambled to his feet and charged at the first man. "You shut up."

Vel motioned for Grit to back away as he did the same. He headed far enough away that they wouldn't be overheard. Of course, being they were still fighting, he doubted they'd hear them even if they charged in on them on horseback.

Grit stood in the shadows. "What's the plan?"

"They're idiots. I think they'll just tell us what we want to hear."

Grit snorted. "Yeah. How about we just hit them a few times?"

"Nah, I think we'll go a little more subtle this time. You're going to get us the information we need."

Grit stilled.

"You got a problem with that?"

Grit spit out the words. "No, no problem."

"Didn't think so. Get going."

She pursed her lips, her eyes narrowing before heading back to them. She yanked off her cap, letting her long blonde hair fall around her shoulders. He followed a few dozen feet behind, watching as Grit's stride shortened. Her shoulders rounded. She hunched over, her steps becoming more hurried, less careful.

She stepped on a branch, letting out a small whimper as she hurried forward. Vel smiled. She was good at this. Had been since she was a kid.

Another branch snapped as Grit hurried forward.

"Who's out there?" a voice demanded.

"M-me," Grit said, her voice shaking.

"Keep your hands where we can see them."

Vel slipped into the trees, making his way to the other side of the fire so he could have a better view. He got into position just as Grit stepped into the light. Instead of the fierce woman who could take down a man twice her size in less time than it took her to lace her boots, she now stood quaking, her eyes darting around the fire, her breathing panicked.

The two men fell for her routine immediately.

One quickly put his sword back in its scabbard. "Hey there. No need to be scared. I'm Aaron, and this here is Ham. What's your name?"

"I'm ... I'm Polly."

"Well, what are you doing out here all alone, Polly?"

She took a shuddering breath. "My-my camp. I lost them. There was an attack. And I ran and I ran." A tear escaped the corner of her eye.

"Hey now, no need for that. I'm sure we can help you find your way back."

Grit shook her head. "No, no. I managed to get back. But they were gone. They were all gone!"

Ham and Aaron exchanged a look before Ham spoke. "You wouldn't be from Camp Attlewood, would you?"

Grit's eyes widened. "Yes. You know us? Do you know where my camp is? My family, I just—" She swallowed, her hand going to her mouth.

"Now, now, don't go getting yourself upset again. Your camp's fine. Well, as far as we know."

"But how can you know that? You don't know what happened."

"Well, your leader Lyla was here just two days ago with that son of hers and one of your Phoenixes."

"They were?"

"Sure were."

"Do you know where they went?"

"Not exactly."

Grit's bottom lip began to tremble.

"B-but we know they moved camps," Aaron said quickly.

"Come to think of it," Ham said, frowning, "Lyla said all her people were accounted for. So how come she didn't know you were missing?"

Grit shrugged her shoulders. "I don't know. My parents, they should have said something."

Aaron frowned, studying her.

Grit shook her head. "You know what? I'm sick of this." She pulled out her sword.

Vel sprang from his hiding spot. Ham spun around. "Wha— What's going on?"

"You sure you don't know where they went?" Vel demanded.

"Somebody said something about an old zoo," Ham stammered out.

Grit smiled. Ham started to smile back. Vel nearly laughed out loud. When Grit smiled, you better start running.

"Hey!"

Vel's head jerked to the side as three men sprinted for them. Damn it. He sliced at Ham's chest as he sprinted past, catching the man on the shoulder. Grit managed to plunge her sword in Aaron's side before disappearing into the trees.

Footsteps stormed after them in the dark. Vel ran through the darkened forest, heading to a patch of closely grown trees that blocked out the moonlight. Eventually the footsteps faded behind him, his pursuers giving up.

He continued on, heading for the border, where he'd meet up with Grit, unless she'd gotten grabbed. He'd give her an hour and then take off without her. Lyla had another camp, an old zoo.

And he thought he might know exactly where that was.

22

Pierce hurried through the gates and handed Ham and Aaron over.

The gash on his right arm that he'd hastily bandaged before taking his horse had loosened, allowing the blood to flow freely down his arm. He'd caught it on a branch of all things.

"Pierce, do you need the doctor?" Angela said as she hurried next to him, handing him a cloth.

"What?"

"Your arm."

He looked down, surprised at the blood flowing there.

Angela pressed a cloth down on the wound. He shook his head. "Not now. I need to speak with Meg."

"Wait. Let me at least tie that off. We can't have you bleeding all over Meg's floor."

Pierce winced at the disgruntled tone in Angela's voice, as he knew her sister would be the one in charge of cleaning that floor. He came to a stop. "Quickly, then."

"Quickly, then," Angela mocked even as her deft fingers pulled a roll of thin fabric from her pockets and began to wind it around the cloth on his arm. Angela always seemed to have a roll of fabric bandages or ointment tucked away. She wasn't the camp's doctor, but she was a pretty good medic.

She tightened the cloth, and he winced in response. She smiled. "There. Now Isolde won't complain to me all night about your blood."

Pierce chuckled because they both knew Isolde never complained. "Thanks, Angela." Pierce took off again, widening his stride and picking up his pace until he was just shy of running. The guards at Meg's saw him coming and held the doors open.

"She's expecting you," one of them said.

He nodded his thanks as he strode through. Isolde was in the hall as he entered. She gave him a small smile.

He smiled back with effort before passing her. The throne room doors were thrown open. He hurried through them. Meg and his father were waiting.

"Report," Meg ordered.

Pierce started speaking when he was barely a quarter of the way to the dais. "Two men on the northern border. Two east. And another two west. The ones on the northern border were killed. The eastern and western infiltrators escaped."

"What were they doing?"

Pierce exchanged a look with Lewis before speaking. "Searching the ground. They were looking for a trail. This was found on the two killed." He stepped forward, placing the bracelet he had yanked from the dead man's wrist into Meg's outstretched hand.

Her face darkened as she examined the smooth, soft rubber bracelet. Although not made of metal, the bracelet was sturdy and inscribed with an alien language.

"Bounty hunters." All her animosity and disgust with humans who would turn on their own kind were laced into her words.

"They were looking for Lyla," Pierce offered.

Meg shook her head. "Stupid. Lyla wouldn't leave a trail. If they wanted to find her they should head back to Attlewood and follow the larger group. *They* will have left a trail."

"What would you like us to do?" Lewis asked.

"What have you done, Lyla?" she said softly before sitting back, the bracelet curled in one hand, the fingers of the other hand drumming on the arm of her throne. "Double the patrols. I want to know every individual, human or otherwise, who steps on our land."

"You think the Unwelcome will come?" Pierce asked.

"Unlikely. They use their pets to do their dirty work. They won't show until they know where Lyla's camp is. That stupid girl," she muttered.

"I would like to ride to Attlewood," Lewis said, "scout around and make sure it is Lyla they're looking for. Make sure there isn't another threat we're overlooking."

"I can't spare a contingent."

"I won't need one. I'll take Pierce."

Meg nodded, a light coming into her eyes. "Very well. You have four days. Find out what you can and report back. And do *not* get killed."

Lewis bowed. "Yes, ma'am."

She waved him away. "Go make your preparations and speak with the guard."

Pierce's father immediately left to work out a schedule for the guards before speaking with the stable to arrange their horses for the morning. He spoke with another half dozen people as he passed, arranging the supplies they'd need.

Pierce didn't want to leave the camp. And his father shouldn't either, not with Meg trying to push him out of the decision-making process. She would undeniably use his absence to agree to the Naku's offer. Imogen and the rest of the Cursed needed them to stay here.

But he never had the chance to tell him any of that. His father sent him to convey his orders to the remaining troops on the edges of their land. By the time he returned home, his father was in counsel with the heads of his guard.

He sat eating the stew his mother had left for him, waiting for his father, and ended up falling asleep at the table.

A kiss on the side of his head woke him the next morning. "Time to rise, sleepyhead."

Pierce straightened, rubbing his eyes and stretching, the blanket that his mother had no doubt placed over him sometime during the night falling from his shoulders.

"That could not have been a good night's sleep," she said. His mother was small of stature and as soft as his father was hard. She always had a comforting word, a supportive phrase. But she also had a spine of steel.

He grimaced, his back supporting her words. "No, it wasn't."

"Your father is waiting by the gate for you. I told him to let you sleep to the last moment. But you should hurry."

Pierce looked out the window. The sun wasn't even up yet. He frowned. Why were they leaving so early? "I don't think I should go. You don't understand what's—"

His mother fixed him with a look. "I know everything. And you need to trust your father." She handed him a bag heavy with food. "That's your and your father's breakfast. You can eat it once you're underway."

"But—"

She kissed his cheek and pushed him out the front door. "Go."

He stood on the threshold for a moment, his mind still a little addled from sleep. But then his mother's words came back to him. *Your father is waiting by the gate for you.* He started to jog toward the front gate. His father wasn't a fan of waiting. He would just have to convince him that they needed to stay.

He rounded the stables and caught sight of his father standing with two horses.

He shot a look at his father, who warned him with a shake of his head not to say anything.

"So, I see you've finally rolled out of bed," Marcus said as he walked toward the gate to unlock it.

Pierce secured the food on one of the horses. "Ha, ha. Very funny, Marcus."

"I am a funny guy," Marcus said as he pulled the gates wide. "Happy hunting."

Lewis had already taken his mount and was heading through the gate by the time Pierce took his mount.

His father took the lead, leaving no room for talking, and he set a brutal pace. Pierce had no chance to eat his breakfast or speak at all. He'd hoped they would be heading toward Lyla's new camp, that his father had been just saying Attlewood for Meg's benefit, but with a sinking feeling he recognized they were heading toward the old camp. An hour later they were heading off Meg's land. Almost as soon as they did, his father pulled the horse to a stop. "Let's have some breakfast."

Pierce frowned. His father had set a blinding pace, and now they were going to relax over breakfast?

He dismounted from his horse. "Dad, we can't leave. You know Meg will accept the—"

His dad removed the bag of food his mother had given him. "See to the horses. They need some water."

Pierce practically swallowed his tongue as he did as his father asked. He led both horses to a nearby stream, tying their reins to a low branch. He took a breath, knowing he needed to be calm when he spoke with his father.

He headed back, determined to get his father to understand the importance of staying close to home.

"Dad, we need to go back. You know Meg is going to agree to the Naku's offer as soon we're gone."

"I know." His father took a bite of jerky.

Pierce stared at him. "You know? Then what are we doing?"

Lewis finished off his jerky and took a sip of water. "It doesn't matter."

"It doesn't matter? How can you say that? She'll turn the Cursed over. Imogen will be killed!"

Lewis stood, wiping his hands on his pants. "It doesn't matter, Pierce. Have some faith."

Pierce gaped at his father. What was wrong with him? Then hoofbeats sounded from the east. Pierce turned, his hand moving to the hilt of his sword. His father placed a hand over his. "You won't need that. *They* are the reason it doesn't matter what Meg decides."

His father strode forward just as four riders crested the top of the hill and started to make their way toward them. In the lead was Imogen, her blonde hair flowing behind her. And following her were the other three Cursed from their camp.

23

The old zoo stood spread out before Vel. It had taken a while to find the place. The information from Meg's people had helped, but Lyla was good at covering her tracks. But they'd seen smoke two nights ago. Following it had led them right here.

Now, he was a half mile away, the binoculars at his eyes giving him a bird's-eye view of the place. It had taken him longer than he'd liked to find it. When he'd found Attlewood abandoned, he'd been sure the trail would be easy to follow and was surprised at how well they had covered their tracks. In fact, the trail they had been following had led them in the completely wrong direction.

But her connections were what doomed her. He had no doubt if she was on her own, he'd still be looking for her. But she wasn't, and those people had spelled her doom.

She'd been a worthy opponent. But like all his targets, she was now his.

"She there?" Grit asked next to him.

Vel lowered the binoculars. "Haven't seen her yet. Looks like they're moving on. But take a look at this." He handed the binoculars over to Grit.

"Where am I looking?"

"Oh, you'll know what I'm talking about when you see it."

Grit frowned, scanning the zoo before her whole body went rigid. "Is that guy blue?"

"There's two of them. One looks like he just got the crap beaten out of him."

Grit's mouth fell open. "So that's what they look like."

"I don't think the Naku even know these guys are here."

"Think they'll pay us extra?"

Vel shook his head. "Not their way."

"Did you contact them?"

"No. I haven't seen Lyla yet."

"You think she's still with them?"

"Oh, she's still with them. I've seen all her kids. She wouldn't leave them on her own. She'll be back."

"And when she is?"

Vel lowered the binoculars with a smile. "Then we get paid."

"Then I think it's payday." Grit smiled as she handed the binoculars back.

Vel focused on where she indicated and saw Lyla's dark-brown hair. "Well, so it is."

24

It had taken a week to arrange for the move. The first small group was sent four days after Frank and Lyla had spoken. They would get the initial area secured and ready for the larger group. The site was a small neighborhood that seemed to have avoided most of the major destruction. There were four buildings still standing and two working wells, but there were no fences or protection, which was why it hadn't been higher on the list. But now that would be taken care of as well.

Yesterday, the first large group had left. This morning, the second. Tomorrow, the last of the group would leave, along with Maisy. She wasn't handling the news well. And the idea of not being with her was killing Lyla.

Addie and Jamal had agreed to keep her with them. Looking after Maisy was also the only way she could get them to agree to go. Most of her Phoenixes had balked at the idea of splitting the camp. Otto and Montell straight up refused to go until Lyla promised she would be back.

But the trip ahead of her terrified her. They didn't know what they were facing and whether or not they could even find this lab. And if they ran into trouble ... The older kids, they could fight. But the younger ones were only twelve years old. They had never truly been tested in a fight. What if the Unwelcome found them and their abilities didn't appear? It would be a bloodbath.

But she locked all those fears down. She could not let anyone see how scared she was for the days to come. She slipped into the medical tent. Arthur was sitting on the edge of the bed, struggling to get into a shirt. His chest was still a mass of dark bruises, although the color had lightened over the last week. Miles didn't think he had any broken ribs but was pretty sure he'd bruised a few. His hand was wrapped in a splint.

Lyla walked over to him. "What are you doing?"

He looked up, his blue eyes locking onto her gaze. "You'll need my help with the move."

With a sigh, Lyla grabbed half his shirt, guiding his arm through. "You're supposed to be resting."

Arthur shook his head. "I'm fine." He paused. "I can go. You can stay with your people."

She shook her head, sitting next to him on the cot. "You're not the problem. The Unwelcome will be trying to track us. But they don't want everyone. Just me and the Cursed. *You* should probably go off somewhere else. It would be safer for you."

He took her hand. "I am staying with you."

She looked into his eyes, and the air between them seem charged.

"Hey, Arthur." Riley barged into the tent, Miles right behind him.

Lyla quickly dropped Arthur's hand and stood up. The two boys came to a standstill looking between them.

"Uh, did we interrupt something?" Miles asked.

"No, no. I was just telling Arthur it would be safer if he didn't come with us."

"She's right. They don't even know you're alive. You could hide out somewhere and be fine," Riley said.

Arthur shook his head. "I'd be alone. That is not fine. What about my sister and Thor?"

Lyla met Riley's gaze before speaking. That topic had been the subject of much debate. The safest thing would be to kill them. But none of them could bring themselves to commit outright murder. "We're letting them go."

Arthur's head snapped to her. "What?"

"Three days after the camp is gone, I will loosen the door locks. It will take them a good long while to break through, by which time I will be long gone. That will give us time to cover the tracks of the camp. Once they're out, they can make their way back to their people. Or disappear. It won't matter. They won't know where we're going. They can't tell them anything of importance."

"Except that you've split up," Arthur said.

Lyla nodded. "And we *want* them to know that. We want them to know that the rest of the camp doesn't have anyone they are interested in, so they'll leave them alone."

"That's ... very decent of you."

Lyla just shrugged. "Well, since you're up, let's go. We were going to have a little meal at the kitchen to say goodbye. Maisy will be heartbroken if you're not there."

Arthur put his hand over his heart. "It hurts to think of not seeing her for a while."

Lyla nodded. "That's love. And yes, it does."

The hair on the back of Lyla's neck rose. She turned slowly to the entrance of the building. Miles and Riley did the same. "You guys feel that?"

They both nodded.

"Feel what?" Arthur stood.

A blasting noise sounded from the front of the camp. Lyla sprinted for the door. "The Unwelcome. They've found us."

25

They were moving the camp. No one had said anything to him, but Thor could read the signs. Now he prowled along the edge of his enclosure, feeling for once like one of the animals for whom it had been intended.

They'll wait until the rest are gone. Wait until there are fewer witnesses. He knew they would come for him. He was a risk to leave behind, and they certainly weren't going to take him. He wasn't sure what exactly had happened, but he suspected that the camp was splitting up.

Ever since the fight with the traitor, the camp had been different. It was as if lines had been drawn amongst the members. Maisy had only been by twice in the last week, and she hadn't sung either time. She'd sat up on the hill and watched his enclosure while pretending to read a book. The traitor had been nowhere around.

Each time he'd seen her she'd been found and taken away shortly after she arrived.

"Hello."

Thor whirled around. It was as if he had conjured her up out of thin air. She stood twenty feet away. Unless someone came all the way down the path, she would be hidden from view.

Thor didn't move closer and didn't say anything. She was the first child who had spoken to him since he was a child himself. For the first few years after they had arrived, he'd been stationed on the ship. Then he'd been sent on rotating patrols. Some days he would be in New City at the research building. Other times he was sent as part of the camp investigations. But children had always cowered from him, and even then it was only at a distance. Why was this child so different?

"We're leaving soon. Most of the camp is already gone. My mom, she won't let me go with her." The girl sniffed. She sat on the ground, her knees pulled to her chest.

Thor took a small step forward and could make out the tears on her cheeks. Unbidden, words fell from his mouth. "Why are you crying?"

The girl looked up at him. She didn't seem surprised when he spoke. "Because she won't take me with her. She says I'll be safer with the rest of the camp. My brothers are going with her. All the Cursed are."

Splitting up. He was right. Had they sent the child to feed him false information? She seemed an unusual choice for a messenger.

She wiped at her eyes. "I'm not useless. I can help. I can fight. My whole family is leaving me behind." She took a deep breath, her whole body seeming to shudder as she looked up at him. "They're going to free you after everyone's been gone a few days. Then you can go back to your family."

"I don't have one."

"Everyone does. I've had two. My first, they were killed by the —" She looked up at him and shrugged. "But then Lyla found me. Her, Miles, Riley, we're a family."

She stood, wiping the dirt from her hands on the sides of her pants. "I should go. They're going to be looking for me."

She shifted from foot to foot, glancing over her shoulder, but made no move to leave. Biting her lip, she looked up at Thor. "When you go back, could you do me a favor?"

He didn't say anything, just watched her.

She took a deep breath. "Don't kill my family if you find them. Please?"

Thor didn't know what to say. She stood there looking up at him with her big eyes, eyes as big as Xe's. Someone called her name in the distance. Maisy looked over her shoulder and then back at him. "Goodbye, Thor. Don't forget me, okay? I won't forget you."

His heart felt heavy as a different little girl's voice cut through his mind. *So you'll have a way to recognize me, even if I'm grown when you see me again.*

A blasting noise sounded from the front of the camp. Thor whirled around, his gut tightening. His compatriots were here.

The girl. He turned around to warn Maisy to run, but she was already gone.

Run fast, child. He pictured Lyla and hoped she reached her in time. Then he strode to the other side of the enclosure to wait for his release.

26

The ride from Meg's camp to Lyla's new one took nearly two full days. Lewis had ridden over these same lands many times before during his patrols, but these last two days he had seen it through new eyes. He saw it through Imogen's and the other Cursed.

The children had rarely left Meg's camp. As Cursed, it was simply too dangerous. He had a trapdoor in the floor of his home that led to a small room where Imogen and the other three Cursed from the camp hid when the Unwelcome stopped for one of their inspections.

All of the Cursed looked at their surroundings with wide-eyed wonder, but Lewis's gaze kept finding its way back to Imogen. Her delight at everything she saw was eye opening. He realized she had been a prisoner for almost all her life. They had kept her hidden for her own good and because they loved her, but it didn't change the fact that she had led her life within the confines of the camp.

Now, she watched deer running through a field with bright eyes. She had laughed in delight at two bunnies that came near their camp this morning. And Lewis felt guilt for not allowing her more freedom while at the same time knowing it had been impossible.

Even with those thoughts, he still wasn't sure if bringing Imogen and the rest of them was a good idea. If an Unwelcome patrol came across them ...

But he feared the camp was no longer safe for them, either. He knew Meg. She would eventually accept the Naku's offer, and he couldn't really blame her. She had an entire camp to think of. He had debated waiting a little longer, but then Meg had called an advisor's meeting two days before when Lewis had been at the edge of their lands. She had never held a meeting without him since she'd made him her second. It meant she was planning on accepting the Naku's offer. After telling his wife about the advisor's meeting, she had insisted he leave as soon as the opportunity presented itself.

And his wife was right. Imogen needed a chance at a life. Which meant they needed answers and a safe place to wait while they got them. And Lyla was their best chance for both of those.

"Dad," Pierce called, a warning in his tone.

Lewis pulled himself from his thoughts, focusing on the area Pierce was pointing to. A herd of deer were racing away from the site. Bunnies and other small creatures were doing the same. He shared a look with Pierce before they both urged their horses farther into the trees.

"What's happening?" Robbie, Isolde's younger brother, asked.

Lewis put his finger to his lips to quiet them all. In the distance, he could just make out the faint sound of a fight and the unmistakable sound of the Unwelcome's weapon.

Pierce led the way, stopping at a tree with lots of branches. He quickly dismounted and tied the reins of his horse to one of the branches. As Imogen dismounted, he did the same for hers. The rest of the Cursed followed suit.

After Lewis had secured his own horse, he nodded at Pierce. "Keep your eyes on them."

Imogen straightened. "We can take care of ourselves."

Lewis softened. "I know, honey. But you still need someone watching your back. And you need to watch Pierce's as well."

"That's better," she muttered.

Pierce rolled his eyes behind his sister's back before looking at Lewis. "Is that coming from Lyla's camp?"

"It's the right direction. We'll go on foot. Stay hidden."

"Do you think it's the Unwelcome?" Imogen asked.

"It sounds like their weapons, so we stay hidden until we know exactly what we're dealing with. If it is the Unwelcome, we'll hide until they're gone, okay?"

Imogen nodded, but Lewis could see the tremor running through her and the other Cursed. Pierce nodded as well, his whole body tense, his eyes narrowed. Lewis looked between all of them and prayed he didn't lose any of them today.

He led the way through the woods, the blasting sounds getting louder. As they got closer, he could hear the yells of some humans as well. He paused at an old garage. The roof had fallen in, and three walls were leaning over as well, but there was enough room inside for at least five people. It was dark and hidden from the air. He nodded toward it. "You guys, inside. I'll scout ahead alone."

Pierce opened his mouth to argue, but Lewis looked at Imogen. Pierce nodded. "Come on, Im."

Lewis waited until they were all hidden from view before continuing on. He stopped at a location that overlooked the old zoo. He crawled to the edge. Only some of the zoo was visible, but he could clearly see the two Unwelcome craft in the field next to it.

Damn. He was too late. There was no reaching Lyla now. And there was also no helping her.

He started to crawl back from the edge when he got the sense that he wasn't alone. He rolled to his feet, crouching low as two Unwelcome stalked toward him.

27

Thor stood, legs braced, arms behind his back at the gate of his enclosure, waiting to be released. He watched and listened through the bars to the sounds of fighting in the distance. There were about two dozen humans left in the zoo. It should not take long to destroy them.

A strange feeling in his chest appeared at the thought. He must have eaten something that did not agree with him.

The heavy pounding of feet approached him. He straightened his back even more, raising his chin. Finally.

From around the curve in the path, four chelvah approached. They marched in unison, their helmets reflecting the images of the cages they passed. They did not hesitate as they headed for Thor. Two peeled off and headed further in toward the other enclosure.

Thor stepped to the side as they raised their romag and blasted the lock. In an explosion of sparks, the gate swung open. With a nod, Thor stepped forward. The soldiers each gripped his arms painfully. He looked up in confusion, but neither said anything. They just started moving forward. Thor got his feet under him and moved along with them.

They moved with purpose along the path. A pile of ash lay to one side. Thor wondered who it had been, an image of Maisy flashing through his mind and the feeling in his chest growing more uncomfortable.

A flash of red hair at the edge of the gift shop pulled his attention from his discomfort. Fear slashed through him as Maisy's head peeked out from the building. Thor was careful to keep his head forward and not indicate he'd seen her.

But then a blast of a romag stopped his two colleagues.

Across from Maisy, a chelvah stumbled into view as Riley jumped and landed a spinning kick in the man's chest. The chelvah flew back, slamming into an old metal railing enclosing an exhibit and tipped over it, disappearing from view.

"Maisy!" Riley yelled.

One of the chelvah holding Thor released him, raising his romag as Maisy dashed from her spot toward Riley. With a lurch, Thor stumbled into the man, forcing his shot to go wide. He crashed to his knees, the rough ground cutting into his skin.

Riley swung around, his eyes going wide. And Thor knew he had not realized they were even there. He pulled Maisy into his arms and sprinted out of view, too fast for any chelvah to catch him.

28

The two Unwelcome stormed toward Lewis, blocking his way. He had a fifty-foot drop behind him with rocks and debris at the base. Even if the fall didn't kill him, he'd be in no shape to fight. He'd barely be in shape to crawl. The kids were about two hundred yards away and hidden well, so if he at least stayed quiet, they'd stay hidden.

He pictured Imogen and Pierce. *Stay safe, you two. Take care of one another.* He tensed as one of the Unwelcome raised its spear.

"No!" Pierce sprinted toward the Unwelcome, his sword raised.

"Pierce, no!" Lewis scrambled to his feet, his heart in his throat, knowing he was about to lose his son.

A flash of yellow hair was all he saw before Imogen appeared right next to one of the Unwelcome. Robbie appeared to the side of the other one. Lewis blinked, thinking his eyes were playing tricks on him. They had moved so fast. Imogen spun, landing a back kick at the base of the creature's back. The Unwelcome's back arched, its arms thrown wide. Imogen grabbed its neck and with a spin, flung it to the ground with a thud that shuddered through Lewis. Then Elise was there and stomping on its face, crashing right through the creature's helmet.

Robbie had climbed the other Unwelcome's back like a monkey and now sat with his legs wrapped around its throat. The Unwelcome reached up with a giant arm to knock him loose, but Hector grabbed the arm, stopping him. He slammed his heel into the being's knee, and it lurched to the side. Robbie squeezed his thighs tighter, and the being dropped to its knees, its arms hanging weakly at its sides before it crashed forward. Robbie leapt off as it fell.

It had all happened so fast that Lewis had barely even had a chance to move from his spot. His gaze shot to Imogen. He'd taught her how to defend herself, but he'd thought she had no feel for fighting. Or at least, no interest in hurting anyone. But the Imogen he'd just seen had been incredible, strong, fluid, instinctive.

They *all* had been. Now all of them stood in silence, staring at the two downed aliens.

Imogen stared at her hands and then at Lewis. "How?"

"The Cursed. They have abilities that allow them to fight the Unwelcome, to defeat them. Lyla, she said—" He whirled back around as a blast of an Unwelcome's spear echoed through the air.

Pierce hurried to his side, staring down at the zoo. "They're in trouble."

29

Lyla all but threw Addie into the saddle of one of the horses near the zoo entrance. Jamal quickly mounted the other one. Lyla had already sent the other camp members through, but there were a few she hadn't been quick enough for, even with her abilities. "Get out of here!"

"What about Maisy?" Addie held on to the reins as the horse pranced.

"We'll get her to you. Go." She slapped the back of the horse, sending her off at a gallop.

"Lyla," Jamal warned from the other horse.

"Go! We'll cover you. Go!"

With one last look, Jamal took off as well.

They'd had no warning about the Unwelcome. It was only Cursed left in the old zoo now, all except one. One Riley had sworn to retrieve.

Come on, Riley. She scanned the area, wanting more than anything to take off after them but knowing that they could easily pass one another. She had to trust him, as much as everything in her screamed that she needed to go find her baby.

A burst of air escaped her as she spied his familiar shape

heading toward her, Maisy wrapped in his arms. Lyla took a deep breath to hold back the tears that wanted to break. She had been unable to find Maisy when the attack began. Her heart had been in her throat ever since, even as she battled six Unwelcome and got as many as she could to safety.

Miles and Petra sprinted up from a separate path. "We need to go," she said as soon as they reached her.

"Arthur?" Petra asked.

Lyla swallowed. She'd lost track of him not long into the fight. "I don't know. But he'll find us. Let's go."

Together, they ran for the exit. A sense of something being wrong jolted through Lyla right before they reached the front entrance. She threw out a hand, slamming to a stop. "Wait!"

An Unwelcome blast slammed into the ground right in front of her. She backpedaled. An Unwelcome stepped through the open gateway.

A giant blue hand reached out from the wall next to it and wrapped around the Unwelcome's helmet. With a ferocious yank, it slammed the helmet into the gate post. The Unwelcome dropped face first to the ground. Arthur stepped out, his chest heaving as he scanned all of them. "Are you—"

Lyla hurried forward, relief rushing through her. "We're fine. Are there any more?"

"Not on this side."

They all sprinted through the exit. Miles and Petra stopped only long enough to grab the Unwelcome's spear. Lyla noted two other Unwelcome down as she ran for the trees.

The sense of danger wafted through her again. "Down!" She dove for the ground, yanking Riley and Maisy with her. Arthur grabbed Petra and Miles, covering them with his body as a blast burst over them.

A returning blast came from the trees ahead. She looked behind her as two Unwelcome took cover behind a trailer behind them.

Then to her surprise, Lewis peered out from around a tree. Pierce was with him. "We'll cover you!" Lewis yelled.

Lyla waited until Lewis and Pierce opened fire before grabbing Riley's arm and yanking him up. Maisy was wrapped around his neck, her eyes closed tight.

Together they ran for the cover of the trees. From the corner of her eye, she saw Petra slip her hand into Arthur's while Miles placed himself directly in front of him to make sure Lewis knew Arthur was with them.

They passed through the path created by Lewis and Pierce. Petra immediately took up position behind one of the trees, adding her own firepower to keep the Unwelcome back.

Riley handed Maisy to Arthur. Maisy resisted at first, clinging to him even tighter. "No, no."

"It's Arthur, Maisy, Arthur," Riley whispered.

She cracked open her eyes. With a little cry, she flung herself at Arthur. He gathered her to him, rocking her in his arms as he stepped behind a tree farther into the forest.

Lyla took up position on Lewis's other side. He raised an eyebrow at her. "Something you forgot to mention?"

She gave him a tight smile. "Oh, I didn't mention having a very tall blue friend?"

"I believe I would have remembered that." Lewis regarded her for another moment before turning back to the current problem.

They needed to take the two advancing Unwelcome out and get the rest of their people out before reinforcements arrived.

"Riley, Petra, with me. We're taking these guys out. Lewis, can you continue with the cover fire?"

"You got it."

Lyla had just stepped to the side when the blasts from the Unwelcome stopped. She frowned, trying to see what was going on when Adros, Rory, and Rory's sister, Tabitha, stepped from around the building. The three of them jogged toward the woods.

Adros grinned at Lyla. "Hey there."

Lyla couldn't help but laugh. "Thanks, Adros."

He nodded. "Everyone else is at the old bridge."

"Okay, let's get moving." She strode through the woods, everyone falling in step behind her. They kept up a fast pace, wanting to put as much distance between the zoo and themselves as possible. Twenty minutes later, they came across the rest of the group. Lyla didn't pause, just continued forward as the rest of the group fell in line with them.

She kept them all moving for two hours. Everyone was quiet, which was pretty amazing being they were now a pretty-good-sized group. Lewis had four Cursed with him, one of whom looked too much like Pierce to be anyone but his sister. After two hours, she slowed the pace, allowing them to speak. Lewis explained about the bounty hunters and how Meg was leaning toward accepting the Naku's offer.

Lyla agreed with his concern.

"I was hoping you might be willing to take them on," he said.

She glanced at him out of the corner of her eye. "I won't turn them away, but I'm not setting up a camp."

He frowned. "You're going to keep moving?"

"Yes, but not aimlessly. We're looking for a place. It's called the Lab. Rory heard rumors about it being out west. So we're heading in that direction and we're hoping we can find it."

Lewis frowned. "The Lab. I've heard of it. You think it's still working?"

She shrugged. "I don't know. But we need some answers about the Cursed. We need to understand these abilities. What we can do. Why we can do it. The more we know, the better off we'll be."

Lewis studied her for a long moment. "I know where it is."

Lyla stopped dead. "What?"

"About ten years back, a group came to us from out west. We do a debrief with anyone who joins us. When we can, we map out where they've been, what's out there. They'd been to a lab. Said there were still docs there. It's a little east of what used to be Dallas, Texas."

Lyla smiled. "That's great." Her gaze strayed to where Arthur was just coming up behind them, Maisy still in his arms. "We'll head there first thing in the morning. But first, I need to get Maisy to our other people. It's too dangerous out here for her."

Lewis looked at where Maisy lay curled up in Arthur's arms. "She looks pretty safe to me."

Lyla shook her head. "No. She needs to be in a camp, with walls and guards. Not out here with us. Now I just need to convince her of that."

He raised an eyebrow. "Think you can?"

"Of course. She'll just have to be reasonable."

Lewis laughed. "Good luck. I'll start setting up for the night with everyone else."

Lyla nodded, keeping her gaze on Maisy and Arthur. She straightened her shoulders. She had faced down the Unwelcome, the Naku, and all sorts of despicable humans. She could handle one little girl.

30

"No." Her arms crossed over her chest, Maisy glared up at Lyla. She stomped the ground for emphasis.

Lyla sighed. She had known this was going to be a difficult conversation. But it was going even worse than she'd expected. "Maisy, it's not safe."

"I don't care! I'm not staying at New Attlewood. I belong with you." She angrily wiped a tear from her eye away.

Lyla's heart broke at the sight. She hated this. She hated not being able to wake up with Maisy cuddled into her side. She hated having to trust that other people would look out for her as well as she did. Addie, Jamal, Emma, and Edna all loved Maisy. She had no doubt they would take care of her, along with a dozen others. But Lyla still wanted Maisy with her.

But with the Naku looking for her, bringing Maisy was the height of selfishness, which only made her angrier. Life had been tough enough before the Naku had arrived with their race of Unwelcome slaves. But now, life was a struggle to try and be with the ones she loved.

"Maisy, try and understand, if you come with me, you would be in constant danger. You could be killed—"

Maisy gave her a look way beyond her years. "Are you kidding? Nowhere is safe. Not New Attlewood, not New City, and not with you. So if I can't be safe, I want to be with you. You are not leaving me behind again."

Lyla reached out a hand for her. "Maisy."

"No." She shook her head, backing away, tears cresting and then falling over. "Families belong together." She ran away.

Arthur, who'd been watching quietly, nodded toward Maisy's disappearing figure. "I'll keep an eye on her." He disappeared after her.

Lyla sank to the ground, leaning her back against a tree. God, she was just so tired. She dropped her head into her hands. She just wanted one thing to be easy. Just one little thing.

"She's not wrong, you know."

Lyla's head jolted up as Lewis took a seat on the downed tree across from her. He shrugged. "Couldn't help but overhear."

"I don't know what to do. Keeping her at New Attlewood is safer, but she acts like I'm abandoning her."

"In a kid's mind, that *is* probably how she views it."

Lyla snorted. "Gee, thanks. More guilt."

He gave her a rare smile. "That is the life of a parent."

"Yes, it is." She paused. "What did you mean she's not wrong?"

"About no place being safe. Our world, it's got dangers around every corner. That one tornado swarm killed nine people in my camp, and it razed crops, which means it will still kill more this winter from hunger. My wife, she's taking care of a little girl whose mom died. Her father, I'm not sure if he'll ever be able to take care of her. He lost the use of his legs, and his heart is broken over Letty's death."

Lyla winced. Sometimes she forgot she was not the only one struggling through this life. That in some ways she was actually one of the lucky ones.

"I know why you want to keep Maisy away, but is it *really*

going to be safer for her? I've kept Imogen locked away for years for her own safety, and I'm only now just beginning to realize how unfair that was to her." Lewis stood. "I'm going to go grab my kids and see if we can catch some fish for dinner."

Lyla nodded absentmindedly, her thoughts on Lewis's words. He was right. Tornado swarms, waves of earthquakes, flash floods, basketball-sized hail. Mother Nature alone was a danger that threatened everyone's life on the regular. She couldn't protect Maisy from that, especially not if she wasn't nearby.

For a moment, she imagined how she would feel if Maisy was killed in the camp by a storm while Lyla was away. Her heart lurched at the thought, and pain cut through her deep. She shoved the idea away, her breathing still a little panicked. *I can't protect her from everything.*

But what happened if the opposite occurred? If Lyla was killed and Maisy was left feeling abandoned? Lyla didn't want that for her, either. There were no easy answers. There was risk on both sides.

So what do you want?

That question cut across her seesawing thoughts. *I want my daughter with me for as long as possible.*

And like sunlight piercing through the clouds, she knew exactly what she needed to do. She stood up, following Arthur and Maisy's trail. They had not made it very far. Lyla could hear Arthur's deep, rumbling voice as he spoke in a low voice. "She loves you more than anything. She just wants to keep you safe."

"She doesn't want me with her."

Lyla's heart broke at the pain in Maisy's voice. She rounded the tree and saw Maisy curled up in Arthur's lap, her little body shaking with emotion.

"Oh no, she wants you with her always. She loves you so much that she can't bear the thought of anything happening to you. And even if it causes her pain, she wants you safe."

"But I want to be with her ... and you."

A small smile crossed his face. "And we want you with us too. We always will."

Maisy sniffed. "Will you always be my friend, Arthur?"

"Always."

Tears pressed against the back of Lyla's eyes at the exchange. Arthur had come into their life an enemy, and now ... Now she didn't know what he was, but she knew he was important to all of them. With a start, she realized that despite the size and difference in skin tone, right now Arthur was the closest person Maisy had to a father.

She needs him as much as she needs me.

Arthur caught her gaze, and the world seemed to stop. She knew in that moment he felt just as strongly about all of them as they did him. And he would stop the world to protect the little girl curled up in his arms. Which meant that there was no safer place for Maisy than with the two of them. Along with Miles and Riley, Maisy would have four people who would do everything in their considerable power to keep her safe.

Lyla walked up to the two of them. Arthur spoke softly. "Lyla's coming."

Maisy's tear-drenched face looked over at her. Lyla knelt down, pushing Maisy's curls back from her face. "I need to keep you safe because my world would end if anything happened to you. You, Riley, and Miles are the most important people in the world to me."

"And Arthur, too," Maisy said, sniffing.

Lyla smiled. "Yes, and Arthur, too. But you're right. There is no perfectly safe place. But with me, Riley, Miles, and Arthur, you're probably safer than you would be anywhere else."

Maisy gasped. "You mean it?"

"I mean it."

Maisy lunged at her, throwing her arms around Lyla. "I love you."

"I love you too, sweet pea."

Lyla was content to sit with her like that forever. But too soon, Maisy pulled back, a giant grin on her face. "I'm going to tell the boys and Petra I'm staying."

Lyla watched her go, doubts still rolling around in her mind. "Guess she's coming."

"I won't let anything happen to her."

Lyla looked up at him, seeing the commitment in his face. "I know. And I'm counting on that. So if you have to choose, choose her."

"You mean if I have to choose between saving you or saving her?"

She nodded. "Yes. Promise me."

He nodded slowly. "I promise."

She knew he would keep his word. She leaned into him, and he wrapped his arms around her. "It won't come to that," he whispered fiercely.

She leaned her face against his chest, feeling safe locked in his arms. "Let's hope so."

31

The right side of Thor's face throbbed. He blinked his eyes, straightening his head. He was strapped into one of the seats on the cruiser. His hands were bound in front of him. Across from him, two chelvah sat, unmoving. The only way to tell them apart was by the numbers on their uniforms: 38-A and 22-A. They hadn't said a word to him.

He felt the cruiser dock. 38-A stood and unbuckled Thor while 22-A went and released the ramp, then moved down and stood at the bottom of the ramp. As soon as Thor appeared, 22-A began to walk. Thor stepped from the ramp and looked around. They were in the loading bay of the mothership. Thor had expected they would bring him here, although he hadn't expected that he would be bound. No doubt his stumble had caused them to view him with suspicion. He still wasn't sure what had come over him. He'd seen Maisy, seen her brother, and he'd just acted. And he'd received a fist across his face for that action.

The door from the loading bay slid open. 22-A walked through without pausing. Thor followed while 38-A brought up the rear. As he stepped into the hallway, a chill ran over his skin. It was cold in here. He'd never noticed that before. In his uniform, he'd never felt it. But in the lightweight human clothes, his skin chilled immediately.

22-A led him through hallway after hallway before they reached the hallway leading toward the Esteemed Leader's throne room. Thor had expected to be questioned, but he did not expect it to be done in the presence of the Esteemed Leader.

Unease slid down his back as he recalled humans being questioned by the Imperial interrogators. They were a shadow of themselves when it was done. He straightened his shoulders.

I have nothing to hide. An image of Maisy flashed across his brain. He squelched it down. *She is nothing to me.*

The doors to the throne room slid open, and Thor stepped through. 22-A and 38-A stepped to his sides, escorting him to the raised dais. The Esteemed Leader was already there. He dropped to a knee ten feet in front of him, bowing his head, as did 22-A and 38-A.

Rise.

The word appeared in his mind. The Esteemed Leader, in fact, all the Naku, did not vocalize. All their communication was telepathic.

Thor got to his feet. 22-A and 38-A took one step back. The Esteemed Leader looked down at him. *Why are you out of uniform?*

"Mine was damaged during the battle. They removed it from me."

And gave you these? The Esteemed Leader's small lips curled.

"Yes."

What else did they give you?

He hesitated. He felt like he was being led into a trap, but he could not see what it would be. But honesty with the Naku had been so well ingrained in him he did not even think about lying. "Food, water, shelter."

Did they question you?

"Yes. They wanted to know how many of us there are, what our plans are, where we are based."

What did you tell them?

"Nothing."

And how did they respond?

"They continued to question me."

And?

"And I still told them nothing."

Did they harm you?

"No."

Even though you told them nothing?

He frowned. That was strange. "I do not think they had the stomach for it."

Why did they not kill you?

"I think they were planning to, but the ground team arrived before they could."

But they held you for weeks. They could have done it at any time.

Thor did not know what to say to that, so he stayed silent. The Esteemed Leader questioned him for another thirty minutes. Thor answered each question honestly, holding nothing back, except for the existence of the traitor. He wasn't sure why he did not mention him. But they did not ask about him. From the Leader's questions, he knew that the other Unwelcome had also been brought back to the ship. But the Leader was not really interested in Thor or her. He wanted to know about the camp where he'd been held and the humans who ran it. He wanted to know their skills and abilities, whether they had any Cursed.

Finally, the Esteemed Leader looked down at him. He felt the strangest fluttering in his brain. Then the leader nodded.

Take him to Interrogation. Level 1.

Thor tensed. The humans might not have the stomach for interrogation, but his colleagues in Interrogation had no such qualms. The one saving grace was that he would only be questioned with physical torture, not mental. The Esteemed Leader's interrogators were not used on level 1.

He followed 22-A once again from the room and down the cold hallway. And he realized that while he had told the humans nothing and they had not lifted a finger against him, he had told the Esteemed Leader everything, and now he was walking toward his own torture.

32

Water crashed against Thor's face, rousing him. He spluttered, shaking his head. 56-I looked at him, his head tilted to the side. Behind him, 67-I made a notation on his chart. Both were fully uniformed, including the helmet. And for once, Thor wanted to see who was underneath. He realized how much he'd gotten used to seeing people's expressions in his time with the humans. Not seeing them, it was jarring. And intimidating.

Which was the point.

"We have completed the test. You will wash in there, and a new uniform will be waiting for you," 56-I said.

Thor took a moment to determine if his legs would hold him. Gripping the sides of the chair, he hoisted himself up.

Without a word to the two in the room, he walked to the shower room. The door automatically slid open as he approached. He stepped inside and the door slid closed behind him. He looked down at himself. His shirt had been reduced to fragments. Burns covered his front, along with blood. He felt the remnants of the shirt stuck to some of the burns and cuts along his back. A glance at his pants showed that he had soiled himself at some point during the interrogation.

But he had passed. If he hadn't, he would not have woken up. He knew it had been days; interrogations always took days. But he had no concept of how much time had actually passed.

To his right, the light above the inoculation site blinked on. *Place hand here.*

He placed his arm along the holder. Bands clamped over his wrist and bicep. A needle descended from the tube above it and plunged into his arm. Once the needle retracted, the bands also retracted.

He pulled his arm out, rolling his fist.

Remain still. Close mouth, the screen to his right now warned. Thor did as he was told. Air blasted him from above, and he winced as it hit his burns. The clothes disintegrated into pieces, falling to the floor.

Continue forward.

The door in front of him slid open, revealing a second tube. He stepped inside, and the door slid shut behind him. Water flowed from above, followed by a soap mixture, then the water once more. Once again, his burns hissed with pain as the soap touched them.

A warm air filled the tube, drying his skin.

Step out, the screen built into the tube announced. A door on the other side of the tube slid open. Arrows on the floor directed him to the left. He followed them into another tube with nozzles on the sides. Once the door closed, the screen flared to life. *Remain still.*

A pink spray emitted from the nozzles level with his chest. The second they touched his cuts and burns, the pain began to fade. More dry air filled the tube, drying the lotion. Thor let out a small sigh of relief.

The doors slid open, and he stepped out and followed the arrows once again. A new uniform was waiting for him on a shelf at the end of the small hall. He ran a hand over the ID on the front of the uniform. 18-F. The uniform did not belong to him. He was simply issued one each time he needed to replace his. This one had no doubt been worn a thousand times already by others. The only thing unique about him was his number, and it was attached with a removable fabric.

He started to dress quickly, not sure why the thoughts were even running through his mind. He pulled the helmet from the shelf last, and the shelf slid back into the wall.

He hesitated, staring at the helmet. He had not worn one in weeks. He found he liked the feel of air on his face.

Weakness. He put the helmet on. The world took on a light-blue hue, and he felt comfort in the anonymity the uniform offered him. He walked to the door and slid his bracelet under the scanner.

Barracks Level 18, Room 3, Bunk 67. A small slot slid out from the wall, two small blue pills resting inside. The Ka Sama. Thor took the pills, clutching them in his hand. The Ka Sama was a sleep aid. All chelvah were required to take them when it was their downtime. It put them to sleep almost immediately. They did not dream.

He palmed the pills as he made his way out of the room and to the lift. It arrived almost immediately, and he rode it to the eighteenth level. The doors slid open. Two individuals were waiting. Thor exited the lift, and they stepped on. Neither said anything to him or each other.

He passed another dozen individuals. No one said a word or even looked in the others' direction. The whole area was completely silent. Even his footfalls were silent due to the padding on the floor.

Room 3 was in the middle of the hall and held one hundred beds, fifty bunks doubled up on either side of the room. He found 67. Someone was already asleep on the bottom bunk, his helmet on the floor next to his bed. There was nothing else there. Bunks were assigned randomly. Thor had never been assigned the same bunk twice. He climbed into his bed.

Once settled in, he carefully removed his helmet and placed it on the shelf next to him. He looked around the room. Only about a quarter of the bunks were filled. Each would sleep until the bracelet on their wrist woke them. No one is this room would be on the same squads. No one is this room would know one another. Camaraderie amongst soldiers was not tolerated. Decisions were to be made on a cost-benefit analysis without emotion. Emotion was the enemy, or at least one of them.

Thor lay down, staring at the ceiling above. It was strange to be back here. Everything on the ship felt different. *He* felt different. Even the air felt strange, false.

But it was right that he was back here. This was where he belonged. He pictured the traitor sitting with Maisy on the hill as she sang. Walking hand in hand with her, his giant hand dwarfing hers. *Don't forget me.*

A strange feeling welled up in his chest. During the interrogation, he had not mentioned the traitor. He was not sure why except that he had not been directly asked about him. At one point, he had seen the other Unwelcome who had also been held. She was being interrogated as well. He wondered for a moment if she had been returned to her duties yet.

Then he blinked at the thought. It did not matter whether she had been returned to duties or destroyed during the interrogation. What was with these thoughts?

He opened his palm and started to lower the pills to his mouth. Then he stopped as an image of Xe drifted across his mind. For years, she had not been a thought. But since his time with the humans, she had been a constant presence, keeping him company. He had liked seeing her, even if it was only in his memories and dreams. It had made him feel like he belonged.

If he took the pills, he knew there was a chance he would not see her again. He palmed the pills, debating for a moment before slipping them up the cuff of his shirt. One more night would not make a difference. He would take the pills tomorrow. He closed his eyes, thinking of his sister. Yet when he fell asleep, it wasn't Xe he dreamed of, but Maisy. Singing to him that life could be better than this.

33

The soft drone of the engine was the only sound in the veerfinah. There were twenty soldiers on this one, including Thor, which made it one of the smaller ships.

When he had been awoken this morning, he had been dreaming that it was he, not the traitor, walking in the camp. Sharing meals, laughing with the humans. As a result, he swore to take his sleeping pills that night. Those were not the dreams he wanted.

He filed out of the room, falling in line with the others on their way to the food hall. He picked up his bowl from the table and sat down. Placing his helmet on the table in front of him, he picked up his spoon. Across the room, thirty others were doing the same, eating in a quiet rhythm. Thor took a spoonful, and the familiar taste coated his tongue. It was bitter, with the consistency of paste.

After one spoonful, his mind flashed on the little round objects Maisy had left him, but he showed no outward sign. He simply finished his bowl. Wiping his mouth, he replaced his helmet before returning his spoon and bowl to the bin. That would be his last meal until he returned to the ship after his shift.

The humans had fed him much larger quantities of food, three times a day. The human food did not have the nutritional punch of the food the Naku had developed, but the Naku's food also did not have any of the appeal of the human food.

Thor scanned his bracelet on the way out the door. He was to report to landing bay GG-7, so he made his way down with a dozen individuals. They all crammed into the lift, everyone shifting to the side to accommodate as many as possible. No one spoke.

At the landing bay, they loaded onto the ship, strapped in, and took off.

All without a word.

Thor stood now, tempted to stretch, his back still sore from his interrogation. But it would only draw attention to himself. His kind did not stretch. They did not do anything but what the Naku ordered. And he needed to make sure he stayed under the radar. Yesterday he had passed, but he knew he would be under observation for a while. Any slipup and he would be terminated without hesitation, so he filed off the ship when it was his turn. A light wind was blowing, and the sun was just coming up over the horizon.

They were on a tall, rocky hilltop. A building had been constructed into the side of it. From the look of it, the building dated to before their arrival but had been added to recently. Strong supports now bolted the building more securely into the ground as well as the tall rock face behind it. It was three stories high with strange peaked points that he saw no purpose in, except perhaps to give a better view of the area surrounding them.

They filed toward the building in a single line. The marchelvah stood at the front of the line with a duty wand. As each soldier passed, he touched their bracelet with the wand.

When Thor came abreast of him, he dutifully held up his arm. The bracelet gave a soft ding as the wand made contact with it. Thor glanced down. "Interior courtyard" was displayed on the wrist unit, followed by a small map of the facility, highlighting the route he was to take.

The first of his group had reached the facility. The two chelvah on duty at the gate headed for the ship as soon as their replacements reached them. That process took place all over the facility. As replacements arrived, those on duty would immediately head for the shuttle.

Thor made his way through the building. It was a strange mix of old and new. The walls and floor were rock, some primitively hewn. But scanners had been added as well as artificial lighting.

Thor didn't pay much attention to his surroundings as he followed the map to the interior courtyard. From the building, he stepped into a large hallway that surrounded the open-air space in the middle of the building. The hallway had cutouts to allow for fresh air to breeze through.

He moved to the Unwelcome standing guard between the hallway and the open-air space. As soon as he arrived, the other guard turned on his heel and disappeared into the building.

Thor took up his spot. The open-air space had grass with flowering trees. Benches and chairs were scattered about, along with a few tarps set up to offer shade. And even though it was early morning, there were half a dozen individuals walking or sitting in the space. All were tall, blue, and female.

But unlike the bulk that dominated the frames of the soldiers, these avad were all incredibly thin, with long fingers, arms, and legs. They all wore long white shifts that covered them from their necks to just below their knees. They wore no shoes but also had bracelets around their wrists.

And the occupants of the courtyard had one other feature in common: All of them had large round, protruding bellies.

Thor had been sent to a breeding facility.

34

Thor knew that there were three options for females: soldiering, breeding, or death. He had never seen a breeding facility before, although he assumed they were somewhere on the ship. He had not realized they had set up a facility on the planet.

The few women in the courtyard took no notice of the changing of the guard. Thor kept his head straight, careful not to watch any of them too closely, lest his attention draw someone's attention. But he could not help but inspect the women from the corner of his eye.

They were so thin, they were almost emaciated. The females in the soldier ranks were barely discernible from the men. But these females were a quarter of their width, with the exception of their bellies. The women walked around or sat, often with one hand on their stomachs.

As the morning wore on, more women joined them, most with extended bellies, although a few were obviously much less farther along in their pregnancies. Each woman was unlike any avad he'd seen. They spoke, although they did so quietly. And they smiled. He'd never seen a smile cross the face of a soldier.

The last smile he'd seen on a chelvah had been during training when one soldier had broken the leg of another. And that smile was nothing like these.

But although the smiles were surprising, it was nothing compared to the surprise still in store for him. Halfway through the morning, a bell rang. All the women immediately got up and made their way into the building, all of them exiting through the same door they had entered. Thor glanced at his bracelet, but there was no warning. And as there was no alarm on the faces of the women, he assumed this was a normal part of their routine.

A door along a different wall opened. A woman stepped out with something clutched to her chest. A second woman followed her, holding the hand of a small child.

For once, Thor was thankful for the helmet as his jaw dropped. Woman after woman appeared, each accompanied by a child. Thirty women were in the courtyard now, with thirty-two children. Thor struggled to not gape at them and to keep his body still. The children ranged in age from newborn to about two years old. Or he thought that might be their age. He had not seen such young children in decades. The older children still seemed to have trouble walking and talking.

These women also smiled. Some even laughed at the antics of the children. Thor caught himself smiling as one little child kept climbing up on a chair as soon as his mother turned away. Every time she turned her back, he climbed up. Because she kept turning her back, he knew it was some sort of game they were playing. The child's laughter echoed through the courtyard at the mother's "outrage" every time she spotted him once again in the chair.

Keeping his movements controlled, he watched the other three guards in the courtyard. From what he could tell, not one of them glanced at the children. Nor did they betray even a twitch of movement indicating any interest in the children.

The women stayed outside for a few hours before once again

switching with the pregnant mothers. In the afternoon, each series of mothers was run through an exercise regimen.

Thor watched it all with increasing confusion. These mothers were different than the soldiers. Their emotions were much less in check. How could that be? How could the chelvah be so unemotional compared to them? Was their emotionality the reason they were chosen to be breeders?

And as he watched the women, he couldn't help but wonder if Xe had become one of them somewhere along the way. Had she looked with happiness at her child? Had she protectively placed her hand over her growing belly?

He also couldn't help but wonder at his own mother. She must have lived in a facility like this, but on the other planet. Had she laughed at his and Xe's antics? What had she thought when they were taken from her? He could vaguely remember arms reaching for him as he was hauled away.

These women all seemed to care for their children. Did they then just simply hand them over?

And even as those thoughts wandered around and around his mind, he wondered at the fact that he was questioning anything the Naku had done. He had never done that before. He had never wondered about anything he had seen during his duties. So what had changed for him?

His bracelet vibrated. "End of shift" splashed across it, seconds before his relief arrived. Saying nothing and not sparing the courtyard a second glance, he headed out of the facility.

He said nothing on the silent flight back to the mothership. He said nothing at dinner, although the guard who had been stationed at the other side of the courtyard sat near him. He couldn't help but watch the man from the corner of his eyes, but the man gave away nothing. He stared straight ahead as he ate and stood up immediately when he was done. Replacing the bowl and spoon in the bin, he walked to the scanner, and after holding out his bracelet to be read, he took the two pills that were dispensed and disappeared into the hallway. He would be asleep almost as soon as his head hit the pillow.

With a start, Thor realized that he was taking his time with his meal, and there were only two others in the room. Both had come in after him. He quickly downed the rest of his meal and disposed of his bowl, but when it came time to take his pills, he palmed them, faking that he had swallowed them as regulations required. He had a new bunk assignment: Level 18, Room 4, Bunk 43.

He told himself he just wanted to make sure he could find his new bunk before he took the pills. There had been incidents of individuals not finding their bunk in time and collapsing on the floor. They were left there until morning. As Thor was still recovering, he wanted to make sure he at least had a comfortable place to sleep. He slid the pills up his sleeve next to the other ones.

He found his bunk, and after removing his helmet, lay down. He stared at the ceiling, his mind replaying and trying to make sense of all he had seen during the day. He just could not wrap his mind around the difference between the soldiers and the breeders. How was it possible for them to be so different?

His eyelids began to close as he remembered the little boy with the infectious laugh. A smile was on Thor's face when he fell asleep.

35

The next morning, Thor was surprised to find that he had fallen asleep before he'd taken his pills. He made sure they were carefully tucked up his sleeve, out of sight, but they felt like an extra weight on his arm. He kept waiting for someone to call him out, but no one did. As usual, no one said a word.

He was not surprised when he was assigned to the breeding facility again the next day. Tours tended to last between ten days and six months depending upon how much interaction there was with humans.

Today his bracelet informed him he was to report to Level 2, East Wing, Room 212. According to his map, each side of the building was designated by a direction: north, south, east, and west. The east wing required him to turn right down the wide hall. The floor in this section was made of a dark wood. His footsteps sounded off the floor, joined a few seconds later by other footsteps behind him.

He kept his head straight, but from his peripheral vision, he took in a large room on the left that had a long wooden table nearly the length of it, some sort of lighting fixture made of similar wood above it. On the other side of the hall was a long room with an odd assortment of what he thought might be chairs. But some were long, as if meant to accommodate more than one individual. All of them were covered in fabric. They looked like the chair version of a bed. Odd.

At the end of the hall, he made a left. There was a stairwell two doors down. He turned into the stairwell and headed to the second floor. These stairs were obviously a new addition, as they were made of metal. He stopped at the metal door and waved his bracelet over the scanner. The door slid open. Although the door and stairwell were new, the floor was made of the same wood as the first floor. Only here there was a distinctive antiseptic smell to the space that reminded him of some of the floors in the research building. Chelvah stood at the entrance of each door.

He checked the numbers above the doors, coming to a halt at a room at the end of the hall, where two soldiers stood. He stopped at the door, and one immediately left. Thor took his place, turning his back to the room. There was a door directly across from him with an additional two soldiers.

But here there were also Naku. In the short walk from the stairwell, he'd seen six. Four through open doorways and two standing and inputting something into handheld devices at a desk at the midpoint of the hall.

The Naku would come in and out of different rooms. From three of the rooms, he heard screams, and he knew by this that they were the labor rooms. One body had been rolled out covered in a sheet and taken to the end of the hall, then dumped down the garbage chute, followed by a smaller bundle.

He kept his gaze straight ahead but watched all the movement from the corner of his eyes. He could not tell what was happening in the room behind him, but every once in a while he would catch a glimpse of the room across from him. Three women lay in beds, their child either in their arms or in a small cart near them.

The women looked exhausted, but every once in a while

when the door opened, he would see a small smile on one of their faces as they held their child to their chest.

The day passed without incident. Thor stood at his post at the door, behaving exactly as he should. But his eyes had been drawn to the door across from him every time it opened. The images of those women cuddling their children to their chests stayed with him through the ride back to the ship and mealtime.

And as he closed his eyes that night, he pictured them again, his blue pills still in his hand.

36

The vibration of Thor's bracelet woke him up the next morning. It took him a moment to recognize where he was. He'd expected to see a blue sky above his head. He jolted up, spying something blue on the ground next to him. He quickly grabbed the Ka Sama before anyone saw them. He had forgotten to take his sleeping pills *again*. He shoved them up his sleeve and stood, grabbing his helmet. The six pills now felt like a giant sign on his forearm. He needed to find a way to get rid of them. He'd have to find something on the planet. Everything was too closely monitored here.

He hurried through breakfast so he could be one of the first on the shuttle to the planet. He chose a seat with the arm hiding the pills along a wall.

The shuttle began to fill. Thor kept his gaze straight ahead. He felt like with any movement, the pills in his sleeve would be detected. Sweat broke out along his body. He breathed carefully, trying to calm down.

The trip to the planet felt torturously long. When they finally landed, he had to keep himself from jumping from his seat. He waited until everyone had filed out before taking his place at the back of the line. He held up his bracelet and received his assignment. East Wing, Level Three, Room 308.

He kept his pace unhurried and carefully slid the pills into his palm and crushed them. As he climbed the steps, he dropped the remains of the pills over the side of the railing. The small blue pieces drifted through the bushes, settling underneath and out of view.

No one said anything. No one made any moves toward him. His shoulders drooped in relief. Tonight, he would take his pills. He would take them as soon as they were issued to him. He would not wait until he was back in his bunk. He could not take that chance again.

He stepped inside the main entrance. Ahead of him was a wide staircase that had not been touched by the renovation. It split into two staircases after twenty steps, leading to the second floor and then the third. He headed up, wondering why the humans had created the stairs like this. It wasn't efficient, although he had to admit, it was impressive to look at.

At the third floor, a wall had been added along with a secure access door. He scanned his bracelet, and the door opened. A guard stood on the other side. He glanced at Thor and then looked away.

Thor checked the numbers above the doorways. These rooms had entry scanners. He made his way to 308.

One of the guards on duty stepped away from the door as Thor approached. Thor took up the guard's position as the avad left. The door behind Thor was different than the others on the floor. There was a scanner, but there was no window in the door.

He had been standing there for only a few minutes when the door opened behind him.

With me. The command rattled through Thor's mind. He gritted his teeth against the intrusion. The Naku doctor headed down the hall. It was taller than some others, standing at almost five feet, but the incredible amount of wrinkles lining his face and arms indicated how old he was, which meant he was also highly ranked.

Thor followed the Naku, as did the other Unwelcome, 36-F. The Naku headed for the first door on the floor, near the stairs. The guard on duty immediately opened the door before the Naku arrived. The Naku ignored him as he strode into the room. Thor and 36-F followed. The guard at the door did the same.

A woman sat in a chair with a small child in her lap. The woman's eyes widened as she caught sight of her visitors. The Naku ignored her.

The woman gripped the child to her, shaking her head.

Restrain her.

Thor moved forward, his limbs not truly moving of his own accord. He grabbed the woman by an arm, pushing her back against the chair. 36-F did the same on the other side, yanking the woman's arm from her child. The guard from outside the door walked over and grabbed the child from the woman's lap. He immediately left the room with the child, who screamed, trying to climb from his arms.

The woman also screamed, trying to fight Thor and 36-F, but with her slim frame it was impossible. Tears rolled down her cheeks as she collapsed back against the chair. The Naku strode forward and plunged a needle into her arm. The woman's eyes rolled back into her head.

Leave her.

The Naku strode for the door. 36-F released the woman and followed the Naku. Thor did as well. But he glanced over his shoulder at the woman, whose tears were still wet on her cheeks.

They removed three more children, following the same process. Then they entered a room where three women lay strapped to beds. Two of the women had their eyes closed. One was trying to force her eyes open. The Naku checked the machines monitoring them before adjusting the dosage of the pale blue drip attached to the women's arms.

The next three rooms contained women sitting up. The Naku reviewed each of their charts and then ordered them to take two blue pills. The women did and were asleep before Thor had left the room.

Thor followed the Naku and did as he was ordered for the entire morning. But he was struggling with the orders. He knew this was their way. Children were born, lived with their mothers for the first two years, and then were shipped to a facility until they were five. At that point, their life path was chosen.

But watching it happen was difficult.

By the time the morning was done, Thor felt beyond uneasy. When the doctor's rounds were completed, his bracelet vibrated. East Wing, Level 1, Room 101.

He let himself out of the ward, noting that one of each of the guards on door duty was doing the same. They made their way down the two flights to the first floor in silence.

Once again, the floor was secured. He had to scan himself onto the floor and then into Room 101, which took up the entire length of the hall. As he stepped inside, he realized why: It was filled with small capsules that were on wheeled tables. They were silver, approximately four feet long with a rounded top. Canisters were attached to each of the capsules with tubes.

Six Naku were in the room. One looked up as the last of the chelvah entered. *Roll the capsules out the bay door and into the ship.*

A large door at the back of the room that Thor had not noticed before rolled up. Each of the chelvah walked to one of the capsules and started to roll it toward the door.

Thor made his way to one of them, noticing a small window on the lid of the capsule that he hadn't been able to see before. He glanced in as he moved toward the head of the capsule.

A small blue face, its eyes closed, lay there. Shock rolled through him. There was a child in each of these capsules. This was how they transported them to the next facility.

He flashed on the laughing boy from the courtyard. Was he in here? He pictured his little sister, Xe. This was how she had been transported. How he had been transported. They were sending these kids to a hellhole where they would be forced to adapt or die. And even if they survived, they could still be killed if it was determined the Naku felt they were unworthy.

He started to push the capsule toward the doorway, his mind racing. At the same time, he struggled to figure out what was wrong with him. Why was he thinking like this? He had never thought about the ramifications of any of his actions before.

But as he pushed the small capsule toward the ship, he knew what the ramifications for this child would be. And he wondered whether there wasn't a better way.

37

X antar glided down the hall. His chair made no noise as it carried him through the wide hallway of the mothership. The air was cool. The silver walls gave off a slight shimmer as the light hit them. He had exerted himself too much these last few weeks, and his body, already weak, could now only stand for a few hours a day.

To compensate, he took the glider. Most of his people had the same physical weaknesses. It was why they utilized the slave race. They had the strength and stamina but lacked the same intellectual capability as the Naku. They were designed to be used as a physical force and lacked the mental acuity that would allow them to responsibly determine their own fate. History had proven that well enough.

The doors at the end of the hall slid open as he approached, operated from the control panel on the armrest of Xantar's glider. Aek looked up from her desk. *You are early.*

There was no censure in her tone. It was merely an observation. *I am. What are the numbers?*

Aek's long, slim bony fingers lightly touched the console in front of her. Data appeared on the wall to Xantar's right. He scanned the lines of numbers. Thirty-seven children had been identified within the last year. Twenty-four had been moved to the first level of testing. He frowned. *Only twenty-four to level one?*

Aek nodded. *Ten terminated prior to reaching age two.*

Cause of death?

Maternal rejection.

Interpretation?

The mothers were impregnated within a shortened window, three months sooner than previously conducted. The time frame was too short to allow them to forget the first child. They were still in mourning. They rejected the new child in self-defense against the pain of the expected future loss.

Xantar grunted. They rejected a child for fear of losing the child, thereby hastening the loss. Emotions were another weakness of these creatures. *Irrational beings. Solution?*

We will need to return to the original timetable.

What about a drug regimen?

Considered and rejected. The drugs interfere with the mother's production of milk and can weaken the child. Any benefits in getting the mother to forget the child would be countered by weakening future offspring.

Xantar sighed. These creatures and their emotions were so taxing, especially where the offspring were concerned. The mothers had to be removed from all drugs to ensure a healthy offspring, which also made them less controllable. Luckily, without the muscle enhancements, they were no match for their guards. *Very well. Return to the previous protocol, but begin inseminating the subjects with more than one egg. If we cannot increase the rate at which they reproduce, we can increase the number they birth each time.*

Yes, Esteemed Leader.

What is the status of 72-A?

The data on the screen shifted. A tall avad's picture was on the right. On the left, the avad's biological information.

Levels remain consistent.

He nodded. The avad in question had been genetically linked to the avad who had helped the humans. They had not known of his existence until she had offered it. The other avad had not reported on the traitor, but a review of his interrogation demonstrated no questions directly related to the traitor's existence. His failure to mention him was therefore not his failure but that of the interrogators. And they had already been punished for such an oversight.

He turned his attention back to the female avad. *Interpretation?*

It appears unaffected by the contact with its genetic similar. The higher levels of suppressant issued to the subject when its similar's betrayal was detected may account for the consistency.

Where is it?

In observation. Aek waved hand, and a ten-foot slice of the wall slid away, revealing the tank behind it. The avad floated there, oxygen tubes connected to its nose and mouth.

Xantar studied the figure. *Maintain the present course, but use her as the test subject for the new protocol. Perhaps she will be of greater use to us in the future.*

Yes, Esteemed Leader.

What of the other avad?

The data on the screen shifted, the picture as well, although Xantar could not detect the physical difference.

Levels varied slightly, but it remains within an acceptable range. No hesitation or change in activities.

Xantar stared at the screen. *What do you account for regarding the variation in levels?*

The stoppage and readministration of suppressant can cause a variation in levels. Once the subject's system has stabilized, the levels will remain consistent.

Keep it under observation.

Do you want it terminated?

Xantar considered it for a moment, but they were having difficulty replenishing the ranks. If it was following the program and its system only needed time to stabilize, it should not be a problem. *No. Should the levels dip, however, remove the subject from duty, examine it, and if the levels cannot be brought back, terminate.* He paused. *Keep the female avad on board in isolation. Test her again, and then up her regimen.*

There is no logical reason to do that.

These creatures are not logical. They are emotional. Do it.

Aek inclined her head. *Yes, Esteemed Leader.*

38

Thor finished his shift by shutting down his emotions. He had never had to do that before. His emotions had never been an issue before. And he couldn't figure out why they were now.

It had to have been his time with the humans. He had spent nearly a month with them. They had done something to him. At first, during his captivity, he had felt the same—which meant to say he had felt nothing. He had simply waited for his rescue. But it never came. During those first few days, he watched the humans, categorizing weaknesses, looking for opportunities to escape. But none materialized.

As time went on, though, he had begun to notice more. He noticed how they always seemed to want to interact with one another. They sought each other out, sometimes just to sit in silence with some person, but they were always looking for one another. And they took great joy in this, it seemed. They talked, they laughed.

And then there was Maisy's singing. He had never heard such an incredible sound. There was nothing like that among his people. He had barely heard any of his people talk the last few years. The closest would be grunts of pain during training.

And thinking back, as time went on, he had even found himself searching for the humans. He did not like being on his own. And Maisy. He watched for her each day, getting joy out of seeing her. Was it the food? Had they put something in it? What was wrong with him? His people did not behave this way ...

Except for the traitor. He interacted with the humans. He sought them out. And some of them sought him out. They enjoyed his company. They were protective of him. *I'm turning into him.*

He wracked his brain trying to figure out what had changed. At the same time, he felt more alive now than he had since he had been with Xe. It was as if he had awoken after a long sleep. He ate dinner that night with one of his legs jiggling under the table. The man next to him turned to watch him, and he immediately stopped. His people did not move unnecessarily.

He quickly finished his food. After putting away his bowl, he scanned his bracelet, and the two pills popped out of the tube next to the scanner. He scooped them up and went to drop them in his mouth when his mind flashed back on the blue liquid in the bags next to the women's beds. He hastily pulled down his hand, pretending to swallow at the same time. He walked to the lift, realizing he had not checked his bunk assignment for the night. He glanced at the reflection of the lift and saw two chelvah heading toward the lift as well. He could not check it now without arousing suspicion.

He stepped onto the lift, scanning his bracelet and getting a quick glance of his assignment. Level 17, Room 18, Bunk 2. He let out a quick breath, feeling the sweat across his back.

The lift stopped on levels 14 and 16 before stopping at 17. He quickly made his way to Room 18 before climbing into his bunk. Removing his helmet, he stared at the ceiling, the pills wrapped tightly in his hands. He closed his eyes, listening to the other

Unwelcome file in. Lights were extinguished a short time later. He opened his eyes in the dark, staring out over the bunks. There were one hundred and forty-nine of his brothers and sisters in here. All of them had followed the rules, taken their pills, and were now asleep. He was the only one awake.

He watched them, picturing each of them as a small child being loaded onto a ship in a capsule. Before that moment, each of them had had emotions. He remembered fear, joy, anger, sadness. He had felt all of those when he was with his sister. Each person in this room had felt those. But now, none of them felt those emotions. Before he'd been captured, he had not felt them, either.

He unrolled his fist, staring at the two little pills. They were almost the same color as the liquid in the bags attached to the IVs. And the same pills had been given to the women. He stared back out over the bunks and knew that somehow the Naku were responsible for their emotions being shut off.

And Thor just could not bring himself to shut his own off again.

THE DAYS PASSED with Thor being shifted from section to section. Each night he promised himself he would take the pills, but the image of those women stopped him each time.

Today he was assigned to West Wing, Level 3, Room 304. He knew as he climbed the stairs that this was the wing that held the women with the children. From what he could tell, the east wing was the medical wing, which held the women after they gave birth as well as the women as they neared birth. The south wing was where the pregnant women stayed. And the north wing, well, he wasn't sure exactly what happened there. He had yet to be assigned there.

He opened the door leading to the hall of the third floor. A shape came flying around the corner at him. He stopped short, stepping back quickly as a child ran into his legs and fell back onto his butt. The little boy stared at Thor's feet before looking up, up, and up at Thor. His mouth fell open.

Thor recognized him as the little boy with the infectious laugh.

His mother ran around the hall, her eyes wide when she caught sight of her son on the ground. "No, he didn't mean anything. Please."

Thor took a step back, not sure what he was supposed to do. Another Unwelcome stormed down the hall. The woman grabbed her son. The Unwelcome latched onto her arm, pulling her down the hall, bunching the material of her sleeve as he did so, revealing the back of her forearm and an old burn, the one seared into his memory as much as her skin.

39

Thor stood frozen in place, watching as Xe was dragged down the hall. At the same time, he memorized everything about her. She was tall and slim like the other avads. But there was a light in her eyes when she looked at her son. He had seen it for days in the courtyard. And her son, he was so full of life and joy. The door opened behind him, pulling him from his thoughts. He hurried toward his assignment, not allowing himself to glance back, but his mind was still picturing every interaction of Xe and her child.

Xe was alive. She was a breeder. She had a son. Thor could think of nothing else all day. He looked for her all day but did not see her again. That night, he'd pretended to take his pills and then stared at the ceiling most of the night, wondering how he could tell her it was him, while simultaneously knowing he never could.

Thor was stationed once again in the courtyard the next morning. He arrived just as dawn was breaking. Three pregnant women were in the space. He watched them, imagining Xe there, her belly growing over the months.

Was this her first child? He thought that unlikely at her age.

How many children had she brought into this world? How many had she reached for, only to be pushed into a drug-induced darkness? He didn't know how long the women were drugged after their children were taken. It would have to be long enough for the women to forget some of the pain.

He flashed on the look on the woman's face from the removal ward. He did not think she would forget that child anytime soon. And if the women were too difficult, they would simply be terminated. Their lives were only worth as much as their roles in the Naku's supply chain. If they could not supply the Naku with children, they were of no worth.

The bell sounded. He realized that he'd been so lost in his thoughts, he had not been paying any attention to the women in the courtyard. His heart rate ticked up. He had never been so careless in his duties.

Those pills. He hadn't been able to take them since seeing the woman injected with that blue solution. He wondered if he should just take one and go back to his other way of living. That existence was easier, without all these thoughts, these doubts running through his mind. He had never had any anxiety then. He'd also though had no awareness, no feelings. But wasn't that better than this constant state of unease?

And now that he knew Xe was alive and at the facility, it was making everything harder. He wanted to grab her and her son and escape. But that would only ensure their deaths.

The women exited through the door of the west wing. When the last one slipped through, the door to the north wing opened. A small blue blur dashed out through the door. Titters of laughter followed him. Xe appeared, hurrying to catch up with her son.

Thor's chest felt tight, and his breathing became uneven. She was so close.

My family. The thought stirred something deep inside of him. They were connected. They belonged together. In a world where he had nothing, not a single possession that was his, and nowhere that he could claim as a home, the idea of belonging with these two people was nearly overwhelming.

He kept his body still, not betraying his interest. But from the corner of his eye, he watched the boy as he roamed through the courtyard. He seemed to find joy in everything. A butterfly drifted by. He let out an excited exclamation, racing with his stumbling steps after it. His small chubby hands reached out to claim it but always fell a little short. He reached too far one time and tripped, sprawling in the dirt. He let out a wail.

Xe hurried over and gathered him in her arms, sitting on the ground and curling him in her lap. He clung to her, his little chest shuddering. Xe rubbed his back, murmuring words into his ear, then leaned her chin on top of his head and rocked back and forth.

Thor's chest ached, remembering doing the same for her when she was just a little older than the boy was now.

Mentally, he shook himself, pulling his gaze from the two of them. Even if he wanted to, a life with them was a fantasy. He had awareness but no power. Xe probably didn't even remember him. It would be better for all of them if he simply forgot.

But even as he thought that, he knew the words were false. It would be better for him, true. But it would not be better for Xe, who would lose her son. And then in the best-case scenario, be forced to have another child, only to lose them too. And eventually when her child-bearing days were over, she would be over as well.

As for her son, he would be thrown into hell. If he survived, he would be made a chelvah.

And he will turn into me.

None of those thoughts mattered, though. There was nothing he could do. He could not save himself from his fate, and he certainly couldn't save them from theirs.

His sister had released her son as his tears had dried. He was once again exploring the courtyard, completely undimmed by his earlier emotions. A second child joined him, who was about the same size. Xe walked behind them, keeping a careful eye on them. Another woman walked with her.

The sun shone off their blonde hair, and they looked so fragile with their slim builds. The children walked a few feet from Thor and then plopped down in the grass, picking at the weeds that had sprung up. The women were standing only six feet away from Thor. He struggled to overhear their quiet conversation. It took him a moment to recognize the old language. They spoke English as well, although he noticed they were more likely to speak the old language when they spoke with each other.

"Did you get any sleep?" the other woman asked.

Xe shook her head. "He turns two in two months."

"I know. You should not have gotten so attached."

"How do I do that, Olera? Can you honestly say that you are any less attached?"

Olera sighed. "I have tried. But it is not easy. We should not have given them names."

"I don't think giving them names make it harder, just as I think nothing will make it easier." Xe's head jolted up and headed to her son as he was about to put a weed in his mouth. "Geothorxed, do not eat that."

Thor went still. Geothorxed, she had named him Geothorxed. *She named him after me.* He was glad for once that he was required to stay perfectly still because he did not think he could move at that moment, even if one of the Naku themselves ordered him to.

She remembers me. He watched with disbelief rolling through him as the women picked up the children and headed away from him. Two months. In two months her son would be taken from her.

He had no idea how he was going to accomplish it, but he was going to save them.

He knew he wouldn't be able to live otherwise.

40

It had been a month since Thor had recognized Xe. A month of not taking the Ka Sama. A month of wracking his brain to figure out a way to protect her and her son. A month of realizing that on his own, he had no options. Tonight, Thor completed his shift feeling as if his skin belonged to someone else. He felt trapped in his helmet, in his uniform. He wanted nothing more than to shred them both. But he couldn't. He felt more trapped right now than he had felt in that cage with the humans.

He focused on keeping his breathing even as he walked back to the ship behind another six chelvah. For the first time, he wondered if he had known any of them on their home planet or in training. Had they had any siblings that had looked out for them, loved them, or had they been on their own even longer than him?

His mind couldn't seem to stop asking questions. It was as if the wall against his curiosity had been destroyed, and now all he had were questions.

He knew nothing of his people's past. He knew nothing of the Naku's past. That information was not anything that would help them with their duties and therefore unnecessary to convey. But right now, he wondered. Had the Naku and the avad always lived together? Had the Naku always been their guardians? Had it always been this way?

A strong wind blew in from the west. Thor had to tuck his head to fight against it on the way to the ship. Eight crates lined up next to the veerfinah toppled over, knocking over the marchelvah.

Thor took a step toward him before realizing no one else had moved to help. He covered the move with a stumble as if the wind had knocked him off balance.

"18-F, 22-C, aid me," the marchelvah called.

Thor and the soldier next to him veered off. They lifted crates and began placing them on the cart. Thor reached for another one and noticed a small disc on the ground. Without a thought, he swiped it into his palm as he reached for the crate's handle. He finished loading the rest of the crates. As he made his way to the veerfinah, he slid the disc up his sleeve.

He took his seat, sweat beading along his back. He had stolen the marchelvah's information tablet. It was a running record of all chelvah's activities. It was updated as orders were issued. Thor had no idea what made him do it.

As the doors opened, he found himself following the other chelvah from the ship, others following behind him. They moved as one unit to the lifts, silently getting on until they filled the space.

Once the doors reached the food level, they all exited in silence. Thor ate his food and palmed his pills, pretending to swallow them before heading to his new bunk assignment. He was on the bottom bunk this time. He placed his helmet on the floor next to the bed and then lay down. The room filled up with the rest of the chelvah, and they all quickly took their bunks. Soon, their even breathing filled the air.

He looked out over his sleeping people. They were sleeping even when they were awake. He pictured Xe at the breeding facility. She was awake, and she needed his help. But he couldn't do it alone. All he would do was get himself killed. And then Xe would be no better off, maybe worse. If they realized they were related, they might kill her and her son just to be sure the genetic flaw did not reappear.

He could not do this alone. He stared at the man sleeping on the bunk next to him. He had a darker hue to his skin and dark hair. He was powerfully built, as were they all. He would be a powerful ally if Thor could get him to wake up. He glanced out across the room. They would all be powerful allies if he could get them to wake up.

But that was well beyond his power. The traitor flashed through his mind. In his gut, he knew the traitor would help him. The one person who would help him was a traitor to their own kind.

But isn't that what I am becoming? Am I not turning into a traitor, too? He didn't want to linger on those thoughts. He focused on what he needed to do: help his sister and her son escape. His fingers traced the outline of the tablet. He knew that the information it relayed could be the only chance he had of saving Xe.

And to do that, I'm going to need help. Now I just need to figure out who would be willing to help me.

41

It had taken two months to find the Lab. One month had been eaten up just by travel. They'd faced a tornado, an earthquake swarm, two flash floods, and one mountain lion attack. None of their abilities had manifested during any of the incidents. Lyla knew they were lucky they didn't lose anyone, though they had come close.

But finally they had made it to what used to be northern Texas. Lewis knew the Lab was somewhere in the northeast corner of the old state. Unfortunately, he didn't have any more specific directions than that. And after three weeks of searching, Lyla was losing hope.

But then Petra had come across an old highway sign that mentioned Allied Laboratories. It took them another three days of searching, but they finally found it.

Now she, Riley, and Miles stood looking at the object of their search. Lewis and Arthur were keeping an eye on everyone else a few miles down the road while Lyla and the boys did the initial search. They didn't think it would endear them too much to the inhabitants if it looked like they were invading. And being most of their group were Cursed, Lyla didn't want to take a chance if the Lab was anything other than friendly.

But it looks like unfriendly inhabitants are going to be the least of our worries.

The building stood silently in the clearing, which nature had been slowly overtaking. A game trail ran through the tall grass. What had once been a long driveway and parking lot was now reduced to a large chunk of asphalt and upturned ground. The building itself was shaped like an L. It was gray and only one story high. A forest seemed to have sprung out of the roof. Vines cascaded over the side.

All the windows were smashed save two in the front. The double front doors were also absent of glass, except for a few diligent shards holding onto the frame.

Wind whistled through the air, rustling the scraps of fabric left from drapes in one of the rooms.

Lyla stared at the building with a sense of despair. Abandoned was not a strong enough word for this place. They had traveled so far, with hope that maybe the Lab might offer some answers. But if this was the Lab, answers were not going to be forthcoming anytime soon.

"Is it possible anyone is still here?" Miles asked.

"I doubt it," Lyla said. "But there may be a sign inside that could tell us where they've gone."

"Maybe this isn't even the Lab," Riley said. "Maybe Lewis got it wrong."

Lyla nodded, but inside she felt despondent at the idea. If this wasn't the right lab, they had no idea where it could be. Which meant answers were even farther out of their reach. The Lab had always been a long shot to begin with, but until she saw the disrepair of the building, she hadn't realized how much she had been clinging to the small hope that they'd find it.

Because the truth was, there was no plan B. They would be relegated to simply running and hiding from the Unwelcome.

Maybe if they survived the next few years, they could put down some roots. But she wanted so much more for these kids than a life constantly on the run.

Lyla made sure none of those concerns could be heard in her voice. "It's possible Lewis got it wrong. But let's check it out anyway. Maybe this is just the wrong building, and the real lab is somewhere nearby."

Neither Miles nor Riley looked comforted by her words. She ignored their dubious looks and kept her voice brisk. "Okay. Let's walk the perimeter. Stay on guard. If there's nothing suspicious, we'll head in through the front doors. All right?"

Riley and Miles nodded. Lyla led the way, staying twenty feet from the edge of the building, which, with the encroachment of the trees, kept her right along the tree line in case they needed to retreat. They walked along the wing. The back was in the same condition as the front but had a few more windows that were intact. Nothing stirred inside the building except for a few birds that had made their nest in one of the windowsills.

"This is a waste of time. We should keep going," Riley said.

"We check it out first," Lyla said. "*Then* we can move on."

Riley grunted but didn't say anything else. Lyla couldn't blame him for his bad mood. They had all been hoping this destination would be the beginning of understanding and maybe defeating the Unwelcome.

They made their way back to the front doors. Lyla paused, listening, but no sound out of the ordinary greeted her. She cautiously stepped through the empty frames, her staff in her hand. Dirt had made its way inside, covering most of the old foyer. An old couch and two chairs sat on the right-hand side, covered in years of bird droppings. An old tall receptionist desk stood along the back wall. The desktop had been peeled back, and a green moss had started to grow along the sides.

"I'll take the right. You guys head left."

The boys nodded, slowly heading off together.

Lyla walked down the hall to the right. Twelve doors lined it, six on each side. There was a large opening at the end, which had probably been a pane-glass window at some point. She stopped at each doorway. All the doors were open, some lying in the hall, the hinges having long since given up the fight to keep the door upright. Others barely hung on. All of the rooms were formerly offices. Each contained a desk and bookshelves but no sign of any recent human presence.

Lyla carefully made her way back to the front foyer and stopped at a large board. Names had been listed on metal tags with office numbers next to them. Nearly half of them were gone.

The room numbers ranged from 100 to 250. She frowned. Why the two hundreds? She glanced to her right and saw a small plague that indicated the hall she'd come through contained rooms that began with one hundred. She glanced at the other side. A dark smudge was on the wall at the same spot. She reached down to the ground, carefully pushing away the dirt and debris on the floor. She found the other sign, indicating the rooms in the other hall began in the two hundreds. A few more pieces of metal stuck out of the ground, and she recognized them as part of the directory. She started to pull them out.

Riley and Miles reappeared. "There's no one here," Riley said, his weapons sheathed behind him.

Miles at least kept his short staff in his hand. "What are you doing?"

She pointed at the display above her. "This is the directory. It lists all the offices. Some of the names fell off." She handed Miles the six she'd found. "You two wipe these off."

She dug out another five, handing them to Riley. Riley started wiping them of dirt as she straightened, wiping the dirt from her hands. "What are the room numbers?"

"Uh, 104, 203, A7—"

Lyla frowned. "A7? Are there any others like that?"

"I've got a B2. And an A1," Miles said.

Lyla turned, examining the area. Along the far wall, a tarp had been thrown over part of it. She walked over and pulled the tarp back. A door stood there, clear footprints in the dirt in front of it. She pulled out her staff. "Somebody's been here."

Behind her, Riley pulled his sword as Miles stepped behind her. Lyla moved to the side of the door and made eye contact with Miles and Riley before opening the door, revealing a stairwell leading down. A metal ladder bolted into the wall led upward. She leaned in, looking down and listening. It was silent.

There was a small hatch in the ceiling. Dirt clung to the rungs leading to it. Lyla put her fingers to her lips and pointed up. The boys nodded back at her.

Lyla stepped into the stairwell as Riley and Miles flanked her. She quickly climbed the ladder and easily pushed open the hatch. With the state of the roof, she'd expected it to be overgrown. But the space around the hatch was clear, increasing her suspicion that someone had been here recently. She glanced around. An explosion of green surrounded her. She carefully climbed up, staying hunched by the opening for a second before waving the boys up.

The boys climbed through, and she closed the hatch.

Dots of red caught her eyes, and she recognized a wild patch of strawberries. The roof was covered in overgrowth, but as she looked closer she could see an order to it. Along the edges were wild growth that cascaded over the sides, but netting had been placed to keep that wildness from crossing into the interior of the space. And everywhere she looked were edible plants. Zucchini, blueberries, watermelon, corn, cauliflower—the list went on and on. It looked like it was growing wild, except there was a small path that wound through it.

"This is someone's garden," Miles whispered.

"Yes, it is." She moved farther in, spying a metal object. It was a large box, four feet by four. It had been cut and had hinges attached. She opened it. A shelf had been put inside, and gardening tools had been placed on it. "Ingenious. If an Unwelcome ship were to fly over, they'd never recognize it as a working garden."

"And from the ground, the whole place looks abandoned," Miles said.

Lyla glanced back at the hatch. "Whoever is responsible for this must live on the lower levels, out of view."

A small screech of metal caught her attention. She pulled the boys behind the makeshift gardening shed, putting her fingers to her lips.

A man with gray hair and dark skin climbed out of the hatch. Carrying a basket, he moved with a slow shuffle. He began to pick some of the strawberries, humming a little tune to himself as he worked. From Lyla's vantage point, it didn't look like he carried any weapons.

Lyla indicated that the boys should stay there. She slipped out from their hiding spot. The man's back was to her. She moved until she was close enough to reach him should she be wrong about him not having a weapon. "Hello."

The man let out a screech, whirling around. The contents of his basket went flying as his hand flew to his chest. He stood staring at her, his chest heaving.

Lyla put up her hands. "I don't mean you any harm."

His eyes were wild as they darted around, his pulse visibly hammering away in his throat. "How ... how did you get here?"

"Through the same hatch as you."

The man looked back at the hatch and then at Lyla. His breathing calmed a little as he took some deep breaths. "Sorry for my reaction. We haven't seen people here in quite some time."

"I can understand why. This place looks abandoned."

"Keeps people away, usually. So how come you came in? There's no storm to try and seek shelter from, and most people would think there was no food to be had." He frowned as if just realizing his garden might be in danger.

"I'm not here for your food," she said quickly. "I'm looking for a place called the Lab."

Once again the man's eyebrows headed north. "The Lab? Why would you be looking for a lab? Science isn't really that important these days."

Something about the man's tone had her studying him closer. He knew something. She spoke slowly, keeping her focus on the man. "I have some questions about the Cursed, their blood. And I was hoping there might be someone there who could help."

He frowned. "The Cursed?"

"The children the aliens are targeting. I think there's something different about their blood."

The man seemed to weigh her words, struggling with some sort of inner debate. Finally, he smiled, extending his hand with a slight tremor in it. "Well, then you're in luck. I'm Dr. Jerrold Stevens, geneticist."

42

Relief and disappointment warred in Lyla for dominance. "So this *is* the Lab?"

The doctor watched Lyla, a smile on his face. "Yes. We were called that for years after the Incident. But no one's used that name for a while. What are you hoping to find?"

"Actually, I think Miles would be able to better explain it. Boys?"

Miles and Riley stepped out, keeping their hands in front of them and walking slowly. "Miles, Riley, this is Dr. Jerrold Stevens, a geneticist."

Jerrold watched them both with more than a little concern. Lyla couldn't really blame him as she tried to view them with unbiased eyes. Although she still thought of them as her boys, they were no longer little. They were both taller than her, and each had the build of a muscular young man now. Both also had weapons peeking out from over their backs and along their sides.

But Miles stepped forward with his usual enthusiastic smile. "Dr. Stevens, I am so happy to meet you. We weren't even sure this place still existed."

At Miles's enthusiastic greeting, the doctor seemed to relax.

"Call me Jerrold. And as I was explaining to your ... sister?" He looked between them.

"More like mom. But I go by Lyla."

He nodded, more of the tension draining from him. "As I was explaining to Lyla, no one's called us that for years."

"But you do still have some lab capabilities?" Miles asked.

Jerrold hesitated. "Some. Perhaps if you told me what you were looking for?"

"We want to look at some blood samples," Miles said quickly. "I managed to get a hold of a microscope and noted some differences in the blood samples I was examining. But I was really hoping you had something a little stronger and maybe a better understanding of what we're looking at."

"Whose samples?"

Miles hesitated, glancing at Lyla, but she nodded. This was why they came, after all. "A sample of a Cursed, a human adult, and an Unwelcome."

Jerrold's eyebrows nearly disappeared into his hairline. "You got an Unwelcome's blood?"

Miles opened his mouth to answer, but Riley jumped in, no doubt worried that Miles in his enthusiasm would mention Arthur. "Yes. We managed to get some after a skirmish with one of them."

Jerrold looked between them. "That's amazing. And intriguing. I've often wondered why it was they targeted such a powerless group. When they arrived, the Cursed were only between the ages of seven and twelve, hardly a threat."

Lyla spoke slowly, studying Jerrold's face. "We've learned the Cursed actually *are* a threat."

Jerrold frowned. "How?"

"Abilities manifest when in confrontation with the Unwelcome that allows the Cursed to truly fight them," Miles said.

"What kind of abilities?"

"Speed, strength," Lyla said.

Jerrold nodded. "All adaptations that would allow an individual to defend themselves."

"And I got my arm back to fight one," Miles said, holding his half arm up. "I—"

Jerrold cut him off. "Excuse me?"

"When I fought the Unwelcome, my arm reappeared, and I could use it as if it had always been there."

Jerrold's jaw dropped, and he stared at Miles. "How long did it last?"

"As soon as the fight was over, it disappeared."

"And how long since you lost your arm?"

"Almost six years now."

"Oh my goodness, this is beyond fascinating. Elaine is going to be beside herself."

"Elaine?" Lyla asked.

"My wife. She's a biochemist. This is going to be right up her alley."

"Are there any other scientists here?"

Jerrold's smile dimmed. "I'm afraid it's just me and my wife. But come on in. Do you have the samples with you?"

Miles nodded.

Jerrold clapped his hands together. "Oh, this is exciting."

Before journeying back inside, Lyla, Miles, and Riley helped Jerrold finish collecting his food supplies.

As they headed to the hatch, Jerrold looked hesitantly between his basket and the three of them. "Um, I know this may look like a lot of food, but we really only have enough for ourselves—"

Lyla spoke quickly. "We do not expect you to feed us. We've already taken care of that."

Relief flashed across Jerrold's face. "When I was younger, my grandmother lived with us and always set out food and drink for any visitors that stopped by. She considered it the height of rudeness to do any less."

"Sadly, the world has changed since her day," Lyla said.

Jerrold nodded his head with a big sigh. "Yes, it has." He bent down for the hatch handle, but Riley beat him to it. "Let me to do that."

"Thank you, son. I don't bend as easily as I used to."

Riley held the hatch open.

"I can take the basket if you want," Lyla said.

Jerrold tucked it a little tighter to his side. "No, no. I'm used to making the climb with it."

Lyla knew that was at least partly true. He simply still didn't trust them. And she couldn't blame him. Even his grandmother would distrust strangers in this world. She was just happy he agreed to help them. But she didn't trust him, either. And at the first sign of danger, she could and would use him to protect her boys.

Jerrold went down first, followed by Lyla, Miles, and then Riley, who shut the hatch after them.

Stepping onto the landing, she wiped her hands on her pants. "You should consider putting a lock of some sort on the hatch."

"We had one. But my hands have gotten a little worse for wear over the years." He held one out, and she again noticed the tremor in it. She'd noticed it up on the roof but had attributed it to nerves.

Miles looked up at the hatch. "I may be able to rig something up for you with a handle release. It wouldn't be too hard to manage."

"Well, I would surely appreciate that, son. Thank you."

Lyla smiled. Miles simply couldn't help himself when it came to helping people. It was one of his most endearing qualities and also the one that those who loved him tried to make sure didn't get him into trouble.

Jerrold headed down the stairs, keeping one hand firmly on the handrail and the other on the basket. No one spoke as they descended. The entry to the lower level had been secured with a large metal door. A large, heavy-looking ball had been attached to a string and hung in front of it.

Jerrold paused at the door. "Um, I think it would probably be best if you left your weapons outside."

The boys looked at Lyla, who immediately placed her staff against a wall and unbuckled her scabbard, placing it next to the staff. "That's fine."

Miles and Riley followed her lead.

Jerrold smiled. "Thank you."

She returned the smile, not feeling the least bit guilty about the knives stashed in her boots. There were steps they needed to take to trust one another, and she was willing to do that, but she would never put herself or the boys at a disadvantage. If, when Jerrold opened the door, someone was waiting to harm them, Jerrold would be the first to die.

Jerrold grabbed the ball and knocked three times, then twice more in a quick succession. He released the ball and waited. "I can't open the door from this side. Only someone from inside can."

"Exactly how many people are inside?" Riley asked.

"Four. My granddaughter, Iris; the twins Michael and Michelle; and my wife, Elaine."

The door began to slide to the side with a screech. The first thing Lyla noticed was the small shaft of light that appeared through the crack. Could it be they had electricity?

A small head appeared in the gap. The woman was tiny. Lyla wasn't sure she would even reach her shoulders. She had large glasses that magnified her eyes, and her dark hair was pulled back into a ponytail. "Jerrold?"

"It's all right, Elaine. They need our help with a scientific inquiry."

Elaine studied each of them for a moment before sliding open the door farther.

Jerrold smiled, stepping through. "Lyla, Riley, Miles, I would like you to meet the most amazing biochemist this side of the Mississippi, my wife, Dr. Elaine Choi."

Elaine waved away his words, a slight blush appearing on her cheeks. As she ducked her head down, Lyla noticed the gray hairs running through the black. Elaine was older than she first appeared.

But it wasn't Elaine that held Lyla's attention. It was the light bulbs that were strung along the hall.

Miles gasped, moving closer. "You have electricity."

"Yes, we do," Jerrold said. "But I'd rather not talk about how that's possible."

Miles opened his mouth to ask out of pure curiosity, but Lyla grabbed his arm before he could. "We understand. We appreciate you allowing us in and helping with our little problem."

"Now let me drop these off in the kitchen, and then we'll head to the lab." He kissed his wife on the forehead as he passed her. A young girl with skin a few shades lighter than Miles sprinted down the hall, coming to an abrupt halt in front of Lyla.

The girl's thick hair fell forward over her face. She shoved it back impatiently. "Hi, I'm Iris. Who are you?"

"That is not how we introduce ourselves," Elaine said.

Iris rolled her eyes theatrically. "How would I know? I've never introduced myself before."

Lyla judged her to be about nine. "I'm Lyla. And this is Riley and Miles."

Iris tilted her head, staring at Miles's half arm. "Did the Unwelcome do that?"

"Iris!" Elaine shook her head. "I'm so sorry. We haven't had visitors in a while. And now that I think about it, she was too young to remember the last time we had visitors."

"It's okay." Miles knelt down so he wasn't towering over the girl. "No. It wasn't the Unwelcome. I got bit by a wolf that had rabies. My arm was cut off so the rabies couldn't spread through my system."

Elaine let out a little gasp. "Whoever did that must have reacted quickly. It spreads so fast."

"Yes, she saved my life." He glanced at Lyla, who gave him a small smile back.

"Ah, good, you've met Iris." Jerrold draped an arm over Iris's shoulder. Iris flung her arms around his waist and snuggled into his side. Jerrold smiled down at her. "All right, Iris, why don't you lead the way to the lab?"

Iris led them down the hall, past the entrance they had come through and to a different hallway.

There were no lights on in this new hallway. Iris hit a switch on the wall, and three bulbs flared to life. Lyla glanced back as Elaine hurried to catch up with them. The lights had been extinguished behind her.

Jerrold noticed Lyla's attention. "We conserve electricity. While we have access to electricity, it is not unlimited."

"You have solar, don't you?" Miles asked.

"What makes you say that?" Jerrold said.

"Well, the only other real option is water. But there aren't moving bodies of water around here strong enough to generate the energy you'd need. So solar makes more sense, especially if you have batteries to store it."

Jerrold watched him. "Very good. But maybe keep that under your hat."

"Sure thing."

"All right." Jerrold stepped into a doorway and flipped on a switch. Lights flared on across the large space, which looked to be the entire length of the hallway. "Welcome to the Lab."

43

The lab consisted of six rows of long metallic tables. All of them had dust on them. A few had drop cloths covering the equipment on top.

"So, I'm guessing you don't use this place very much," Riley said.

"Not as much as we used to," said Elaine, "but the equipment is all still good. We just need to tidy up a little bit first."

Lyla rolled up her sleeves. "All right, let's get to it."

They focused on cleaning up the first table. Riley, Miles, and Lyla moved the heavier equipment off while Jerrold and Elaine searched for the equipment they would need. Iris trailed after Elaine, doing whatever her grandmother asked.

While they worked, Jerrold explained about how they'd come to be at the Lab.

"We were working here when the Incident occurred. We hunkered down, riding it out along with about two dozen of our colleagues. We escaped most of the damage. But after a while, most people left. They went to find their families. Some returned. Most didn't."

"You two didn't leave?" Lyla asked.

"We did. Elaine's family was in California. Mine was on the East Coast. We headed to California. It was under water. Her family was in San Francisco. Before the tsunami, a 9.2 earthquake hit. We knew we wouldn't find them."

"What about your family?" Lyla asked.

"It was only my mom. She lived in Queens. I spoke with her the day before the Incident, tried to talk her into flying out to be with us. She said she'd come the next week. I never spoke to her again."

"I'm sorry."

Jerrold gave her a tight smile. "It was a tough time. Elaine and I had only started at the Lab six months earlier. We met in grad school. I'm pretty sure they hired me just to entice her into the job."

"Not true," Elaine yelled from the back of the lab.

"Yes, it is," he yelled back before smiling at Lyla. "They had another geneticist on staff. They really didn't need me."

"What did you do here?" Lyla asked.

"We investigated human mutations."

"Mutations?"

"Humans as we know them today are not what they were thousands of years ago or even hundreds of years ago. Each new generation demonstrates a new mutation, most subtle, but the effect accumulates over time. Seventy-three percent of the 1.15 million variants have been found in the last five thousand years."

"What did you focus on?"

"Longevity. There are genetic mutations that shorten an individual's life span and others that lengthen it. We were identifying different strands to create a process that would remove the damaging mutations while leaving the beneficial ones."

"You could do that?"

"Not quite, but we were getting pretty close before ... Well, you know. The company had just gotten a huge government contract. Everyone was excited, and then ..." He shrugged.

"So it's only been you guys since then?" Lyla asked.

Jerrold shook his head. "No. We came back because we had nowhere else to go. A few of the scientists came back a year or so later." Jerrold shook his head. "They weren't the same people they were before. They'd seen too much."

"What happened?"

"Two took their lives. Three succumbed to illness. Some just wandered off and never came back. Soon it was just me, Elaine, our daughter Tiffany, Michael, Michelle, and Harold, the twins' father. We managed for a long time on our own. Every once in a while, someone would find us. Some were good people. Some weren't. Tiffany, she became pregnant after some not-so-good people came calling."

Lyla's head jolted up, and she looked at Iris.

"Iris is a blessing," Jerrold said firmly. "No matter how she came to be, we never looked at her as anything other than a gift."

After a bit of silence, he continued. "Harold, he died from the flu. Tiffany ... she was out hunting. She didn't notice the bear."

"I'm sorry."

Jerrold shook himself from his memories. "It was a long time ago, and I'm sure you have stories just as difficult." He nodded to where Riley and Miles were helping Elaine. "They might call you their mom, but I don't think you gave birth to either of them. You're lucky to have found one another."

"Yes, we are."

"You two are way too serious," Elaine said, walking over with a box of slides. "And I think this is the last of it. I think we're ready."

A tingle of anticipation rolled through Lyla. Finally, some answers.

44

Miles was having trouble keeping himself from just grabbing the microscope from Elaine. He had given Jerrold the slide of the Unwelcome blood first. That had been ten minutes ago. Jerrold had examined the slide silently, making some illegible notes on a notepad before moving over for Elaine to look. Finally, she moved back, and they conferred quietly.

Miles rolled his hand into a fist. He so wanted to butt into their conversation. Lyla was sitting patiently in a chair, waiting. Riley had actually curled up in the corner of the lab and gone to sleep.

"Calm down, Miles," Riley said.

Miles turned to him. "I thought you were asleep."

"Nope. Just relaxing while I can."

"How can you relax right now?"

Riley cracked open one eye. "Exactly how is your frenetic pacing helping things?"

"It's not," Miles grumbled.

Riley started to stand. "Showtime."

Miles whirled around to find Jerrold waving them over. Jerrold and Elaine remained seated on their stools.

"We've examined the sample, and we have some questions," he said.

Lyla leaned against the table across from them. "Shoot."

"Was the Unwelcome alive or dead when you retrieved the sample?"

"Alive."

"How long ago did you take the sample?"

Lyla hesitated for a moment. "This morning."

Surprise flashed across both the scientists' faces. "My good-ness." Elaine's hand flew to her neck. Miles noted the slight tremble in it.

Jerrold just nodded. "Uh-huh." He looked at Elaine. She turned to Lyla. "Have you seen what they look like under their suits?"

Another pause. "Yes."

"Is their skin blue, perchance?"

This time it was Lyla's face that flashed surprise. "Yes."

"How did you know that?" Miles asked, taking a step forward. Riley moved a little closer as well.

Jerrold waved Miles to the microscope. "Take a look."

Miles looked through, his eyes taking moment to adjust. The blood sample was much clearer than when he'd seen it before. The higher magnification made everything stand out more. He frowned. The little dots he'd thought he'd seen before were much more clear under this magnification. "What is that?"

"We'll need to do some follow-up tests to be sure, but we think it's silver," Elaine said.

"Silver?" Lyla asked.

"Yes. This sample is littered with it. We think that's why they're blue," Elaine said.

Miles frowned. "I don't understand. You mean the blue color isn't genetic?"

Jerrold shook his head. "I don't think so. I think the color is the result of an environmental contamination. Wherever they are from, silver was most likely in the air, the water, the food. And it changed their skin color."

"So what color *should* they be?" Riley asked.

"That's the other thing. It's been a while since we've looked at blood cells, but this one is extremely close to human."

Lyla narrowed her eyes. "What are you saying?"

But Miles knew exactly what they were getting at. His mouth fell open. "You mean, if they hadn't been living in a silver-saturated environment, their skin would be like ours. They'd look human."

Jerrold nodded. "Yes."

45

Miles's mind raced through all his conversations with Arthur. He struggled to say what he had to say without giving away Arthur in his excitement. "We actually believe that they're not all the same shade of blue. That there is a variation in tone, like you see in humans."

"Races," Elaine said, looking at Jerrold with bright eyes. "It's possible they have different races and ethnicities as well."

"Okay," Riley said, drawing out the word. "But humans have been exposed to silver in the past, and none of *them* are blue."

"They would have to *ingest* the silver to change their skin tone," Elaine said. "And humans who have done that have, in fact, turned blue."

Lyla, Riley, and Miles gaped at her.

"There are blue humans?" Riley asked.

Elaine gave them a small smile. "It wasn't common, but some people ingested silver as a health remedy. They believed that it boosted a person's immune system and even treated cancer. Of course, there was no scientific research supporting that."

"There's even a genetic link," Jerrold said. "Some humans have a recessive genetic condition called methemoglobinemia. It essentially means the individual produces too much hemoglobin. The result is the blood struggles to carry oxygen throughout the individual's body, resulting in blue skin and lips and an almost brown-colored blood."

"That happens?" Riley asked.

"Rarely. It's not a common genetic condition. It seems to be pretty isolated and sadly is the result of inbreeding. There was a famous family called the Fugates where three quarters of the family was blue," Elaine said.

"So humans have been blue," Lyla said. "But you're not saying the Unwelcome are humans?"

"I am not prepared to go that far. I'm not even prepared to say they have our skin tone, although we feel confident that the blue hue is the result of environmental factors."

Miles stared at them. They'd looked at one sample for a few minutes and had just blown their minds. He quickly reached into his pack and pulled out the box Judith Carolina had made for him. He pulled out the slides of Lyla's blood and Petra's. "Can you look at some other samples?"

Jerrold rubbed his hands together. "You'd have a hard time stopping us."

46

The Unwelcome were not naturally blue. Lyla pictured Arthur with human skin. Incredible. How different things might have been had his size been the only physical attribute that separated him from humans.

A laugh erupted from the hallway. Lyla whirled around, the hairs on the back of her neck standing on end. A man and a woman stood there. Both had long dark hair and a sallowness to their complexion. Body odor wafted toward Lyla as they stepped into the room.

"What's this?" the woman demanded.

Jerrold nodded at them, tension in his shoulders. "Michelle, Michael. Glad you're here. This is Lyla and her sons, Riley and Miles. They were looking for the Lab."

"Is that so?" Michelle crossed her arms over her chest. In contrast, her brother stood in the doorway alternating between smiling and scowling.

"Uh, yes," Jerrold said, playing with the collar of his shirt. Lyla looked between the twins and the two scientists. Iris had disappeared underneath a table. All three of them seemed nervous.

Michelle leaned against one of the tables. "You can't just let people in here, Jerrold. It's not safe. We don't know anything about them."

Michael slid in the door, angling toward her boys.

Lyla stepped between them. "Well, I'd be happy to answer any questions you have."

A laugh burst out of Michael.

Riley's gaze narrowed. "What's so funny?"

Michael just grinned at him before scowling again.

Miles kept looking between the two of them, his brain no doubt categorizing every strange quirk.

Elaine brushed off the twins' concerns. "No need for that. We're just—"

Michelle cut her off. "*We* decide what's necessary for our home's security."

Elaine blanched.

Lyla took a step forward. "Look, why don't we step outside? You guys can ask me whatever questions you want, and they can finish up their work."

Michelle gave her a hard stare before turning on her heel and marching into the hall. Michael followed her with a strange bobbing walk, as if he couldn't touch the heels of his feet on the floor.

Riley stepped next to her. "I'll go with you."

Lyla shook her head, nodding to Miles and the others in the room. "You keep an eye out in here, okay?"

Riley glanced at the doorway. "Be careful."

She squeezed his arm. "Always."

Raising her voice, she addressed Jerrold and Elaine. "I'll be right back."

Squaring her shoulders, she headed for the twins, not sure what to expect.

47

Miles paced along the aisles between the tables, categorizing everything he knew about the Unwelcome and trying not to worry about Lyla. She could handle two people easily, but something was off with those two.

But concerned as he was, his mind kept going back to what Elaine and Jerrold had said before the twins had interrupted. The Unwelcome would probably look human if not for a silver-saturated environment.

He knew people had theorized that other life-forms could be similar to humans. Which made sense if the universe was seeded as some theorists argued. Which would mean that they would develop from the same DNA. DNA changed over time, adapting to the environment. Would that account for the Unwelcome's size? Was their strength also an adaptation?

But even as he thought that, he wondered about their emotional state. According to Arthur, they never spoke or interacted socially. And they obviously had no difficulty with killing humans, even children. Of course, history was also littered with humans who had done the same. Had the Naku weeded out the

Unwelcome who might be too sympathetic or too emotional? But then how did Arthur slip through?

They had one answer, and now he had dozens of additional questions rolling around in his brain.

"This can't be right," Jerrold muttered.

Miles turned to the doctor. "What's the matter?"

"Are you sure you didn't mislabel these samples?"

Miles shook his head, a sense of déjà vu coming over him. "No. But when I first looked at the samples, I thought I had as well. The shape of the nucleus, right?"

Jerrold nodded. "Would you be willing to give me another sample? You're a Cursed, right?"

Miles felt light-headed at the idea. Blood was not his favorite thing.

"I'll do it," Riley offered, stepping forward.

Jerrold walked over to one of the cupboards and pulled out a bottle of rubbing alcohol. He moved to the sink and ran the alcohol over a scalpel. He walked back to Riley. "Hand, please."

Riley proffered his hand. Jerrold held it, the hand with the scalpel shaking as it moved toward Riley's finger.

Riley placed his hand over the doctor's. "How about I do the cut?"

"Yes, that would probably be for the best." Jerrold handed the scalpel to him.

Miles looked away as Riley made a small cut on the tip of one of his fingers. He turned back when Jerrold said, "All set."

Riley held his finger to his mouth. Jerrold slid the slide back under the microscope. "Huh. Elaine, take a look."

She slid her stool over. When she looked up, she said, "We need an adult sample."

Riley spoke quickly. "Lyla's not great with blood, either."

Jerrold raised an eyebrow. "All right. Well, I'm game. Mind sterilizing that?"

Riley nodded before walking to the sink and running the

alcohol over the scalpel. He walked back to Jerrold and took his extended left hand. "Ready?"

Jerrold nodded, looking away.

Riley made a tiny swipe. Jerrold sucked in a breath. Elaine quickly placed Jerrold's finger over the slide, and two drops splattered onto it. She released Jerrold's hand, and he immediately pressed the edge of his shirt to it.

Elaine slid the other slide out and the one with Jerrold's blood in. She looked through the eyepiece, adjusting the focus. Finally she sat back. "I'm not sure what to make of this."

Miles leaned forward. "What is it?"

She flipped her pad to a new page and drew three separate shapes. "Okay, these are the shapes of the nuclei in the three samples."

Miles nodded. Two of the shapes were essentially the same, barring Elaine's poor artistic ability. But the third was noticeably different, with a more squarelike shape to the nucleus.

"Which one is the Unwelcome's?" Elaine asked.

Riley pointed to the squared nucleus. "That one, obviously."

Elaine spoke slowly. "Yes, that one is noticeably different, while the other two are identical."

"That's not the Unwelcome's nucleus, is it?" Miles asked.

Elaine shook her head. "No. According to these samples, it's not the Unwelcome that is a different species. It's the Cursed."

48

Lyla stepped into the hall and found it empty. She frowned, walking slowly toward the living quarters. She glanced into the kitchen, but there was no one there. A search of the bedrooms showed the same. She stepped back into the hall, looking around. Where had the twins gone?

She made her way to the stairwell door. It had been left ajar. Lyla raised an eyebrow. If the twins were actually concerned about safety, they had a funny way of showing it. She opened the door. The stairs leading down were dark, and a strange smell drifted up toward her. She had no intention of going down there.

Noting their weapons hadn't been touched, she quickly belted her sword around her waist and looped her staff across her chest. She headed up the stairs, searching the dark corners of the stairwell as she moved until she reached the door leading to the first floor. A low murmur of voices and then Michael's laugh came from the other side of the door.

She opened the door and peered out. The foyer was empty, but she could hear voices from just outside. Lyla moved forward slowly, frowning as the words became more recognizable. Were they singing? She reached the edge of the room and peered through the missing panes of glass. The twins were on the other side of the clearing playing patty-cake. Lyla stared at them, not sure what the heck was going on.

Michelle turned and caught sight of Lyla as she stepped out of the building. A smile burst across her face as she skipped over to Lyla. "Oh, hey, there you are. I'm Michelle." She extended her hand.

Lyla shook it slowly. "Lyla."

"Lyla, what a pretty name." She grabbed onto Lyla's arm and dragged her over to some logs that had been pulled into a circle. "Come on. Tell me all about yourself."

"Uh ..."

Michelle let go of her and took a seat. Michael sat across from her, rocking back and forth. Both of them looked up at Lyla. Lyla was struggling to figure out what had just happened. The two siblings sitting in front of her now were nothing like the people she had met downstairs.

"So, where are you guys from?" Michelle tapped her leg on the ground.

Lyla carefully sat down, the twins' emotional shift leaving her on edge. "We're from out east."

Lyla explained to the twins about Attlewood and the Unwelcome. Michelle stared at her the whole time she spoke, barely blinking. Michael just laughed every now and then. Finally, Lyla stopped speaking.

Michelle's smile disappeared. "You expect us to believe that?"

"Which part?"

"That you took kids in who weren't yours?" Michael asked.

Lyla wasn't sure how to answer that. After all, Riley and Miles were right downstairs. They'd seen them. But before she could reply, Michelle and Michael stood up and walked into the woods. Lyla sat staring after them, her mouth hanging open.

While she'd been speaking, Michael had rocked in place the entire time. Michelle had stared at her, but her whole body had been tense and shaky, even as she smiled at Lyla. And then that shift at the end. What was with those two?

It was possible that being stuck in the lab in the dark had driven them a little crazy. Lyla glanced back at the lab. Jerrold and Elaine seemed fine, but they did seem nervous around the twins. They must know something was wrong with them.

Lyla stood up, a crick in her back. She'd been talking for a long time, intentionally. She'd been afraid the twins would cause problems and get in the way of Elaine and Jerrold's work. Hopefully she'd bought them enough time to get some answers. She scanned the area, feeling eyes on her and knowing it was the twins. She walked slowly back to the building and ducked in.

She needed to get Riley and Miles and get them out of here.

49

Words seemed to be tough to come by as Lyla stepped out into the fresh air with Riley and Miles a few minutes later. Riley ducked through one of the broken windows as Lyla and Miles exited through the door. Lyla's mind was spinning as Miles explained what Elaine and Jerrold had suggested: the Cursed were a different species.

The docs had promised to continue researching tonight. They'd talked about a range of possibilities for their abilities, including some sort of pheromone/hormone combination.

Lyla took the lead, and Riley fell back with Miles in between. It hadn't been a conscious decision they made, but Lyla always took lead, wanting to face the danger first. And Riley would always watch her back. And they both knew Miles's mind was racing, trying to figure out angles on what the docs had said that Lyla and Riley wouldn't even consider, which meant he would not be paying close attention to his surroundings.

They made camp not too far from the Lab but far enough that they wouldn't be seen. An image of the twins flashed through her mind again followed by the memory of Michael's laugh. It was just creepy. She was a little worried for the docs and Iris. But the twins had been with them for years. They were probably safe.

Lyla left the boys to scan for anybody in the area they weren't aware of, but she hadn't sensed anyone. She walked slowly, carefully. She'd checked the area twice, but she wasn't quite ready to go back to the camp. She needed a little time on her own to process everything.

Whatever answers she thought she'd find, she and the Cursed being a different species hadn't been it. What did that even mean?

But the other part of the puzzle was no less confusing: The Unwelcome's blood looked human. Miles had said something about humanoids on other planets, but come on.

It all felt unreal. But then again, everything felt unreal. Her early life had been about survival. Her parents and Muriel had given her a sense of security and love. But her mother had died when she was only six. She'd gotten a small cut, and it had become infected. Two weeks later, she was gone. Even at that young age, she'd recognized the sense of safety her family had created for her had been an illusion. So she had started looking for ways to actually protect them. She'd learned to fight, to hunt. She paid attention so she could read people beyond their words.

But through all of that, she never doubted she belonged in this world. That she was one of the humans struggling to survive.

So what am I really?

And if she was struggling with this information, how were the Cursed going to be able to adapt to it? What about the world at large? The first reaction differences usually generated was fear. The fear the members of Attlewood demonstrated whenever they looked at Arthur. And then that fear had shifted into violence.

She'd seen fear in Jerrold and Elaine, although not of either her or the boys. But it was Iris who had shown the greatest amount of fear at the presence of the twins. Something about them really scared her.

Lyla's long-honed ability to read people told her they were

right to be afraid. It was part of the reason she was out here scouting. She wanted to make sure the twins hadn't followed them. She didn't trust those two.

Lyla looped back around the camp so that she was now between the Lab and her boys. She backtracked toward the Lab but saw no indication that the twins had attempted to follow them.

She wasn't quite ready to let down her guard, but it was at least a good sign. That night, she slept little and was up before dawn doing another search, replacing Miles, who looked asleep on his feet. All the questions she had yesterday returned with force. She hoped today might lead to some additional answers.

Crashing sounded from the direction of the Lab. Lyla immediately thought of the twins. She climbed a tree nearby. While her money was on the twins, she'd seen evidence of bears in the area. She wasn't taking any chances.

She crouched down low on a branch fifteen feet up. She scanned the ground but kept returning to the direction of the Lab. Minutes passed, and the noises got louder, but whoever it was wasn't moving very fast.

A figure stepped into view, leaning one hand against a tree, doubling over. It wasn't one of the twins. Lyla quickly climbed down and jogged over to the person. "Jerrold?"

Jerrold's head snapped up. His shirt was soaked in sweat, his eyes wild. "Lyla, thank God."

"What's the matter?"

"It's Iris. She's gone."

50

The hole was almost two hundred feet wide and seemed to go another few hundred into the ground. Maisy sat on the edge, peering into it. She leaned forward a little more. Arthur's hand immediately gripped her shoulder. "Not too far."

"I won't." But she didn't lean back. She leaned a little more forward, staring into the dark depths, knowing Arthur wouldn't let her fall. "I've never seen a hole so deep."

"It's called a sinkhole. The ground underneath slowly empties out until the ground along the surface collapses in on itself."

Maisy shivered at the idea. The one thing you should be able to count on was the ground under your feet remaining solid. She imagined walking along and the ground suddenly opening up underneath her. And then she would be falling and falling, maybe forever. "No one would be safe."

Arthur pulled her onto his lap. "I will never let anything happen to you."

She shook her head. "You wouldn't be able to protect me."

"Then I would fall with you."

She hugged his arm closer to her, knowing he was telling her the truth. If a sinkhole opened underneath her, Arthur would dive in after her. He would not leave her alone. She leaned her arm against him with a sigh.

The two of them sat there just listening to the quiet. The camp was a few hundred yards back. The Cursed were training under Lewis's instruction. He was as tough as Lyla when it came to training. Maisy and Arthur had gone for a walk. Maisy had secretly hoped they might find her mom and the boys. They hadn't come back to the camp last night, although her mom had said they probably wouldn't if they found something. She didn't like being separated from them. She was always worried something would happen to them. Not that she could do much to help them, but like Arthur said, she'd rather fall with them than stay safe up on the surface.

Arthur rubbed her arm. "We should get back."

Maisy climbed from his lap. "Okay."

She took Arthur's hand, and they headed back to the camp. She sighed, peeking up at Arthur, who was scanning the area for any threats. She didn't want to go back to the camp. She was the youngest person there, and everyone except Petra and Arthur treated her like she was. She could do stuff. No, she wasn't a Cursed with special abilities, but she wasn't completely helpless. She grabbed her water skin and took a drink, then shook it. "Hey, Arthur?"

"Hmm?"

"Maybe we should fill up the water skins. Mine's pretty low."

He smiled down at her. "Good idea. I think I heard water this way."

Maisy smiled, skipping next to him. A little more time away from the camp. Good.

51

Lyla left Jerrold where he was and ran to retrieve Miles and Riley. She let out a whistle when she was in range. The two of them were running in her direction when she met them a short distance later.

Riley scanned the ground behind her, looking for a threat. "What is it?"

Lyla jolted to a stop. "Iris. She disappeared just after breakfast. Jerrold searched the Lab but couldn't find her, but he found the door to the stairwell open."

"Where are the twins?" Miles asked.

Obviously the twins had made the same impression on her boys as they had on her. She started to jog back to Jerrold. The boys fell in line next to her. "They were with Elaine since breakfast. Jerrold thinks she might have gone looking for us."

"Has she been in the woods much?" Miles asked.

"No. According to Jerrold, she's barely left the Lab. She's never left on her own. I had him start back to the lab. We're heading that way, and we'll try to pick up her trail."

The boys didn't say anything else, just kept their eyes peeled as they moved swiftly through the forest. Jerrold appeared up ahead. He hadn't gotten very far. "Miles, get Jerrold back to the Lab. Riley, we're going ahead to see what we can find."

Miles veered off toward Jerrold. Lyla picked up the pace, noting there was no warmth surging through her. Her abilities weren't kicking in. But even without them, she was fast. Riley stayed right behind her.

They burst into the clearing outside the Lab. Lyla slowed to a walk, scanning the ground. Iris was small, but she would still leave a trail.

"The twins went this way," Riley said. A series of footprints were clear in the dirt. Lyla nodded. "Look for signs of Iris."

Lyla scoured the ground around the entrance but saw nothing. But Iris would have been sneaking out. Lyla moved to the windows. At the last window along the front foyer, she found the first footprint. "Over here." She crouched down low, scanning the ground.

Riley jogged over. "Which way?"

"It looks like she went that way." She pointed along the side of the building.

"Wrong way," Riley said softly.

"Yeah. And the twins are going the wrong way too." She started to move quickly in the direction Iris had gone.

"How long's she been gone now?"

"Close to two hours." Lyla picked up her pace.

Riley didn't say anything. He didn't need to, because they were both thinking the same thing: Two hours was a very long time for a child not used to the dangers of this world.

52

The woods, which had at first enamored Iris, had taken on a more sinister edge as the sun rose in the sky and clouds moved in. Earlier she had seen a baby bunny hopping with its mom. Squirrels had dashed across the path in front of her and up trees. It had been awesome! She couldn't understand why her grandparents didn't let her come out here more. There was no one around.

Now she trailed her hand through a field of daisies. She even grabbed a handful and made herself a necklace as she walked. But then she realized she had been walking for a long time. She had thought it would be easy to find Lyla's camp. She just wanted to ask them some more questions. Maybe see if Lyla would agree to bring her daughter to visit soon.

Iris had never seen another child except in books. In the books they always looked like they were having fun. Her grandparents played with her, but she always had to tell them what to do. They were really smart, but they didn't seem to understand how to play make believe.

Iris stopped where she was, as she heard something howl in the distance. The hair along the back of her neck stood up. She looked around, noticing how few trees there were in this section. She didn't like it.

She must have passed Lyla's camp. She turned around and started to walk back. But she didn't recognize anything she was passing. She walked faster, hoping she would see something familiar sooner. But the farther she traveled the more worried she became. She didn't remember any of this.

She burst through a row of low bushes that pulled at her pants. She stopped quickly on the other side in front of a creek. She definitely hadn't been here.

Her head whipped from side to side, looking for something, anything that would tell her which way to go. Tears pressed against the back of her eyes, and her chest felt tight. *I'm lost.*

Her grandparents would never find her. She'd walked so far, and they couldn't walk that far. And if the twins found her ... She shivered. She did not want the twins to find her. She turned around and bolted into the woods. She ran fast, flying over the ground. A howl sounded behind her. She turned to look. Her feet caught on a root in the ground. She pitched forward with a cry, sprawling on the ground. A low growl came from her right. She scampered backward with a whimper.

Two glowing eyes appeared from the shadows. They grew larger until the mountain lion's face could be seen. It slunk out of the shadows, its ribs poking through its thin coat. But any pity she might feel for its hunger disappeared when she recognized she was its plan to feed that hunger.

It let out a loud screech and lunged. A second shadow burst out from the left, tackling the cat away before it could reach her. She screamed, scrambling back farther and hitting a tree.

She gasped as a girl darted out from the trees. She had pale red hair and bright blue eyes. She knelt down, staring into Iris's eyes. "We need to run."

Iris just stared at the girl. She had heard what she said, but it was as if her limbs couldn't move. The girl stood, grabbing onto

Iris's arm and yanking her to her feet. The girl was a head shorter than Iris but surprisingly strong. Iris took a step and let out a whimper as pain shot through her ankle.

"What's wrong?"

"My ankle."

The girl slipped Iris's arm over her shoulders. "Lean on me. Hurry." The girl was already moving them forward.

Iris glanced over her shoulder. A cry came from the bushes where the other shadow had tackled the cat. Then the mountain lion flew through the air, slamming into a tree.

But before Iris could feel any relief, she spotted a second lion stalking from the trees toward them.

"Hurry," the girl urged her on.

Iris limped along, leaning on the other girl and praying as hard as she could.

A screech echoed through the air behind them. The girl shot a glance back. With a gasp, she shoved Iris away. A giant cat leaped over them, landing where they had just been.

The girl leapt to her feet, pulling a knife from the sheath at her belt. "Stay behind me!" she yelled at Iris, not taking her gaze from the cat in front of her.

Iris watched with wide eyes as the girl planted herself in front of Iris. The cat got to its feet and let out a bone-chilling cry.

But the girl didn't move. She stayed where she was. She waved the knife. "Get out of here!"

The cat sprang at her. The girl ducked, rolling out of the way as the cat landed. With shock, Iris realized she had cut the cat along one of its legs. The girl rolled to her feet. "Over here!" she cried, taunting the cat.

But the cat had caught sight of Iris. Iris shut her eyes, knowing she was about to die. She tensed, waiting for the cat to pounce.

A thud and then the sound of a snap was all she heard. A

small hand touched her shoulder. "Hey, it's okay. You're okay now."

Iris opened her eyes slowly to see the girl.

"Arthur took care of it."

"Arthur?" Iris looked at where the cat lay, its body at an unnatural angle. But it wasn't the cat that drew her attention or her fear. It was the giant that stood up from behind him. She had never seen anyone so large in her whole life.

And he was blue. He walked over and knelt down next to the girl but kept his gaze on Iris. "Are you all right?"

Iris screamed.

53

The scream was soft and distant. If Lyla and Riley hadn't stopped for a moment they might not have even heard it.

Lyla took off in the direction of it. They had lost Iris's trail twice, but once they got back on it they realized that Iris herself had been lost. She had actually turned back toward the Lab. If the twins kept on their trajectory, there was a good chance they would come across her.

But that scream meant they hadn't found her soon enough. *Or maybe they had.* Lyla shook away the thought. She had no reason to suspect the twins would hurt Iris. But still, the idea of them finding her did not sit well with Lyla.

Lyla lengthened her stride, her gaze straying from the horizon to the ground to make sure she didn't trip. Riley kept pace with her.

"No! No!"

Lyla's heart nearly stopped. Maisy? She put on a burst of speed. And this time her heart did stop at the scene in front of her.

Arthur was crouched down low. The two girls were hunched down behind him as the twins attacked Arthur. Arthur managed to deflect their knives with his staff, but he didn't move himself out of the way, because if he did, he would leave the girls exposed.

Lyla sprinted forward. She thrust her staff in front of Arthur, blocking Michelle's attack. With a sweep of her arm, she disarmed her, sending the woman's knife flying.

Riley swept his staff at the back of Michael's legs, sweeping him off his feet with a thud. He slammed the end of his staff at the wrist holding the blade. Michael cried out, releasing the knife. Riley kicked it away.

"What are you doing?" Michelle demanded, her face murderous.

"He is not a threat."

Michael tried to get up, but Riley placed the end of the staff at his throat. "He took Iris," Michael said.

Michelle stepped toward Lyla.

"Step back," Lyla said. "Now." Lyla gripped her staff hard, the urge to punch the woman becoming harder to resist.

Michelle glared at her for a long moment before taking a step back. Lyla didn't turn her back on the woman as she spoke. "Arthur, are you all right?"

He stood slowly. "I'm all right."

Lyla flicked a glance at him. She shouldn't have. Her anger only spiked higher at the cuts along his arms and ribs. He'd just finished healing from the last assault.

"Maisy, what the heck are you doing here?" Riley asked.

"I ... we ..."

"They saved me," Iris said quietly, her face abnormally pale. "The cats would have gotten me."

For the first time, Lyla noticed the large mountain lion lying behind Michelle. From its strangely angled back, she knew Arthur had killed it. "How many cats were there?" she whispered.

"Four," Arthur said.

Lyla's knees buckled for a second. She took a deep breath. "Maisy, come here."

Maisy peeked around Arthur before walking toward her. Lyla lowered herself down to her knees. Maisy had a scrape along her cheek. And there was blood on the knife she still clutched in her hand. "Are you okay?"

Tears welled up in Maisy's eyes. She nodded and then flung herself at Lyla. Lyla held her tightly, rocking back and forth and trying to hold her own tears back.

"She protected Iris until I could get there. She was very brave," Arthur said.

Lyla just nodded, not ready to say anything quite yet. Lyla wanted to hear the whole story, but right now, she just needed to assure herself that Maisy was okay.

Riley was leaning down, speaking quietly with Iris, who gestured to her ankle. Lyla closed her eyes, taking a deep breath. "Are you all right, Iris?"

"She hurt her ankle," Maisy said.

Iris nodded.

"Okay, let's get you back to your grandparents."

"I'll take her." Michelle strode past Lyla. She had nearly forgotten the twins were there. Michael let out a laugh as he gathered up his knife.

Lyla gently pushed Maisy toward Arthur. Arthur immediately picked Maisy up and held her close, whispering in her ear. Maisy nodded, resting her head on his shoulder.

Michelle reached for Iris, but the girl shrank away from her, shaking her head. "No."

"Iris, let's go," Michelle said sharply, reaching for her again.

Iris cringed away from her. "I don't want to go with you."

Michelle's mouth was a tight line. "*Now, Iris.*"

"Enough," Lyla said. "Michelle, leave her alone."

Michelle whirled toward Lyla. "You don't tell me what to do. You don't know me. Don't pretend you know me."

Lyla frowned. What was wrong with these two? She put up her hands. "You're right. I don't know you. But Iris is scared right now. How about we let her decide who she wants to carry her, okay?"

Michele tightened her lips together, her eyes narrowing. She stood with her legs braced, her arms crossed over her chest. "Fine."

"Iris, who would you like to carry you?" Riley asked.

Iris looked from each adult, her gaze constantly darting back to Arthur. Finally her gaze stayed on him.

Surprise flitted through Lyla. "Would you like Arthur to carry you?"

Iris nodded.

"No!" Michelle burst out. "You cannot let that animal near her."

"He saved her life," Riley said, his voice taking on a hard edge.

Michael glared at them but then gave off another one of his strange laughs.

"Iris has chosen. And I assure you, Arthur is perfectly safe," Lyla said.

"If anything happens to her, it's on you," Michelle said before stalking away.

Lyla shook her head, watching the woman head back toward the Lab. Her even stranger brother followed her. They didn't even look back to make sure Iris was all right. They just disappeared from view.

"Apparently they're not actually that concerned about Iris's safety," Riley drawled.

Lyla shook her head. "I cannot figure those two out."

"I doubt anyone could." Riley walked over and tweaked Maisy on the nose. "Good job, sis."

Maisy smiled shyly at him.

Riley turned to Iris. "All right, Miss Iris. Let me help you up."

He picked her up and handed her over to Arthur. He eyed the three of them. "You all right with those two?"

Arthur smiled. "They barely weigh anything."

"I'm sorry I screamed," Iris said softly.

"It's okay, little one. I understand," Arthur said.

Iris snuggled into Arthur's other shoulder.

"Riley, take lead," Lyla said.

He nodded and headed forward. Lyla motioned Arthur ahead of her as she took up the rear. As Arthur passed, she couldn't help but notice the look of absolute contentment on his face. Even with the violence that had been visited on him, she knew he wouldn't hold a grudge. And right now, the fact that Iris had accepted him had made Arthur's whole world.

Their plan had been to keep Arthur away from the Lab. But his existence was now out of the bag. Lyla sighed, scanning the woods, and she realized it wasn't the wildlife she was concerned about sneaking up on them. It was the twins. She glanced over to where Iris lay with her head on Arthur's shoulder. She had just met Arthur, a being from a different planet, and she felt safer with him than she did with people she had known her whole life.

Lyla shook her head. They needed to figure out what was wrong with the twins. Because right now, Lyla was pretty sure neither Iris nor her grandparents would be safe if they left them behind.

54

The reaction of Elaine and Jerrold to Iris's arrival in Arthur's arms was practically comical. Miles caught sight of Riley and grinned at the expression on his face. He called out to Elaine, who turned. Elaine tapped Jerrold, who was looking off in a different direction. They both hurried forward only to stop dead a few feet later as Arthur emerged with Iris and Maisy in his arms. Jerrold's mouth fell open. Elaine stepped forward, her hand to her open mouth.

Arthur leaned down and spoke quietly with Iris. Iris's eyes opened. "Grandma! Grandpa!" She scrambled to get out of Arthur's arms. He carefully placed her on the ground. She hobbled forward, and the Stevenses rushed to meet her. They wrapped her in their arms, holding her tight. Elaine's chin wobbled as she looked at Lyla and Riley. "Thank you."

"It was actually Arthur and Maisy who found her," Riley said.

Jerrold looked up at Arthur. Maisy now stood on the ground next to him, holding his hand, looking fiercely protective of the giant. "Um, th-thank you."

"You are very welcome," Arthur said.

"You, um, I—"

Lyla stepped forward. "How about if we chat inside? I think Iris's ankle may need to be wrapped."

Jerrold darted a look at Iris before nodding. "Yes, um, okay."

Riley looked around. "Are the twins back?"

"What?" Elaine yanked her gaze from Arthur. "Um, no. Should we send someone to tell them Iris's back?"

Lyla frowned. "They know. They should have been back ahead of us."

Jerrold shrugged. "They sometimes wander."

Lyla frowned again. "Uh, okay. Iris, let's get you—" She hobbled from her grandparents to Arthur, looking up at him expectantly. He reached down and picked her up.

Elaine stumbled back, her hand at her throat again.

"He, um—" Jerrold couldn't seem to find words.

"We'll explain everything. Shall we?" Lyla gestured to the building.

Elaine just nodded, her mouth still open.

Lyla waited until Jerrold and Elaine followed Arthur and the girls in before turning to Riley and Miles. "Go get the rest of the group. I want them camped out here tonight."

"Why the change?" Miles asked.

"Well, they already know about Arthur, and ..."

"And you don't trust the twins," Riley finished.

Lyla nodded. "Yes. Now go. And get back here quickly, okay?"

55

By the time Lyla reached the lower level, Arthur had deposited Iris on her bed and was standing against the far wall. Elaine was ripping up some linen strips. Jerrold had her boot off and was examining her ankle while Maisy had plopped down on the bed next to Iris, looking around with big eyes.

Lyla stood just outside the doorway, listening to the girls explain to poor Jerrold and Elaine what had happened.

"And then we heard the lion screech. Arthur, he started to run and tackled it just before it got Iris."

"And then Maisy showed up and grabbed my hand. She helped me run. Another cat came, and Maisy shoved me out of the way. It jumped right over us as we hit the ground."

"But I got in a swipe at its paw."

Iris nodded. "She did."

Lyla felt light-headed. She hadn't known one had gotten that close.

"And then Maisy, she dared the cat to come get her. It was so brave."

Lyla looked at her daughter. She had been training her for years, but she hadn't realized how much she had actually learned. She was split between being so incredibly proud of her and completely terrified of what could have happened to her.

"And then the last one came, but Arthur got that one too," Maisy said.

"And then I screamed." Iris looked over at Arthur, biting her lip.

"Then those other two came. I didn't like them. They hurt Arthur." Maisy crossed her arms over her chest with a frown.

Iris mimicked the expression. "I don't like them, either."

"Iris!" Jerrold admonished.

She uncrossed her arms. "They were mean to Arthur, and all he did was help me."

"They thought I was a threat to you," Arthur said. "It is understandable."

"Still don't like them," Maisy muttered.

Lyla couldn't help but smile. *Me either, sweetheart, me either.* She stepped forward. "How's the patient?"

Jerrold looked up as Lyla entered, looking relieved. "It's just a little sprain. She should be fine in a few days."

Elaine crouched down next to her, wrapping linens around her ankle. "You hear that? We'll keep this nice and tight, and it should be good as new in a few days."

Lyla walked over and stood next to Arthur as Elaine finished up. "You okay?" She kept her voice low.

He nodded. "Just a few scratches. Nothing critical. I'm just glad the girls are all right."

"You're a good man, Arthur."

Even in the dim light, she could see the color heat up his cheeks.

"There you go." Elaine stood. "Now I'd like you to rest for a little bit."

"Aw, Grandma. I wanted to show Maisy around."

"Just rest for a little bit, and then you can show her around, okay?"

Iris pouted. "Fine."

"Maisy, why don't you stay with Iris? Arthur and I are going to speak in the other room with Iris's grandparents."

"Okay." Maisy pulled over a pillow, stuffing it behind her head.

Lyla smiled at how comfortable she looked already.

"Uh, this way." Elaine led them out of the room and toward the lab.

When they stepped in, Lyla nodded to Arthur. "This is Arthur. He's our friend. He is also an Unwelcome."

Jerrold sat down heavily. "My goodness."

Elaine looked up at him. "So you *are* blue."

"The Unwelcome are. The Naku are gray."

She frowned. "The Naku? Are you and the Naku the same species?"

Arthur shook his head. "I don't believe so. They are much smaller."

"The Naku are the overlords of the Unwelcome. The Unwelcome, they're a slave race," Lyla said.

"Oh." Elaine jerked back.

"The Naku call us avad," Arthur said.

"Avad," Jerrold murmured. "An interesting name."

"How so?" Lyla asked.

"Hm?" Jerrold pulled his gaze from Arthur.

"Avad. You said it was an interesting name," Lyla prodded.

"Oh, yes. It's very similar to the old Hebrew word for slave—ebed. But it's also pronounced abad."

"That is unusual," Lyla said, struck by the similarity.

"Huh." Elaine's eyes scanned Arthur, and she jolted. "You're hurt."

Lyla noted the rips in his shirt, the slight stain of blood.

Arthur shook his head. "It's nothing."

Elaine tutted. "Animal wounds are nothing to brush off. All

sorts of bacteria could get in there. Come." She marched to the other side of the room.

Arthur gave Lyla a helpless look before following her. Elaine had him sit on a stool and remove his shirt as she inspected his scratches. They really weren't too bad, but Lyla liked that Elaine wanted to take care of him.

Jerrold stepped next to Lyla. "He's, um, a friend?"

Lyla smiled. "He saved my children. Come on, I'll tell you and Elaine the story at the same time."

56

Maisy lay on Iris's bed, staring up at the vents above her. Iris's home was so different from hers. "I can't believe you live here. It's so cool! It's like a secret hideout."

Iris smiled shyly, looking around. "I guess."

Maisy sat up. "So you don't go up to the surface much?"

"I sometimes help my grandpa with the garden on the roof, but he doesn't like letting me out to wander around anywhere else. The only ones that do that are Michelle and Michael."

Maisy studied her new friend. "What's wrong?"

"I—" Iris looked around, leaning toward Maisy. "They're really bad people."

"Yeah, I don't like how they treated Arthur."

"No, it's more than that." She looked down the hall, her voice dropping to a whisper. "I think they've hurt people."

"What?"

"Michael and Michelle keep saying that there haven't been any people around here. But I know there have been. Sometimes I sneak out on the roof."

"And you saw people?"

Iris nodded. "And one time I saw Michael and Michelle talking to them. They know there are people. And they lie."

"Lie?"

"Yeah. We had this really bad winter last year. And they said they found some deer one day. But I saw them come back. They didn't have a deer with them."

"Why'd they lie?"

"I don't know."

Maisy looked around the room. "Where do they sleep?"

"Below us."

Maisy drummed her fingers on the bed. She did not like that her new friend was scared. "They're not back yet, right?"

"No," Iris said slowly.

Maisy stood up. "I'm going to see where they live."

"What? Why?"

"If we can show my mom something that shows they're bad people, she'll make sure they leave here."

"Really?"

Maisy nodded. "My mom would never let anyone get hurt if she could help them. Now, how do I get down to their place?"

Iris scrambled off the bed. "I'll show you."

"Are you sure? What about your ankle?"

"It's not too bad. Come on."

57

Once Lyla had finished her story about meeting Arthur and what they had been through, Elaine and Jerrold sat staring at them. Elaine was the first to recover. "My goodness. You've really been through a lot."

"It's been a *long* couple of months," Lyla said.

"And you really learned about humanity by reading about us?" Jerrold asked.

Arthur nodded. "For me, it was a joy. The life of the avad, or the Unwelcome as you call them, is devoid of joy. We own nothing. Our lives are completely at the mercy of the Naku. Until I started reading about humans, I never even considered that it could be a different way."

"And when you saw Miles with that girl, you wanted to help them?" Jerrold asked.

Arthur nodded.

"Had you ever wanted to do something like that before?" Elaine asked.

Arthur frowned. "I-I don't think so. It's strange, but before that point, I don't recall truly feeling anything. I did not think for myself. I did not feel. We are not built that way."

"Huh," Elaine murmured.

"What?" Jerrold asked.

"People don't just develop emotions if they've never had them before. The only way for that to happen was for them to have been blocked somehow." Elaine shook her head. "Sorry. That is just some unsubstantiated theorizing on my part. It's been a while since we've had a scientific mystery to dive into."

Jerrold took her hand. "We've missed it. Do you mind if I ask you some questions?"

"I'd be happy to answer them."

"Are all your people blue?"

"Yes.

"And are you all so ... large?"

Arthur shook his head. "No. The charat are not as muscular as the chelvah."

Lyla frowned. "The charat?"

Arthur looked at her. "The breeders. They are impregnated and produce the next generation of chelvah and charat."

"And you are a chelvah?" Jerrold asked.

Arthur nodded.

"When do you begin to achieve your size?" Jerrold asked.

"Not until we have made it through the shedar. You would call it a culling."

Elaine blanched.

Arthur continued. "Once we are initiated into the rovac program, we are given supplements and operations to make us larger."

"Operations?" Jerrold asked.

"Our bones are broken and lengthened."

Lyla gasped.

But Elaine only nodded. "They actually have done that with humans as well, but generally only to help someone achieve normal height."

"Why would they be so cruel?" Arthur asked. "It is a very painful process."

"With painkillers, it shouldn't be ..." Jerrold's voice faded away as he watched Arthur. "They didn't use anything to mediate the pain?"

Arthur shook his head.

"How old were you?" Lyla asked.

"The process began when I was a little younger than Maisy."

Lyla listened in horror, picturing a small child being tortured. But it wasn't just one small child. It was generations of them. She reached out and took Arthur's hand, squeezing it gently. He returned the squeeze and then held her hand firmly in his.

Elaine was obviously having the same issue, as her voice was shaky when she spoke. "And the women, the charat, are they as tall as you?"

"They are taller than most human women, but they are not as tall as the chelvah."

Jerrold took off his glasses and wiped his eyes. "This is just ... it's a lot to take in." He returned his glasses to his face. "I assume you are the source of the blood sample?"

Arthur nodded. "We were hoping it might explain why the Naku are trying to eradicate the Cursed."

"I can understand that. Well, how about if we take some fresh samples? Elaine and I were theorizing that perhaps there is something in your skin that might trigger the Cursed abilities, a pheromone that in combination with adrenaline results in the manifestation. And I'm feeling rather energized to help you get some answers at this moment."

Arthur smiled. "That would be great."

58

Maisy and Iris managed to make it to the stairwell without her mom, Arthur, or Iris's grandparents noticing. Iris paused at the top of the staircase. It was dark down the stairs, with only a dim light somewhere below. Maisy didn't really want to go down there, but her new friend needed her help. And her mom wouldn't be scared. She put a hand on Iris's arm. "It's okay. I'll go. You can stay here."

Iris shook her head, her voice shaking a little. "No. I'm going with you."

Maisy gripped the handrail and started down the stairs. After a short hesitation, Iris followed her. Maisy was glad. She would have gone down there on her own, but she'd rather not have to.

It was only about twelve steps to the lower level, but to Maisy it was like entering a whole different world. It even smelled different. "What's that smell?"

"I don't know."

Maisy paused at the door to the twins' level. The smell definitely originated from behind the door. She reached out and pulled it open. A few dim lights were on, casting shadows around the halls. It looked like the same hallways as upstairs but somehow creepier.

Iris gripped Maisy's hand as Maisy stepped forward. Maisy thought for a moment she was trying to stop her. But she wasn't. She just didn't want to walk in there alone. Maisy gripped Iris's hand back just as tightly.

The hallway to the right was completely blocked by old furniture, so they headed left. Together they walked along the hall until it turned.

"That's their bedroom," Iris whispered, pointing to the first door a little along the hall. Maisy walked toward it. Iris stayed behind her. The door was open, a small light on a table along the wall illuminating the room. Instead of beds, there were two hammocks strung up on opposite walls. And the room was covered in clothes, old boxes, and other junk.

"They're slobs," Maisy whispered in disgust. How could they live like this? Even the animals at Attlewood would have refused to live in this filth.

"Is this where the smell is coming from?"

Maisy sniffed deeply and then shook her head. It didn't smell good in there, but it wasn't the source of the really bad smell. "Do you want to go check in there?"

Maisy stared at the room, taking another deep sniff before turning to look down the hall. The smell was coming from down there. "Not right now."

Iris followed her gaze. "I don't want to go down there."

"Me either." She held out a hand. Iris took it. Together, hand in hand, they walked down the hall. There were two doors on the other side of the hall that led to one large room. Maisy stopped in front of the first closed door. The smell was definitely coming from in there.

Maisy reached out a trembling hand and opened the door. The smell of decay washed over her, almost making her gag. Iris stumbled back a step. "That's gross."

Maisy nodded her agreement and stepped inside. There were shelves and shelves of junk, most wrapped in plastic.

"We should—" Iris's voice cut off as her head whipped to the side. "Oh God, they're back."

Maisy reached out and grabbed Iris, dragging her into the room as she heard Michelle's voice. "... think she is ordering us around."

She couldn't hear what Michael said in response, only his creepy little laugh.

"Hey, did you leave the storage room open?"

Maisy and Iris exchanged a terrified glance before dashing around the first row of shelves. Maisy grabbed Iris's arm and dragged her farther into the mess, trying not to look too hard at the junk they were passing. Goosebumps broke out across her skin, only partly from fear. The back of the room was really, really cold.

"Who's in here?" Michelle yelled.

Iris jumped, her eyes growing impossibly large. Maisy yanked her down. Crouching, Maisy struggled to listen above her pounding heart. Footsteps were one row over and heading toward them. Keeping low, she tugged Iris over another row. They were as far back in the room as they could go. And god was it cold. She could practically see her breath.

The footsteps drew closer. Maisy looked around wildly, seeing a little space on one of the shelves a few feet to their left. She pushed Iris in that direction, quickly following after her, trying to avoid the plastic on her side. Iris backed in next to her, rustling the plastic. Maisy looked over, her whole body going still.

"Who's there?" Michelle demanded again.

Neither Maisy nor Iris moved, but Maisy's eyes locked on the bag next to Iris that had shifted with her movements, revealing a small piece of its contents. Maisy frowned, trying to make it out. Was it a doll?

Then she noticed the hair still on the arm.

Iris followed her gaze, the fear plain on her face. Her mouth dropped open.

Maisy slapped her hand over Iris's mouth before she could scream.

Tears dripped onto Maisy's hand, and both of them were shaking so hard that Maisy was sure they would be found any minute. *Mom, please find us. Mom, please.*

But it wasn't her mom who found them.

Michael reached in and yanked Maisy out. She screamed and kicked him in the groin. He let out a yell, doubling over as he released her.

"Run, Iris!" Maisy yelled. Together they sprinted down the narrow path between the shelves. Michelle darted out from between the shelves, standing in front of them and blocking the way.

Both girls leaped back. Maisy slammed into a shelf, and one of the bags from the top tumbled off, spilling its contents onto the floor right next to Iris.

Iris took one look at the body and screamed.

59

Lyla bolted out into the hallway, heading toward Iris's room, but it was empty. They had been just about to examine Arthur's blood when the screams reached them.

"It came from downstairs!" Jerrold yelled.

Lyla sprinted for the stairwell. Arthur was already heading down them. "Maisy!"

His deafening yell echoed through the stairwell as he leaped down the last three steps. He yanked on the door leading to the lower level so hard that the bottom hinge was pulled from the wall.

Lyla's stomach bottomed out as the smell hit them. She knew that smell: death.

"Arthur!"

Another scream came from the left. The hairs on Lyla's whole body seemed to stand at attention as she ran down the hall. She could hear the sounds of a struggle ahead. Arthur ducked into the room ahead of her, and she nearly slammed into him as she followed. He'd come to a dead stop only a few feet in.

Lyla moved to his side as Michael let out a laugh. Michelle stood behind Maisy, a blade to Maisy's throat. Iris was cowering on the ground, Michael standing over her with a wooden bat over his shoulder. Arthur was closer to Maisy while Lyla was positioned closer to Iris.

Michael laughed, inching forward.

"Stop!" Lyla yelled. "What are you doing?"

Michelle didn't answer, just tightened her grip on the knife. Lyla flicked her gaze at Maisy, who was watching her with complete trust. "Maisy, stomp."

Maisy immediately pushed the blade away from her neck and stomped on the instep of Michelle's foot. Michelle let out a yell, reflexively loosening her grip. That was all the opening Arthur needed. He wrapped his hand around Michelle's wrist, yanking the knife farther from Maisy, who dropped to the ground and crawled away as Michelle screamed, finally dropping the knife. Arthur grabbed Michelle by the throat and threw her across the room.

Lyla saw all of it from the corner of her eye. As Michelle screamed, Michael charged at Lyla and swung. She ducked the first swing. As he swung back toward her, she grabbed his wrist and shoulder and kept the momentum of his swing going. Not expecting the move, he stumbled. Before he could recover, she rolled her forearm along the back of his elbow, forcing it up. Pressing down on the elbow of the now straightened arm, she forced him down, slamming his wrist into the ground. He screamed, the bat rolling from his hand.

He lay on his stomach, squirming and laughing hysterically. *He is not right*, Lyla thought as she held him down.

"Mom?"

Maisy stood in the doorway. Lyla turned to look at her. "It's okay, honey. Take Iris to her grandparents, okay?"

Iris was sitting on the ground, her knees pulled to her chest, rocking in place as she stared down the rows. Maisy helped Iris to her feet, holding on to the bigger girl and helping her from the room.

"Arthur?"

He walked over. "She is dead."

Michael's laughs increased, and he started to bang his head into the ground, hard. Blood stained the ground under him.

Shocked, Lyla released her hold. "What the—"

Arthur grabbed her and pulled her back as Michael reared up, his face covered in blood. He ran for his sister until he stood a foot away from her. Then he reached into the shelves and pulled out a shard of metal.

Lyla started forward. "No."

Michael laughed as he plunged it into his neck.

Lyla's mouth fell open, and her breath left her. Michael crashed to his knees and toppled forward, his blood spreading around him and reaching his sister.

"I just— I don't understand." She looked up at Arthur, but he was looking at the shelves.

"I think perhaps that might explain it."

Lyla straightened and walked over to the shelves. Something pale and white was in the bag in the middle shelf. She recoiled when she realized it was part of a leg. She looked down the row of shelves and the similar plastic bags lined there. There were dozens of them.

Oh my God.

60

The discovery of dozens of bodies in the basement of the Lab should have been the worst discovery they made.

It wasn't.

It didn't take long to realize that not only had Michael and Michele killed those people—they had also been eating them. After they investigated the room, Lyla and Arthur went up to get the Stevenses. Riley and Miles arrived shortly after and learned about what had happened. The rest of the group was breaking up the camp and would join them shortly.

Miles accompanied Lyla and Arthur back to the basement with the Stevenses while Riley stayed with the girls.

Even before they made the trip down the stairs, Jerrold and Elaine looked like they were in shock. Lyla took them down to the twins' level and showed them the bodies. Elaine immediately left the room, her hand to her mouth. Miles went with her.

But Lyla and Arthur stayed with Jerrold. He paled a few shades as he walked along the shelves, looking at each of the faces of the bodies. But he didn't leave until he had seen the last one. Then he turned to them both and nodded. "I've seen enough."

They left the level after Arthur secured the door. Lyla stopped at the first level, but Jerrold shook his head. "I think I need some air."

"Of course." Arthur headed up the stairs.

As they stepped through the shattered remains of the front door, Lyla spied Elaine sitting on a log at the edge of the treeline, her head in her hands. Miles sat next to her, rubbing her back. The girls were playing hopscotch while Riley kept watch.

Zombielike, Jerrold stumbled over to his wife. He collapsed onto the log next to her, staring straight ahead. Without looking up, Elaine reached over and grabbed his hand. Miles stepped away, giving them some privacy. He made his way over to Lyla and Arthur.

"How is she?" Lyla asked.

"On the border of shock. That was ... a lot to take in."

"For all of us," Lyla muttered.

"I'm going to go get them some blankets." Miles headed inside.

"How could humans do that? Isn't it taboo?" Arthur asked.

"It is. But people in desperate situations will take desperate measures. Jerrold mentioned that the twins' father disappeared one rough winter. The twins said he went out to find some game and never returned. But a short time later, the twins found a deer. The meat from that deer kept them alive." Lyla went quiet.

"You think their father was their first meal?"

Lyla shrugged. "There's no way of knowing, not now." She glanced at Arthur, who was watching the Stevenses with a concerned look. "Are you all right?"

He turned his gaze to her. "It's just ... I never imagined humans were capable of such things. The Naku said humans were capable of atrocities, but this—"

"No. You were taught that *all* humans were capable of these types of atrocities. That's not true. But not all humans are good or even sane. I have to believe there was something fundamentally wrong with the twins."

Arthur nodded slowly, his gaze focusing on the girls as they laughed together, though Maisy's smile was not as wide as usual. "They're not bothered by this?"

"They are. Children have an amazing capacity to adapt. But this will haunt them. For now, I'm glad they can smile, if only a little. Why don't you go over there? I think you could use some of their joy."

"I think I could to." He started over to the girls and then turned back and hugged Lyla tightly. "I am glad I found you all first." He released her and walked quickly away.

Lyla watched him go, her insides feeling unsettled. There was something about Arthur, a comfort, a security she rarely felt with anyone else. With a shock, she realized that Arthur felt like home.

Miles stepped back through the doors, blankets in his arms, and made his way to the Stevenses, pulling Lyla from her thoughts. Following him, she reached the group as Miles was wrapping the second blanket around Jerrold.

"Thank you, Miles," Jerrold said.

"How are you two?" Lyla asked.

Jerrold opened his mouth and then shut it. Shaking his head, he said, "I really don't know how to answer that."

Lyla knelt down. "I'm sorry."

"I don't know how we didn't see it." Elaine clutched the blanket tightly around herself. "When I look back, I can see how much they've changed over the years. But when it's happening right in front of you, it's like you're blind to it."

"How did they change?" Miles sat cross-legged in front of them.

"We've known them since they were children. They were always very close, very quiet. But after their father disappeared, they got even quieter."

"Iris seemed uncomfortable around them," Miles said.

Jerrold looked at his wife. "We never understood that. She refused to be alone with them. How did we not see it?"

"Did Michael always have that strange laugh? I mean, it seemed almost involuntary," Lyla said.

"No. That started about a year ago. I thought the stress of living underground might be getting to him. But whenever I went to bring it up, I just didn't." Jerrold shook his head. "I don't know why."

"I think you knew that something was wrong but that you were also not in a position to do anything about it," Miles said.

Elaine's head snapped up, her mouth falling open. "Michael's laughing. I think he had the laughing disease."

Lyla frowned and looked at Miles, who shrugged at her. "What's that?" he asked.

But Jerrold's mouth had fallen open as well, his eyes wide.

Lyla reached up and gently touched his shoulder. "Jerrold?"

His gaze slowly moved back to her. "Kuru. Elaine thinks they had kuru."

"Oh my God." Miles's voice was shaky when he spoke. "Kuru is an illness that a person can get from eating another human. It comes from ingesting infected brain tissue."

Jerrold nodded, taking over the explanation. "It causes a loss of coordination, tremors, and neurodegeneration. It's called the laughing disease because for some, as the brain deteriorates, it causes the individual to laugh for no apparent reason. There's no cure, not even in the Before. It's fatal."

"Then there's nothing you could have done," Lyla said.

Elaine shook her head, holding up her hand, which noticeably shook. "No, I'm afraid there's nothing we *can* do."

61

The tremor in Elaine's hand was obvious. And Lyla remembered the tremors she had seen in Jerrold throughout the afternoon yesterday. "Are you sure that's not just fright?"

Elaine shook her head slowly, her gaze on her husband. "For both of us, the tremors began a few months ago. I thought maybe it was the beginning of a neurodegenerative disease, like Parkinson's. I never imagined ..."

Lyla's gaze shifted to Iris. "What about—"

"No, no," Jerrold said. "She's never shown any signs. And she would never eat any of the food the twins prepared."

"So she should be all right?" Miles asked.

Elaine watched her granddaughter, sadness splashed across her face. "From kuru, she should be. But Jerrold and I, we won't be able to take care of her as the disease progresses. What will—"

"We'll look out for her," Miles said quickly, glancing at Lyla, who nodded in return. "She'll always have a home."

"If you hadn't come looking for the Lab, she would have been alone. She would have—" Elaine's hand flew to her mouth.

Jerrold fumbled for the other one and held it tightly.

"Don't do that," Lyla said softly. "That didn't happen. She won't go through that. And we'll make sure she's safe."

Elaine took a shaky breath, her eyes glassy. "But you're on the run. How will she be safe?"

"We have friends in a camp," Lyla said. "They're good people. They'll look after her. Treat her like she's their own. She won't be alone."

"Like they did for me," Miles said.

Surprise fluttered through Lyla. Miles was such a part of her life, it was hard to remember that he hadn't always been. "And you'll stay with us too."

"But when the disease progresses—"

"We'll deal with it then," Lyla said firmly. "Iris deserves to have her grandparents for as long as she can."

Jerrold and Elaine stared into each other's eyes, waging a silent conversation before Elaine nodded and turned to Lyla. "Okay."

"Lyla." Miles pointed behind her as he got to his feet.

Lewis stepped through the trees, Rory and the rest of the group right behind him.

Lyla nodded at them. "Now, let me introduce you to some of those good people."

AFTER MAKING some of the introductions, Lyla pulled Lewis aside and quickly explained what they had found underneath the lab. Usually stoic, Lewis blanched at the news.

"I'll get started on digging some graves out back," he said when she was done. "Once we've got a few dug, we'll start bringing up the bodies."

Overwhelmed by what they'd found, Lyla hadn't even thought about what to do with the bodies. But Lewis was right.

They deserved to be put to rest. "I'll see if the Stevenses have any shovels."

Luckily, there was a storage shed at the back of the building that contained a few shovels. Each of the Cursed took turns digging graves. They dug twenty and filled each one with a body or at least parts of a body. It was not easy work, but Lyla felt better when the bodies were out of the lab. It took them a few hours to finish up, and everyone was quiet when they were done.

Everyone had drifted off to get cleaned up, Lyla as well. When she returned, she spotted Elaine with the girls, but she didn't see Jerrold. She had a feeling she knew where he would be. She made her way around to the back of the building. Jerrold stood near the graves, his head bowed. Lyla approached quietly, not wanting to interrupt his prayers.

He finally looked up. "Thank you for doing this." He took a shaky breath, looking out over the mounds. "So many lives lost."

Lyla wasn't sure what to say. The twins hadn't truly been responsible for their actions once the kuru took effect. But that had only happened after they had eaten an infected human. She had no idea what made them take that first step. They might not have had kuru after the first dozen kills. It was hard to know when the kuru became responsible for their actions and when they had been. In the end she supposed it didn't matter, because they were killers either way.

"Their father, he was strict. I thought too strict. Maybe I should have said something. Protected them a little more."

"You're doing it again. Playing what if. No one ever wins that game. You can't know. Sometimes people are just wrong. No one's to blame. It just is."

He nodded, his gaze drifting back yet again to the mounds. "I don't know what to do. This has been our home, and yet I can't bear the idea of being in there again."

"You don't have to be. We'll get the stuff you need and head out."

His gaze darted away from her as he shook his head. "You should leave us here. We'll only slow you down. You should take Iris and—"

"No. Iris deserves to have you for as long as she can."

Jerrold took a shaky breath. "We're putting you in danger. We'll hold you back."

"No, you won't." Lyla looked out over the graves, realizing she was telling the truth. They would not be slowing them down. "We don't have anywhere to be."

62

Riley watched Lyla speaking with Jerrold. The man seemed to have aged in the last few hours. And even so, Riley knew that the horror of what the twins had done hadn't completely hit him yet. The next few days were going to be extremely rough.

Miles, Imogen, and Petra helped the doctors pack up the supplies they would need for the trip to Meg's camp. Lewis thought Meg would appreciate the doctors' science background. And seeing as New Attlewood was just getting started, it might be a better place for them to get settled.

Riley had started distributing the docs' stuff amongst the different packs to lessen the load. Rory had offered to help, but Riley needed something to do. He wanted to have a reason to not go back into the lab. It was creepy for all of them, but Riley kept remembering Michael's odd laugh, which was making it even tougher. He wasn't alone in not wanting to be inside. No one was going in unless they had to. Everyone was happy to put a little distance between themselves and the building.

They started out as soon as they said a few words over the graves, even though it was late in the day. Everyone just needed a little space from the Lab. They didn't make it far. Lyla called for a break after only two hours. Rory and Riley had been sent to see if they could find some game for dinner that evening.

Rory glanced over his shoulder once they were out of earshot of the camp. "It's going to take forever to get to Meg's at this pace."

Riley nodded. At the same time, he wasn't sure that mattered. The truth was, they didn't really have a plan after they reached Meg's and dropped off the Stevenses. The only plan they'd had when they set off from the zoo was to find the Lab and get some answers. Now they had some answers but also a whole lot more questions. And with the grisly discovery in the basement, they hadn't had a chance to discuss what they should do now. But being it was going to be a painfully slow walk, they should definitely have more than enough time to come up with a plan. And with the docs along for the ride, maybe they could even come up with more answers.

"Think Arthur could carry the docs?" Rory asked.

Riley grinned at the mental image. "Probably. But I don't think the docs will go for that."

"Did the docs really eat people?" Rory shuddered.

"Yeah. They didn't know it at the time. The twins ... I don't even know how to explain them. There was something wrong with them even before the kuru messed with their brains."

"There's no chance for the docs?"

"No. They said it's only a matter of time."

"Poor Iris."

Riley nodded. She was going to be alone. When Riley had lost his mom, he'd had Lyla. Then Maisy and then Miles. Heck, he had a dozen people who he'd known his whole life still with him. Iris had known only her grandparents and the twins. She'd already lost the twins. Homicidal and crazy though they might have been, they were literally half of her world. And when she lost her grandparents, that *would* be her whole world.

Another unnecessary reminder of how difficult this life could be.

"Hey." Rory nudged his head toward the clearing ahead. Riley peered past him and saw the group of horses. There were five of them.

Riley grinned. "I think you might have just solved our speed problem."

~

RILEY AND RORY SPLIT UP, each circling the clearing to come at the horses from different angles. Wild horses were notoriously skittish. He just prayed they didn't catch his scent before he was closer.

He crept around the edge of the clearing, keeping low. He couldn't see Rory, but he assumed he was closing in from the other side. As he got closer, he noticed a long, thin line of rope attaching the horses to the tree.

Oh no. He slipped his staff from around his back, clutching it in his hands. Not wild horses. He scanned the area but saw no sign of anyone. He needed to grab Rory and get back to everyone else to warn them. Experience had taught him that groups on horseback tended not to be friendly.

He moved forward, straining to hear anything as the horses began to stir. *Come on, Rory. Where are you?*

Wood striking wood rang out through the air, followed by a muffled cry.

Riley bolted forward, moving as fast as he could while keeping track of his surroundings. He shifted past the agitated horses, who stirred even more at his appearance. He sprinted into the trees on the other side of them, catching sight of a staff swinging above the tall bushes there. He slowed, creeping closer and peeking through.

Rory was holding his own against two men. But there was a third that charged out of the trees, aiming for Rory's back with his sword. Riley sprinted forward, catching the tip of the man's blade with his staff. He brought the other end of the staff around, slamming it into the man's temple. One hit was good enough for light's out.

One of the men fighting Rory paused, his attention diverted by Riley's appearance. Rory wasted no time. The end of his staff slammed into the man's stomach before crashing into his throat and sending the man flying off his feet and onto his back. Riley slammed his staff into the back of the other man's legs, twirling it back into the man's face. Blood sprayed as his nose broke. He crashed to his knees. After one last hit to the back of the man's head, he toppled forward.

Riley scanned the area, his blood thrumming.

"What?" Rory asked, catching onto Riley's concern.

"There were five horses. There's two more."

Rory immediately went back to back with Riley, scanning the area as well.

A low chuckle sounded from Riley's left. He turned as a man stepped from the woods. "That was pretty good, kid. You've got some real talent."

The man was tall and broad with a burn down the right half of his face and a scar along the left side.

Riley didn't take his gaze from the man, but his senses were attuned. He knew the second the man's accomplice appeared in front of Rory.

The man cast a glance at his downed men. "It appears I could use people with your skills. Perhaps you boys would be interested in joining up with me. I can make it worth your while."

"Don't think so," Riley said.

The man shrugged. "It's not a good idea to try and go it alone. Everyone needs some people to watch their back."

"We have people," Rory spit out.

The man smiled even wider, holding up his bracelet. It was the same one Brendan had worn, the one that communicated with the Unwelcome. "Not for much longer."

63

Lyla was worried. The doctors were older and not used to physical exercise. Already they looked exhausted from just the short walk from the Lab. They would have to take lots of breaks.

But that wasn't the only issue. Lyla was not familiar with the lands they'd be traveling through. If there was a problem, moving the doctors quickly wasn't going to be easy. Then they had Maisy and Iris. Arthur could carry both of them, but it would tire him, which meant he wouldn't be at his best if there was a problem.

Lyla had no intention of leaving the doctors, though. That would be a death sentence. But they needed to figure out something.

The bigger problem was what they were supposed to do in general. They'd found the Lab and gotten the information they sought, or at least some of it. But now what were they supposed to do with it? They still didn't know why she and the Cursed were different. They just knew they were.

Miles mentioned the ash that had covered the world while most of the Cursed had been born. Jerrold thought it was possible something in the ash had changed the Cursed at a genetic level. If it was genetic, shouldn't all children have the abilities? Why would the change occur for only some of them?

But why then would she and possibly Muriel also have abilities? The existence of their abilities was the anomaly. There hadn't been ash before she and Muriel were born. So what accounted for their abilities? And how had the Naku known to target those kids? No one had any clue about their abilities when the Unwelcome arrived. So how did the Naku know they would eventually develop them?

Lyla wanted to ask the docs more questions, but neither of them were up for questions. But they had a long, long walk ahead of them that should give them plenty of time to discuss the Cursed and a million other things. In the back of her mind, a vague idea was forming about trying to find a university. Maybe they could hide out there while the docs conducted a little more research.

About twenty feet away, Maisy unrolled her bedroll. She handed one to Iris and showed her where to place hers, which of course was right next to Maisy's.

Lyla smiled. Well, at least Maisy was getting a friend out of this. And Iris too. Even though Iris was a little older and a lot taller, she was looking to Maisy. And Maisy was really stepping up to the plate and helping the girl. She was growing up.

A pang hit Lyla. She hadn't given birth to any of her children, but she couldn't imagine her feelings for them being any deeper if she had. She wanted to keep them all young and with her forever. But that was not the way life worked. And she supposed the sooner Maisy grew up and was able to defend herself, the safer she would be.

But Lyla couldn't help but selfishly wish she'd stay little just a bit longer. The girls flopped down on their bedrolls with a giggle, then they leaned their heads together, whispering eagerly with wide grins on their faces.

Lyla wanted nothing more than to sit with them and just

listen to them chat. She headed toward them, intending to do just that but got waylaid by Miles.

"Lyla."

With a sigh, she turned. "Hey, hon. How are Elaine and Jerrold?"

"Tired."

"How much traveling do you honestly think they can do each day?" she asked. "What's a realistic goal?"

"I think the first few days will be tough, and not just because of their physical limitations. They're still reeling from learning about the twins and their own probable diagnosis. And Jerrold keeps mentioning how they're going to be a burden. I keep trying to talk him out of it, but ..." He shrugged.

"I know. He said the same to me."

"Well, it's going to take them a little while to adjust," said Miles. "But they're both actually in pretty good shape. No major issues, just age. So, if we can help them kind of get past what's happened, they can handle a good few miles a day."

It was a better prognosis than she had hoped for. "I sent Riley and Rory to see if they could track down some dinner. Who knows? Maybe they'll even come across some horses. Lewis said it wasn't unusual in this area. It's a long shot, but ..." Her words drifted off as the hairs on the back of her neck rose. She turned her head slowly to the right. She noticed more than one Cursed do the same.

"Lyla." Miles's voice was filled with warning.

But Lyla didn't answer. She was already running. "Get the girls and the Stevenses out of here! Grab the spears!"

She pulled her sword just as the first Unwelcome stepped from the trees.

64

R iley stared at the man in front of him. "What did you do?"
"What I was paid to do. It's really quite lucrative to work with—"

Riley slipped the knife from his sleeve and hurled it at the man. The man let out a yell as he dodged, but the knife embedded itself in his left shoulder.

Riley raced forward, but the man ducked back into the trees. Riley whirled around as Rory yelled. He barely caught sight of a boot as a second person ducked into the woods on that side. Blood dripped down the side of Rory's arm.

"Rory, are you—"

Rory slapped his hand over the wound, already moving. "Let's go!"

Riley didn't need to be told twice. He sprinted back toward the camp, heedless of any danger in the immediate area, his only focus on getting to his family and his friends in time.

Rory was right behind him, the wound in his arm not seeming to slow him down any.

Whoever the hell that group had been, they had contacted the Unwelcome. He focused on a picture of the Unwelcome in his mind, recalling the ones he'd fought on the bridge before he'd tumbled over the edge. He waited for the sense of warmth to spread through him, but nothing happened.

Damn it! He put on a burst of speed. He needed to get there. He needed to get to them before it was too late. Then the burst of an Unwelcome spear sounded from the direction of the camp, and he had a horrible feeling he might already be too late.

65

The familiar feeling of warmth spread over Lyla as she swung her sword at the Unwelcome. She felt a sense of satisfaction as the sword cut through the material. The Unwelcome doubled over. Lyla hefted the sword up, ripping through bone. She jumped out of the way as he collapsed at her feet.

The blast of a spear sounded. She dove for the ground. The bush near her dissolved into dust. On her stomach, she saw the rest of the camp was embroiled in battle. Miles had locked arms with an Unwelcome that towered three feet over him. She did a double take at his fully formed left arm. Petra leaped, wrapping her legs around an Unwelcome eight feet tall that had lurched toward Iris and Maisy. She threw her body weight to the side, her legs still wrapped around the being's throat, and it tilted to the ground. Petra jumped from its shoulders before it hit and then stomped on its neck.

Holding on to Iris's hand, Maisy looked toward Lyla with large eyes.

"Run!" Lyla yelled at them.

An Unwelcome stepped into Lyla's path and swung its spear at her head. She ducked and, still moving forward, grabbed the back of its calf, slamming her shoulder into its knee. She heard the crack as she forced the knee straight.

It fell backward. Lyla shielded her head with her arm as its leg involuntarily came up when it crashed to the ground. Shoving the leg back, she slid forward, slamming her knee into its groin and praying it was a male.

It jerked, curling over, and she knew her prayers had been answered. She crawled up his body, punching him with everything she was worth in the throat before scrambling off of him.

She grabbed the spear that had flown from his hand as she sprinted in the direction the girls had gone. She took aim at three Unwelcome as she ran, hitting two and sending one behind a tree. Blasts from ahead of her told her there were Unwelcome somewhere near the girls' location.

She put on an extra burst of speed, feeling as if she was flying through the trees. She was moving so fast, she nearly collided with them, but at the last second, she vaulted over them and rolled as she hit the ground, lying stunned for a second.

"Mom!" Maisy cried.

Lyla looked up as an Unwelcome stepped from the trees, its spear aimed at the two girls.

66

Lyla scrounged for her spear, time seeming to slow down. Her hand wrapped around the shaft just as the sound of a spear emitting its deadly ray sounded.

Time snapped back to normal speed as Lyla whipped the spear into her hand and pulled the trigger. "No!"

The Unwelcome stumbled back a second before Lyla's blast hit it.

Trembling, she scrambled to where she'd last seen the girls. A log hid the ground from view. *Please God, no. Please God, no.*

Red curls peeked out from the top of the log, followed by Maisy's blue eyes. Lyla's legs weakened. She grabbed the log for support.

The blast of an Unwelcome's spear caused her to whirl. The Unwelcome she'd hit had gotten to his knees. Now it flew back, a gaping hole in its chest. Lyla vaulted over the log, coming to stand in front of the two girls as a second Unwelcome stepped from the woods.

It put up its hands. "Don't shoot."

Maisy tugged on Lyla's hand. "He helped us. Look."

To her left, Lyla could just make out another pair of Unwelcome boots. Realization at how close she had come to losing Maisy crawled through her. "Who are you? What do you want?"

Slowly, the Unwelcome lowered his spear to the ground. Just as slowly, he reached up, unbuckled his helmet, and pulled it off.

Lyla's mouth fell open in shock. She had no voice.

But Maisy's voice was full of joy. "Thor!"

67

By the time Riley reached the camp, the battle was in full swing. Petra was going toe to toe with one of the beings and holding her own. Adros let out a roar as he threw one of the Unwelcome ten feet. Arthur tackled one around the waist as he aimed for Tabitha.

Lewis and Pierce were working together using the Unwelcome spears to wound as many Unwelcome as they could, thus giving the Cursed a better chance. Riley did a double take at quiet little Imogen as she leaped off a log, driving both her feet into the back of an Unwelcome. She rode it to the ground before rolling and running to tackle another one at the knees.

There were eight Unwelcome he could see. No, nine. One stepped out from behind a tree, aiming at Imogen.

Lewis and Pierce's attention was elsewhere.

"Imo—" Riley didn't even get her name out before the trigger was pulled. Then Jerrold appeared out of nowhere. He stepped into the blast and disappeared in a puff of dust.

Riley gasped. It had happened so quickly. It took him a moment to accept that it had happened at all. And at the same time he recognized that Jerrold had not gotten in the way. He'd stepped in front of the beam intentionally.

Riley's head whipped to where Elaine lay crouched near a bush. She met Riley's gaze and nodded. *Protect her*, she mouthed.

Riley felt his throat close as she jumped from her spot.

"No!" Riley bolted forward, but he knew even with his enhanced speed he wouldn't make it in time. She grabbed the arm of an Unwelcome targeting Lewis. The being shook her free. Turning, it blasted her with the spear, and she was gone.

Lewis whirled, bringing his own weapon up.

The Unwelcome started to raise its spear. The only other Unwelcome still standing joined it, its spear by its side, but its whole body tensed.

The Cursed encircled them, moving in.

"Don't do it," Riley warned. "Just put the spears down. You don't have to die." For a fraction of a second, he thought they might listen.

But then they yanked their spears up.

Blasts ripped into each of the beings before they could pull the triggers. They both fell back, the spears rolling from their hands. Riley closed his eyes. *Damn it.*

Miles appeared at Riley's side, his arm back to its normal state. "Why didn't they retreat? They knew they couldn't win."

Arthur stopped at his other side. "We are not allowed to retreat. They would not have even considered it."

One of the Unwelcome groaned. Petra stepped forward, but Arthur held out a hand. "Wait. They are already down. Can we not leave them?"

Riley scanned the area. The Unwelcome were all down, but he saw life in most of them. He nodded. "Gather them up. I want four people with spears watching them while we figure out what to do with them."

"Thank you," Arthur said quietly as Riley passed him, heading toward one of the fallen Unwelcome. He could only nod in response. He liked Arthur. He really did. But that affection didn't extend to the people he had just seen obliterate Jerrold and Elaine without a word. He paused, looking around the camp. "Adros."

Adros hurried over. "Yeah?"

"Where are Lyla and the girls?"

He frowned, his gaze scanning the camp. "She went after Maisy and Iris. That way."

It was quiet in the forest, but that didn't mean it was safe. Riley swallowed. He knew his aunt was capable, but the Naku wanted her badly. "We need to find her."

68

Lyla stared at the Unwelcome. She hadn't had much interaction with him other than on the trip to the zoo, and she would not classify any of those interactions as positive. After the zoo attack, Riley said Thor had tripped into one of the Unwelcome that had been aiming at Maisy, but he couldn't be sure if it had been an accident or intentional.

Lyla held Maisy back when she made a move toward him. She knew Maisy liked him for some reason, but Lyla had no reason to trust him. She flicked a gaze at the two downed Unwelcome, wary.

Except he had saved them, *and* he had removed his helmet. The only other one who had ever done that was Arthur.

Still, Lyla held her spear on him. "What do you want?"

"I ..." His gaze shifted to Maisy and then back to Lyla again. "I came to help."

Of all the words Lyla expected to come out of his mouth, those were probably the last she expected. "What?"

"I ..." He looked around. "We should not stay here. They will most likely send more when the marchelvah fails to report in."

Maisy waved at him. "Hi, Thor."

Thor gave Maisy a small smile. Iris said nothing. She just stared at him, looking completely confused. Lyla felt exactly the same way.

Crashing sounded through the trees. Lyla kept her gaze on Thor but darted a quick gaze toward the noise. Adros burst from the trees before coming to an abrupt halt. He glanced at Thor. "Uh, what's going on?"

"How's the camp?" Lyla asked.

"We're good. The Unwelcome, they're all down."

"Good. Any casualties?"

Adros flicked a gaze at Iris before shifting back to Lyla. "Two." Lyla's heart dropped. *Oh no.*

"Take the girls back to camp." She paused. "Take them to Miles and Petra. Send Riley and Arthur here."

Adros nodded, holding out his hands. "Come on, girls."

Maisy shook her head. "But I want to—"

Lyla didn't take her gaze from Thor. "Maisy, you go with Adros. Now."

Maisy grunted before taking Iris's hand. "Come on, Iris. See you later, Thor." She glared at Lyla after she said it, almost daring Lyla to contradict her.

Lyla almost smiled at her gumption. Almost. "Go."

Maisy strode across the space, ignoring Adros's outstretched hand. "Come on, Iris. We'll go find your grandparents."

Lyla winced.

Adros disappeared into the trees. Thor watched them go. "Why did you make that expression?" he asked.

"What expression?"

"Maisy said something about the girl's parents, and you made a strange expression."

"Her grandparents, the only family she has in the world, were just killed by your people's attack."

"Oh," he said, looking down. "I am sorry."

Lyla frowned. I am sorry? Those words were not words she ever thought he would say. "Why would you say that?"

"Because she lost someone."

"Why do you care? You were part of the reason she lost them."

"No. I—"

"Lyla?" Riley called.

"Over here." Lyla kept her focus on Thor. There was something very different about him. When they had marched him from the old camp, he'd been almost robotic in his movements, and his expression had stayed the same. She'd seen more expressions on his face in the last few minutes than she had that entire walk. What had they done to him?

Riley materialized from the woods with Arthur right behind him. Riley centered in on Thor, but Arthur's entire focus was on Lyla. He pushed past Riley.

"Hey," Riley said, stumbling to the side.

Arthur didn't even seem to hear him. He looked like he wanted to reach for her but stopped himself at the last second. "You are all right?"

She nodded, taking her gaze from Thor and reading the concern in Arthur's eyes. She ignored the strange way her stomach moved at the sight of him. "You?"

"I'm fine." He turned, a jolt running through him as if he was just noticing Thor for the first time. "What is going on?"

"That's what I'm trying to find out."

Arthur moved to stand directly behind Lyla. She could feel the heat of him along her back.

Riley had his own spear trained on Thor. "Yeah, I'd like to know that, too."

"He says he came to help."

"*Help*?" Riley demanded. "You just tried to kill us."

"I didn't. I didn't come with them. I came in a separate ship. When I learned they were coming for you, I commandeered a veerfinah and came to help. And I did." Thor turned and looked at Lyla.

Lyla nodded slowly. "He saved Maisy and Iris. There was an Unwelcome already down when I appeared. And he also saved me."

Riley stared him down. "What do you want?"

"I need help. And you are the only people I could think of who might help me."

"Help you with what?" Lyla asked.

"My sister. I need you to help save my sister. And her son."

And for the third time, Lyla was completely shocked by the words coming out of Thor's mouth.

69

"We can't stay here," Thor said, looking around. "They will be sending more."

"Well, then you better talk fast," Lyla said.

Thor shot a glance at Arthur before he began. "When we are kids, we are sent to a training ground. It's a culling. If we survive, we are initiated into the rank of the avad. There are only two options: soldier or breeder. My sister, she was sent to the breeder program."

Even the sound of it made Lyla uncomfortable.

"After I was rescued, I was stationed at the facility she's in. Here. On Earth. I didn't realize it was her at first. She looks so different. It's been so long since I last saw her. But she's there with her son. He's coming up on his second birthday soon. He has maybe six weeks."

Arthur sucked in a breath.

"What?" Lyla asked.

"Two is the age the children are taken from their mothers. They spend a year in a health program. Those that are healthy enough enter the culling when they are three."

"That's barbaric," Riley said.

"My sister, she loves her son. I can't get her out on my own."

"Why do you even care if she gets out? When we first met you, you didn't care about anything," Riley said.

"No, I didn't. But I do now."

Lyla studied him. He seemed sincere, which again made no sense. He had been defiant, taciturn, and stubborn in their custody. But now, the being before her was worried, stressed, and desperate. Lyla was struggling to accept that this was the same Unwelcome they'd taken with them from Attlewood. Maybe he'd been—

"You stopped taking the Ka Sama," Arthur said softly.

Thor nodded slowly. "Yes."

"Ka Sama?" Lyla asked.

"Two blue pills we are given each night as a sleep supplement. It ensures that we sleep continuously until woken. I stopped taking mine before I met you," Arthur said.

"Why?" Riley asked.

"I read about the impact dreams had on humans. I thought it would help me to better understand them. I stopped taking my pills, thinking perhaps it would allow me to dream."

"Did it?" Riley asked.

Arthur kept his gaze on Thor as he answered Riley's question. "Yes. I was off them for almost two months when I came across Riley and Miles on the old road. Thor was off them for a month when he was with us."

"How do you know it was the pills?" Lyla asked.

"I wasn't sure at first," Arthur said. "I was trying to figure out why I was different from the rest of my people. At first, I thought it was the books I read. But others have read the same books. That's when I began to suspect it might be the pills. Thor seems to confirm it was them. But it was Elaine who gave me the idea."

Lyla turned to Thor. "Why didn't you start taking them again once you were returned?"

"I meant to," Thor said. "The first night I was so tired I fell asleep with them in my hand. The next day I was sent to the breeding facility. It was the first time I had been on duty without the pills in my system."

"And?"

"It was difficult. I ..." Thor shook his head.

"You felt things. Had thoughts you had never had before," Arthur said.

Thor nodded. "I didn't take them again that night. I don't know why. And the next day I was sent to the removal ward." He sucked in a breath. "It's where they take the children from the mothers. I had to hold women down while they were drugged and their children were ripped from their arms. I couldn't bring myself to take the pills after that. Then I realized Xe was there. And that her child would be taken from her."

Lyla shook her head. What Thor was describing was barbaric, but she couldn't risk her people to save them. They were already in such danger. To tackle a facility guarded by the Unwelcome would be absolute suicide.

Arthur frowned. "When I was with the Naku, I read a report once. It spoke about the rovac program. The class size has been going down each year."

"Why?" Lyla asked.

"The breeders have been dying, so there are less children being born each year."

"So?" Riley demanded.

Arthur darted a quick glance at him, his face tight. "The Naku are logical. We chelvah are their safety, their bodyguards. They will not allow the numbers to dip too low. They will look for another source."

Lyla mouth fell open. "You think they'll take humans."

"I believe they might, at some point," Arthur said.

"I have not seen any human at the facility," Thor added.

Lyla nodded, but her mind was racing. Elaine and Jerrold said the Unwelcome and humans were extremely similar. If that was true, then human females would be a perfect replacement for the dropping numbers. She shuddered at the thought.

"Look, I really think we need to move," Riley said. "We need to be long gone before the Unwelcome return."

"I have a ship," Thor said. "I can fly you, drop you off wherever you want."

"Will they be able to follow our flight path?" Lyla asked.

"No, they can only check where we are. Not where we have been."

Lyla looked to Arthur, who nodded back at her.

Riley frowned. "Why? That seems stupid."

"There has never been a need to track where we have been. We always follow orders. They need to know where we are. They've always known where we've been."

Lyla struggled to understand that, but Arthur had explained how the Naku were logical creatures. Order and efficiency were their focus. And they had fine-tuned their control of the Unwelcome over centuries. From that perspective, there was no need to track ships.

Accepting Thor's offer was still a risk, but truth be told, there was a danger in just about everything they did. She looked at Arthur. "Can you fly one of them?"

"A veerfinah? Yes." He nodded.

"All right. Then let's get everyone loaded up."

It took little time to load everyone on the veerfinah. It took longer to convince everyone to get on board. But after a little persuasion, everyone was strapped in, and they were taking off with Arthur at the controls. They left the Unwelcome who were still breathing bound.

Lyla sat in the cockpit with Arthur after getting Iris and Maisy settled in the back with Petra and Imogen. Iris looked like she was in shock. She hadn't even cried yet.

As they flew through the air, she thought on what Thor had said. If Thor was on the up and up, he could be an asset. She wasn't ready to go all in on that yet, though. He'd protected Maisy, which counted for a lot in her book, but she still needed a little more proof of his conversion.

But his conversion alone was eye opening. Miles was fascinated by his change and the suspected impact of the Ka Sama on the Unwelcome. As a result, he was in the back grilling Thor, along with Riley and Lewis.

Lyla expected Miles to come to her and argue for helping Thor. Lyla had to admit, the idea of children being sent off to slaughter didn't sit well with her. But she didn't see saving them at this moment as in her people's best interest or even in the realm of possibility.

And she also realized exactly how heartless that made her sound. She hadn't completely written the idea off, but convincing anyone besides Arthur and Miles to help would be a tough sell.

"Is there a way Thor can contact us? A radio or device of some sort?"

Arthur shook his head. "No. The only contact is between the Naku and the marchelvah. There is no need for the rest of us to contact one another because we are just expected to follow orders."

It was disturbing to think of a group of beings whose entire existence was to serve another species. They had no thoughts of their own, no will of their own. Everything about them was dedicated to serving the Naku.

Miles knocked on the cockpit doorframe. "Um, hey."

"Hey, honey. What's up?" Lyla asked.

"I was just speaking with Thor. He's *really* different than he used to be."

"That's the general consensus," Lyla said.

"I was asking him about his thoughts and feelings, kind of when they came into being. He said it actually started when he was with us. He really liked Maisy's singing."

Lyla turned around in her seat suddenly. "What?"

Arthur smiled. "Maisy would sing every day. I thought it was just something she enjoyed doing. But eventually I realized she was actually doing it for Thor's benefit. I think she thought he might like it."

"Well, he did," said Miles. "And I think he's sincere about being worried about his sister."

"Even if he is, we can't simply storm the place. Even if we trust the intel Thor gives us, the odds are too high."

Miles nodded. "I know. And I agree that's too big a risk."

Lyla looked at him in surprise. She'd thought Miles would be leading the argument to help Thor.

"But," Miles continued, "what if we were able to get a few of the Unwelcome on our side, or at least conflicted about which side they supported?"

Lyla frowned. "How on earth would we do that?"

Miles grinned. "What if we take them *all* off the blue pills?"

70

Lyla walked slowly toward New Attlewood. She and the rest of her group had been dropped off an hour from the camp. Riley and Arthur were now taking Thor a distance away on the veerfinah, and then they would head back here. They most likely wouldn't make it back before morning.

According to Thor, he had stolen the veerfinah and needed to get it back before it was discovered. He had taken a big risk coming to help them. And he'd saved them a very long walk back. What should have taken a month of travel had taken less than an hour. He'd shown them the information tablet that had alerted him to their position. Apparently that bounty hunter Riley and Rory had run into had tipped them off. Lyla shook her head. Bad enough the Naku were after them. Humans taking their side was beyond wrong.

Lyla was alone as she approached the camp. She wanted to get a sense of how New Attlewood was doing before she brought Maisy and Iris over. They hadn't been banished, but some people had been very happy to have the camp split up. She wasn't sure what kind of a reception they would receive, and she didn't want to expose the kids to any more difficulties than she had to.

Most of the kids from New Attlewood still had family in the camp. She hoped they'd be happy to see their kids again, even for a short visit. But she knew even some of them had been relieved when they'd left.

Instead of hurrying, she took her time. Thor's appearance had unsettled her. But she couldn't deny it had also lit a spark of hope in her. If the Unwelcome could be awakened, could they turn them to the humans' side? Or at the very least, could they get them to not do the bidding of the Naku?

The possibility of that was probably worth the risk. But they were going to need some help.

She spied the top of the fence surrounding New Attlewood through the trees. She hoped that their short absence had allowed the camp to calm down and allowed people to see things more clearly. She also hoped in the not-too-distant future she could bring them all back together. But that wasn't the point of today's incursion. Today she needed to make sure it was safe to leave Maisy and Iris with Emma and Edna when, *if* they decided to make a move against the Naku.

And she needed to speak with Max Turner.

She crept closer, noting the changes the group had made. She was impressed. In the time since Frank and their people had taken up residence, they had managed to erect a complete fence with four turrets. It looked secure. *Good.*

She walked around the edge of the camp, keeping in the tree line, out of view. The main gate had two guards. One was Angela, a Phoenix. But the other wasn't a Phoenix. She recognized him, though. He was one of the farmers. Lyla didn't want to try to talk her way in with someone she didn't fully trust. She continued on to one of the smaller side entrances with only a single guard. She smiled when she saw the familiar face.

She threw a pebble at his back. He turned around with a frown. Before he could speak, Lyla peeked out from a tree, letting Otto see her face.

He hustled over to her, pulling her off her feet into a hug. "Where have you been?"

"All over," she said with a small laugh. It was so good to see him. Contentment filled her at how good he looked. "How's the camp?"

He lowered her back to the ground. "It's okay. We've had to fend off a few groups, but it went all right. Although the new guards aren't as disciplined as the Phoenixes."

Lyla frowned. "Who's training them?"

"Addie and Jamal. They're doing a good job," he said quickly. "It's not them. It's the new recruits. They don't have the same work ethic that the original Phoenixes have. They don't understand how dangerous this world can be. Guess we protected them too much."

Lyla understood what he meant. She and her Phoenixes had fought off many threats to the camp, but they hadn't broadcast those threats, wanting people to feel safe. But apparently they had done their job too well. "How's Frank?"

Otto pinched his lips, looking away. "Good."

"Otto," Lyla said.

He sighed. "He came down with a fever a few days after we arrived. He's been slow to recover, and Justin has used that as an excuse to try and push him out."

Lyla growled. Justin again.

"But Frank's finally on the mend. He'll get everyone in line. Montell's been holding the line in his absence."

Lyla knew that Montell would take the lead. But she didn't like the idea of Frank being pushed aside.

"What are you doing here?" he asked.

"Two things. First, I have Maisy with me. I need to get her to Emma and Edna."

A giant smile split Otto's face. "They will be so happy to see her. They are going to stuff her so full of cookies she'll burst."

"Well, they're going to have two girls to stuff full of cookies."

She quickly explained about Iris and what had happened to her grandparents. The plan had been to send her to Meg's, but once her grandparents were gone, it seemed cruel to separate her from Maisy, who seemed to have taken on the role of Iris's protector.

"You said there were two reasons."

Lyla nodded. "I need to speak with Max Turner."

Otto frowned. "Max? Why?"

She gave him a small smile. "Because I'm hoping he may be able to help us turn the Unwelcome against the Naku."

71

At the change of shift, Otto snuck Lyla into the camp. It was already dark, and with her hood up it was hard to tell who she was. They walked quickly to Frank's cabin. Otto left her there and went to go get Max.

She knocked quietly on the door. It opened a few seconds later. Montell's hair had grown longer and he had started to braid it. It looked good on him. He scowled down at Lyla. "What do you ... Lyla?"

She smiled as she pushed her hood back. "Hey."

Montell's gaze darted past her as he pulled her in. He took one last look outside before closing the door. He leaned against it and held out his arms. "Knew you'd be back."

She slipped into the hug, realizing how much she'd missed the Phoenixes. They had trained and fought together for years. She never questioned whether they had her back, the same way they never questioned whether she had theirs. Being without them these last weeks had been difficult. It made everything feel off.

She finally stepped back, looking up at him. As happy as she was to see him, she could see the strain on his face. And his worry about someone seeing her at Frank's door hadn't exactly been subtle. "What's wrong?"

He ran a hand through his hair. "Just about everything. You heard Frank got sick?"

Lyla nodded. "Is he ..."

"He's fine, or at least he will be. But Justin tried to take over. He started making decisions that are Frank's to make: what to trade, what the priorities are."

"And what are his priorities?"

"Everyone must work equal amounts. Those who don't will receive smaller food rations and be put last on the list for housing."

"But not everyone can physically do that."

"I know. As for the Phoenixes, we're considered mid-level workers. Because, you know, we just stand around all day."

"And let me guess, the people in the fields are ranked highest."

Montell nodded.

"Frank hit the ceiling when he found out. But I think Justin was his own worst enemy. One of the first people he downsized was Judith Carolina."

"You're kidding."

"Nope."

Judith took care of any stray kids they come across. She currently had ten. And she was extremely well liked.

"As soon as Frank was up to it, he called a camp meeting and announced in no uncertain terms that we were going back to the old way."

"I'm guessing Justin had a problem with that?"

"He did. But Frank's in charge. Everybody agrees with that. But Justin's been putting up resistance to every little thing."

Lyla sighed, knowing the stress that would place on Frank and wishing she could help. But at the same time, she recognized that her and the Cursed reappearing were only going to be one more headache for Frank.

"Don't you even think it."

Lyla turned. Frank stood highlighted in the doorway. He was thinner, paler, and his hair even seemed to have grayed a little more.

"Think what?" she asked.

He shuffled forward, his shoulders stooped. He gripped the back of the tall wingback chair. "Leaving. I shouldn't have let you go in the first place. You wouldn't be here if something big hadn't happened. And we're not letting Justin get in the way of that."

Frank's speech and the short walk seemed to sap him of a large part of his energy. He slumped into the chair.

Lyla exchanged a concerned look with Montell before he shooed her forward.

Lyla sat down across from Frank, disturbed at how weak he looked. He also had a hacking cough, but he managed to sit upright.

"Stop looking at me like that," Frank ordered after she'd caught him up on how everyone was doing.

"Like what?"

"Like you expect me to keel over at any moment."

She forced a smile to her face. "Just preparing myself to leap forward and catch you if necessary."

He grunted. "Disrespectful."

She smiled wider at his surly tone. "I'm just worried."

"Hey, I'm the one surrounded by people. You're the one out there on your own."

"Not completely."

His smile dimmed. "I don't like you all being out there. You should come back."

"Well, actually, we have a plan that just might help us do that."

The front door burst open. Lyla leaped to her feet, her staff in her hand. But it wasn't an enemy.

Addie hurled herself across the room, pulling Lyla into a bone-crushing hug. "I have missed you so much!"

Lyla hugged her back just as fiercely, tears flooding her eyes. "Same."

"Okay, enough of that." Jamal elbowed Addie out of the way and wrapped Lyla in another hug.

Emma tapped Jamal on the shoulder. "Our turn."

Jamal grinned as he let her go. Emma and Edna hugged Lyla at the same time. Lyla breathed them all in. She had missed this —the sense of family, of security. She finally stepped back, wiping at her eyes. "A few minutes with you guys, and I'm a blubbering mess."

They all grinned back at her, everyone's eyes just as shiny. She looked past them, spying Max standing by the door. She smiled. "Come on in, Max. Join the hug fest."

Max made his way forward shyly. "Hi, Lyla."

Lyla hugged him. "Hey, Max." She pulled back. "How's Sean Jr.?"

"He's doing great. He's made some friends. He's even started training with Jamal."

"That's great."

"What about Petra? How's she?" Edna asked anxiously.

"She's good. They're all good." She looked over the group. "Why don't you all take a seat, and I'll explain."

Everybody scattered around the small room except Montell and Otto, who took up positions by the windows, keeping an eye out in case anyone tried to intrude.

Lyla told them everything—about finding the Lab, the twins, heading back with the Stevenses only to be found by the Unwelcome thanks to some bounty hunter, and then Thor showing up out of nowhere.

"Do you believe him?" Frank asked.

Lyla paused, mulling over her answer. "I'm not sure. I think my head is telling me it's crazy, but there's something very different about him. You'd have to see him to understand. I think he's telling the truth. And I think the change is because of the Ka Sama, or rather his *not* taking the Ka Sama."

She explained what Arthur and Miles thought the blue pills might be doing. "So we thought if we could interrupt the manufacturing of the pills, we could actually turn some of the Unwelcome to our side."

No one spoke for a moment. Finally, Addie broke the silence. "That's a lot to take in."

Lyla gave a small laugh. "Yup. We've been busy."

"Do you really think it would work?" Emma asked.

"I don't know. But if there's a chance, I think we need to take it. But we need to do this very carefully."

Frank nodded slowly. "We need to interrupt the supply in such a way that they don't realize we've done it."

"And that's where you come in." Lyla turned to Max.

Max reared back. "Me?"

"Do you have any idea where they are manufacturing the Ka Sama? We figured it was probably in New City."

"Uh ..." Max frowned, his eyes shifting back and forth as if searching his memory banks. "I don't remember hearing about anything like that. Of course, I didn't know the pills existed, so even if someone said something, it would have been meaningless to me."

Lyla's hopes deflated. She had been hoping that maybe he would have some idea.

"But, actually, I have a friend. Jane. She lives in the Fringe. She might know something. She works at a place called the dispensary."

72

Taking all the Unwelcome off the blue pills. When Miles had first mentioned the idea, Riley had thought he was crazy. But after they'd dropped everyone off, Riley had been able to think of little else. It was crazy but also incredibly appealing. If they could turn the Unwelcome against the Naku, or at least get them to think for themselves, things could really change.

They had dropped Lyla and everyone else a short distance from New Attlewood. Now it was just Riley, Arthur, and Thor.

They set down in a clearing miles from the camp and removed the blindfold from Thor's eyes. He blinked rapidly. Riley gestured for him to put his hands up. Riley sliced through the binds at his wrist.

Thor rubbed them while he rolled his wrists. "So what now?"

"Now, we let you go back."

Thor's face fell. "You won't help me?"

"We haven't decided." Riley paused. "It's not that we don't want to. But it's a huge risk for all of us."

Thor bowed his head. "I know."

"Good. We need you to keep in touch with us. Let us know

what you can about the Naku's movements, any plans they might have. Meet us here in a week."

Thor paused.

"Is that a problem?" Riley asked.

"No. It's just a serious risk to take another ship."

"Well, you're asking us to risk a lot as well, aren't you?" Riley demanded, his temper rising.

Arthur put a hand on his shoulder.

Riley looked up at him.

"We're all risking a lot," Arthur said gently.

Riley took a breath. "Right. Can you meet us again?"

Thor nodded. "Okay."

Riley stood. "You should get back."

Arthur stood as well, extending his hand. "Good luck, Thor."

Thor stared at it, a puzzled expression on his face.

"It's how people, humans, say hello or goodbye." Riley shook Arthur's hand. "See?"

Arthur extended his hand again to Thor. Slowly Thor reached out, gripping Arthur's.

Arthur nodded and released his hand.

Thor turned to Riley. Riley raised his eyebrows as Thor extended his hand to

Riley. He hesitated for a moment. Was Thor really a non-enemy? In the end he figured it was a good first step if they were going to start on the road to trust. He gripped Thor's hand. "Have a safe trip back."

He released Thor's hand and stepped back. Thor stared down at his hand. "That was ... strange."

"Good strange or bad strange?" Riley asked.

"Good ... I think."

Two minutes later, Riley and Arthur stepped off the ship, backing away as it raised up into the air and headed toward New City.

Riley watched until the ship was a speck in the air. "Do you really think he wants our help saving his sister?"

Arthur kept his gaze on the ship. "I do. You have to understand, with the Ka Sama in our systems, we feel nothing. But when we are not on them, we feel everything. We have thoughts, dreams. We become who we are supposed to be. We're not very different from you."

Riley remembered what Jerrold and Elaine had said. "Will he get caught?"

Arthur hesitated. "It is difficult to say. The Naku, they are so used to us following orders that they would not think to look for those of us doing something outside of our orders. Those safeguards are simply not in place. Thor, he is breaking all sorts of rules. And because he is the first to do that, he may very well succeed."

"But if someone realizes what he's done?"

Arthur looked back to where the ship had disappeared. "Then he will be terminated."

73

Vel was not happy. First, those two kids had gotten the drop on them. His shoulder still ached. He took his time bandaging it, figuring he had time until the Unwelcome swooped in and grabbed them or killed them.

But that wasn't what happened. When they'd arrived at the scene, the Unwelcome were removing the bodies of other Unwelcome. There were two dust piles that he could see, but he had expected much more than that.

He had been careful to keep himself and Grit from being seen. The Unwelcome didn't think well for themselves. And if they had been sent to retrieve humans, they would not differentiate.

So they had waited until the Unwelcome had left and then searched for a trail. If the humans hadn't been killed, they had undeniably run off in a panic. They had kids, old people. A trail shouldn't be hard to find.

And yet it was. He couldn't find any trail leading from the site. All he saw was the trail leading to it, which made no sense. He knew Lyla was supposed to be good, but with a group of that size, someone was going to break a branch, step on a soft piece of ground, do something that showed their passage, especially in a panic.

Which meant they didn't walk away from the site.

"Where are they?" Grit growled.

"Check for landing sites."

"I already did. There were three. Why?"

"If they didn't walk away from here, they must have flown."

"You think they took one of the veerfinah?"

"Maybe." He'd seen that tall blue guy with them. He could have flown them. And the Naku were stupid when it came to security. Of course, they had an army of giants who did every single thing they said, so they'd been lulled into a *false* sense of security.

And now it looked like that was going to bite them in the ass.

"Get the horses. We're going to find that camp they used to be a part of. If they're running, they'll turn to people they know."

Grit balked. "But that will take forever."

"No, it won't. We'll run the horses into the ground."

"Okay. Uh, what about the guys? They're hurt."

"Well, they shouldn't have gotten hurt, should they? Just get the damn horses."

"Sure." Grit disappeared into the woods.

He'd lost his prey. He did not like that. But he'd find them again soon. It was just a matter of time.

74

There was a great deal of arguing over who would get to go into the Fringe. Finally, it was agreed that Lyla, Adros, Riley, Miles, and Max would head into the Fringe to speak with Jane. Addie and Jamal would accompany them down and wait outside the boundary of the Fringe with Rory, Arthur, and Petra.

Lyla wanted to keep the Cursed as far from New City as possible. But they had all argued that they had as much to gain by this action as anyone else. And that if the Unwelcome discovered them, they'd be better in a fight than anyone else.

Besides, the only other realistic options were the Phoenixes, and they couldn't leave New Attlewood without people realizing something was going on. So Lyla had conceded.

The rest of the Cursed would be staying at New Attlewood. Lewis was going to get them settled before slipping back into Meg's camp and checking on his wife.

So far, the presence of the Cursed had gone undetected. But Lyla knew it was only a matter of time before they were discovered. Lyla hated that they had to hide kids who should be protected, but apparently that's the point they were at now.

But hopefully not for long, she thought as she stared down at the Fringe.

The journey to the Fringe had been long and uneasy, but they still arrived too early to head right to Jane's. They would need to wait until nightfall.

No one spoke much as they waited for the sun to disappear behind the horizon and for the lights to twinkle on in the homes below. Lyla watched those lights with an odd sense of nostalgia for a time she had never known. When she was little, though, she'd seen a TV show in one of the camps where the streetlights would come on at night and kids would know it was time to head home. Before that, they had played out in the streets with their friends, not worried about anything. Just being a kid. She wanted that for Maisy. Riley and Miles were beyond the age for playing ball in the street, but she wanted them to sit out under the stars not listening for every creak of a branch or whisper in the trees.

Arthur leaned down. "You all right?"

"Yeah, just thinking about how I wish things could be."

He took her hand. "It will be one day. You humans have a way of turning wishes into reality."

She looked up into his bright blue eyes, wondering again how this man who had traveled thousands of miles from another planet had somehow become someone very important to her. Arthur often said that humans were incredible creatures. But Arthur was no less amazing. He had spent his life as a slave. But still, when he had been able to think on his own, the first thing he had done was protect two helpless humans. She wasn't sure what the rest of the Unwelcome would be like if they managed to remove the effects of the Ka Sama, but if they turned out even a little bit like Arthur, then all of their lives were going to get a lot better.

Max spoke quietly in the dark. "I think we can go now."

Lyla squeezed Arthur's hand before slipping hers from his.

She turned to Addie and Jamal. Addie nodded at her. "You've got this, but if there's any trouble, we'll come running."

"I know. Just keep an ear out here too." She glanced at Arthur.

Arthur had donned an Unwelcome uniform and had the helmet tucked into his side. "I'll keep them safe."

And maybe it was simply wishful thinking, but she believed him. Without another word, she started down the hill with Max. Adros, Miles, and Riley would follow a minute behind.

Lyla wasn't comfortable bringing the boys, but Adros and Riley had been to the Fringe before. And they needed Miles in case Jane could tell them anything about the science of the Ka Sama.

Nerves coated Lyla's skin. She tried to ignore them, keeping her pace leisurely as she and Max stepped onto the street that ran through the middle of the Fringe.

A couple walked past on the other side of the street. Lyla watched them from the corner of her eye. At first glance she thought they were a couple out for a carefree evening stroll. But as they neared she saw the dark circles under their eyes. And they were holding on to each other more out of necessity than affection. Apparently, despite the comforts it offered, it was not all happiness and joy in the Fringe.

Max turned down the second street they passed. Jane had one of the only single-family dwellings. It wasn't large, just a single story without any outward appeal. It looked like a large box.

Max started to hasten his pace, but Lyla put a hand on his arm to slow him down. "Casual, Max, remember?"

He nodded, but Lyla could feel the tremble in his arm. They made their way up the dirt path to the front door. There were no flowers or bushes by the house, just overgrown grass. The blinds had been pulled closed, but a little light shone through at the edges.

Max stepped up to the front door. After only a short hesitation to take a deep breath, he knocked.

No sound came from inside for a few seconds. Then Lyla could make out a shuffling step. "Who is it?"

"It's, um, Max. Max Turner."

There was a pause before the lock was undone. The door only slightly opened. "Max?"

"Hey, Jane."

The door swung open wide, and Lyla got her first look at Jane. She was medium height but extremely thin, giving her an almost birdlike appearance. Her white hair was pulled back into a pony-tail, accentuating bright blue eyes that shone from a face lined by a full life. "Well, get in here." She stepped back.

Max followed her, gesturing to Lyla. "Um, this is my friend Lyla."

Jane's eyebrows rose. "What's going on, Max?"

"Um, we need to talk to you. There's a few of us, and I'm hoping you'll just hear us out."

Jane's eyes skipped past Lyla and back to the path. "These the rest of your group?"

Max turned around, nodded. "Yes."

Jane looked from Lyla to Max. "Will this get me in trouble?"

"Hopefully not," Lyla said.

Jane sighed. "Well, come on back to the kitchen. I'll put on some coffee."

JANE SET out some pound cake while she got the coffee together. Lyla was tempted to turn down the offer of food, but the white icing on top of the cake was making her mouth water. She gladly took the slice Max placed on a plate for her.

She took a tentative bite, and sweetness exploded in her mouth. She struggled to contain her groan. She hadn't had sugar in months.

Adros was less reserved in his response. "I think I love you, Jane."

"I *know* I do," Miles said, all but licking his plate.

Jane tittered as she took her seat, some of her initial concern replaced by a smile as she watched the boys. "Well, a girl always likes to hear that. Now, why don't you tell me what's going on? Where'd you go, Max? One day you were here, and the next you were gone."

Max gripped his mug. "Sorry about that, Jane. I, um, I never told you, but my grandson was inside New City."

Jane started. "Oh, Max. I'm so sorry."

He nodded. "I was living here because I just wanted to be near him. He was placed on one of the work duties."

Jane looked like she wanted to spit. "I can't stand seeing those kids treated that way. Little more than slaves."

"How come you work for them, then?" Adros asked.

Jane looked him right in the eyes. "I lost my husband, my three children, their spouses, and both of my grandchildren when the Unwelcome arrived. I was sixty years old with a bum leg and had no one. So what exactly should I have done? No groups wanted to take me in. Should I have starved to death to prove a point?"

"Um, sorry, no." Adros stared at the tabletop.

Lyla studied the woman across from her. She wasn't a pushover. She was a survivor. And she obviously had no love for the Unwelcome. They could work with that.

"Your grandson?" Jane asked, looking back at Max. "He still inside?"

Max shook his head with a smile. "These two here"—he indicated Riley and Adros—"they helped me get him out. We've been living at a camp. He's safe. We're both safe."

She smiled at him. "I'm happy to hear that. Was that all that commotion down by the research building just before you disappeared? It was the first time I'd seen Unwelcome go running."

Adros grinned broadly. "Yup, that was us."

"How many kids did you get out?"

"Four," said Riley. "We lost one, but the rest are all at the camp. They're doing really well."

Lyla took a breath. "You're welcome to join us. You don't have to stay here."

Jane met her gaze directly, crossing her arms over her chest. "I'm assuming you're not going door to door offering people refuge, so what's the catch?"

"We need some information," Lyla asked. "You work at a place called the dispensary?"

Jane nodded slowly. "Yes."

"Does the dispensary make little blue pills?" Lyla asked.

"They're called Ka Sama, and yes."

Riley's mouth dropped open. "You know the name?"

"Of course I know their name. After all, I'm in charge of their production."

75

Lyla stared at the woman across from her, not sure she'd heard her correctly. "*You're* in charge of the Naku's production of Ka Sama?"

Jane scanned each of their faces. "Yes."

"How's that possible? Why would they trust you with that?" Riley asked.

Jane shrugged. "From what I can tell, trust isn't really a Naku concept. Humans, Unwelcome, we're told what to do, and they expect we will do it. They don't seem to have any concept of resistance."

Lyla nodded, thinking of what Arthur and Thor had said. *Which hopefully will make our job a little easier.*

"Do you know what the Ka Sama does?" Miles asked.

Jane nodded. "It's used by the Unwelcome as a sort of sleep aid."

"It does more than that," Miles said.

Jane studied him. "I had a feeling it might. It reduces their emotions and makes them more pliable to orders, doesn't it?"

"Yes," he said eagerly. "How'd you know that?"

"I was a chemist in the Before. The Naku were looking for

specific chemical compositions. They were almost out of their current supply. I think that might have been one of the reasons they came here. Anyway, I helped figure out how to manufacture them. And I keep the process working. That's how I earned this place."

Excitement rolled through Lyla. "Is there a way to change the formula? Switch out some of the chemicals or their composition to render the pill useless?"

Jane didn't speak for a moment. Then she smiled. "I've actually given that some thought over the last few years. Just in case, you understand."

"Of course," Max said, returning the smile.

Jane raised an eyebrow at Lyla. "What exactly are you planning?"

Lyla wasn't sure what to say. But Adros leaned forward, a grin on his face. "A revolution."

76

Jane said she'd need a little time to figure out exactly what needed to be done. She had given it some thought, but it was more in the form of wishful daydreaming than actual planning. Adros volunteered to stay with her and then report back when she had a plan.

Adros returned from the Fringe three nights later with good news: The process for neutralizing the Ka Sama was actually pretty easy. Jane had figured out a way to make the pill harmless, basically a placebo. She was going to need help moving some of the vats and pipes, however. Lyla would aid her along with Otto, Arthur, Adros, and Riley.

The plan was to sneak into the factory in two days. Jane knew of an entrance where the scanner was down. With Arthur's help, they should be able to send Riley over to open the gate and admit the rest of them. Then they would hide in the shed on the roof of the factory until lunch.

Lyla still felt uncomfortable with Adros and Riley's presence. But the two of them had grown so muscular in the last year that they could easily pass for older. Add in the beards they had grown over the last few days, and you would be hard pressed to identify them as teenagers.

Even so, Lyla tried to talk them out of it. But they were adamant. And honestly, if things went sideways, she could definitely use their help. So now, the five of them were standing in the shed on the roof of the factory. It was a pretty tight squeeze, especially with Arthur and Otto.

Everyone was glad when Jane finally opened the door. "All clear. You guys good?"

Riley stepped out first, stretching his back. "Happy to never do that again, but yes."

"Everyone go to lunch?" Lyla asked.

"Yes. We should have ninety minutes."

Arthur frowned. "Ninety? I thought we had only sixty."

Jane grinned. "I might have suggested they take a little extra time. That I would need some time to set things up for the afternoon diagnostics."

FORTY-FIVE MINUTES LATER, Lyla was feeling pretty optimistic. They had managed to remove one of the large vats down to the basement as well as rearrange six of the pipes. Otto, Arthur, and Adros were carting up the new vat to one floor below while Lyla got to work on loosening the other vat they would have to change out. Those were the last steps, and then they were good to go.

Jane stood below Lyla, pointing to a large joist hanging ten feet up. "You'll need to get up there to get the next one. That blue tube needs to attach to that red interface. And the red tube needs to attach to the blue one."

"Got it." Lyla climbed on top of the large metal vat. Her tools were secured in a pack on her back. She looked up, and then scrunching down, leapt. Her fingers wrapped around the metal tube. Swinging her legs over, she climbed upside down to the interface Jane had pointed to and then pulled herself up to straddle the tube. She pulled her bag around front and dug through it for the wrench.

"Ah, to be young again," Jane said.

Lyla laughed, glancing down at the woman as a flash of yellow caught her eye. Lyla immediately lay flat, her heart racing.

"There you are, Jane. I've been looking for you." The man crossed the floor toward them.

Jane hastened away from her position and crossed the room to intercept him. "Brandon, what can I do for you?"

Lyla held her breath, waiting for the man to call her out, but he simply smiled. "I was hoping we could talk about your salvation."

77

Lyla stayed flat on the beam. The man had been dressed in mustard yellow robes, which meant he was a McGovern. The McGoverns had sworn their loyalty to the Unwelcome. They turned in other humans for any hint of disloyalty or rule breaking. They viewed the Unwelcome as saviors.

Jane took him back to her glass-walled office, keeping his attention away from the beam where Lyla lay still. Lyla sat up slowly. She could see the man's back through the glass windows of Jane's office as she quickly worked at loosening the bolt. She managed to get it done quickly, slipping the bolts into her pack. As quietly as she could manage, she arranged the tubes as Jane had explained. Every once in a while, Jane would dart a gaze her way, but she didn't seem to be in distress, and more importantly she was keeping Brandon's attention on her.

Carefully, Lyla lowered herself to the ground and silently moved toward the office. The boys would be coming back soon.

As she drew nearer to Jane's office, she could hear the conversation through the thin walls of Jane's office.

"We are disheartened to hear that you're still living in the

Fringe. A woman of your education should be inside New City, taking advantage of all the Naku are offering us."

"I have all I need."

Lyla could hear the patronizing tone in the man's voice. "Ah, but Jane, you could have so much more. You should join us. The Naku, they have saved us from a life of toil. We owe them a great debt, and yet instead of asking for anything, they offer us more."

Lyla stood against the wall, peering in the window. Jane's arms were crossed over her chest, anger slashed across her face. "Except for the lives of our children."

"Not all our children. Only a few. All gods require sacrifices."

Jane's eyes narrowed to slits, her mouth a tight line.

"But you needn't worry about that. We can arrange for a child to be brought for you. You would not have to do a thing except, of course, join us."

Lyla's skin crawled. He was offering children up like their lives meant nothing.

Brandon sat back, stretching out his legs. "I have decided that I am not leaving until I have convinced you. Join us and accept the beneficence the Naku have so generously shared with us."

"I will not kill a child."

"No child dies. Their soul is merely freed from its physical restraints. They are happy."

Vomit threatened to rise along Lyla's throat.

Brandon's tone turned a little harder. "Of course, those who do not join us are always a bit suspicious, aren't they? Perhaps I should suggest to the Naku that they take a closer look at your work here. They'll go over this place with a fine-toothed comb. And no matter how good someone is at their job, there's always something that's not quite right."

"You wouldn't dare."

"Try me. I told you, Jane, I'm not leaving until you agree to join us."

Lyla had heard enough. She pushed through the door. "Oh, you're leaving all right."

Brandon bolted to his feet and lashed out with his fist, surprisingly fast. Lyla avoided the backswing with a quick jump back, placing one hand on his wrist and the other on his shoulder.

He let out a yell as she pulled him off balance before putting him in an arm bar and slamming him forward. She cringed as his head slammed into the corner of the desk.

Lyla felt the fight drain out of him and let him drop to the floor. He collapsed in a heap, blood running from the wound in his forehead. Lyla frowned, looking at his chest. It wasn't rising. She reached down and felt for a pulse, but there wasn't one.

Jane peered from around the desk. "Is he …"

"Dead." She hadn't planned on killing him. She wasn't sure what she'd planned. She'd known she was going to have to keep him from informing on Jane, but she hadn't meant to do this. It was just an unfortunate hit. She didn't like killing, especially not like this. But if this man was going around offering kids up like lambs to the slaughter, she didn't think he qualified as an innocent.

Jane looked pale as she slumped back into her chair. Lyla winced. "I'm sorry you had to be here for that. I know—"

Jane shook her head. "It's not that. He's not a good person. They've been trying to recruit me for months. I don't know why. But that's the first time he ever said they would give me a kid to trade in. I didn't realize they were that far gone. I mean, trading kids like that? How do they sleep?"

Lyla glanced over her shoulder at the elevator. The car was one floor away. "All right, let's get this—"

A feeling of warmth spread over Lyla as Jane called out. "Lyla!"

She whirled around just as the Unwelcome stepped into the room.

78

The Unwelcome paused for only a split second before it raised its spear. Lyla leapt across the desk, pushing Jane down. With one hand, she flipped the metal desk, hiding Jane behind it.

"He ... he must have come with Brandon. They sometimes have an escort when they expect problems."

Damn it. The Unwelcome had seen Brandon's body. There was no way to avoid it reporting it back. "Stay here!"

Lyla slid to the edge and peeked out. A blast sent her jolting back. She barely missed getting dusted.

An answering blast from the other side of the room sounded. Lyla peered out as the Unwelcome whirled to face the new threat. Adros sent another shot, catching him in the side. The Unwelcome aimed at him, but Riley appeared behind him. He stomped on the back of its knees, sending it to the ground, and then with one quick movement broke its neck.

Lyla stood, her hope crashing. Riley had done the right thing. But right now, all their plans were as dead as the Unwelcome and Brandon.

79

Lyla crept out from behind the desk and made her way over. Riley looked up. "What happened?"

"One of the McGoverns came to try and recruit Jane. He was going to rat her out, have the Unwelcome search the facility. They would have found the changes. I killed him."

"You did?" Adros asked.

"Not intentionally."

Otto and Arthur came to an abrupt halt after bolting into the room. "We heard blasts," Otto said.

"Yeah." Lyla quickly recounted what had happened. She shook her head. "We can hide Brandon's death, but the Unwelcome's ..."

Otto and Riley moved across the room. "We'll take this guy down to the furnace," Riley said.

Lyla nodded. All their careful plans, and now they had nothing. The Unwelcome would investigate the facility once they realized one of their own had died here. Maybe they could try again in a few months, but they'd be too late to save Thor's family then. It was just dumb luck that Brandon chose today, at this time, to stop by. She felt a crushing loss. She didn't realize how much she needed this to work, how much she needed the hope of a better future to cling to.

"I'm going to check on Jane," Adros said before heading for the office.

Arthur knelt down next to the Unwelcome and checked his pulse. But Lyla knew he was gone. She frowned as Arthur unsnapped the bracelet from the Unwelcome's wrist. "What are you doing?"

With a click, he snapped it around his own before pulling the ID number from the Unwelcome's uniform and replacing it with his own as he stood.

Lyla's mouth fell open, and she grabbed his arm. "Arthur, *what are you doing?*"

He looked down at her. "What needs to be done. I'll go in his place."

Lyla shook her head, panic rising in her chest to replace the feeling of loss. "No, you can't. They'll know it's not him."

He kept his gaze on her as he spoke. "No. The bracelets are our identity. Right now, I am 78-E. If I go, they'll never know he died."

"Arthur, we'll think of another way. We'll—"

He cut her off. "Not in time to help Thor and his family."

"That doesn't matter!"

"You don't actually mean that. And if they discover that we were attempting to interfere with the Ka Sama manufacturing, they'll wrap the whole process up in so much security that we'll never get another chance. But if I go in his place, they'll never know we were here."

She waved her hand to where Otto and Riley had disappeared with the body. "But Brandon ..."

"They don't care about the deaths of humans. And they won't know he's dead, only missing."

She stared up at him, trying to think of something to say to keep him from doing this. "I won't let you."

He smiled. "You can fight the Unwelcome. But not me. You know I'm not a threat to you. I would never hurt you."

Tears pressed against the back of her eyes. "Please, please don't do this. You *can't* do this. If they find out—"

"They won't. And as soon as I can, I'll come back to you."

"Arthur, no." A single tear slipped down her cheek.

He ran a hand along her cheek, wiping it away. "I'll come back to you." He leaned forward and brushed his lips across her forehead. Then he disappeared out the doorway.

Lyla stared after him, watching the empty doorway.

Arthur was gone. He was gone.

She couldn't seem to think of anything else. She barely heard Riley and Otto return. She just stared at the empty doorway, willing Arthur to reappear.

But he didn't, and Adros finally pulled her away.

80

It took the four of them to get the body of the Unwelcome into the elevator and then the furnace in the basement. Jane looked shell-shocked at the turn of events, and Lyla prayed she'd be able to keep it together.

They managed to slip out of the dispensary minutes before the rest of the crew returned. All of their nerves were frayed as they made their way out of New City.

Even as Lyla scanned for any threats, she felt detached from what was happening around her. Arthur had sacrificed himself for them. He had put chains back on himself. If he was discovered, he would be killed. And if they managed to learn where they had been hiding, they would all be killed.

Worries and fears dogged Lyla's mind, weighing her down. Even being safely ensconced in Jane's home didn't offer any relief. All she could picture was Arthur disappearing out that doorway. Without a word, she walked into Jane's bedroom and closed the door. She curled up on the bed but didn't sleep. She just stared straight ahead, wishing she could turn back time.

~

JANE ARRIVED HOME JUST before dark that evening. No one at the plant suspected anything, and as far as Jane could tell, no sort of alarm seemed to have been raised among the Unwelcome. Even so, it was a somber meal that evening. The dishes were cleared away, and the Fringe was quiet as Lyla, Adros, and Jane waited. Otto and Riley had already left and would wait for them outside the Fringe.

Finally, Lyla pulled on her pack. "All right. I'll head out first. Then—"

"I'm not going," Jane said.

Lyla stared at her. "What?"

Jane gave her tight smile. "If I leave now, it will set off alarm bells. But if I stay, it will help guarantee that the changes we've made won't be discovered."

"But if they figure it out and you're still here..." Lyla said.

Jane gave her a tight smile. "I know. But this is my way of fighting back. I might not be able to swing those swords like you guys, but I can do this. And if all goes well, in a month's time, I can leave. After first making sure everyone thinks I'm suicidal."

Lyla looked into the woman's eyes. "Are you sure?"

Jane nodded. "I am."

Lyla stared at her for a moment longer before nodding. "Okay. We'll come back for you in four weeks."

Jane nodded, a slight tremble in her chin. "Counting on it. Now, I'm not much for goodbyes, so you can let yourselves out." Jane slipped from the living room. A few seconds later, her bedroom door closed.

The weight on Lyla's shoulders got a little heavier at the sound. "Okay, Adros, let's—"

"I'm staying, too," Adros announced.

"What?" Lyla asked.

"Look, she's risking a lot by helping us. And after what happened, she looks a little shaky. Plus she's on her own. If something goes wrong, someone needs to be here to help her. So I'm staying."

"What about your sisters?"

"Until we get things settled, I can't really be with them anyway. Besides, you guys will take care of them if anything happens to me." He looked back down the hall. "But Jane doesn't have anyone to take care of her. She needs me."

Lyla looked at Adros and realized how much he had changed. He was not the boy who'd gone out of his way to bully other kids. Somewhere along the way, he'd turned into a good man. Tears threatened to bubble over. She leaned up and hugged him tight. "I'm proud of you, Adros."

Adros ducked his head away, but she could tell her words made him feel good. "Just doing my part."

"Okay, you stay and look out for Jane. But in a month, I expect you two to head for New Attlewood, okay?"

"You got it," Adros said.

Lyla cinched her straps a little tighter. A few minutes later, she was heading out of the Fringe. A veerfinah flew overhead, heading for the mothership. She stopped to watch it, wondering where Arthur was right now and if he was all right. She also wondered if, like Thor, he'd be able to avoid taking the Ka Sama. Because if he couldn't and their plan at the dispensary didn't work, she would lose him just as certainly as if the Naku discovered him.

81

Lyla returned to New Attlewood that night feeling numb. When she'd pictured them returning, it had been with a sense of hope for the future. But right now, she wasn't sure if the cost of the mission was going to be worth it, all she could picture was the empty doorway after Arthur had disappeared.

Riley started to turn toward one of the side entrances as they approached the camp so they could sneak in.

"No." She headed for the front entrance. She was tired of sneaking around. They had to sneak around the Naku and the Unwelcome. That was necessary. But she was damned well done sneaking around her own people.

A minute later, they rode through the front entrance of New Attlewood. The dozen or so people just inside the gate stopped what they were doing to watch.

"Lyla." Riley nudged her leg, having already dismounted. She looked up. Sheldon and Justin hustled toward them, then stopped a dozen or so feet away, a group of people behind them. Two of the men behind him were those who'd attacked Arthur and Maisy.

And suddenly, all her melancholy and despair shifted straight into white-hot rage. She jumped from her horse and stormed over to the group.

Justin stepped forward. "You and your people are *not* welcome—"

"Shut. *Up.*" Lyla rolled her hands into fists.

Justin backed up from the venom in her voice. She stepped toward him. "I've had it with you. Communities work because everyone pulls their full share. You are no better than anyone else, and you don't get to decide who belongs and who doesn't."

"You're not part of this community anymore."

Lyla laughed. "Is that so? Why don't you ask the Phoenixes if I'm still part of it?"

Justin's gaze darted around. "They're only a small part of this group."

"Yeah, the small part that has kept you safe. They wanted to go with me when I left. But I told them to stay to keep *you* safe. Now I will be staying until my business here is done. But if anyone wants to come with me when I go, anyone at all, they are all welcome. Except you. Justin. You can stay."

She continued walking. Justin nearly tripped over his own feet trying to get out of her way. Her group fell in line behind her, walking right through the crowd that had gathered. Most simply walked away, but more than a few glanced down at their feet.

Lyla was done with this garbage. She had protected these people with her life. The Phoenixes had protected these people with their lives. Even now, Arthur was risking his life for a chance to make all their lives better. And now these same people whom they'd protected were trying to make them feel less than. Well, she was done with that. She and her Cursed were staying in New Attlewood until they knew if the Ka Sama plan had worked.

And then Lyla would find a place for those who wanted to go with her. Making sure everyone had a say in their governance was important, but letting some people become empowered and vaulting themselves above others was not how they were going to move forward, especially not when those who were sacrificing the most were being treated like second-class citizens. The Phoenixes had risked too much to accept that. Lyla had risked too much to accept that.

She kept her shoulders straight and her head high as she headed for Frank's to give him a report. And she prayed the image of Arthur would disappear for a little while so she didn't break down and cry in front of the whole camp.

82

Thor took his bowl and spoon and made his way to the nearest empty seat. It had been two weeks since the dispensary had been compromised. Or at least, he thought it had been compromised. He had no confirmation of that. For all he knew, they could have decided it was too risky to attempt.

He'd met with them three times so far. Each time he asked them to help save his sister. Each time they said they needed to wait to see if the Ka Sama plan worked. And when he asked when it was going into place, they clammed up.

He couldn't really blame them. He wouldn't trust one of them if they'd come to him the way he'd gone to them. But he really wished he had a better idea of what was going on.

Their plan could have already been uncovered, and the pills everyone had been taking could have been the regular Ka Sama. He had not seen anything that indicated that any of the chelvah were feeling any different. He'd even toyed with the idea of taking the Ka Sama himself to see if he felt any effects. But he worried that if he tried it again, it would overtake him. He couldn't risk it. Because he needed to help Xe. And if he went back to the way he was, he would never be able to.

He wouldn't even want to.

It was getting harder each day to keep his silence around Xe. He wanted so much to tell her that it was him, that he remembered her too. But each time the thought crossed his mind, he would remind himself how difficult it was for him to keep himself under control. And he'd had a lifetime of practice. Asking Xe not to talk to him, not to look at him after revealing who he was was just cruel.

So he bit his tongue each time the thought crossed his mind. And he memorized every detail of Xe and her son as they went about their lives, not knowing he was so close.

Thor took his seat, conscious about not moving too much. He sat with efficient movements and immediately placed his spoon in the bowl and then raised it to his mouth. He hated this stuff now. It was bland except for the bitter aftertaste.

But he could not show any emotion. He was too close now to ruin everything over a lousy meal. He ate silently, lost in his thoughts of Xe and picturing them living a quiet life with her son after they had been liberated. He was not surprised to picture them living with Maisy and her group. Maisy had somehow become an image of all that was good and innocent in this world. And he wanted that for both Xe and her son.

A light tapping intruded on his thoughts. He turned his head slightly. The avad next to him was jiggling his leg under the table. Thor had to catch himself quickly before a smile burst out across his face.

OVER THE COURSE of the next week, Thor noticed more and more abnormalities in the routine of the avad. He'd seen a few shifting their stance after standing for too long. More than one glanced around in the food hall and on the ship. They were waking up.

More than ever, Thor knew how important it was for him not

to stand out. He made sure to stand straight, to not fidget, to look straight ahead, and to not call attention to himself in any way, shape, or form.

He ate his food, his distaste for it growing by the day. He was to go down and give the humans a report in a few days. It had been almost four weeks since he had first spoken with them. If they were going to help him, now was the time. He'd seen the changes in the avad. He knew they had managed to sabotage the Ka Sama. If all went well, in a few days he could have his sister and her son out.

And I'll be a traitor.

He still bristled at that thought. He knew he was doing the right thing, but his training was so ingrained, it was hard not to buckle. Even now with all his thoughts his own, he still followed his orders. But when he took this next step, he would be turning his back on everything he knew and throwing in with a group of people who may not even accept him. He was placing his trust in them. More than that, he was placing the fate of Xe and her son in their hands. Yet he knew with the humans they stood a far better chance than with the Naku.

Dispensing of his bowl and spoon, he scanned his bracelet and palmed his Ka Sama. He once again acted as if he had swallowed them while shoving them up his sleeve. He made his way to the lift and then to his room. His bunk was at the back of the room this time. Once again, he was on the lower level. He sat on the edge of the mattress and removed his helmet, placing it on the floor before lying down. The room started to fill. Within a few minutes, the lights went out, only the emergency lights offering a dim glow along the floor.

Thor stared at the bunk above him, wondering if the person above him felt any different. A creak sounded from across the room. Thor went still. He'd never heard a noise after the lights went out. Heart pounding, he turned his head. Two rows over, a man sat up, looking around. Beyond him he saw at least two more rolling in their sleep.

Thor rolled onto his back. He felt as if eyes were on him. He turned and found the woman in the bunk next to him staring at him. She licked her lips, looking around. "What's happening?" she whispered.

He paused, trying to think of what to say. "We're finally waking up."

She stared at him, and he read the fear in her eyes.

"It's all right. It's a good thing."

She just stared at him for a long time before her eyelids closed. Thor watched as she drifted off to sleep. And he realized that she was the first chelvah he had looked in the eyes.

He closed his own. One way or another, it was time.

83

Waiting to see if their work on the factory in New City had succeeded wasn't easy. Even if the Unwelcome woke up, there was no guarantee they would help them.

And if it didn't work? Well, then they were right back where they started—running, hiding. Regardless of whether it worked or not, Lyla knew she needed to find some kind of home base for the Cursed. She could see how the constant movement had gotten to them. They needed the sense of security that came from being able to call a place home, even if that sense was more illusion than fact.

And New Attlewood wasn't going to be it. The camp was tense. The air felt downright brittle. No one would turn them in, she believed that, at least for the moment. But they also would no longer accept the Cursed amongst them. Lyla needed a new place, a fresh start for all of them.

So while they waited, she searched. She took a few different Cursed with her on different days to get them out of Attlewood for a little while. But so far, she'd had no luck finding a new spot that met their needs. Some were too run down, others too close to other settlements, but most were discounted because they didn't have close enough access to a water source to be viable.

For some, the futile searching was frustrating. But Lyla was happy to have something to focus on. Because when she wasn't searching, she was thinking about Arthur. They'd heard nothing from him. Thor, whom they met once a week, hadn't mentioned anything about him either.

Each time they met Thor, he asked for help. And each time Lyla had to say not yet. She could tell how much he was hurting, and she knew that soon she would say yes, even if it meant going alone. She couldn't get the images Thor described out of her head. So whether the Ka Sama plan worked or not, she planned on helping him.

But she shoved those thoughts aside, because today she was feeling hopeful. While she'd been out searching, Lewis and a different group searched as well. And yesterday Lewis had returned thinking he might have found a spot.

It had taken her, Riley, and Lewis most of the day to ride here. Now, the three of them rode through a pair of broken iron gates. The wrought-iron fence surrounding the estate was mostly fallen over. Lewis pointed to it as they passed through the gates. "Parts of the fence are down, but a large portion is actually in good condition. With some repairs, it could be made sturdy."

Lyla nodded, but her attention was drawn to the home in front of them, although "home" seemed too small a word for the grandeur she was seeing. A large, wide stairwell had been built into the small rise in front of the building, leading to a set of massive old iron doors. The building was four stories high and stretched out on either side with twelve windows in each wing.

Riley pointed to the top of the building. "What are those?"

"Gargoyles. They were believed to scare off evil spirits," Lewis said.

"Did they?" he asked.

"Well, being the Unwelcome arrived, I'm guessing not," Lewis replied.

They rode around the left side of the building. A few windows were broken, but most had escaped damage. The backyard, if that's what it could be called, was tiered and about the size of ten crop fields. Another giant stone stairwell led to the back of the house and a veranda that was the length of the house.

"This place is massive. Who lived here?" Lyla asked.

Lewis shrugged. "Someone very rich."

"A single person lived here? Oh, this is like a home from *The Great Gatsby* or the English aristocracy in a Jane Austen book Arthur told us—" Riley's voice cut off, and he darted a quick apologetic look at Lyla.

"It's okay," she said.

Lewis shook his head. "It's hard to accept that he's better read than most humans, but yes, I think it's from that era."

Lyla stopped her horse, trying to imagine living here, having people wait on you hand and foot. She couldn't do it. The sheer size made it impossible for her to imagine anyone wanting to live here with a single family. "The size is good. Really good."

"And there's three working wells," Lewis said.

She glanced around. There were a few more buildings scattered around the edges of the large yard, which could be used for individual homes or working buildings. There was even a stable. From the roof, they'd have good sight lines, and being they were on the top of a hill, they'd actually be given a lot of notice if anyone came at them from either the air or ground.

And most importantly, there was absolutely no one living nearby. New Attlewood was the closest, and it was almost a day's ride away. It was completely isolated. "This could really work."

She stared at the space, an idea forming in her mind. "I know we were talking about this being the home for the Cursed, but how would you feel if we added a few more?"

"Who?" Lewis asked.

She pictured Thor. "Some women and children who need a place to hide."

84

It was time. Lyla had put off telling Frank about the breeding facility. If the Ka Sama manufacturing had been disrupted, she needed to move soon, before the disruption was noticed. She, Riley, Addie, and Jamal were heading to New City to pick up Jane and Adros tomorrow.

They would meet with Thor in a few days, and she wanted to be able to tell him something. In the back of her mind, she hoped Thor would be able to tell her something about Arthur. With that communication device of his, he might at least know if Arthur had been caught, although he had not mentioned anything so far. But they had not told him that Arthur was in New City. Lyla had decided to tell him in hopes that maybe he knew something. She had been torturing herself imagining what was happening to Arthur. She needed to know he was all right. And if she couldn't save him, she could at least help the women and children at the facility. She knew Arthur would approve.

She spied Frank's cabin up ahead, pushing aside her fears for Arthur. She needed to focus on the task at hand, and that was convincing Frank that rescuing the women and children from the breeding facility was in everyone's best interest.

When she entered Frank's cabin, she expected him to be alone, but Montell and Max were also there. She debated for a moment waiting to catch him later. But they'd each learn about it eventually, so she sat down with all of them. She explained about the breeding facility, Thor's sister, and Arthur's idea that they might start doing the same to humans. Then she sat back to wait for their reactions.

It didn't take long.

Frank crossed his arms over his chest. "You can't be serious."

"We're *helping* Thor?" Montell asked.

"Not just him. Those women, they're being forced to breed children for the Naku. Besides the horror of that act, by saving those women, those children, we're removing future Unwelcome. And if they *are* planning on targeting humans, we'll remove that threat before it can even begin."

"You're declaring war," Frank said.

"We're *already* at war. We have been since the Unwelcome arrived. The only difference is now we're fighting back. And they're children."

"There are other children at risk," Max said quietly. "There are more kids that could use our help in New City. Human kids."

"I know," Lyla said. And she knew it very well. The kids she had seen in New City tugged at her heartstrings. But they couldn't take on New City in their first attack. It was too well defended, too large. And the humans in New City had chosen to be there, had turned in a child to gain admittance, which meant they could fight against them as well.

The breeding facility, on the other hand, was in an isolated location, which meant it would take time for reinforcements to arrive. Plus, they had a much smaller number of guards than New City. So if the guards hadn't been changed by the Ka Sama, at least there'd be fewer to fight.

"We *will* do something about the children in New City. But we need a test fight, for lack of a better phrase. We need to know how the Unwelcome are going to respond. If they're going to fight us or help us. And the breeding facility is a better test case."

"You know they're going to fight you. Their training will kick in," Montell said.

"It's possible. But I'm hoping that's where Thor will come in. That he'll be able to talk at least some of them out of hurting us or maybe even into helping us."

"That's a big hope," Frank said.

"Yes, it is. But it's either that or accept that this is our life. That the Cursed and I will always be hunted. That the rest of humanity will exist or disappear simply on the whims of the Naku. And I'm not willing to accept that." She looked Frank dead in the eyes. "Are you?"

He blew out a breath. "I agree with you in principle, Lyla. I don't agree with what the Naku are doing to those women. But I can't agree with risking our people's lives to save them."

"They're children, Frank."

He ran a hand through his hair. "I know. But some of our Phoenixes have children, too. What do we tell them if their parents don't come home?"

"That they died trying to make this world a better place for them?"

He shook his head, giving her a sad smile. "That may be true, but it's also true that you're asking our people to risk their lives to save the enemy."

"We *need* to test if the Ka Sama plan worked," Lyla said. "Going into New City, it's too big a risk until we know how the Unwelcome will respond. The breeding facility is isolated. It has a small contingent. Plus, if we're helping women and children, that might win us a little good will amongst the Unwelcome."

"*If* they realize that's what we're doing. They could just as easily think we're trying to hurt them," Montell said.

"That's true," Lyla conceded. But she couldn't help but think of the risk Arthur had taken in helping Miles, in the risk Miles had taken in turn to help him. That risk had saved her life, saved *their* lives.

This risk was no smaller. But it could have just as large an impact. It could change everything. She looked at each of them. "It *is* a risk. There is no doubt about that. And we need to do everything to minimize that. But if we succeed, it can change everything. Those women aren't the enemy."

"But they look a lot like them, don't they?" Max said softly.

Frank cringed but didn't correct Max. "Lyla, this camp is barely holding it together as is. If the Phoenix go off and help the Unwelcome, it will break this place apart. We can't risk it. I'm sorry."

Lyla looked at Montell, who shook his head. "I'm sorry, Lyla, Frank's right. We can't help, not right now."

Lyla knew arguing further wouldn't change their minds. And she could see their point. It had taken her a good long time to come around to the realization that helping the women at the breeding facility was in everyone's favor. She stood and headed for the door.

"Lyla," Frank called.

She stopped with her hand on the doorknob and glanced back at him. "Yeah?"

"What are you going to do?"

"You made your choice, and I respect that. But now I have to make mine and live with it." She opened the door and headed out into the night.

85

It had been a rough night. Lyla had gotten very little sleep. Maisy had crawled into her bed and snuggled up next to her. Lyla had watched her sleep, wondering how it would feel to have someone rip her away and not being able to stop it. Unwelcome, human—it didn't matter. What was happening in that facility was wrong. Now Lyla just needed to figure out a way to stop it with less people than she had hoped.

But there was some good news. They had agreed that the site Lewis found would be their new camp. They were calling it the Gatsby. Lewis and most of the Cursed had left this morning to start getting it set up.

Lyla would join them tomorrow, after going down to get Adros and Jane. Then she'd swing by New Attlewood to get Maisy and Iris.

About a dozen people had already said they wanted to join her. She would bring them over once the Gatsby was in better shape.

She was very grateful and not surprised that Emma, Edna, and Saul had been the first non-Phoenixes to agree. Once they got some sort of kitchen rigged up, they'd be the first ones brought over.

"Earth to Lyla," Addie said.

Lyla blinked, looking over at her oldest friend. They were on their way down to meet Adros. Jamal was on Addie's other side. Riley and Otto were riding a few feet behind them. "Hey, sorry."

"It's okay. I get it. That breeding facility makes me sick too. You know Jamal and I are in, right?"

"I know. Thanks." She frowned, studying her friend. "Are you okay? You look a little tired."

Addie laughed. "Well, thanks. Actually, though, I wanted to talk to you about that—"

"*We* want to talk to you about that," Jamal cut in.

Addie smiled. "Yes, we—"

A birdcall caused all of them to go silent before Jamal returned the call. A few seconds, later, Adros stepped out of the trees two hundred yards to their right, waving.

"He was supposed to wait for us in the Fringe. Why would he ..." Lyla's words faded as a second figure stepped out of the woods behind him.

Lyla gasped, setting her horse to a gallop, her eyes glued to the second figure. She yanked on the reins to stop her horse and leapt for the ground.

She never touched it as Arthur gathered her into his arms.

86

Lyla wanted to stay wrapped in Arthur's arms. But Riley appeared, leaping off his horse to greet Arthur. With reluctance, Lyla released Arthur to Riley's embrace. She stepped to the side while Jamal and Addie greeted him as well.

"What happened?" Lyla asked.

Adros grinned. "He showed up two days ago at Jane's in the middle of the night. I thought Jane was going to pass out."

Jane grunted. "Yeah, well, I'm betting you didn't exactly handle it well when you first saw him."

Adros laughed. "And you would be correct. Anyway, we hid him at Jane's until it was time to go."

Lyla smiled at Arthur, who even as he'd been greeting everyone else, kept his gaze on her. He walked over to her now. She leaned into him, feeling like she could finally breathe again. "I was so worried."

Adros cleared his throat. "You know, Jane packed some food, so I'm going to set up lunch in the trees *way* over there. Come join us when you're ready."

Lyla barely noticed them leaving. "You're okay?"

Arthur nodded. "Yes. I was stationed in New City. I actually did patrols around the dispensary for the first two weeks. Then I was stationed at one of the gates."

"No one suspected anything?"

"No. Like I said, I was just a number."

Lyla held him a little tighter. "I'm sorry you had to do that."

"It was a good reminder of why I need to help my people."

She looked up at him. "Did you see any effects of the Ka Sama?"

"I think so. I saw some fidgets, restlessness at night. All good signs."

"And you didn't take the Ka Sama?"

"No, I didn't want to risk it."

"How did you get out?"

"I waited until everyone had fallen asleep and made my way to the loading dock. I was planning on stealing a veerfinah like Thor did, but I didn't have to. A squadron was heading down. I boarded with them. When I reached the planet, they went one way, I went another."

"They didn't question you?"

Arthur shook his head. "No. We don't question. If someone is there, they are supposed to be there."

Lyla let out a shaky breath. "If you had been caught …"

"I wasn't, and now I'm back."

Lyla rested her head on his chest. "Right where you belong."

87

Lyla and Arthur joined everyone under the trees. They all sat, ate, and laughed. Lyla sat near Arthur, wanting to assure herself that he was truly here and all right. Jamal, Addie, and Otto took the horses to scout as the rest of them cleared up the food.

"So no one suspects anything?" Lyla asked.

Adros shook his head. "Jane was awesome. At work, she started talking about how futile existence was and how she thought she might take a long walk in the woods."

Lyla looked at Jane with raised eyebrows.

"One of the guys in the Fringe, he did that. Got really depressed and then disappeared into the woods. He left a note, and his body was discovered a few months later."

Lyla shuddered. "That's horrible."

"Yes, but it also helped me figure out how to leave without raising any suspicions."

"You're okay with that? Leaving everything behind?" Lyla asked.

Jane shrugged. "Didn't really leave anything of importance."

"Jane and I were talking," said Adros, "and I thought maybe once we get set up at the new camp, maybe she could stay with me and the girls? You know, just to get her settled in."

Lyla looked between the two of them. They had obviously bonded during their time together. During the meal, Jane had handed Adros an extra serving without even asking him, and Adros had grinned his thanks. There was definitely a mother-son relationship forming there, and Lyla was happy to see it. She thought they both could use it. "I think that sounds great."

Adros grinned broadly. "Hey, Arthur, can you grab the—" Adros cut off as Arthur's head jerked up.

Lyla turned in the direction he was looking. "What is it?"

"Ship."

And then like a phantom, the veerfinah appeared over the hill. Jane gasped. From the corner of her eye, Lyla saw Adros take Jane's hand. Then no one moved, no one dared to even breathe deeply.

With the trees tightly covering them from the air, the ship wouldn't even know they were there. They all sat in tense silence, watching it head away from them. Once it was just a speck in the sky, they all gave a small, tense laugh.

"Well, that was stressful," Otto said.

"Yeah, I wonder what—"

Lyla put up a hand, standing. "Hold on."

Someone was yelling, but she couldn't make out what they were saying. She stepped out from the trees.

"Addie!" Jamal burst from the trees, riding his horse like the devil itself was chasing him.

Addie's not with him. Lyla turned and ran for the pack horse. She pulled her knife from her sheath and sliced through the ropes holding the supplies, sending them crashing to the ground.

She grabbed its mane, but Riley pushed her aside. "I'll go."

Before she could utter a protest, he was swinging himself onto the horse and taking off after Jamal. Lyla started after him, but when Otto emerged from over the hill, she changed direction and sprinted for him. "Otto, what happened?"

Otto, his face red, dropped to his knees, gulping in the air. "They ... they took Addie."

88

For once, Thor was glad to be wearing his helmet. Last night, he'd barely slept. And every time he did, he dreamed of Xe. He imagined her dying back on their home planet. Then she died in the culling. Over and over again his imagination tortured him with images of her meeting her final demise. And then when he would go to look at the body, she was always holding her son.

Each time, he would lie awake, trying to figure out a way to help her. He could not take the facility on by himself, even with the Ka Sama sabotage. He needed help. He needed Lyla and her people to help him. But he could not think of any way to convince them. He would be asking them all to risk their lives for the race that had decimated their population and continued to do so.

He had finally stopped trying to go back to sleep. He simply stared up at the bunk above him. Then he'd gone through the motions of showering, breakfast, and heading down to the planet.

When he stepped off the veerfinah, he struggled to swallow his yawns. He wasn't sure how he was going to make it through the day. He was already so tired. He took his place in line, and when he reached the marchelvah, he raised his bracelet.

Medical Ward, Level 2, Section 11.

His gut tightened. He hated that duty. The women he saw were almost always drugged beyond recognition of anyone or anything. The ones that were cognizant were generally terrified because their children were about to be taken from them. He'd never been to Section ii, though. He hoped it was not something like body removal. He wasn't sure how he would bluff his way through that today.

He walked up the stairs, crushing the Ka Sama from last night and dropping it over the side of the bannister, careful not to drop it until he was little higher up today. He'd need to find another spot soon. The dust was beginning to accumulate behind the bushes.

He headed for the medical ward, careful to keep his shoulders straight and his steps even. He made it to the second level without incident. When he reached the scanner, though, he had to wave his bracelet a second time past the scanner to enter. He'd moved too fast the first time. The chelvah behind him had tilted his head slightly to watch him.

Sweat broke out over Thor's body. *Careless. I need to be more careful.* He pulled open the door. The chelvah behind him followed him in. Thor was more aware of him behind him than he liked. It was a struggle to keep his breathing even. And he realized he had not glanced at his bracelet to see what room he was supposed to head to.

The hair along Thor's neck stood on end. He couldn't just walk around. He needed to check his station.

He was reaching the end of the hall. The chelvah behind him peeled off and entered the room to his right. Thor quickly checked his wrist. His room was at the end of the hall.

His heart still raced as he replaced the avad at the door. He stood straight, keeping his focus in front of him while taking slow, easy breaths.

I can do this. I just need to focus.

~

THOR NEARLY FELL ASLEEP STANDING up. He jerked his eyes open. He'd let his mind drift off. He'd thought about Xe and the dreams he'd had last night. Before he knew it, his eyelids were closing.

He watched the other chelvah in the hall, but none had turned toward him. At least his security lapse had gone undetected. But he desperately needed to stretch out his legs. They felt stiff from standing in the same position. How had he done this before? Did the Ka Sama also have some sort of pain relief in it?

His bracelet vibrated, making him frown as he glanced down. He flicked his wrist over. Landing Pad.

His heart began to race. Had they figured him out? Were they finally—

Two chelvah from down the hall peeled off from the doorway and headed for the exit. Thor did the same, once again taking more deep breaths. He could not function like this. He might have to take the Ka Sama tonight just to make sure he got some sleep. He was making too many mistakes.

He followed the other chelvah down the stairs, through the halls, and out the front door. The air was a little cooler, which helped clear his head. He wanted to yank off his helmet and gulp in huge lungfuls of the stuff, but he had to settle for enjoying the coolness slipping through the rim of his helmet.

A veerfinah was landing up ahead. Thor frowned. What was going on? The veerfinah arrived at the beginning and end of each shift. In between, it flew back to the mothership.

The marchelvah stood waiting, his legs braced as the veerfinah touched down. Dust blew up, but the marchelvah did not move. Thor took his place and lined up behind him next to the other avad.

The ramp of the veerfinah lowered. Thor peered inside the dark interior, curious as to what was responsible for this change to the schedule. Two chelvah appeared, a human woman with long blonde hair between them. She was shaking so hard Thor did not think she would be able to stand on her own. The chelvah pulled her along, Her feet dragged in the ground, leaving tracks.

They walked up to the first two chelvah and handed her off. The Unwelcome stood with her clasped between their arms. Then the chelvah disappeared into the ship, reappearing with another woman. They made four more trips, handing over six women—all *human* women. Thor gripped the woman he had been handed by the arm. He watched her from the corner of his eyes. Unlike the others, she did not cower. She looked straight ahead, her face resolved. But he could see her pulse pounding away in her neck.

He felt his own pulse moving rapidly, because unlike the other women, he knew this one.

She was one of Lyla's.

89

As soon as the women were offloaded from the ship, the marchelvah took the lead and headed into the breeding facility. One by one, each of the pairs of chelvahs followed, dragging their prisoner with them.

Thor did the same when it was his turn, his mind racing. If they were bringing the women here, it had to be for breeding purposes. Arthur had mentioned that the classes of chelvah had been growing smaller in number over the last few years. The Naku must have decided they needed a new source.

Fear for his sister flashed through him. Did that mean they would get rid of the other breeders? It was possible. But he knew that would take a little time. They would need to make sure this new pool worked first. But getting his sister out of here was no longer a hope; it was now a necessity.

They followed the marchelvah up to the third level of the medical wing. Each pair of chelvahs pulled their prisoner into a separate room. Thor headed to the last room. His partner went through the door first, pulling the woman with him. The woman slammed a sidekick into his knee as soon as they crossed the threshold. Surprised by the move, he loosened his grip on her.

She wrenched her arm from his grip before landing a brutal kick to the avad's groin.

His knees buckled. She tried to yank her arm from Thor, but he held on. The other chelvah was hurt but not down. He stood, his hand curling into a fist. Thor grabbed the woman, wrapping his arms around her in a bear hug while placing himself between her and the other chelvah. The woman struggled in his arms.

He tightened his hold, lowering his head to her ear. "Do not fight. You will only get yourself killed. I will tell Lyla where you are."

She went still, her gaze flying to his helmet. A Naku bustled in with guards. *Keep her still.*

Thor cringed against the mental intrusion but did as he was ordered. One of the Naku's chelvah plunged a needle into the woman's arm. Her eyes closed, and had Thor not held her, she would have crumpled to the ground.

He picked her up and placed her in the bed. The chelvah she'd struck secured her arms to the bed with the restraints. Thor did the same on his side before moving to strap down her legs.

Then he stepped out of the room, taking position outside the door. It looked like he would not be getting that good night's sleep tonight after all.

90

Riley was worried. Jamal was not acting like himself. He had raced off after the ship, continuing at a breakneck pace even long after they had lost it. And once they lost visual, there was no hope they'd find it again.

But Riley had followed him, not sure he'd be able to stop Jamal from continuing to search. They'd ridden for hours before Jamal slowed. The direction they had found themselves heading in led near the meeting spot with Thor. Riley didn't want to take Jamal back to the camp. He was so worked up, he needed time to cool off. So he headed in that direction. Thor wasn't supposed to make contact for a few days, but it was the only safe location he knew nearby.

"Where are we going?" Jamal asked as Riley turned toward the meeting site.

"I thought we'd camp out here. I know a spot."

Jamal shook his head. "No. We need to get back to the camp, make a plan to—"

"Jamal, Lyla will be doing everything she can from there to find Addie. It's hours away. The best thing we can do is get a good night's sleep so we're rested for whatever rescue plan Lyla comes up with."

"Sleep? I can't sleep."

"You need to try. For Addie's sake. Besides, the horses need a rest. Now come on."

Jamal looked ready to argue again, but then his shoulders slumped, and he simply nodded. Riley would have preferred if he had argued. Right now, he just looked broken.

Riley set about making camp while Jamal sat up on a rock, not even offering to help. Riley wasn't even sure he was aware what Riley was doing. He glanced over at Jamal. "Hey, are you hungry? Do you want to—"

"A ship!" Jamal jumped off the rock and sprinted into the woods.

Damn it. Riley took off after him. Jamal was moving incredibly fast ... and loudly. It was like he had forgotten absolutely everything he'd ever been taught. Riley caught sight of the veerfinah ahead, and it was landing.

Oh no. He put on a burst of speed, tackling Jamal around the waist. Jamal went down with a grunt. "What are you doing? Let me go! We need to—"

Riley held him down. "Stop it! What are *you* doing? You don't know if she's in that ship. The only people we know for sure are in that ship are Unwelcome. And if you run at them, you'll get dusted."

"But Addie—"

"We don't know she's in there. Most likely, she's not. But we'll check it out. Do this smart. I mean, what would Addie say if she saw you now?"

A ghost of a smile crossed his face. "She'd tell me I'm an idiot."

"Yes, she would." Riley climbed off him and held out his hand. "Now let's go see what's going on."

Jamal gripped Riley's hand and let him help him up. "But we are getting on that ship."

"Yes, we are." Riley started moving quickly through the woods, listening intently for any sounds that didn't belong around him. Jamal stayed behind him, relieving a little of Riley's worry about him.

The veerfinah had landed in a clearing. Riley realized it was the same clearing where he met Thor. He slowed as he approached. The ramp was just lowering. Was it possible Thor had—

Jamal shoved past him, bursting into the clearing. "Addie!"

Riley raced after him as an Unwelcome stepped off the ramp. Jamal swung his staff at the Unwelcome's head. He ducked and caught the staff on the back swing, wrenching it from Jamal's hand. Jamal charged, but the Unwelcome slipped the move and grabbed him from behind.

"Stop," the Unwelcome ordered.

Riley reached the two of them, not sure what to do. No power rolled through him. "Thor?"

The Unwelcome nodded. "Yes."

Jamal struggled in his arms. "Let me go!"

But Thor held on to him, apparently not sure that Jamal wouldn't launch himself at him again. Riley walked up and grabbed Jamal's arms. "Jamal. Jamal!"

Jamal quit his struggles, his chest heaving, and stared at Riley.

"It's Thor, okay? Now, he's going to let you go." Riley glanced up at Thor.

Thor released Jamal, taking a step back. Jamal crumpled to the ground. Thor removed his helmet, tucking it into his side. "What's going on?"

"His ..." Riley struggled for the right word to use for Addie and Jamal's relationship. They had never officially declared they were together, but everyone knew they were. "Friend was taken by a patrol this morning."

"I know. That's why I'm here. I know where she is."

Jamal's head jolted up. "What? Where is she? Is she all right?"

"I'm not sure how all right she is. She was"—he paused —"okay when I last saw her."

"Where is she?" Riley asked.

"The breeding facility."

Riley's mouth fell open. "What?"

The idea of it staggered and disgusted Riley. He looked down at Jamal, whose face was frozen in a look of horror before he lunged for Thor. "You did this! You knew we wouldn't help you, so you told them where Addie was!"

Thor grabbed Jamal's hands, gripping him tightly. "No. I did not."

Jamal struggled against him. "You did! It's the only way—"

"I did not!" Thor yelled before lowering his voice. "I couldn't. I didn't know they were taking humans. This is the first time I've seen any humans at the facility."

"Why would they bring humans?" Riley asked.

"Our births have been on the decline for the last few years. I believe they may be looking for a new source." He slowly released Jamal, who stumbled back, his chest heaving. "She was brought in earlier today along with five other human women."

"Can you tell us exactly where it is?" Riley asked.

Thor nodded. "As well as the security on site."

"Good. We'll need all of that."

Thor took a breath. "You'll stage a rescue?"

Riley nodded. "As soon as we can. I need all the information you can give me."

"Will you rescue all the women?"

Riley nodded again, wondering at Thor's tone. "Of course."

Thor stared at him. "*All* the women? And the children?"

Riley looked up into his face. Thor didn't have to come tell them about Addie. He didn't have to help them outside the Lab, either, but he had. "Yes. We're saving all of them."

∼

RILEY GOT every detail he could think of out of Thor. He made him repeat the layout, the numbers, and the schedules over and over again. Only when he was convinced that Thor had told him everything was he content to let him go. He and Jamal had set off immediately for their camp.

Thor was going to meet them each night until they came up with a rescue plan. He pictured Thor's face when he asked about helping his sister. And for the first time, Riley felt a connection to the man. The idea of Addie being in that facility twisted him up inside. Thor had watched his sister in there, not being able to help. He tried to imagine trading places with him, watching Maisy be in there. It was too painful to even think about.

And he realized that his inability to imagine himself in Thor's place had made him immune to Thor's pain. But his pain was no different than Riley's. But unlike Thor's sister, Addie had people who would risk life and limb to get her back. Thor was the only one fighting for his sister and nephew, and he hadn't been able to figure out how to help them on his own.

What a helpless feeling. Guilt roared through him. The Unwelcome had killed people he loved, but they were slaves. Most were still asleep, but Thor wasn't. And he had come to help them at great risk to himself. Even telling them about Addie was a risk. From what Arthur said, every aspect of their lives was controlled. Sneaking out to meet with them and warn them meant he was risking his life every single time. And Riley had never truly appreciated that until now.

He was going to convince Lyla and the rest of the people that they needed to help the other women at the facility. At the end of the day, it was the right thing to do.

91

The loading bay was empty as Thor stepped out of the veerfinah. He quickly punched in the code to raise the ramp and winced as it shut with a thump. He felt hot and cold at the same time. He had felt this way the last three times he had taken the veerfinah. He was not sure, but he thought it was what the humans called nerves.

He quickly made his way through the bay. It was dark with only emergency lights on at the edge of the large room. He hurried down the main path between the ships, not liking being out in the open. He had never run into anyone, but it still made him nervous. Until he was back in his bunk, he would not relax. He reached for the keypad next to the door to the hall.

"What are you doing?"

Thor snatched his hand back and whirled around.

An Unwelcome stood there, its helmet obscuring its features. Thor's helmet was tucked into his side. He had not wanted to put it on until the very last moment. He hated the blasted thing now.

His mind scrambled, but he could not think of anything to say. And avad did not speak to one another. The fact that this one *was* speaking ... "Why do you want to know?"

The avad hesitated and then reached up and removed its helmet. He recognized her. She had been the avad in the bunk next to him that one night. The one who had asked what was going on. "I have watched you sneak out of your bunk three times now."

"And you followed me? Why?"

She frowned before shaking her head. "I do not know. I do not even know why I am awake."

Thor could tell she was confused. He remembered feeling the same way when the effects of the Ka Sama had started to fade. "You are no longer controlled by the Naku as you once were."

"But why?"

He wanted to tell her. He wanted to feel like he was in this with someone. But he could not risk his sister's life on a stranger keeping his secret. But he also did not want to lie to her. "I cannot say."

She studied him for a long moment before she spoke. "I ... I find myself having thoughts that I don't understand. They are not thoughts I have had before."

"I have had the same thing."

Fear flashed across her face. "What if the Naku find out?"

"We cannot let them know. You must behave as you always have."

"It will be difficult. It *has* been difficult."

"I know. But it is the only way. We should go before someone finds us."

"Yes." She placed her helmet back on. Thor did the same. "What is your name?"

"I-It's Pxedlin."

"I am Geothorxed. But I prefer Thor."

She nodded and reached for the door controls. Her hand paused, hovering in the air next to the panel. Her voice was so low, Thor had to strain to hear her. "I find myself wanting."

He stared down at her. "What do you want?"
She ran her bracelet under the scanner. "More."

92

Riley and Jamal stumbled into New Attlewood just as dawn was breaking. Otto and Angela were on duty at the front gate. Angela disappeared as soon as she caught sight of them while Otto hurried out to meet them. "Any luck?"

Riley nodded. "We know where she is."

Jamal said nothing. In fact, he'd said nothing ever since they'd left Thor. Angela reappeared at the gate, Lyla at her side. Ten minutes later, Riley and Jamal were sitting at a table in the kitchen area. Frank, Arthur, Montel, Miles, and Petra met them there. Emma and Edna were already there and placed heavy pots of coffee on the table.

Riley drank some thankfully and quickly explained every-thing they had learned from Thor. He shot glances at Jamal throughout his report, but he simply sat with his hands wrapped around his coffee mug. He didn't drink from it, just held it as it grew cold, his gaze unfocused.

Riley fielded the questions that everyone raised until finally everyone fell silent. He knew they needed a chance to digest everything. But now he had a question of his own. "Thor asked us to help save his sister as well as the other women in the facility. I know not everyone thinks that's a priority, but I think we should do it."

Lyla raised an eyebrow. "That's a bigger rescue. It would be easier to just rescue the human women."

Riley met her gaze. "I know. But I also know that those other women are no less prisoners than Addie. And no one's coming for them."

Lyla studied him for a long moment. "I agree."

"Wait, wait." Frank put up his hands. "How do we know Addie's even there? Isn't it convenient that she showed up in the exact place his sister is? Maybe he tipped them off."

Otto shook his head. "That patrol wasn't looking for us. It was just plain bad luck."

"And I don't think he's lying," Riley said. "And you know what, if it was Maisy, I'd damn well lie, cheat, and steal to help her. I don't blame Thor for using this opportunity to help his sister."

Everyone went quiet. More than a few kept their gazes on the tabletop. Finally, Miles spoke. "Did Thor say anything about the Ka Sama? Is he seeing any changes in behavior?"

Riley nodded. "A little." They spoke for another hour, drafting out the rough outline of a plan. And it was rough. But he and Lyla would go back and speak with Thor and have him fill in a few necessary details tonight, and hopefully then they'd have a fully fleshed out plan.

The entire time they spoke, Jamal said nothing. He didn't even move. Montell finally walked over and touched his shoulder. "Jamal? Why don't I take you back to your cabin so you can get some sleep?"

Jamal's shoulders began to shake. Montell's hand hovered in the air behind Jamal's back for a moment before he placed it again on his shoulder. "It's going to be okay. We'll get her—"

Jamal threw back his head and laughed. He laughed until tears rolled down his cheek. Everyone stared at him, not sure what to do. He had lost it.

Finally, Jamal stopped laughing. He stood up, wiping the tears from his cheeks. "She's at a breeding facility." He looked around the table. "Don't you see? That's the funny part. She doesn't need a breeding facility."

His face crumpled. "Because she's already pregnant."

93

Addie was pregnant. Jamal's announcement landed with the impact of a bomb. *Oh my God. No wonder Jamal was in such a state.* After his announcement, sobs tore through him. Montell gathered him up and led him away.

Lyla watched him go with a sense of disbelief. She, Jamal, and Addie had been the closest of friends for years. When the two of them had finally admitted what everyone else had known, no one had been happier for them than Lyla. Addie hadn't told her about the baby, but she also wasn't showing, which meant she had to be very early on.

But the idea of Addie and Jamal's child being in the hands of the Naku ... everything in her tensed up at the thought. She remembered the Naku she'd killed on the ship. He had been without care, without emotions. And from what Arthur described, the lives of the children of his people were more of a struggle to survive than what even they had experienced here on Earth.

And she remembered what that human trashcan Chad Keyes had said about the Naku's mental gifts. How they burrowed holes through an individual's brain as they sought their answers. If they realized how Addie was connected to them …

Lyla forced herself to stay seated even though she wanted to stand and scream. "Okay. Riley and I will meet with Thor tonight and finish up the rest of the details. I'm going to need a list of volunteers to see who is willing to help."

"You'll have all the Phoenixes, I have no doubt," Frank said.

Lyla shook her head. "We can't take them all and leave the camp defenseless."

Frank leaned forward. "You will take absolutely everyone that volunteers. Those bastards don't get to—" He took a deep breath, his hands shaking and his eyes suspiciously bright. "We're getting Addie back."

"We are."

Frank stood, staring her in the eyes before he strode away. Lyla watched him go. Addie was like another daughter to him. God, she was so well liked and respected in the camp that the news of her abduction would hit everyone hard. And Frank was right. Lyla wasn't going to leave anyone behind that wanted to help.

She turned to Riley. "You need to get some sleep."

"No, I'm—"

"Riley, you did great. And I'm going to need you tonight, so please, get some sleep?"

His shoulders drooped. "Okay."

Lyla glanced over at Miles. "I need you to gather some medical supplies, whatever you think we'll need for the mission."

"You got it."

Petra stood as well. "I'll help him."

Lyla nodded. Now it was only her and Arthur. Her fears and worries were pressing against the back of her eyes. She had slept little last night, going over and over again what she could have done differently for Addie not to be taken. And then she had imagined everything she could do to find her. There had been precious little.

"Okay. I'm going to go check on our weapon supplies. I'll see you later." She didn't meet his eyes as she hurried from the table. She kept her face neutral as she headed for the nearest camp exit. She nodded at people who met her gaze, but no one was really smiling this morning.

She slipped through the gate, nodding at Rory, who stood guarding the entrance.

"Everything okay, Lyla?" he asked.

"Yup," she said but didn't stop. She headed for the tree line. She walked twenty feet in, then leaned against a tall oak and bowed her head. *Addie.*

Her arms wrapped around her waist. Her chest felt like it was being carved open. A breeding facility. Horror, disgust, and terror rolled through her. Tears rolled down her cheeks.

And then she was being pulled into an embrace. Arthur's arms wrapped around her. She leaned into his strength. She didn't say anything, and neither did he. Nothing needed to be said. It was all horrible. And there was nothing to do except share the horror.

94

Thor barely remembered the trip back to the mothership last night. He had crashed on his bunk and slept hard. So hard he had not even felt his bracelet vibrate. A kick to his leg woke him. He jolted upright, recognizing Pxedlin as she moved past him.

He quickly sat up and grabbed his helmet, falling in line with the other avads. He still felt like he was sleepwalking as he made his way through breakfast and onto the veerfinah. He found himself sitting next to Pxedlin. He reached for his strap. "Thank you," he said quietly.

She nodded her head in response.

That small acknowledgement somehow changed everything about that trip down to the planet. He found himself shifting the slightest bit closer to her, his arm resting against hers. And she didn't pull away.

It was stupid, such a small little thing, one arm leaning against another, and yet the comfort it offered was immense. He felt like maybe for the first time, he wasn't completely alone here.

The day went by quickly. He was stationed in the supply room. He spent most of the day moving crates and carrying them to the correct department. It was an ideal time for it because it allowed him glimpses of different parts of the facility. He tucked all the new information away to relay to Riley that night.

He was on the last run of the day. He deposited a load of fresh blankets to one of the women's dorms. He had just dropped them off and was returning when a shout went up.

A small blue figure tore down the hall, a larger Unwelcome running after him. Thor quickly moved to intercept and grabbed the child, pulling him into his arms.

It was his nephew.

Little Geothorxed's mouth fell open, and he stared at Thor. But then Thor realized it wasn't him he was staring at, but his own reflection. He wondered if the boy had ever seen himself before.

Xe hurried around the corner, stopping short when she saw her son in Thor's arm. She began to shake. "Please, let me have him."

The marchelvah intercepted her. "Your child is unruly. He will be written up, as will you." The marchelvah waved Thor forward. "Return him to his ward."

Thor strode down the hall, the boy incredibly light in his arms. Xe fell in step next to him. Thor's heart rate picked up. She was right there. His sister was right there. Slowly, he slid the cuff up on his sleeve.

They reached the door to their ward. Thor reached for the door handle, turning his arm so the scar would be visible. Xe gave a little gasp.

Thor opened the door and handed her son to her. "I remember you, Xe," he said quietly before letting the door close between them.

95

Lyla stood in front of the group of volunteers in front of the stables. Justin, his arms crossed over his chest, stood with his people toward the back of the group. Not as volunteers but watching to see what she was up to. She ignored them.

As expected, all of the Phoenixes had volunteered, as had all of the Cursed. The younger Cursed wouldn't be allowed to join them, but she appreciated the enthusiasm. She and Lewis had gone over the plan, looking for flaws. He had also agreed to join them, as had both his children. Lyla was glad to have him. One extra seasoned warrior made it easier to delegate responsibilities. He stood next to her now, much like she had seen him stand next to Meg. Arthur stood on her other side.

Emma and Edna stood along the side, their arms wrapped around Maisy and Iris. Other non-Phoenixes also lined up, including Frank. They would be leaving with the volunteers and heading to establish the new camp at the estate.

Maisy gave her a small smile. Lyla returned it, then searched the crowd for Riley and Miles. They stood with Adros, Rory, Petra, and Tabitha. For a moment it wasn't them as they were now, but five years ago, all gangly and young. Her breath caught.

She didn't want any of them to be a part of this fight. But this fight was coming to them no matter what. Lyla had at least given them the tools to fight back. And each one was a formidable warrior in their own right. She took solace in that as she turned back to scan the crowd one more time, making eye contact with as many as she could. "None of you have to go. This is purely voluntary."

No one said anything.

"We won't only be saving Addie and the other human women at the facility. We will also be saving the Unwelcome women who have been imprisoned there."

The grumbling she expected began. She held up a hand, cutting off anyone's chance to speak. "I know what you're thinking. Why should we help them? They certainly haven't helped us."

More than a few heads nodded in agreement.

"The Unwelcome women at the facility are not like the other Unwelcome. They are slaves, but they are not drugged. It is believed they did not because the drug would interfere with their ability to reproduce. So they are left drug-free while they are impregnated, during their pregnancy, and for the two years after the birth of their child. Then their child is taken from them, and they are drugged into accepting that loss. They remain in that state for a year."

All eyes were on Lyla now. "These women are slaves. They have no say in what happens to themselves or their children. And that is a future the Naku are trying to begin for the women of our planet. If you cannot wrap your head around the idea of helping the Unwelcome, think of taking the women and children from their facility as a way of defeating the Naku. Their lives depend on having the Unwelcome to protect them. We're going to take one very large brick out of the wall they have built around themselves. Because make no mistake, our assault on the facility is only the beginning of us taking back our planet."

She paused. "Now I ask again, who is with me?"

Hands raised.

"Who is with me?" she asked louder.

Yells greeted her.

She shook her head, yelling. "Who is with me?"

Almost every person yelled.

She nodded, her voice strong, not betraying any of her doubts or fears, and led the way toward the entrance of the camp.

Justin hustled around the group to intercept her. "You can't do this. Those women aren't worth risking all our protections."

"Addie is up there."

"I know, I know. But still—" He reached out to grab her arm. She stopped him with a look.

His hand curled back as if singed. "You're leaving us without any protection."

"You have walls and the guards you trained. I'm not making anyone go with us. Maybe you should have treated people differently."

Justin's face screwed up, his mouth pinching, his eyes becoming slits. "You never should have been allowed back in, you or any of the Cursed."

Lyla ignored him.

"Maybe I'll have a conversation with the Naku. Tell them where there's a group of Cursed who—"

Lyla's hand shot out and grabbed Justin's throat. She kicked the inside of his right knee before shooting her heel into his left. He crashed to the ground. Keeping her hand on his throat, she angled his head up. "If I ever think you pose a threat to me or my people, I will end you."

He scrabbled at her hand.

"Do you understand me?"

He nodded, his face reddening. She shoved him away. He crumbled back, gasping for breath. She eyed each of the people with him. "That goes for all of you."

They all nodded back at her. With a final glare, she headed for the entrance. Lewis fell in step with her, arching an eyebrow. "So we're not playing nice anymore?"

"I've never played nice with people who threaten mine."

Lewis smiled. "Me, either."

96

L yla sent half the group on to the estate. Frank, along with Montell, a handful of the Phoenixes, and the younger Cursed were all going along. Montell had balked at the idea of staying out of the fight, but Lyla knew she needed fighters who could teach the younger ones if this mission went badly.

Now the rest of the group stood waiting on the edge of a clearing. Lyla stood, her arms clasped behind her back, watching the sky for Thor. Lewis and Arthur were once again at her sides. Behind her, another three dozen volunteers waited. She knew what each of them was capable of, but this mission was different from any other.

Arthur had been a great ambassador for his people, but many in her group still wondered if this was the right move. But in her gut, she knew it was. They needed to see if the Ka Sama was having the effect they thought it was. And they couldn't risk an assault on a larger, better defended target. All told, the breeding facility only had about two dozen guards. They should be able to take it relatively easily.

And besides, with Addie there, even if the rest of them hadn't agreed, she would have gone. She wasn't leaving her there to be experimented on. She glanced over to where Jamal stood, fingering his knife. She was worried about him. Since Addie had been taken, he had been beside himself. She just prayed he kept it together.

Arthur nudged her shoulder. "Lyla."

Her gaze flew to the sky. A veerfinah was approaching. As it grew near, she realized it was larger than the one Thor usually stole. It made its way steadily toward them, growing in size. Lyla swallowed, nerves crawling over her. She was about to tell her people to willingly step into an Unwelcome ship. What if this was just a huge trap to get her and the Cursed?

She didn't think the Unwelcome or the Naku had that kind of imagination, though. But they did work with humans. She was putting a lot of faith in an Unwelcome who had been their captive not that long ago.

"Having second thoughts?" Lewis asked.

"Second, third, and fourth as well," she murmured low enough for only him and Arthur to hear.

"What does your gut tell you? Is he on the level?" Lewis asked.

"Yes."

"Then I guess we're doing this. One side's got to take the first step to trust, right?"

"Right."

"And actually he came to us. That shows a little trust on his part, too."

"I guess it does."

Everyone got to their feet as the veerfinah started to land in the clearing.

Lyla took a breath and turned to Lewis. "Keep everyone here." She caught Riley's gaze across the clearing. He headed toward her. Arthur joined them as well. The three of them crossed the clearing as the ramp began to lower.

As soon as the ramp touched the ground, Thor walked down it.

"He never wears his helmet when he meets us anymore," Riley observed.

"Probably so we can identify him," Lyla said.

"No," Arthur said softly. "Once the helmet is off and your eyes are open, it is the most difficult thing in the world to put it back on."

Lyla glanced up at him and knew it wasn't just Thor he was talking about.

Thor's whole body was rigid until he caught sight of the three of them walking toward him. "You came."

"You thought we wouldn't?" Riley asked.

"I wasn't sure."

"Everything okay on your part?"

Thor nodded. "So far. But the chelvah, they're different. Whatever you did, it seems to be working."

"Have any said anything or done anything to indicate they're against the Naku?"

"No, but neither have I. I can only hope that when the opportunity presents itself, they do."

Lyla nodded. That was the best they could hope for. She had hoped maybe a small rebellion was brewing, but that was probably too much to expect in such a small time period.

"We should get everyone on board. It's not a short trip."

Lyla studied him and then the quiet ship. "Riley, Arthur, check the ship."

Riley immediately headed up the ramp. Arthur hesitated for only a moment before following.

She looked at Thor. "Does this bother you?"

He shook his head. "I wouldn't trust me, either."

Riley and Arthur were back just a few minutes later. "It's all clear. There's no one on board."

Lyla took a deep breath and then looked back at the woods where her people were waiting for her signal. She raised her hand. "Then let's get everyone on board."

97

It was difficult to make out what exactly was happening in the clearing, which only made Vel's frustration grow. First, he had wasted time trekking back to Attlewood. There'd been no sign of Lyla or her Cursed. He'd headed over to Meg's encampment, but Lewis had left days earlier. He'd seen his wife with a baby and had contemplated grabbing them. But Lewis and Pierce would track them down and make them pay for such a violation.

But then luck had shined on them. Lewis returned with his son. They only stayed a few hours before leaving again. He contemplated grabbing them as they left. But he wasn't stupid enough to take Lewis and Pierce on. Grit was good in a fight, so it would be an even match between the four of them.

But Vel didn't do even matches. He only did matches where he was all but guaranteed a win. And just like that, they led him to New Attlewood. A few hours later, Lewis and Pierce rode back out with Lyla and a group of close to a hundred people. An hour later, the group split. He'd debated following the other group, but it had few fighters. He was pretty sure the action was going to be with Lyla.

So he followed her instead.

They'd continued north for four hours before they stopped in the middle of nowhere. At first, he'd thought they were merely taking a break. But an hour passed, and they didn't move. Then an Unwelcome ship appeared in the sky. At first Vel had grown angry, thinking he'd lost out on the bounty. The Unwelcome had already found them.

But by the time he moved to a better spot to see what was going on, the veerfinah had landed. Dusk had hit, but there was still enough light to make out what was happening. He'd hunkered down, waiting for the fight or a chase. But neither happened.

Instead of running from the veerfinah, Lyla had walked up to it with that Unwelcome of hers and one of the Cursed. The ramp lowered, and an Unwelcome appeared. But there was something different about him.

"He's not wearing a helmet," Grit whispered next to him. And he realized she was right.

He frowned. Two Unwelcome who weren't behaving the way Unwelcome were supposed to. What made these two so different? And what exactly were they up to?

Vel watched in disbelief as the humans began to step into the clearing and head for the veerfinah. They all walked up the ramp and disappeared inside.

"Shouldn't we contact the Unwelcome? She's right there," Grit hissed.

Vel shook his head. "Be quiet." He needed to think. Calling the Unwelcome was useless because if they were taking off in a veerfinah, they'd be long gone before they arrived. And he knew that trying to explain what had happened would be equally useless. They were mindless drones.

At least, they usually are.

His gaze focused on the two Unwelcome standing with the humans as the last of Lyla's group entered the ship and disappeared inside and the two Unwelcome followed. After scanning the area, Lyla joined them. The ramp raised, and seconds later, the veerfinah rose into the sky.

"We lost her." Grit stood up.

"We never had her." He stood up, hurrying past her. "Come on."

"Where are we going?" she asked, keeping pace with him.

"New City. We need to talk to someone in charge."

98

The veerfinah gave off a slight hum as they soared through the sky. The first time she had been in a veerfinah, she had been overwhelmed by all the newness of it to take everything in. But now she settled in, enjoying the feel of being high above the earth. As a child, her father had told her stories of planes. They had sounded magical. Now she was standing behind the chair Arthur sat in as he piloted the veerfinah, watching the ground below fly by. It was exhilarating, awe-inspiring, and terrifying all at once.

But the view didn't pull her thoughts from what lay ahead of them: the breeding facility. Even the phrase made Lyla's skin crawl. As a woman, the predilection for certain men to control women through their bodies was a real factor in most women's struggle to survive. It was why her father had started teaching both her and Muriel how to defend themselves from the time they were very young.

But the women in the facility had no protections, no choice but to let their bodies be used to further the Naku's goals.

She wanted to think she would be helping even if Addie and other human women weren't inside. At the same time, she wasn't sure that was true. The idea of Addie being in there, it lit something inside of her and the rest of her people. But the humans wouldn't be their only focus.

While the fact that women were being used against their will angered Lyla, she couldn't help but be amazed that she was actually leading a mission to save Unwelcome. Because, breeders or not, they weren't from Earth. They were part of the species that had stepped off of that mothership and decimated what was left of human society.

When she first saw them back at their old camp at the mill, her mind had almost frozen, trying to categorize who or what they were. And then she had been so busy fighting that what they were gave way to thoughts about what their weaknesses were. Then for the next five years, she was on guard looking out for them, teaching her people, and most importantly the children, how to protect themselves against them. They were the boogeyman come to life.

And now she considered one of them her closest friend. And Thor? She wasn't sure what she considered him. But the term enemy no longer applied.

And that made her worried. She now knew they were a slave race. More than that, they were drugged into submission. They weren't choosing to harm humans. They were being ordered to, and they were helpless to resist. She could feel compassion for them because of it.

But that didn't change the fact that if given the order, they would kill everyone on this ship without a thought. Which meant she couldn't hesitate. Her people couldn't hesitate.

Arthur sat at the controls of the veerfinah. One more test of trust for Thor, allowing Arthur to pilot his ship. Thor, meanwhile, was slumped against the side of the cockpit with dark circles under his eyes. He looked like he hadn't slept much in the last week. Or month. Riley kept his gaze on Thor, a romag snuggled in his arms. Lyla had no doubt how quickly Riley would respond if needed.

"Have you had any problems taking the ship?" she asked, breaking the silence.

He shook his head. "No. I wait until maintenance has been through and then slip out. No one goes into that bay after maintenance until the next shift begins. As long as I am back on time, no one is aware."

"And what about the other Unwelcome?" Riley asked. "Any more changes?"

Thor nodded, running a hand through his hair, an action that just looked so human. "Yes. Almost everyone I've seen is a little different."

"How?" Riley asked.

"They fidget more, a few have had trouble waking in the morning. Many have trouble falling asleep. A few have dropped things and tripped."

"That's it? A little restlessness, a lack of coordination, and poor sleeping habits?" Riley said.

"That's actually quite a lot," Arthur said. "Everything in a chelvah's life is controlled by the Naku, all movements. They do not stumble. They do not fidget without a direct order. This is a good sign."

While Arthur might sound heartened by Thor's report, Lyla's thinking was more in line with Riley's. A few stumbles and shifts of someone's shoulders did not sound very encouraging.

But in her interactions with the Unwelcome, she had to admit she'd never seen such behavior. Of course, they were usually trying to kill her, so she couldn't really be sure.

"And I ..." continued Thor, "I spoke with one."

"You did?" Lyla asked.

Thor nodded. "She helped me this morning when I did not hear the alarm. And she was in the loading bay when I returned the other night."

"She didn't give you away?" Riley asked.

"No."

"Did you tell her about our plans for the facility?" Lyla asked.

He shook his head. "No. And I did not tell her where I had been. She wanted to talk more about what was happening to all of us."

"Do you think she's a threat?" Riley asked.

Thor frowned. "Actually, I think she might be an ally. She is assigned to the breeding facility as well."

Lyla nodded. It was exactly what they had been hoping for.

"We're coming up on the coordinates," Arthur said.

Thor leaned forward. "It's a clearing. The facility is just on the other side of the large southern hill. It should offer us good cover to land without anyone at the facility noticing."

"They aren't monitoring here?" Lyla asked.

"No," Thor said.

"Why not?" Riley asked, his frustration evident. "I mean, if they've got, what, twenty Unwelcome stationed at the facility, they must be concerned about security."

"They are. But not in the way you are thinking," Thor said.

Lyla frowned. "I don't understand."

"They are not worried about an outside force, human or otherwise, breaking into the breeding facility," Thor said.

"Then what's with all the guards?" Riley demanded.

Thor looked at Arthur, who answered for him. "The guards are there to make sure no one gets out."

99

Xantar awoke, his eyelids slowly rising. He floated softly, the substance surrounding him, holding him aloft. He tapped his wrist. The substance shifted beneath him, raising his back and head while lowering his legs. By the time the sleeping capsule opened, he was sitting upright. He stepped from the capsule, holding the railing next to him tightly. He walked toward the cleaning room, contemplating calling for his glider. He felt particularly weak this morning. He would need to increase his nutritional supplements.

He stepped into the cleaning tube, closing his eyes as the foam fell over him before the water washed it away. Keeping his eyes closed as the dry air blew on him, the capsule door slid open as it stopped. Sliding into his tunic and pants, he sat down, tapping on his wrist unit. The door to the room opened, and his glider appeared. He stepped onto it, leaning back, his legs already feeling the relief.

His tablet glowed to life next to him. He frowned as he reviewed it. The human bounty hunter wanted to speak with him. He did not understand these humans. They always needed to talk things over. Things should be done efficiently. Any consideration beyond efficiency was unnecessary.

He could admit, though, that the need to talk things over did highlight one of the Naku's weaknesses: understanding emotions. It required that they rely on the very creatures they were trying to understand to explain their motivations and thereby determine the most efficient means of getting what you needed from them. Generally, reward was enough to get most humans to capitulate. Of course, there were always a few that would not bend. But that was what they had the Unwelcome for.

But the Cursed and Lyla Richards were something even more dangerous than a few stubborn humans. Had he known they existed here, he would have bypassed this planet. But their supplies were low. They would need to replenish before they moved on. And he was beginning to suspect that the warnings he'd been given may have been overblown. While the Cursed had been successful in skirmishes with the avad, they had all been directly related to the welfare of the Cursed.

His new human aide stood at the end of the hall, his head bowed. He looked up. His face was thin, sallow. This one would probably not last much longer than the last one. The humans' minds were so weak, so fragile. They never lasted long.

The human bowed and scraped as Xantar floated past. Xantar ignored him. The doors ahead opened, and he slid into his position on the dais while his mind slipped into the human's.

The human walked to the edge of the platform. "Why are you here?"

Vel, the bounty hunter, stepped forward. "A situation has arisen that you need to be aware of."

"What is it?"

"I found Lyla Richards, but I was unable to track her because she was taken into a veerfinah."

Confusion rippled through Xantar. He had not been

informed of this. He would have been told immediately if she had been brought into custody.

"You are mistaken."

"I am not. She and a group of at least twenty boarded a veer-finah and then flew off, heading north. Two Unwelcome were with them. You have a second traitor."

For a moment, the man's words did not compute. The avad followed the orders of the Naku. They were bred to do so unhesitatingly. The Naku had perfected the selection and training regimen. There were no mistakes.

"You are mistaken," Xantar repeated.

"I am not."

These humans. Weak, imperfect. This one was supposed to be good at his job. He was another example of why the humans needed to be taken firmly in control. The avad were perfect soldiers. They would not conspire with the humans. It was illogical. The Naku held the keys to their survival.

Vel stepped forward. "You asked me to find the woman, and I have—three times. Your people are the ones who let her get away the first time. And now one of your people is helping her. I have done my job. Now I expect to get paid."

Xantar stared down at the man. Disrespect could never be tolerated. Nor could a lack of fear. And there was no fear in this man's face. Once the humans reached that level, there was no turning back.

The man's knees buckled. He dropped to the ground, holding on to his head. A keening wail rose from him before he toppled over to the side. Blood flowed from his ears and his nose.

Xantar's glider turned for the doors. Behind him, the human aide rushed to get the cleaning unit.

The man's words rolled over in Xantar's mind. *You have a second traitor.* It was not possible. They had analyzed the first case extensively and concluded that the avad's exposure to human thought had opened his mind. He had developed empathy for them. They had not foreseen that possibility. But they had already taken the steps to make sure it did not happen again: They had terminated everyone in the translation corps, including the younger ones who had just begun. Flaws were not acceptable.

Besides, they did not need the interpreters anymore. The humans were under control. And there were more like Vel who would report on their own people to benefit themselves. At their heart, humans were simple. They were either driven by love or by reward. They simply had to use the ones driven by reward to keep the ones driven by love in line.

But a second traitor would be a significant flaw. The original flaw had been eradicated entirely. The problem, therefore, should no longer exist. Was the human mistaken? They were a people given to hyperbole and false statements and poor interpretations. Chances were he was mistaken at the very least or lying.

But Xantar could not entirely rule out the possibility that he was not. And that did not sit well with him. He said a ship had been used. That was easy enough to check. Xantar made his way down the hall. He turned the corner and entered the lift in his glider. He rose four levels and headed toward the large room at the end. Glass walls showed the panels inside, the Naku monitoring the ships' operation. He floated through the door. Each Naku stopped what they were doing, putting one finger to their forehead before returning to their work.

The Naku supervisor, Jgohnse walked over. *Leader. What may I do for you?*

I need a readout on the location of all veerfinah.

Xantar could sense Jgohnse's confusion. *They are all located where they should be.*

There have been no derivations?

No. He tapped his tablet, the blue light of the screen reflecting back on his face. Half of the veerfinah were placed on duty, and the other half were in the loading bay. *All is normal.*

Xantar knew Jgohnse's words were accurate. Yet Vel had

spoken of subterfuge. Subterfuge was not the Naku way. It was not part of their genetic makeup. But it was part of the avad's before they were brought into the rovac program.

Xantar found his aide's mind. *Find me a human who is not honest.*

100

A wind blew lightly, and the sun was now high in the blue sky. It was a beautiful day, which just added to the sense of unreality of the whole situation. But at least so far, there was no indication of alarm at the facility. The building remained quiet. Riley sat in a tree two hundred yards from the facility. With his cloak on, no one would even know he was there. Petra was a few trees over, keeping watch as well.

Lyla had stationed people in the trees last night to keep an eye on the facility. So far, it seemed to be exactly as Thor had described. The building itself was one of the buildings from the Before, an old gray square monstrosity made of brick. It stretched up three floors on each of its sides. Lights had shone through the first floor since they had first taken up watch. The night before, lights had blared through some of the other floors, although they had all eventually been extinguished as the night wore on. There were no guards stationed outside the building at any other spot except the front door, supporting Arthur's arguments that the guards were there to keep people in.

He took a shaky breath, fatigue weighing on him. Before he'd come on duty, he'd barely slept, thinking of everything that could go wrong, thinking of Addie and what was happening to her. Jamal had been quiet on the trip here. There was a look in his eyes that made Riley nervous. Otto promised to stay by his side and knock him out if he looked like he was losing it. Riley hoped it didn't come to that.

From Riley's perch, he had seen very little movement since the transport arrived with a group of Unwelcome a few minutes ago. He had watched the line of Unwelcome file out, trying to pick out Thor from amongst them. But with their uniforms, they all looked identical: large, imposing, and terrifyingly anonymous.

Riley was still having trouble accepting that this Thor was the real Thor. He knew that the Ka Sama muted their emotions. He didn't understand how, but Miles did, and he supposed that was good enough for him. But still this plan relied exclusively on Thor's info. What if he was tricking them? Granted, it was a pretty extensive ruse, but it wasn't impossible.

As Thor had said, a second group exited the building as soon as Thor's group replaced them inside. The veerfinah took off, and Riley knew the time was getting close.

An hour later, a bird called out through the trees. He looked over at Petra, who gave him a thumbs-up. He carefully lowered himself to the ground and backtracked, making sure to keep his steps silent. Lyla stood waiting for him. "Well?"

"Everything's quiet. Nothing since this morning's transport."

She nodded, glancing toward the breeding facility. "Then it's time to go."

101

When Thor had stepped off the veerfinah that morning, he'd kept his gaze straight ahead. But the desire to look around to see if he could spot Lyla and her group was almost overwhelming. He'd clenched his fists so hard, he'd nearly drawn blood. He knew the assault wouldn't begin for a few hours, but there had to be someone watching. It had been almost a relief to step into the building and not be able to look for them.

He walked behind Pxedlin. They had sat next to each other on the veerfinah as well. It was strange, knowing who was beneath the helmet. He felt a connection to her. Just a few words exchanged, and all of a sudden he wasn't completely on his own. He didn't know how she would react when everything happened, but he hoped, at the very least, she wouldn't be hurt.

Ahead, the marchelvah scanned bracelets, but he wasn't as efficient as he usually was. The lack of Ka Sama was affecting him or her as well.

When it was his turn, Thor held up his arm. He was assigned to the courtyard. Thor didn't let his relief show. He had been hoping he would be near Xe when the assault began. She would be outside at that time. That was good.

He headed into the building, sliding the Ka Sama from his sleeve. Crushing them, he dropped the dust over the bannister of the front stairs as he climbed, staying focused on keeping his stride unhurried.

He walked out into the courtyard, scanning the space. Two pregnant women he had not seen before were sitting out in the early morning sun.

Across the courtyard, Pxedlin stood guard. She gave him a small nod. He nodded back, careful to make sure no one was watching them. That was the last indication he gave of anything being different.

He focused on the courtyard, keeping his gaze roving, not stopping for too long on any particular spot.

The next hour moved agonizingly slow. Despite his attempts to appear calm, his heart raced. He clenched and unclenched his fists before realizing Pxedlin was watching him. He immediately relaxed his hands.

The bell sounded, and the dozen pregnant women rose from their seats or stopped their walks and headed for the door to their dormitory. Thor watched them go, his anticipation growing.

The door to the mothers' dormitory opened. Expecting his nephew to sprint out first, he was surprised to see two women walk out with their newborns in their arms. He watched as woman after woman entered, each with a child. Eighteen women and nineteen children entered the courtyard. He watched the door expectantly but realized that was all the women who would be entering. His gut tightened. Where was Xe?

He scanned the group. The woman whom Xe often walked with was not there either. His gaze flew back to the two women he had not seen before with their newborns.

No. His heart felt like it dropped to his knees. His gaze flew to the medical wing. They had moved up the shedar. They were taking her son from her right now.

102

Lyla stood on the edge of the trees, hidden from the facility but still able to see it. Riley darted another glance toward it, a frown on his face. Lyla knew Riley had doubts. She had doubts as well. Truth was, in situations like this, there were always doubts.

But what she had said to the volunteers was true: War had already been declared. They had just been losing. This was the first step in seeing how they did at fighting back. She raised her hand, and her people began to appear from the trees. Arthur immediately made his way to her side, wearing an Unwelcome uniform, the helmet tucked into his side. Lyla didn't say anything to any of them. They all knew the plan. They all knew their roles. They all had chosen to be part of this fight.

She placed her wrists together. Arthur slipped the rope over them. She grabbed the end of the rope, holding it in between her palms, giving her the appearance of being bound.

Arthur looked down at her. "Ready?"

She nodded. "Lead the way."

He placed his helmet on. Lyla had to hold back a shudder. He looked like one of them. He gently grabbed her by the upper arm and led her through the trees. The rest of their people kept pace behind them. They'd stay hidden in the trees until Lyla gave the signal.

Arthur paused at the edge of the tree line, looking down at her.

She glanced back at her people, meeting their gazes before nodding at Arthur. He gripped her arm a little more forcefully, pulling her out into view.

The two Unwelcome on duty immediately swung their romags up. Lyla ducked her head, hunching her shoulders, shuffling her steps to look as beaten down as possible.

Arthur kept a tight grip on Lyla's arm as they moved forward. His pace caused her to stumble. He hesitated for the briefest of seconds.

"Don't," Lyla warned, knowing he was going to slow down.

Instead Arthur tightened his grip, pulling her along. Lyla struggled to keep up with him. The marchelvah held up a hand, stopping them as a feeling of warmth spread through Lyla. The marchelvah glanced at its bracelet, looking for the order related to their appearance.

Lyla launched herself at it. Dropping the ropes, her arms sliding around its neck, her elbows digging into its chest as she clasped it by the back of the head and rammed her knee into its chest. She felt at least two ribs crack. It buckled over, and she kneed it two more times before ripping the helmet from it and slamming the side of her hand into its throat. Both hands flew to its throat, its eyes bulging. Lyla slammed her knee into its face, and it toppled back, unconscious.

Arthur had his guard in a choke hold, his arm tight against the guard's throat. The guard sagged, all fight gone. Arthur held it for another second and then let it drop to the ground.

Not a sound came from inside the facility. No one had noticed a thing. Lyla raised her hand. Her people silently sprinted across the open grass toward them.

With a nod at Arthur, she climbed the steps.

103

Thor felt like he was going to jump out of his skin. He wanted to storm into the medical ward and grab Xe and her son, but on his own all he would do is get all of them killed. So he waited, feeling like he was being torn apart as he imagined what was happening in the removal ward. The morning crawled by as if time had intentionally slowed. But finally, he could tell by the height of the sun that the attack should have begun.

Yet everything remained quiet, normal. He had barely been able to hold himself together by waiting for the sun to rise above the wall. Now that it was in position, he could barely think.

Come on. Come on. Where are you? He was having trouble standing still. He strained to hear anything from outside the building.

The door to the courtyard flew open. Thor whirled around as Lyla appeared, two other Cursed behind her, followed by Riley and Arthur, who'd removed his helmet. The women let out a cry at the sight, pulling their children near them.

Pxedlin raised her romag from the opposite side of the courtyard, but Thor yelled out as he stepped in front of them. "No!"

Confused, Pxedlin hesitated.

Thor removed his helmet. "They are here to help. They are rescuing these women. Their lives don't have to be this way. *We* do not have to be this way."

Pxedlin shook her head. "How, then? How are we to be?"

Lyla stepped from behind Thor, putting her hands in the air. "Free. You can be free. Making decisions for yourselves, not spending your lives under the yoke of the Naku, only to be killed when they believe you have outlived your usefulness."

Arthur, Riley, and the Cursed headed for the women across the courtyard. Pxedlin raised her romag again, tracking them, but Thor moved in front of her again. "They are going to help them. Get them out of here. Give them a chance to live."

"Where?"

"We have a place for them to go, for you to go. You can live there. You can help protect the children of your people," Lyla said.

"I—" There was uncertainty in Pxedlin's voice.

He stepped forward. "You said you wanted more. That's what you are being offered."

"Help us. Help us to help them. Please," Lyla said.

Pxedlin stepped forward, lowering her spear. Then she reached up and removed her helmet. Lyla smiled at her before alarm flashed across her face. "Behind you!"

The door opened.

Two Unwelcome stormed in with a Naku behind them. The Unwelcome raised their weapons.

Lyla let off a blast from the romag she carried while Pxedlin did the same.

The Unwelcome fell to the ground. Lyla aimed her own romag at the Naku and burned a hole through its chest.

She turned to the Unwelcome on the ground.

"No." Pxedlin stepped in front of them. "You said we could

have a life. That includes them." She knelt down, keeping Lyla in her view.

"Can you hear me?" Pxedlin asked.

Both the Unwelcome nodded. "You can be free of the Naku if you wish."

The Unwelcome hesitated. Pxedlin leaned forward slowly, reaching for the helmet of the Unwelcome closest to her. It reared back, and Pxedlin stilled. But the Unwelcome then leaned forward. Pxedlin unstrapped the helmet. The Unwelcome had large almond-shaped eyes and short dark hair. He looked between Thor and Pxedlin. "You trust them with our lives?"

Thor nodded. "I do, more than I trust the Naku. You know what will happen to these children. To these women. Help me save them. And in doing so, we can save ourselves as well."

The other Unwelcome took off its own helmet. She had light brown hair and green eyes. There was something about the Unwelcome being unmasked that made them, despite their size, seem human.

"We need to go," Lyla said quietly.

Thor nodded, keeping his gaze on the two in front of Pxedlin. "I know you are in pain, but that pain will keep you from being controlled by the Naku. You can stay here and wait for them to retrieve you. Or you can come with us. The choice is yours."

The female looked down at her side. "They will terminate us rather than heal us."

"Yes," Pxedlin agreed.

"I will go with you," she said.

"Me too," the man said.

The woman got to her feet, but Pxedlin had to help the man to his. Lyla moved to the door. "Okay, let's get these women and children out of here. We've emptied the dormitory and the first wing."

Thor let out a breath, knowing the danger from Pxedlin had

passed. Arthur was already hurrying toward the women, two of the Cursed with him. Riley moved to Thor's side. "Everything's set. We just need to get them—"

"My sister's not here. She's been taken to the medical ward."

Riley nodded. "Then let's go get her."

104

It was an hour before the thief was brought before Xantar. The man stood in the audience room. Xantar stared down at him from the elevated dais. He was thin, his skin pockmarked, and his gaze seemed incapable of staying focused on one spot for too long. It continuously flittered around the room.

"You have been charged with theft from four other humans in New City," his human aide said.

The man jumped. "No, no. I didn't do it. Someone is trying to frame me."

Xantar was not familiar with the term. "'Frame' you?"

"Yeah, exactly."

"If I may speak, Your Excellency?" Alan, the man who had replaced Chad Keyes as the human liaison, stepped forward from the edge of the room, where he'd been in shadow. When the lights caught his velvet robe, it shimmered.

"You may speak."

"This ... human," Alan said, his words dripping with disgust, "is saying that he is not responsible for his crimes. That others are attempting to make him look guilty."

"Is this possible?"

The man looked at Alan hopefully.

"No," Alan said with finality. The hope fled the man's face. "He was seen entering the domiciles of each of the victims and then seen trying to sell the items he stole from them."

Xantar did not understand this aspect of humans. Jobs were given. They were provided with enough sustenance to survive. Why would they need or want more than that?

"That matter is of no concern to me. A human has claimed that there is a traitor amongst the avad. He claims the traitor has taken one of our ships to give aid to an enemy. The ships that are on duty and in maintenance have all been accounted for. Can you explain how a traitor would have possibly used a ship?"

"This is why you brought me here?" the man asked.

"Yes."

"Uh, what do I get out of this?"

"You will not be held responsible for your crimes."

The man smiled. "All right, then. So you got somebody saying one of your guys used a ship and you can't figure out how?"

"Yes."

"Where are the ships kept?"

"When they are not in use, in the loading bay."

"Hm. And when they're not in use, are they watched?"

"No. There is no need, for they are not in use."

"Does anybody go into the bay?"

"Maintenance checks the ships when they are taken off duty."

"How long is maintenance there?"

"Two hours."

"So how long is no one in the bay with the ships?"

"Ten hours."

"Well, there you go." The man crossed his arms over his chest.

Xantar did not understand, and he did not like the feeling. "Explain."

"You're kidding, right?"

Xantar sent a tendril of pain through the man's skull.

The man winced, doubling over. "Okay, okay."

Xantar removed the pain, and the man stood. Sweat had broken across his forehead. "Somebody's probably sneaking into the bay after maintenance and stealing a ship."

"The ships are all accounted for at the start of each shift."

The man shrugged. "So whoever it is returns them before the shift. Kind of like taking it out for a joy ride."

"All the avad are sleeping at that time."

"You sure about that?"

They did not monitor the avad's sleep. There was no need. They took the Ka Sama and went to sleep. It had been that way for centuries. This made no sense.

"If I may, sir," Alan said, inclining his head.

"What is it?"

"I have heard that there was a problem with one of the other avad. Perhaps another one has been infected with the same affliction."

"We eradicated that affliction and any opportunity for it."

"Of course, of course," Alan said quickly. "I am suggesting that another, similar type of affliction may have befallen some-one. Are there any avad you have had concerns about?"

Xantar stared down at the man and then turned and left the room. He tapped on his bracelet, summoning Aek to his office.

As he settled himself at his console, his monitor beeped. Aek inclined her head. *I am on Earth. What can I do for you, Esteemed Leader?*

The two avad that were taken prisoner. The female remains in observation?

Yes.

Send me the schedule for the male.

Aek looked down. *Done.*

Xantar scanned it as soon as it arrived. The avad was in his sittu at the times they believed the veerfinah was taken. He was currently at one of their breeding facilities.

Send a retrieval team for Avad 18-F. When he returns, I want a complete medical assessment done on him.

Aek nodded. *Yes, Esteemed Leader. What am I looking for?*

Free will.

105

Riley stood in the stairwell outside the medical ward. They'd made it there without any problems. The humans had already been evacuated. Addie and the others were on the ship, and he'd grabbed Rory and Pierce on the way up.

Thor reached for the door, but Riley gripped his arm. "You realize to save your sister, you may have to shoot some of your people?"

Thor shook him off. "She and her son are all that matter."

"And us," Riley muttered. "Protecting the guys helping you, that matters too."

Thor turned back to him. "What?"

"I'm just saying, maybe ... you know what, never mind. Let's just go."

Thor waved his bracelet over the scanner. The light stayed red. He waved it again. Nothing. Thor looked up at Riley, concerned.

"Back up." Riley aimed his romag at the door lock. Thor stepped to the side, and Riley pulled the trigger. The lock disappeared in a cloud of sparks.

Thor yanked the door open and rushed through. Riley was

right behind him. Three Unwelcome were in the hall just beyond the doorway, along with a Naku.

Riley paused for a split second at the sight of the Naku. He'd barely gotten a glance at the one in the courtyard before Lyla took it out. Even though Lyla and Arthur had described them, he was shocked at how fragile looking they were. These were the boogeymen that had destroyed so many lives? The architects of the New World?

This one let out a squeal and rushed into a nearby room. Two Unwelcome followed it, leaving one in the hall.

"We've got them!" Rory yelled as he and Pierce followed them in.

With a roar, Thor tackled the Unwelcome, slamming its head to the floor. Yanking off the helmet, he slammed his fist into the being's chin. Riley glanced in the first door. Three female Unwelcome lay in beds, attached to drips of some sort. Riley ran into the room. He disconnected each of the drips, not sure how long it would take the women to come around. He'd need help getting them downstairs.

He headed to the other room and found three more. By the time he'd disconnected the third drip, the woman in the first bed had her eyes open. Riley looked into her bright green eyes. He slowly put up his hands. "I'm not here to hurt you. I'm here to help. Can you walk?"

She nodded slowly.

"Can you try to help these other women? I need to check in the other rooms."

"O-okay." She paused. "You are a human."

He shook his head. "Not exactly. But that's a long story for another time. We need to go. We're taking all of you somewhere safe."

"My ... my child. They took her."

"When?"

"Not long. This morning, I think."

"If she's still here, we'll find her."

The woman nodded, sitting up. She stepped onto the floor and swayed for a moment. Riley quickly steadied her.

She looked down at him. "Th-thank you."

He nodded. "You all right?"

"Yes. I'll get the others."

He released her and slipped into the other room. He was finishing up in the third room when a romag blast sounded from down the hall.

106

R iley skidded to a stop in the doorway two doors down. Thor was on the ground, just getting to his feet. A tall, thin Unwelcome stood with a romag in her arms. Twirling it around, she pulled the trigger, sending the Naku soaring across the room with a shriek.

Thor looked up at her.

She smiled. "We've all been holding our children for the last two years. We might not be as strong as the chelvah, but we're not weak either."

Thor got to his feet. "No, I guess you're not."

Riley raised an eyebrow at Thor. "This is your sister? I think I like her."

The woman turned the romag on him.

"Whoa!" Riley put his hands up, jumping back.

Thor put his hand on the tip of the spear. "He's actually with me."

She looked Riley up and down. "Really?"

Thor shrugged. "Yes."

Riley rolled his eyes. "Well, your effusive praise aside, we need to get moving. I have the other women off their drips. There are twelve. Half are okay to walk, but the other half are going to need help. "

"Okay." Thor looked at Xe.

Xe looked around, her eyes becoming wild. "My son. Where is my son?"

"Another woman asked about her daughter."

Riley met Thor's gaze. And although millions of miles separated their births, right now they had the same thought.

Please don't let us be too late.

107

Lyla had left Riley and Thor to empty the ward on the other floor while she took the first floor of the last wing they needed to clear. Unfortunately, the guards had the better positions, and she had been unable to make any progress. She could feel time ticking away. She knew they would have notified someone by now of the attack. They needed to get gone. But she wouldn't leave until they had gotten everyone they could.

Now she stood at the edge of the hallway. Every time she peeked out, the blast of an Unwelcome weapon forced her back. Petra was crouched next to her.

"What do you want to do?" Petra asked.

Lyla frowned. The rest of the assault had gone well. But this hallway, they weren't moving. They were just making sure Lyla couldn't get down it.

Movement behind Lyla caused her to turn, her heart racing as she caught sight of an Unwelcome uniform.

"Lyla!" Petra yelled as she raised her romag.

Lyla grabbed the spear, shaking her head. "She's with us."

"You're sure?" Petra eyed the tall muscular woman.

"Pretty sure." Lyla nodded at Pxedlin, who had her helmet in her hand.

"I got the others outside, but I think you may need help," Pxedlin said.

"You're not wrong. What's down this hall?"

"It's where they keep the children before they are sent to shedar."

Lyla swallowed. Arthur had explained shedar. She looked at Petra. "Go get Miles. We're going to need him."

Petra glanced at Pxedlin. "But—"

"We need him. I'll be fine." And she actually did believe that. There was something in Pxedlin's eyes.

With one last look, Petra sprinted back for the main entrance.

Lyla studied Pxedlin. "So there are two guards at the end of the hall that are trying their best to blow my head off every time I even look around the corner. Any ideas?"

Pxedlin flicked a gaze down the hall and then nodded. She raised her romag. "I'm going to shoot you."

108

Before Lyla could utter a response, Pxedlin pulled the trigger. Lyla's hands gripped the sides of her head as she ducked. The wall next to her shuddered under the impact, the smell of scorched rock permeating the air. Pxedlin slammed her helmet back on and stepped out into the hall. She nodded at the Unwelcome at the end of the hall.

Heavy footfalls hurried toward Lyla's location. She stood, her back against the wall, waiting. Pxedlin kept her focus on the oncoming Unwelcome. The first one reached the corner and stepped into Lyla's view. It reared back as it caught sight of her. Lyla slammed a side kick into its mid-section that sent it flying into the opposite wall. At the same time, Pxedlin twirled her romag, crashing it into the back of the helmet of the other one. The Unwelcome pitched forward, reminding Lyla of a tree that had just been cut down.

Lyla strode to the Unwelcome, grabbing its spear from the ground and moving toward the Unwelcome.

"Don't," Pxedlin said, stepping in her way.

"Why not?"

"If they are too injured, they will be killed."

The Unwelcome on the ground stirred. Lyla stepped around Pxedlin and slammed the romag into the side of its helmet. It stopped moving.

"Let's go." Lyla took off at a run. After a moment's hesitation, Pxedlin followed.

Lyla kicked open the door of the first room. Nothing moved inside. It was quiet except for a small hum that came from dozens of capsules that lay in rows across the long room.

A movement from the corner of her eye drew her attention. A Naku sat crouched in the corner, frantically typing into a tablet. The lights on the capsules went from green to red.

"No!" Lyla blasted the Naku in the head.

Its tablet dropped to the ground, and the Naku's body followed a second later. The humming in the room stopped.

Lyla left the body where it was, turning her attention to the small capsules lining the room. They looked like little coffins. She stepped to the closest one and peered through the glass lid. A small little blue face lay still inside, its eyes closed.

Pxedlin gasped as she looked into one close to the door. "They look so small."

Lyla dropped the romag and quickly found the release to open the lid. Miles and Petra sprinted into the room.

"Open the capsules! I think the Naku turned off their oxygen." Lyla felt the neck of the boy in the first capsule. His pulse was slow but there. She quickly moved to the next and opened it. By the time she reached the third, she felt better. Maybe she had been wrong about what the Naku had been doing.

"No, no, no, no," Miles moaned, pulling a little body from a capsule at the back of the room. It hung lifelessly in his arms. He quickly lowered him to the ground and started pressing down on its little tiny chest.

Petra had pulled one of the other children out, holding the

girl close to her chest. The child was awake but shaking. Petra rubbed her back as she watched Miles with large eyes.

"Come on, little guy. Come on," Miles urged. "Don't do this. Fight."

Riley clambered in the door, followed by Thor.

Thor let out a gasp and lunged forward, but Riley held him back. "Let Miles help him."

Thor fell to his knees, anguish written over his face, and Lyla knew this was his nephew.

Oh please, Miles, Lyla begged silently. The little body was so tiny, and each time Miles pressed on his chest, he jumped a little bit. A few of the other children were beginning to stir. Lyla grabbed one who looked like he was about to climb out of the capsule.

She moved closer. A tear slipped down Miles's cheek. He sat back, stopping the compressions, wiping the tear from his cheek.

Then the little boy let out a small sound. Lyla gripped Miles's shoulder. The little chest rose once and then again.

Lyla put a hand to her mouth, tears flooding her eyes. She hadn't been sure if this was the right mission, the right first step. But right now, she had absolutely no doubt about the rightness of their actions.

Miles put two fingers to the boy's neck and then looked up. He nodded. "He's breathing on his own."

Lyla cleared her throat. "Okay. Let's get these kids out of here. And ourselves. Someone must have called for help by now." She looked at Thor. "Why don't you take your nephew?"

He nodded slowly, getting to his feet with Riley's help. Miles picked up the boy and handed him over to Thor. Thor stared down at him with wonder on his face.

"Come on, everybody. Grab a little one, and let's get going." Lyla reached in and picked up a second one, this one a little girl. The girl looked at her with big eyes. "It's okay, little one. It's okay."

The girl leaned her head against Lyla's shoulder and put her thumb into her mouth. Lyla grasped both children and headed out of the room. She caught the gaze of an Unwelcome who had shed her helmet and was carrying a child as well. Lyla nodded at her, and the woman nodded back. Then they headed for the front door.

109

While everyone else finished getting the kids from the canisters outside, Miles and Petra, along with Rory and Adros, volunteered to check the third floor. They crept up the stairs, but everything was quiet above them.

Miles felt on edge. He couldn't get the image of Thor's nephew out of his mind. If they had been just a few seconds late, those canisters would have become the coffins they already looked like.

Petra nudged him. "Hey, head in the game."

He frowned at her. "What?"

She shrugged. "Another one of my grandpa's sayings. It means stay focused."

"I know, it's just ..."

She nodded. "I know, the kids. But let's just finish our sweep and get the heck out of this creepshow, okay?"

She was right. The faster they cleared this floor, the faster they could leave all of this behind. From the landing below the third floor, they could see the doorway. It was unguarded.

"Good sign?" Adros asked.

"Guess we'll find out." Petra went first, Adros close behind her. She waved the bracelet Pxedlin had given her over the scan. The light flared green. She pulled the door open just an inch, looking back at the rest of them.

They all nodded back at her, getting on either side of the door. Miles got behind the door and grabbed the handle with a nod. He yanked it open. Petra peered inside and then stepped in.

The floor was quiet. It was set up like a hospital ward with a desk along one wall, six rooms on either side of the hall in front of them and another locked door to their left. Oxygen tanks were on the right-hand side of the desk across from the locked door. A cart with medical supplies had been abandoned in the middle of the hall.

Petra nodded down the hall. "Check those rooms first."

Each door had a small window in it. Adros moved to the door at the end of the hall and shook his head. But across from him, Rory nodded. "Got two."

He opened the door. The women on the bed were both tall, thin, and blue. Neither moved as Rory stepped into the room. Miles hurried over to the first woman. Her chest moved slowly, but even as he touched her arm to check her pulse, her eyes stayed closed. He eyed the thin blue line attached to her arm. "Alive but drugged."

"Is it safe to take her?" Adros asked.

"Safer than leaving her." He pulled a bandage from his pocket and handed it to Adros. "When I pull the needle out, you put pressure on it with that, okay?"

Adros nodded. Miles pulled the needle from her arm, red blood rushing to the surface. Adros quickly covered it with the bandage, tying it firmly around the woman's arm. "I keep expecting the blood to be blue."

Miles didn't answer, just hurried to the other bed. This woman's chest wasn't moving. Miles tried for a pulse but found nothing. He shook his head. "She's gone."

Adros pulled the other woman into his arms. "I'll get her out."

"We could use some help here," Petra called from across the hall.

Miles hurried over to her and stopped in the doorway, his stomach dropping to his feet. The room held four cribs, each with a small blue child. But each of these children had some sort of physical disability. Two had completely white eyes. One had the appearance of dwarfism. The fourth was missing part of his arm.

Rory grabbed the two blind children. "What the hell is this?"

Miles shook his head, not liking where his thoughts were going. It wasn't the children's disabilities that had stopped him in his tracks. It was the bandages and old scars on the children's bodies that made his blood run cold.

Petra picked up the dwarf child. "They experimented on them, didn't they?"

"I think so." Miles moved to the fourth crib. The child looked up at him with deep-blue eyes. He looked to be about two. He reared back.

"Hey, hey, it's okay." Miles picked the child up, and the diaper fell off. And he realized he was a she. "It's okay, sweetheart. I won't hurt you."

"Miles, you good?" Petra asked.

"We're good." He turned for the door, and the little girl snuggled into his shoulder with a little sigh. He rested his hand against her back. "I've got you."

By the time he reached the hall, Rory was already heading out the ward door. Petra was almost at the door when the locked door flew open. An Unwelcome stood there, his weapon pointed at Petra. Petra dove for the floor. The Unwelcome pulled the trigger, just missing Petra and the child she carried.

The blast hit the oxygen tanks dead on. They exploded, sending out a concussive blast that sent Miles flying.

110

The crying woke Miles. His head pounded, and everything was dark. Something lay on top of him. He pushed up. Part of the fallen ceiling shifted to the side with a crash. He winced as he straightened.

The crying was coming from somewhere to his right. He scrambled over the debris, avoiding the sparking wires as he searched for the child. He let out a breath when he saw her. She had flown from his arms and landed on a mattress. The frame of the bed had crashed over her, keeping her protected from the worst of the damage. He reached in and gently pulled her out. "You're one lucky little kid."

She screamed louder in response.

He winced. "Yeah, I'd probably be annoyed if someone called me lucky in this situation too."

Using his feet to hold down a sheet, he ripped it and then wrapped it around the child. She calmed down as the material touched her skin, her big eyes looking up at Miles. He smiled. "Okay, that's better. Now let's see about getting out of here."

He picked her up and carefully climbed from the remnants of the room into the hall. The roof had completely collapsed in front of the door to the stairs. The locked door was also blocked. He noticed a Naku lying under a pile of rubble. He glanced around, not seeing the Unwelcome.

Uh-oh.

Warmth flowed through him, and his missing arm began to materialize. Crashing debris sounded from the other room. Miles hustled to the blocked door, looking for any way through, but it was well and fully blocked. He squinted. Actually, there was a small opening. He could squirm his way through. He looked down at the child in his arms. But not while carrying her.

A loud thump came from behind him. He whirled around as the Unwelcome ducked through the shattered doorway, all nine feet of him.

The Unwelcome seemed to fill the entire hallway. And despite the warmth surging through him and the appearance of his arm, he knew he was in trouble. He could still escape. But he'd have to leave the child behind. And he just couldn't do that. Miles hugged the child to him and then placed her in the opening.

He grabbed a shard of metal and faced the Unwelcome. He pictured Petra and figured if someone was going to give him courage, it was her. So he channeled her and gave the Unwelcome his cockiest grin. "Let's dance."

111

The Unwelcome had been recording the experiments on the defects for the Naku. It was just good luck that he also happened to come across one of the Cursed in action.

Xantar now sat and watched as the Cursed stood in front of the chelvah. Xantar spotted the small hole in the debris. The boy would be able to escape through it, but he had chosen not to. Instead he had placed the child in that spot. Strange.

The chelvah was three feet taller than the Cursed. It should be an easy win for the chelvah. Yet Xantar watched in disbelief as the smaller opponent overpowered the larger. The chelvah threw a fist at the boy's head, but he ducked it easily, pushing the chelvah's forearm back toward his chest as he ducked under the arm and punched him in the stomach, then the back. He stomped on the avad's knee, forcing him to drop low enough for the boy to reach him with an uppercut. Surprise flowed through Xantar as the punch sent the chelvah off his feet.

The boy moved with a swiftness and strength that did not coordinate with his size. Instead, it was the smaller opponent who easily bested the larger. The boy now stood over the downed chelvah. Xantar waited for the kill shot, but it never came. Instead the boy kicked him in the side of the head, rendering him unconscious.

The boy backed away and soon was out of frame.

Xantar tapped the controls quickly, rewinding to just before he vanished from view. The boy's arm was disappearing.

Fascinating. Xantar debated for a moment the dangers in the next move weighed against the potential gains. The gains were too great to ignore. He tapped out a message to the retrieval team he'd sent for 18-F.

Bring me the Cursed from the third level of the lab. Alive.

112

Miles's heart was beating hard. His arm had gone back to normal, which meant the threat had passed. The girl let out a little cry. Miles hurried back to her. "Hey, hey, it's okay."

He pulled her from the hole and smiled down at her. "You did great. We did great."

"Miles!" Petra's yell was muffled from the other side of the debris pile.

"Here!" he yelled back.

"Thank God. Are you okay?"

"I'm good. We're both good."

"Adros is with me. We'll get you out in a few minutes."

"Okay." The pile shifted, and Miles stepped back with the girl, watching it warily. To distract himself, he focused on the girl. "So, I think you need a name. Grace?"

No response.

"Annabelle?"

Small grimace.

"Okay, okay. Something else." He glanced around. The little girl had been through a lot in her short life. And in the life to come she would still go through much more. And then he knew the exact name. "Gasira. It was my grandmother's name. She was the toughest, smartest, kindest woman. I think she would like for you to carry on her name."

Movement by the window caught Miles's attention. He went still as he recognized the veerfinah seconds before the exterior wall disappeared in a blast.

113

Lyla had been loading children onto the veerfinah when the explosion rang out. She'd immediately sprinted back inside, knowing Miles was in that part of the building. She ran into Rory coming down with two children. Adros had a woman in his arms who he unceremoniously dumped in Lyla's before she could even say a word. He sprinted away.

Lyla hurried the woman outside, handing her off to Lewis before heading back inside. She sprinted up the stairs two at a time to catch the end of Petra and Miles's conversation. She let out a breath. He was okay. Trapped, but okay.

She grabbed a large piece of drywall and flung it over the bannister. Adros whipped around. "Hey, didn't see you there."

She eyed him. "Next time, how about you carry the victim outside?"

"That was you? I just handed her over, I didn't realize—" He winced. "Sorry. It's just it seemed faster for me to get back here rather than trying to explain where he was and everything."

She shook her head, not faulting his motives.

"Miles has a little girl with him as well," Petra said. "We think this was the ward where they put the children who weren't perfect."

Lyla shook her head, picturing the white eyes of the children Rory had carried out. "This place just gets worse and worse."

An explosion sounded from the other side of the debris wall. Lyla's head jerked up. "Miles?"

"Down here!" he yelled "Take Gasira, quick!"

Petra scrambled down, reached through the small opening below. She thrust her hands in and yanked, a small blanket appearing. She tugged on it, and a small girl appeared. "Miles, what's going—"

Warmth spread through Lyla, and she knew. She yanked a large piece of metal from the top of the pile, flinging it down the stairwell. Two more pieces flew after it as blasts from the Unwelcome's spears rang out and Miles cried out.

"Miles!" Petra yelled. All three of them were digging frantically. Finally, Lyla had created a hole big enough to crawl through. She dove in, catching her thigh on a piece of metal but not caring about the gash it left.

At the end of the hall, a veerfinah hovered outside the remnants of the wall. A metal bridge extended from it to the ward. Two Unwelcome stood on the ward on either side of it as a tall Unwelcome crossed it, Miles slung over his shoulder.

"No!" Lyla sprinted forward. The two Unwelcome opened fire. Lyla avoided the bursts as if they told her where they would land. She heard Adros and Petra behind her.

Ahead, the Unwelcome continued to fire even as the veerfinah pulled away. Lyla bowled through both of the Unwelcome, and they flew from the third floor, heading for the ground below while Lyla latched her fingertips onto the edge of the retracting ramp.

"Lyla! No!" Adros yelled, grabbing her legs.

"Let me—" Her grip broke free. Adros yanked her back. They collapsed into heap on the floor.

She scrambled to her feet, standing at the edge of floor watching as, with a burst of speed, the veerfinah disappeared.

114

The trip back to the estate was subdued. Between the "patients" from the facility who were on the edge of shock to Lyla and her people, who were still trying to wrap their heads around the idea that Miles had been taken, the veerfinah had been silent.

Montell stood waiting as they landed. He immediately started ordering the Cursed to help settle everyone. People did, although there was hesitation on both the humans' and the Unwelcome's part. But Arthur was there to help soothe over the humans while Thor and Pxedlin took the lead with the Unwelcome.

Montell had arranged for beds to be set up in one wing of the main estate for the Unwelcome, and a separate wing had been set up for the humans. Later they'd see about merging groups, but Lyla agreed that right now, separate areas were the best approach.

Montell looked around as Thor helped one of the wounded off the ship. "We should get Miles to take a look at—" His words died away as he looked at Lyla's face. "Oh God, Lyla."

"He's not dead," she said quickly. "But they took him."

"Do you know where?"

"Not yet. But we will find him."

He nodded. "Whatever you need."

"Thank you." She stepped away, taking a deep breath. She covered her mouth, not wanting anyone to see her trembling lips.

Whatever I need. What I need is Miles back.

Before they left the breeding facility, Pxedlin had ripped the trackers from the ship, making them untraceable. They would be able to keep it for future use, as Pxedlin apparently was well versed in their maintenance, so they moved it into the stable.

Lyla pulled Thor aside as soon as she had people assigned to duties, leading him away from the commotion. Petra and Riley followed. She didn't bother with small talk. "Where would they take him?"

"I'm not sure. New City or the mothership are the most likely."

"What about that radio thing you had?" Riley asked.

"It won't mention that. The Naku tablets would have that information."

"Wait, is that a rectangular thing about this big?" Petra held up her hands.

Thor nodded.

Petra turned and ran for one of the veerfinahs. She appeared a few seconds later, handing the tablet to Thor. "I saw Miles put this on the ship earlier."

Thor took it, his hands pausing above the tablet. "I can't read this."

"Get Arthur," Lyla ordered. But Riley was already sprinting away.

Lyla paced, waiting for Arthur to appear, her mind spinning away with her. They had taken Miles, not killed him. That meant they wanted information from him.

Thor must have been reading her thoughts or at least the worry splashed across her face. "They won't kill him. Not right away, not if they went to the trouble of taking him."

"So what will they do?" Petra demanded.

"If he's injured, they'll heal him. They'll want him to be in perfect health before they begin ... their interrogation."

Lyla swallowed, looking away and breathing deeply.

"But first, they'll check him over medically," Thor continued.

"He was shot. I saw the wound in his side," Lyla said slowly.

"It will take at least a few days to heal that. And then another few for the physical. You have time."

Arthur jogged up. Thor handed him the tablet without a word. Arthur's hands flew over it. A crease appeared between his eyes as he focused. Finally, he stopped and looked up. "They're taking him to the mothership."

"Why not New City and the research building?" Petra asked.

"Probably because it has proven too insecure," Lyla said quietly.

Arthur nodded. "I believe that is correct."

Lyla turned to Thor. "You said they'd physically examine him first. Then what?"

Thor flicked a gaze at Arthur. Arthur answered for him. "They'll want to know about his abilities. They'll trigger him to manifest them."

"They'll attack him," Lyla said.

"Once they've figured that out, they'll bring in a special interrogator to see what he knows, what's hidden in his mind. And when they have everything ..." Arthur's voice faded away.

"What? What happens then?" Petra demanded.

"They'll kill him," Lyla said softly.

115

The glider hummed as Xantar made his way to Aek's lab. The door slid open silently as he approached. He rolled through the doorway, ignoring Aek, who stood over at her panel. Instead, he made his way across to the other side of the room, where a large clear glass cylinder with the latest test subject stood. The cylinder was eight feet tall and filled with healing fluid. Suspended in the middle was a male human, age seventeen.

Xantar's gaze roamed over the subject. He was strong with a muscular build and dark skin. Two burns were on his left-hand side, additional scrapes and cuts along his hand. Xantar tilted his head, studying the human's malformed arm. It was not a birth defect. It had been cut off sometime during his childhood. He was not surprised they cut it off. Humans were barely above beasts of the field. But they had kept him alive afterward. Why?

No doubt sentiment played a role. The human could not possibly offer any true productive assistance to any community.

But none of that was truly Xantar's concern. He wanted to know how these creatures were able to manifest their abilities.

Aek walked silently up to him. *He is an intriguing subject.*

You mean the arm?

Yes. There have been reports that the arm becomes whole when his abilities manifest.

Xantar nodded. *Are there any additional manifestations that you have uncovered?*

Speed and strength are all that have been reported. I will put him through a complete battery of tests once he is healed, varying environments, threats, weapons.

Good. I want reports immediately.

Of course. Aek returned to her console.

Xantar studied the human for a few seconds longer. *You will reveal all of your secrets. And your weaknesses.*

He turned his gaze to the other test subject. The female avad lay suspended in the fluid. She had been here ever since she had been recovered. They had made quite a few discoveries in that time.

And you will help us.

EPILOGUE

It had been twenty-four hours since they had set up residence at the Gatsby. Both groups were keeping to themselves for the most part. Except, of course, for Emma and Edna, who had taken it as their personal mission to fatten up all the Unwelcome mothers and their kids.

Maisy and Iris were completely in love with all the children. They were constantly playing with them. The Unwelcomes seemed just as enamored with them. They had not had a chance to see children of their age. Between Emma, Edna, Maisy, and Iris, Lyla hoped a bridge could be developed that would bring the two groups together.

Lyla stood now on the second floor of the east wing, looking out the front. Montell, Max, and Angela rode by on horseback and out the front gates. They were heading to the Fringe to see what they could learn. They were going to stake out the mother-ship as best they could from the ground. Numbers, patterns, anything they could figure out. Max was going to speak with some people inside the Fringe to see what he could learn. Lyla would meet up with them in three days' time.

Three days. It seemed like a lifetime.

Lyla rubbed her arms, even though it wasn't cold, but she couldn't seem to warm up. Miles was on the mothership. *Which means I need to find a way up there.*

A knock sounded at the door. She turned. Arthur hovered in the doorway, the Naku tablet in his hands. Lyla cleared her throat. "Can they trace us on that?"

"No. As long as I don't try to communicate with anyone, they won't know we have it."

She nodded.

"I've been looking through it."

"Anything about Miles?"

"No, not yet."

She sank into a chair. "Oh."

"It does have a record of the Naku's history. And the avad's."

Lyla just looked at him.

He backed away. "I'm sorry. It's not a good time to discuss this. I'll come back later when—"

"No, no." Lyla crossed the room to him, shaking herself from her melancholy. "No, now's good. I could use something to distract me. Tell me what you found." She led him back to the couch.

He sat down next to her, the tablet looking tiny in his hands. "I wanted to know who my people really are."

She couldn't blame him. She wanted answers about herself and the Cursed just as badly as Arthur wanted answers about his people.

"I managed to trace our history. The Naku, they've moved with us from planet to planet. We've been to dozens. They use up all the resources on a planet and then we move on to the next."

"How long have they been doing that?"

"Thousands of years. They were doing it even before they made us their slaves. But their bodies began to weaken until they became too fragile to do much more than walk, think, and eat. They landed on a planet. They weren't planning on staying. They had been called home. But they were so weak. Luckily, the inhabitants of the planet were primitive. They thought the Naku were gods. They fed them, honored them. The Naku stayed for a thousand years and then headed home. They took hundreds of the natives of the planet and made them their slaves. That's where the avad began."

"So you have a home. A place where you're from."

Arthur nodded, an expression she couldn't quite decipher on his face. "Does your home planet still exist?"

Arthur nodded. "Yes. I've read this and reread it, seeing if I made any mistakes in the translation, but I didn't. The Naku call our planet Arak. It's beautiful—oceans, trees, and my people are still there. They still exist."

"That's great," she said, even though she felt a rip in her chest at the idea of Arthur leaving to find his people. "Do you know where it is?"

Arthur nodded slowly. "Yes, and so do you."

She frowned. "I do?"

"We're standing on it."

She stared at him, not understanding. "What?"

Arthur took a deep breath. "The Unwelcome were taken from here. Arak is Earth."

The story continues in Proxy, Book Three of The Unwelcome Trilogy, available now for pre-order on Amazon.

Thank you for reading Seek, Book Two in The Unwelcome Trilogy. If you enjoyed it, please consider leaving a review.

AUTHOR'S NOTE

Between 1997 and 2003, my favorite TV show was beyond a doubt *Buffy the Vampire Slayer*. I absolutely loved it. Strong kick ass female who had friends and family she loved. She faced each battle no mater the odds. Oh, I loved that show!

My love for all things Buffy is well known amongst my friends. A good friend even picked up a Buffy drawing for me at Boston Comic-Con. It sits in pride of place in my office. (I'll put a snapshot of it up on my Facebook page. Take a look!)

But then the worst happened: *Buffy* ended. I think I have seen that finale a dozen times. But afterwards, I felt this keen sense of loss. I had laughed, loved and cried along with these characters. And now, I was never going to see a new adventure. A few months later, Joss Whedon announced he was creating a new series called *Firefly*.

I wasn't ready.

I was still mourning the loss of Buffy, Xander, Willow, Niles, and Spike. (Spike!) I wasn't ready to open my heart to a whole new group of characters. Besides, it couldn't possibly be as good, right? So I didn't watch *Firefly*. Then I learned it was cancelled. Proof positive in my mind that I had made the right decision.

Years passed and one rainy Saturday, I was seriously bored. And the first episode of *Firefly* was on TV. I finally sat down to watch it.

I loved it! It was another group of fun characters, all very different, all incredibly likeable, even Jayne. I watched the entire season and was kicking myself for not watching it when it was on air. Maybe if I had, there'd be more than one season.

You're probably wondering why I'm taking you on this little stroll down Memory Lane. It is my round about way of saying thank you for taking a chance on my new series. I truly know how difficult it is to jump in. So thank you!

I also need to thank my incredible editor Crystal Wantanabe and her team at Pikko's House. You guys have been a godsend.

And to the creative minds at Damonza, thank you for the incredible covers. I am absolutely in love with them!

I also want to thank my incredible Beta Reading Team. I held off creating one for multiple reasons, the biggest one being fear. Now, just like with *Firefly*, I am kicking myself for not doing it sooner. You guys have been such a gift!

To my four furry co-writing partners, you make my days brighter.

To my three furless little ones, never forget you are loved, always and forever.

And to my husband, thank you for your support. Thank you for being an incredible father, husband and partner. You make this all possible. Thank you.

And a special thank you to everyone who has mentioned my book to a friend or left a <u>review</u>. You have helped spread my books far and wide. I am humbled by it.

Until next time,
    R.D.

ABOUT THE AUTHOR

R.D. Brady is an American writer who grew up on Long Island, NY but has made her home in both the South and Midwest before settling in upstate New York. On her way to becoming a full-time writer, R.D. received a Ph.D. in Criminology and taught for ten years at a small liberal arts college.

R.D. left the glamorous life of grading papers behind in 2013 with the publication of her first novel, the supernatural action adventure, *The Belial Stone*. Over ten novels later and hundreds of thousands of books sold, and she hasn't looked back. Her novels tap into her criminological background, her years spent studying martial arts, and the unexplained aspects of our history. Join her on her next adventure!

To learn about her upcoming publications, sign up for her newsletter here or on her website (rdbradybooks.com).

BOOKS BY R.D. BRADY

The Belial Series (in order)

The Belial Stone

The Belial Library

The Belial Ring

Recruit: A Belial Series Novella

The Belial Children

The Belial Origins

The Belial Search

The Belial Guard

The Belial Warrior

The Belial Plan

The Belial Witches

The Belial War

The Belial Fall

The Belial Sacrifice

Stand-Alone Books

Runs Deep

Hominid

The A.L.I.V.E. Series

B.E.G.I.N.

A.L.I.V.E.

D.E.A.D.

The Unwelcome Series

Protect

Seek

Proxy

Be sure to sign up for R.D.'s mailing list to be the first to hear when she has a new release!